D0466339

LP DEL
De la Bere, Imogen
The welcoming committee /
Imogen De la Bere.
ASHCROFT LIBRARY

WITHDRAWN
WITHDRAWN

LOGAN LAKE LIBRARY

SPECIAL MESSAGE TO READERS

This book is published under the auspices of

THE ULVERSCROFT FOUNDATION

(registered charity No. 264873 UK)

Established in 1972 to provide funds for research, diagnosis and treatment of eye diseases. Examples of contributions made are: —

A Children's Assessment Unit at Moorfield's Hospital, London.

●

Twin operating theatres at the Western Ophthalmic Hospital, London.

●

A Chair of Ophthalmology at the Royal Australian College of Ophthalmologists.

●

The Ulverscroft Children's Eye Unit at the Great Ormond Street Hospital For Sick Children, London.

You can help further the work of the Foundation by making a donation or leaving a legacy. Every contribution, no matter how small, is received with gratitude. Please write for details to:

THE ULVERSCROFT FOUNDATION,
The Green, Bradgate Road, Anstey,
Leicester LE7 7FU, England.
Telephone: (0116) 236 4325

In Australia write to:
THE ULVERSCROFT FOUNDATION,
c/o The Royal Australian and New Zealand
College of Ophthalmologists,
94-98 Chalmers Street, Surry Hills,
N.S.W. 2010, Australia

Imogen de la Bere is the author of two previous novels, one of which was shortlisted for the David Higham Prize. She divides her time between England and New Zealand.

THE WELCOMING COMMITTEE

A twentieth-century Faust, musician turned wine merchant Crawford Hollander has done well from his deal with the Devil.

Successful, charming, surrounded by a circle of adoring women, he has cajoled, manipulated and cheated his way to riches. But Crawford has also accumulated enemies. On his return to his native New Zealand, three men are waiting for him. They have formed the Welcoming Committee, and have prepared a very special form of revenge . . .

IMOGEN DE LA BERE

◆

THE
WELCOMING
COMMITTEE

Complete and Unabridged

ULVERSCROFT
Leicester

Thompson-Nicola Regional District
Library System
300-465 VICTORIA STREET
KAMLOOPS, BC   V2C 2A9

First published in Great Britain in 2002 by
Jonathan Cape
London

First Large Print Edition
published 2003
by arrangement with
Jonathan Cape
a division of
Random House Group Limited
London

The moral right of the author has been asserted

Copyright © 2002 by Imogen de la Bere
All rights reserved

British Library CIP Data

De la Bere, Imogen
   The welcoming committee.—Large print ed.—
Ulverscroft large print series: general fiction
1. Large type books
I. Title
823.9'14 [F]

ISBN 1–8439–5039–1

Published by
F. A. Thorpe (Publishing)
Anstey, Leicestershire

Set by Words & Graphics Ltd.
Anstey, Leicestershire
Printed and bound in Great Britain by
T. J. International Ltd., Padstow, Cornwall

This book is printed on acid-free paper

Thompson-Nicola Regional District
Library System
300-465 VICTORIA STREET
KAMLOOPS, BC   V2C 2A9

101597980X

Source of story,
Source of strength,
With love.

Part I

Part I

1

Faust. In a grey cardigan. He lay spread-eagled in the centre of the bare stage, pole-axed by love. Over him swept the insidiously pretty strains of a waltz, Berlioz at his most subversive.

Crawford closed his eyes. He let the beloved music flood his mind, bearing on the tide images of all kinds, like the miscellaneous contents of a household picked at random by the waters. Ah, he thought, ah Berlioz. He let himself forget the offensively avant-garde production, the halting translation, the slightly less than perfect intonation of Faust, the absurd casting of Mephistopheles as a black man. All the irritations were washed away in the darkness of his closed eyes by the charm of the music. Nothing, he thought, nothing, can destroy this!

He didn't know why he opened his eyes, when the darkness was so alluring. He could have kept the unpleasantness on the stage at bay for minutes longer, and salvaged some delight from the wreckage of his evening. It was, he afterwards reflected, the last pleasant moment he was to enjoy for hours and hours.

It was a form of masochism, perhaps, not to miss any of the director's contortions. He opened his eyes. The waltz continued as gracious as ever, and Faust lay twitching slightly in time. But from out of the wings had emerged, thirty feet high, a pair of woman's legs. They were two-dimensional, jointed at the knee and driven by some monster puppet master in the flies. In seamed stockings and red high-heeled shoes, she picked her way slowly, slowly, precisely in time to the music across the empty stage towards the hero. The progress was agonizing, not only for Crawford, for whom the travesty was unbearable, but for any onlooker conscious of the fact that Faust was directly in the path of those six-foot spikes. But as she approached him, Faust jerked suddenly in a masturbatory paroxysm, and narrowly avoided impalement. Instead, as she passed, he gazed up into the darkness between her legs, up up in the velvet heavens.

Crawford could take no more. He rose from his seat, whispering to Genista that this was the four hundredth blow, and they were leaving. He pushed past his neighbours in a manner that would normally be unthinkable, and made for the door.

The corridor outside the circle was curved and lined with red velvet. He leant against the

4

wall for a moment, his heart beating at his own temerity and rudeness. He waited for the door to sigh closed behind Genista. He waited. A young woman in a sadly unflattering uniform came to his assistance. Even in his troubled state, he noted that she normally wore glasses and that her seriousness was locked in an unequal struggle with her overflowing bosom.

'Are you unwell, sir? Can I take you down to the rest room? Or alternatively, the Gents is just round here, can I call the first-aider?'

'My wife,' Crawford cried, 'my wife.'

'Shall I fetch her out? What was your seat number, sir?'

'No, no, no,' he replied, conscious as he said it of all the possible meanings of that little word. 'No, you misunderstand. I am not unwell. I am devastated. And my wife — '

The young woman took him by the elbow. Crawford was offended by the assumption of aged infirmity this implied. He was after all only a decade or two older than the girl, maybe three, and quite capable of fascinating and delighting her. More capable than a callow youth of her own generation, but oh for the chance to prove it. She conducted him along the corridor into the area demarked by the stairways, bars and lavatories. The barman, smearing glasses with a tea-towel, looked up eagerly, as if glad of a distraction. The young woman sat him down as if he were fussy grandpa just in time for his favourite programme.

'No, no, no, no!' he cried. In the trivia of his disturbed mind he thought what an excellent singing exercise it might make. *No no no no no* trilled the girls in his head in various shades of dissent. *No no no no!*

'You are mistaken. I am not unwell or incapable. I simply loathe this production of the opera.'

The young woman looked at him sharply.

'Oh. I thought — the critics — '

'If you have the time, I could explain to you in detail exactly what is wrong with this whole regrettable enterprise, from the notion of staging *La Damnation de Faust* at all, to the pink top hat atop the devil. Perhaps after your duties I could buy you a small night-time drink?'

The young woman surveyed him, took in his brown velvet jacket, his brown velvet eyes, his hand-made shoes. He watched her re-evaluate him and enjoyed the small triumph.

'O, gosh. Thanks. How very kind. I don't know though, you see . . . My boyfriend's in the chorus, and after the performance, we, well usually — '

'No no. I quite understand! I could not under any circumstances interfere with the course of young love.'

'Well, I'm sure just this once — '

But Crawford had lost interest in this young woman, for he had suddenly remembered his wife. There was no sign of Genista; she had not followed him out of the auditorium. She was sitting there still, with his seat empty beside her, presumably enjoying the opera. If not enjoying it, at least not disliking it sufficiently to join him. He could not easily decide which was worse — her not hating the experience as she should or her dereliction of her wifely duty. He sat in the red velvet chair seeing and not seeing the barman about his duties, the over-heated concern of the young woman in front of him, but his head was full of the awfulness of the sights he had seen, and the horror of his wife sitting there of her own volition through more of the same. Genista did not like opera; she did not like modern theatre; she did not like Berlioz. She could only be sitting there to vex him — Genista, who had never so much as questioned their pact of mutual tolerance, by a snappish word or a sharp look. Genista, who smiled at his eccentricity like an eighteenth-century aristocrat contemplating the parson at his peculiar, who turned a wondrously well-bred blind eye to his more unusual behaviour.

Why would Genista wish to vex him? She did not argue, she made a little joke instead. She did not lose her temper, she tossed her head and reduced him to a schoolboy jelly. It was this entirely civilized conduct that had persuaded him that she was the perfect wife — he had after all the choice of many, and Genista was not young, wealthy or beautiful, though as he sometimes chaffed her, had she been born a man she would have been regarded as handsome. Genista's superb grown-upness was her salient feature, her dowry.

Now she was behaving unreasonably. What did she expect him to do, suspended in London at an hour too late for dinner and too early for supper? Wait for her in a coffee house nearby? Go to his club?

The young woman brought him a glass of water. It was tap water in a smeared glass, but he smiled at her with his eyes, and just touched her hand while accepting it. He read in her shimmer of a smile in return that she was weighing up his fascination against his age. But it did not matter which way her deliberations led her, for he was weary of the contest. There was major political conflict brewing, if Genista was set on a course to thwart him.

He sipped as much of the water as was consistent with politeness — one never knew when one might feel the need to charm this young woman further — and went down to the cloakroom to collect his wrappings. The autumn had set in early this year — somehow it set in just a little earlier each year. He had provided himself with a scarf and gloves as well as an overcoat, and was glad of these as he vested himself under the eyes of the cloakroom attendants. *See, I am not unwell, I am displeased. Make the management aware.*

He was glad of his coverings as he stepped out into the evening. This time of the year, when the dread of winter darkness hung in the air, twanged the last remaining string of homesickness in his heart. He wished to be in Canterbury once more, where the daylight, even in the depths of winter, seared the vision, where the nights were as black and hard as coal. As always he wished this only for a moment, heard the string twang and fall silent. He did not want to be anywhere but here, walking along St Martin's Lane as if he owned it. In his own small way, he reflected, he did have ownership — there wasn't a bar or restaurant in the whole parade that didn't sell at least one wine that had passed through his hands.

He did not want to be anywhere but here, but he did not care to be alone. He never went out alone; there was always a woman on his arm, always a companion to be had. He had a system, he had a book, and it was indeed, as Genista often pointed out to her friends, little and black. But it must not be described, she continued, as a little black book, for Crawford did not like the implication. His friendships were platonic.

He was, he declared over many a dinner table, uxorious to a fault.

> *Bei dir allein.*
> *Ich fühl mich mein,*
> *Bei dir allein.*

With you only, I am myself only with you.

But he knew that his wife — his helpmeet as he liked to call her as a wry joke, for she winced at the term — was not his soul mate. He doubted such a thing existed, or that he could endure it if she did. Genista, though so eminently satisfactory as a wife, was not a soul mate. She did not even care for opera. She had only agreed to go with him because *La Damnation de Faust* was not really an opera, and she was intrigued. He had scarcely bothered to mention it to her, but his own rules dictated that he mention absolutely everything. He was scrupulously fair. Genista had first refusal on all occasions. Chamber music she liked, and song cycles, and organ music, for reasons unfathomable to Crawford. But large choral works, orchestral pieces and opera she generally gave a miss. However, he could never be quite sure, and it was Crawford's policy always to ask Genista first. On her refusal, he rang around his harem in punctilious order — if one woman had missed her turn, she was the first to be asked. Everyone was kept informed. There was no favouritism. When a new candidate joined the charmed circle, she had to endure a probation period, flirting sweetly, but not improperly. Three refusals without water-tight cause would strike one off the invitation list, though Crawford did not necessarily strike her off his internal list — his *cataloga* as he liked to quip.

He had been taken by surprise, that first Sunday in September, standing there, elbow on the mantelpiece, his diary open in one hand, g&t in the other, going through the engagements for the month. Genista was energetic and cheerful from walking the dogs back from church by way of the Green, full of neighbourly chat. She breezed into the drawing-room, where he had lit a little fire, and laughed at him for his softness. One of the dogs had jumped into Crawford's leather armchair and she sent it out of the room, desolate. He had poured her the drink that was standing ready across the room, and took up his position by the fire.

'It's that time again,' he said, opening his diary.

She threw herself into her matching chair, legs thrust out before her. He noted the residual mud on her walking shoes, poised above his Afghan rug, but said nothing. She would have to arrange the cleaning of the rug, after all. Crawford was proud of his even temper.

'September,' he said, 'is a very nice month. I have a little expedition planned to the Argolid. A little fellow there, trapped by the Byzantine laws of Greek wine denomination. I think I can help him out. Lovely wine, nice label. Needs better cork and lighter glass. Dreadful clunky stuff. You don't want to come too?'

'No, I don't want to go to Greece. There are too many German tourists. I like to remember it the way it was.'

'Then in September we have the Chillingarian — Tippett and Haydn — how odd. Yes? *The Damnation of Faust*. No. *Death and the Maiden*. Yes — '

'*Faust*,' interrupted Genista, over the rim

of her glass. 'I'm intrigued by that. I read an absolutely swingeing attack on it in the *Spectator*, and I did hope you had tickets. Goody.'

'It's unstageable,' Crawford said mildly. 'I had a good mind to give the tickets away; this is the disadvantage of being a sponsor. I think I may have to review my level of support.'

He had earmarked this one for Mercy, as an object lesson in the absurdity of modern culture. Perhaps it was not quite Mercy's turn, in strict rotation, but she alone would benefit from the experience. Genista would not; nor decidedly would Crawford. He had only not given the tickets away because he wished to clarify Mercy's mind on certain things. There had been a little disagreement over a certain production of a Handel opera in which the chorus made hand signals and shadows were projected on to the backdrop, thus making thorough mock of Handel. Crawford did not feel quite sure that he had won the argument; but he felt sure that the ghastly modernization of the Berlioz *Faust* would seal his victory.

When Genista decided to come with him, he was trapped. He didn't wish to attend the Berlioz personally, and his sacrifice would be in vain, for Genista would learn nothing.

'Are you quite sure?' he said, never one to make a fuss.

'I always know my mind, Crawford, you should have learnt that by now.'

Of course she did. Genista's jolly crowd of friends all agreed on one thing — that she was the sanest person in the world, and knew her own mind. It was only this, some asserted, that kept her married to that womanizing serpent; it was this, according to others, that kept Crawford interested in her now that her looks, at their best idiosyncratic, had faded, and middle age crept spiderlike across her skin. Genista understood perfectly well why she and Crawford were still married to each other, but this was the one piece of information she did not pass on to her concatenation of friends all over the world — or her cattery or claque or coven in Crawford terminology. As opposed to your harem, seraglio, flock, or gaggle of groupies, rejoined Genista, who liked a good crossword, and laughed.

'You wish to go to the *Faust*,' Crawford repeated, not attempting to argue.

It was Genista's palpable sanity that made her behaviour that evening, both at the opera house and afterwards, all the more remarkable. Genista had never done anything unpredictable before. Their marriage was founded upon her sanity and his little indulgences — it was a pact, a binding covenant of mutual agreeability, a *quid pro quo* of his charm and money and sexuality for her strength and humour.

He forgot that some treaties have expiry dates.

He walked along St Martin's Lane, alone, the only person on his own in the entirety of Covent Garden — swarms of friends, youths and girls, smoking and making more collective noise than humanly possible, couples, couples everywhere, curved at bars, bent towards each other over tables, peering into the glass of restaurants trying to determine if the atmosphere would outweigh the prices. Ordinary middle-aged couples, gloriously distinguished by being together.

Crawford felt lonely. He wanted a drink with serious urgency, but he could not go into a bar or even a pub by himself, not on a Saturday evening in deepest Covent Garden. Instead he shut himself in a telephone box. He ignored the vulgar display of flesh with which the box was papered, and dialled a memorized number.

Even her telephone purred, he thought, but repeated often enough, even purring becomes an irritant.

'Yes,' she said, implying in that monosyllable a whole dossier of negatives.

'Crawford.'

'Crawford, darling, it's the weekend. Sat'day night. Call me on Monday.'

She put down the phone. He knew better than to try again. He reflected on the artfulness of intonation, whereby the word *darling* could be persuaded to convey its opposite.

Crawford contemplated the calling cards which adhered cheek by jowl to the panes of the phone box. He had no taste for such vulgarities and no illusions about what would rise up to greet him at the other end. But the devil entered into him, and he dialled a number.

'Personal Services,' said a man with a foreign accent. Or possibly a woman.

'How young have you got?' asked Crawford.

'Seventeen, sir.'

'I was thinking a bit less than that.'

'Sixteen, perhaps, if sir can wait a little.'

'No, sixteen-year-olds are far too knowing. Especially where your girls come from.'

He liked the gratuitous insult contained in this remark, even though the man appeared not to have registered it.

'Well, if sir cares to make a date with us, we

will see what we can do.'

'Hah! Got you,' said Crawford, 'either defrauding your customers or breaking the law. In yet another respect, of course.'

He hung up, and wondered what sort of perverted mind derived pleasure from pestering pimps. He supposed it was a vicarious pleasure to go as far as the pretence of an arrangement. He was not, at fifty-three, going to waste his essence on a putative seventeen-year-old, no matter her age, but he allowed himself to recall the last time he had caressed the body of a seventeen-year-old. And it seemed to him, though possibly his memory was now defective, that it had been that of Mercy. A decade ago. You dirty old dog, he told himself smugly, and cheered himself with the memory as he pushed his way towards Covent Garden station.

But his memories were jostled along with his person, and it was not until he was sitting safe inside his car in the station car park at Harpenden that the past could be properly enjoyed.

Mercy. In his unguarded moments it was a name to conjure with, as now in the dark. Mercy.

Even if she were a plain girl with a thin voice and no bosom, he would have quivered at her name. But Mercy Fisher is a spankingly fine girl with a Paul Robeson voice and breasts to match.

Mercy, he thinks, and smiles, for after all these years he has not grown out of her name.

I will go and call on Mercy.

When he first encountered her, a girl, even then endowed with that voice and those breasts, he was agog. Rosalia had mentioned her name often, but many girls' names tripped off Rosalia's tongue amidst the many that were dropped. *Mercy* alone engendered curiosity. What sort of parents sent their defenceless girl out into the world with a name like that? How did she live up to it? How could one resist copulating with her, just for the paradoxical pleasure of crying out her name?

You . . . will dote on Mercy. You will want to eat her for breakfast.

And indeed he had.

That was many years ago, but her name, now loaded with its special memories, still induced a tremor. He sat in the darkness of the car park and allowed the past to wash over him. He knew this was a mistake, for the dark grew darker, even though the events that he recalled had taken place in brilliant light. It seemed to him that the brilliance of those past days invalidated the light of nowadays, as when the sun is in eclipse — the sky is light

18

and yet one feels surrounded by darkness. In the bright light of then, the pain and the pleasure had been as intense as the light. Surely it was not simply his memory painting melodramatic pictures? It struck him for a moment that everything afterwards had been a campaign to regain the intensity of that time when he first battened upon Mercy.

He thought this, and dismissed it immediately as fanciful. Only a woman would think like that, a woman with precious little to occupy her. Men generally knew better; men knew that life was packed with incident and opportunity, that passing incidents of fleshly pleasure, though delicious, were exactly that — incidental. The passage of time tended to seal certain episodes and shrink them into lovely little things, which one could not look at without sighing, but that did not make them important, any more than a postage stamp was important — compare the artist's original of the label for the 1987 Pinot Noir, with Wolf's signature scrawled across it — now *that* was important.

Nonetheless, he could not pretend that he responded to the words *Pinot Noir* in quite the same way as he did to the word *Mercy*, or that at this moment in the car park he wished for nothing more than a tope of his best Merlot. But if there had tapped upon his window at that moment an acquaintance with an interesting offer to discuss — exclusive supply of a supermarket's own brand, a warehouse full of confiscated South African — his thoughts of Mercy would not detain him.

There was no sign of a business acquaintance, or any man in a suit good enough to do business with Hollander Wines, maker and breaker of vintners the world over. Crawford slid his car out of the car park.

En route to Mercy's, he drove past his own house — slowing as he did so to admire it. A lovely Lutyens thing, overlooking the Green. You can hardly fail to admire it as you drive through Harpenden, so satisfyingly domestic, so well-proportioned and quintessentially English. It was perhaps this latter quality that sealed its purchase in Crawford's heart; no one could deny his Englishness if he lived in such a house, for those colonials who were not English in their hearts, but only aped the manners of Englishmen, they bought Olde Worlde houses, fifteenth-, sixteenth-century, and boasted about it. A true Englishman took antiquity for granted, set little store by it. A Lutyens house had far more style than something merely old. Crawford let it be believed that the garden was designed by the great man also, but Genista, if she were in earshot, would pooh-pooh this rather loudly. Genista rather fancied herself as a garden historian and Crawford let her have her fancies. If the house were to be on the market, however, it would be quite a different matter.

The house — his house — had enraptured him like a siren the first time he laid eyes upon it, and had called to him like a lover ever since. It was a marriage made in real-estate heaven — he had been driving through Harpenden looking for a broad parking space near the church, for he was deputed as the family's representative to attend the funeral of the Commander, a man briefly his brother-in-law and business partner, and spectacularly unsuccessful at both.

Indeed, Crawford was happy to go to the funeral, for the Commander in his coffin could tell no tales.

Cruising into the town, he had spotted the For Sale sign on this most desirable of houses, and was almost subverted from his family duty by the necessity to pursue it.

Standing in the ex-Commander's parlour, sipping sherry from a battered eighteenth-century glass, a sherry so dry it cauterized his throat, he raised the matter of the house with Genista, the sort-of-sister-in-law, whom he not met before. The contours of Genista's accent and the inclination of her gracious head, so very Joshua Reynolds, confirmed in his heart his love for the house. As its master he would woo and win this wonderful woman, born to grace its drawing-room.

She was exactly the wife he wanted. She was head and shoulders above other women, but it wasn't just her magnificent presence, the casually aristocratic profile, the manly height, or the deep voice with all its harmonics, as much as the clear presentation of upper-class credentials, which came to her as naturally as music came to Crawford.

Then he'd have everything.

'Why yes, you must settle in Harpenden, it's a charming place,' she said. 'I am so grateful that Mother had the foresight to buy this little place before anyone *noticed* the village. One can live beyond one's means. And of course you are musical — this is just the place for you! Positively bursting with musical ladies! We have such a jolly time down at the Gleeful Ladies. I'm a bass, you know. The Commander would pretend to find that quite spicy, the naughty old darling.'

Crawford, whose memories of the Commander were rather mixed, smiled his most encouraging smile. He wondered briefly then, as he wondered for much of his life, what on earth could have drawn two such women as his sister, Rosalia, and this excellent woman, Genista, with her old silver and casual antique glass, to marry the drunken, venial life-incompetent they called the Commander.

As long as Crawford could remember, he had been called the Commander, even though he'd never been to sea. Someone, somewhere, in a fly-beaten bar in the back of nowhere, had got their wires crossed, and the title had stuck. The old boy had a knife-box full of medals and a gaze that went right out to sea, and as the locals said of him, he'd have looked a cracker in a white uniform, in his young days, being so tall, and as craggily handsome as a film star, though nowadays rather gone to seed. Back home in New Zealand, he'd been employed sporadically in the harbour master's office, over on the Coast, and then on the wharves at Lyttelton, so it was assumed he had a nautical connection. The Commander he'd become and the Commander he stayed, from the vaguely defined back-blocks of Westport to the tidy confines of the Harpenden Golf Club. As far as anyone knew, he did not mean to perpetrate a falsehood, nor, it must be said, did he go to any lengths to clear things up. Clearing things up was not the Commander's strong point.

Marvelling at his find, Crawford fed the

recent widow tidbits of his charm, as she fed him dainty sandwiches and traditional cakes. He had come to the funeral to do his duty, and to reassure himself that the old boy was gone, and perhaps if absolutely necessary to make some gesture towards provision for his widow. He had expected — what had he expected? — another crazy child-bride like his sister? An ageing harridan whose last hope was a soak who could be propped up and called a husband? He had no conception, except to do his duty and flee.

Instead he found himself lingering after the other guests had gone, reluctant to tear himself from this golden corner of England. He broached the subject delicately. Was there anything Crawford might do? One was family after all, however oddly related.

Genista threw back her head and laughed. He listened to the roaring gurgle and imagined it rolling around the drawing-room of *that house*, and sighed with pleasure.

'The poor old dear didn't have a bean,' she said. 'Apart from his various pensions, army and what not. They more or less kept him in gin and golf-clubs. I'm afraid if we'd been reliant on that source we'd have hocked off the family silver years ago. No, no, one will get by, rather better I should imagine without the gin and golf-clubs, but it's awfully kind of you.'

This answer pleased Crawford, who did not want her to be penniless, nor especially comfortable. It seemed to him that the Commander had, once again, as in New Zealand with Rosalia, been exceptionally lucky, and he marvelled that fate should deal such a poltroon so good a hand. He, on the other hand, had given his life-blood, drop by drop, for his success, sacrificing all the ordinary human comforts, first to grow successful, and then to seal his position in society. He believed that it cost him meticulous effort and self-discipline, and the costs still mounted.

Crawford, on the night he fled from *La Damnation de Faust*, slipped past his house, observing it as an outsider might, drinking in the affluence and simple good taste suggested by its very outline, the well-oiled wrought-iron gates giving a moonlit view of a well-ordered garden, with broad flags leading up to the porch. Genista's experimental jungle behind the house was mercifully hidden from view. He noted that the house was rather obviously unoccupied, but took comfort in the dual protection of electronics and dogs. His neighbours would know of any untoward happenings almost at once; the

25

dogs would bark, the alarms explode, the lights of half a dozen fine houses would blaze out on to the Green, the local constable be on his way round *instanter*!

He passed on, reassured, through a brief passage of fields, and then into narrower and narrower streets, where the houses began to squeeze up to one another for comfort, frontages so restricted that it was a wonder a household could be contained behind them. He always had the same sense of distaste as he turned into Mercy's street, with its long brick terraces, sliced up into so many thin dwellings like a block of processed meat that must go round the whole table. There was of course nowhere to park. Cars filled either side of the mean little street, leaving room for cars to pass by in single file. Crawford's usual expedient was to double-park flank to flank with another car at the point where another little street joined at right angles. As he rarely stayed at Mercy's house above ten or fifteen minutes this strategy had so far succeeded. His paintwork had not once been scratched.

He grimaced with pain as he parked, as always. *I could not live in England if I were poor*, he repeated, his mantra. *But I would not be living in England if I were poor.* If he were poor — which he would not be, only impoverished — he would live as he used to do, on his farm in New Zealand, making a style statement out of his muddy Land Rover and his ancient Jag. He liked to think of those days of struggle, as a moderately successful artist likes to recall the sweet excruciating time when he plugged away at his work, knowing he had what it took. Crawford had always known he had what it took, even in the days of overdraft and dissembling. He was no longer poor, nor ever likely to be, come recessions, Asian, Russian, Brazilian, or *heaven forfend!* European. There was always a market for wine — good wine, cheap wine, wine that was cheap but didn't look it, wine that looked cheap but was good. Funeral direction, wine-shipping, brothels — three businesses that never fail. Of course, he thought, as he let close the car door and pointed the device to lock it, one could be outmanoeuvred. One knew how that was done — and there was bound to be someone out there cleverer and more charming, with better French. Then one would retire to the farm, as if by design, and start again. And nowadays, with all the contacts and the credibility, one could set up a little boutique vineyard from scratch and command a splendid price from the outset, for one thing was certain — and that was Wolf's commitment.

Wolf's commitment, Crawford thought, stronger than any marriage, made in heaven or hell. Born from love and sealed by hatred. Wolfgang, his wine-maker, his self-maker. The cleverest, most mercurial spirit, a troll powered by lightning. The man without whom he would not be who he was, and yet whom he chose, and delighted, to ignore. Back down there, in New Zealand, in his cave, Wolfgang made the reluctant magic that kept Crawford rich. But as with all magics, reluctant or willing, there is a price to pay.

Mercy's curtains were not drawn and her lights were on. Anyone on the street could see straight into her front room and her bedroom. Such a silly girl. Anyone who cared to could see that she was there — and how vulnerable her defences — all alone without a dog or a burglar alarm or even a chain on the door.

Except that she was not alone. Crawford stood by her front window, a three-sided bay, too sharp on the angles, the windows poorly seated and jammed in with inexpert putty. A late rose scraped itself to and fro against the glass. Inside Mercy's sitting-room was a young man.

He was a short-haired, bullet-headed man, about thirty, a working man by the look of him, sharp-eyed and nimble-fingered. You knew the sort.

Crawford had never seen him before, but that did not prevent him from disliking him.

Mercy and the man had glasses and bottles of beer, and a tube of crisps. She was sitting on the floor by her gas fire, and he was sitting on the chair. Mercy only had one chair that worked. The others were flourishes of gentility that no one sat in.

Mercy was wearing jeans and a check shirt. The top two buttons were undone. She was cross-legged and her bare feet curled up in front of her. She was arguing a point with the man; neither was smiling but Crawford was aware that they were enjoying themselves. He knocked on the door. She would recognize his knock.

'Oh it's you,' she said, throwing the door wide. As always he winced microscopically at her vowels and abruptness. 'I suppose you need a drink. What the hell do you think you're doing here this time on a Saturday?'

'I trust you haven't given that man any of my brandy?'

'Would I? His name is Ron and we're about to go to bed.'

'Excellent.'

'I don't need you here screwing it up.'

'I need a drink, Mercy, and I need some of

your company. A few minutes to calm down.'

'Go into the kitchen and help yourself.'

Crawford was obedient. He glanced into the sitting-room as he passed, fielding a bemused and angry look from the man called Ron, who was clearly quite drunk. Mercy's hall was painted soviet red, but most of the paint was concealed by paperback books, stacked two deep on rickety wooden shelves, stuck in on their sides above others, teetering in piles on the very top shelf, but all spines out, in subject and alphabetic order, with the sort of comprehensiveness which makes you long to be a good reader. Crawford was familiar with the contents of these shelves. He often pointed out to her that if she didn't spend all her money on books she could have the car she so lusted after. He pointed out to her that she lived in everybody else's make-believe world, reading so many novels. He pointed out to her that part of her inability to get a grip on her own relationships was her addiction to other people's.

Mercy's kitchen was just large enough to accommodate an electronic keyboard and a two-person table, a small library of books on cookery and herbs, stacks of jars and packets in home-made shelves right up to the ceiling, which was covered with laminated photographs of New Zealand overlapping one another, so that you felt pressed down upon by the impossible beauty of somewhere else.

Crawford would have been uncomfortable here had it not been for the many, if fleeting, moments of pleasure enjoyed by the keyboard, and the lingering sensation of biting into Mercy's savoury muffins, still warm from the oven, and light and salty as a spring dawn on his very own sea-shore.

In the painted cupboard under the sink there was a wine rack of his choicest discoveries, and a good stock of brandies and ports which he never had to share with his neighbours.

He had to find himself a clean glass worthy of the contents. Mercy's housekeeping was not wanting, merely haphazard. The brandy balloons on the top shelf were clean, without any of the water-based residue common on hand-washed crystal in these parts, but they were dusty. The tea-towel with which he wiped out the dust was also clean, but grey and unironed. Mercy talked about tea-towels quite often — she had something of an obsession about them.

'They're clean!' she'd shout. 'But they never look clean. You hang them on the line in the sun and they stay grey. Sometimes they get greyer because of the filthy rain. At home — don't you remember? Blinding white linen — five minutes on the line in the sea breeze — blinding. And smelling so wonderful — '

But Crawford had never hung washing on a line, nor gathered it in, nor folded it, though he occasionally took it out of the cupboard.

'Buy new ones,' he would say, and Mercy would laugh.

He wiped the glass, poured himself a brandy, had a look at the wine rack to see if he fancied something. A bottle, at ten on a Saturday night — was that wise? Would Mercy join him? He heard footsteps going upstairs, accompanied by playful chat in low voices. This was only to be expected, but Crawford sighed. The man called Ron was stumbling and making a joke of it. Crawford surmised that he would be enthusiastic but not up to much and decided, on balance, it was worth his while to open something. He found a nice Zinfandel from Stellenbosch, smiled at the recollection of buying them — straw-covered and neglected from the back of the barn, a charming coloured man who found the possession of wine an embarrassment, and was only too glad to take his cash then and there and help him load them into the Rangie and its trailer. Aah, beautiful place — very much his spiritual home, had it not been so complicated by Afrikaaners.

He opened the wine carefully and set it to warm gently just the right distance from a radiator. Turned up the central heating, wondering why Mercy would wish to go to bed in the cold.

He walked about the kitchen, prevented from enjoying his drink by the thought of his wife, by now emerging from the opera house. She would look about her to scout the way to the station. It was her custom to let Crawford steer her through the side-streets, pretending confusion in the lanes and byways, though ordinarily she was as competent as a scout leader in every aspect of her life. As a consequence she never quite got to grips with central London and tended to stand in the middle of the pavements looking up and down for landmarks, like a romantic traveller on the misty moor.

★   ★   ★

He was pleased in a way to have the time alone in Mercy's house. He liked to discover if there were any corners of her life that she was hiding from him. He did not go so far as to read her emails, but he scouted about for receipts, programmes, tickets, greetings cards, withered flowers carefully preserved — anything that might suggest an event that she had not chosen to share with him. The man Ron had been a surprise, but only a little one; new men spun in and out of orbit, some of them mere asteroids. Crawford was only interested in the planets, he feared a massy dark one as yet unnamed by astronomers. Crawford wanted Mercy to have a man in her life, and told her so often. But he must be the *right* man, especially after the long-running soap opera of Mercy's disasters.

He pulled books out of the shelves and carefully returned them as they proved dissatisfying; he sampled tracks from various CDs, hearing the minuscule defects of diction and timing even in the very best choral groups, and the excruciating liberties that soloists took with intonation. Was this sloppiness increasing or was it simply the perfection of modern technology which made everyone's imperfections plain? It seemed so simple a thing — perfection in music, and yet, how many fell short. There was very little new to be found in Mercy's house. But then, there was so much *in* Mercy's house that the vital clue might take days to unearth. She kept several calendars — one for work, a laminated photograph of children in smocks gluing straws together, with the legend *Your*

Local Education Authority Art Works! On this she had meetings and workshops and what days she was at which school carefully annotated in different coloured pens. From the middle of December until the middle of January there were no events. Instead the words NEW ZEALAND danced across the blank days in a riot of feltpen.

Another calendar issued by her church was spotted with line drawings of dancing people who had found Jesus and printed up with details of Alpha courses, study groups, Healing Events and Prophecies and Rock of Ages sessions. Mercy had added her own annotations: *Get Harvest Festival mess ready today. Boot Camp at Chellington 16:30. Taizé chaos 17:00.* She had another calendar, featuring the cats of Rome, for musical and social events. Every Monday night was marked *Glee!* as if Mercy was determined to enjoy herself. On this were marked lunches and nights out with the girls, and film and theatre trips and concerts with Crawford.

There was little of use to be found on the calendars, no matter how informative they pretended to be. There were too many unlikely gaps — tonight, if the calendar was to be believed was a complete blank. Crawford supposed she must have vulgarly picked Ron up at the pub. How many other

Rons? — or more worryingly, what about the unhappily married Inspector of Schools or adulterous Music Group Leader — offering Mercy a simulacrum of love and future commitment in return for present pneumatic bliss and excellent omelettes?

★ ★ ★

Having given the lovers a head start, he carried the bottle of wine and a pair of glasses upstairs, stepping delicately, and picked his way to the bedroom. Mercy's upstairs hall was narrow enough without the small architectural miracle of coloured cardboard boxes that filled it. REMNANTS — B&W REMNANTS — PL. COLOUR REMNANTS — PATTERNED RMN QUILT PATTERNED TOO SML FLOWERS STRAW RIBBONS BUTTONS METAL BTNS FANCY in Mercy's bold capitals.

'I brought you up some wine,' Crawford said. 'South African. Very good.'

'Go away, Crawford,' said Mercy.

The front bedroom overlooked the street. Mercy had not drawn the curtains and the light blazed out. Crawford padded into the room and put the wine on the mantelpiece amid the chapter of teddy bears which Mercy had made or renovated. He crossed to the

36

window to reassure himself over the safety of his car, and looked out at the street and wondered in how many of the curtained bedrooms opposite strange occurrences took on the lineaments of ordinariness.

He stood by the window, elbow on the sill, glass in hand, and watched for a while. *Piss off, Crawford,* Mercy's mouth said. He ignored the mouth, that lovely orifice, too big and handsome for her face. 'What's he doing here?' asked the man called Ron.

Mercy's bedroom was painted first flush cherry blossom white with an Edwardian stencilled frieze in aubergine around the picture rail. It had taken her weeks, and Crawford felt he had lived through every purple spot of it. The room otherwise was uncluttered and comfortable — old Indian and Greek rugs and bright abstract ones of Mercy's weaving, and cream New Zealand sheepskins covered worn bits of the carpet and provided an inviting alternative to the bed.

Crawford saw a small car weaving its way slowly around the dark bulk of his Jaguar, and drew anxious breath. The car nosed around for a park. He decided it posed him no threat and closed the curtains. He went over to the bed, bent over, turned on the bedside light, and gave Mercy a light kiss on the contorted forehead.

'After a certain age, bright light is simply too cruel.'

'What the fuck is he doing here?' said Ron again.

'Just protecting my investment,' said Crawford, civilly, and turned out the bedroom light as he left.

2

Crawford drove home, still hurt over Genista's betrayal, but on balance cheerful — a muscular thirty-year-old had been entirely routed. Possibly a night of excellent strenuous sex lay before him — but tomorrow, what would the man called Ron remember? Crawford's fantasies were fuelled for the night.

Would that things were so simple.

When he got back to his house, all the lights were blazing. He opened the garage door with the device, and docked safely in his garage. He noticed as he got out of his Jag that Genista's black Polo was ticking as if it had been driven and were cooling down. He could make no sense of this. He went towards the door which led from the garage into the house and heard, much too loudly, the *Ride to Hell* from *Faust*. This seemed to him rather tedious. He unlocked the door. But it was bolted on the inside. He went out of the garage to the front door and unlocked both its locks. It was secured on the chain. He pushed it loudly on its chain to alert Genista to his presence. He went round the outside to the garden door and tried there. Those doors also were bolted from within. He banged on the glass.

The dogs, roused from their slumber, greeted him genially, but could not let him in. He went round to the drawing-room, from whence the music issued, and banged on the window. He noticed that the track was on endless repeat. How inexpressibly tedious. He went to the front door and leant on the bell push. There was no corresponding ring from the depths of the house. Was it possible that Genista had disconnected it? He had not credited her with so much practical forethought, nor so much malice. He hammered on the door from the garage, slammed the garage door once or twice, leaned on the front-door chain, threw an ineffectual stone or two at the master bedroom window.

A light went on in the upper reaches of his neighbour's house. Crawford froze in the shadow of a cypress. The humiliation of being discovered in this state by a neighbour crept over him like a hot flush, and he felt almost nauseous with embarrassment. How they would drop their voices at the tennis club, and whisper around the cocktail circuit. He could never hold up his head before the ladies of his glee club again.

He stood in his own front garden, flanked

by his rose bushes, conscious of the noise and the neighbours, and considered what would be consistent with his dignity. A man of fifty-three years, with soft skin and a delicate constitution, dressed for an evening out could not spend the night in his summer house. He considered driving back into St Albans and putting up at the Red Lion, but remembered from the irritating occasion that he delivered a Rumanian wine merchant rather late, that they shut up shop at eleven o'clock. This, he thought crossly, is England. We are not deemed to have a night life unless we are ravers in Leeds. Even in New Zealand one might stay out late. He considered driving out to one of the ghastly motorway hotels where you could get a bed at any time. He considered going back to town and knocking up his club. But in both cases, without an overnight bag?

He took the car out once more and drove into the village to the telephone box. He despised the mobile phone. He dialled his own number and heard his own silver voice making soothing apology. He despised the answerphone also, but the ladies had begged him so. Genista bought one and often left the phone switched over, for the fun of replaying messages left for him. *She must be a new one. About to divorce, perchance?* she'd say, chuckling at a message. *Bit of a tiff at the coffee morning*, she'd say, rippling with laughter, *I think you must have shown undue favour*.

He cursed the answerphone; at least if the phone were now resounding through the house she might eventually be forced to react. He was mystified by her behaviour. Until now she had been so tolerant and amused. There were, naturally, things he did not trouble her with, but there had never been deceit worthy of the name. He would have said rather that his marriage was characterized by an exemplary frankness. Genista had never exhibited jealousy; she knew there was no cause and she was far too well adjusted to invent one. They had their pact and both of them had been happy with it. What on earth had happened to disrupt it?

Crawford stood in the phone box, pulling his coat around him against the encroaching cold, and tried to make sense of his evening. *Dies irae dies illa*. Had he upset her so much by leaving the theatre? But by the same token she had upset him terribly by staying behind. He had visited Mercy — but he had done that a thousand times. There was no secret in that. Genista positively encouraged him in his care of Mercy. She sent him round with lemon drinks when Mercy had the flu, made

42

him take Mercy to the hospital when she had bad period pains, bought him flowers to take her on her birthday, invited Mercy at Christmas and Easter and to all their little *soirées*. She probably knew he kept a stock of wine in Mercy's kitchen and that he often went by to partake some of it after choir practice. She knew that he and Mercy had a shared history from New Zealand farm days, and while she might be shielded from the particular details, she had never exhibited any unnecessary nosiness.

For his part, he had never asked her personal questions about her first husband, the egregious Commander. Not that there was much need, for Crawford had locked in his innermost parts his own secret knowledge of the Commander. He had never shared this with Genista, nor had she ever described how she came to marry so unsuitable a man. They had agreed to start from scratch — *tabulae rasae*, he said; like a Mormon marriage, she said, and they laughed at the very difference in their little jokes.

He dialled Mercy's number. After a very long time she answered, her voice more Chaliapinesque than usual.

'Oh, you.'

'I am sorry to disturb you, Mercy, but I'm on my way to your house. I thought you

43

would like to be warned. I shan't venture upstairs this time, but make myself comfortable by the fire, if you leave me a blanket.'

'What the — '

'I'm locked out of my house.'

This time he parked around the corner in the supermarket car park, noting that it alone was bright and open. Perhaps I should shop instead, he thought, wondering what one would buy at midnight. What sort of desperation drove people to buy frozen peas and cornflakes at night time . . . perhaps the same out-of-kilter life that he was suddenly tipped into. He hesitated by the bright doors, thinking what he might buy for Mercy — chocolates, flowers — did they sell such things? He spent so much money on Mercy it scarcely seemed necessary.

She opened the door in her African robe, yellow suns and brown monkeys, pushing her amber hair out of her eyes. She was still half asleep. She went straight up the stairs.

'Most of that wine's left, and your glass is still up there.'

'No, I won't intrude.'

'You already did. Anyway he's gone.'

Crawford followed her up the stairs.

'Already?'

'It's none of your business.'

'I am deeply sorry, Mercy — it's a simple

misunderstanding — '

'I'm asleep. Tell me tomorrow.'

He looked into the back bedroom, hardly more than a glorified box room. On the narrow bed stood a good-sized loom, with a rug in russets half woven. The rest of the room was taken up by the sewing table and bags and boxes and baskets of stuff. The vacuum cleaner, the cello, the old Apple Macintosh were allotted their share of the small space. On the walls were framed photos of home — up the valley, across the bay, bush walks, waterfall, ski slope. No room for Crawford.

He went back into the main bedroom, now in darkness.

He stood in the doorway listening. She was crying. He could not have explained why he had expected this. She was crying as secretly as possible, but he was not to be deceived.

He stepped into the room and took off his clothes with care. He found an empty hanger in the bottom of the bursting wardrobe and hung up his jacket and trousers. He folded his shirt and underpants and laid them on a chair-back. He folded his socks together and slipped naked into Mercy's bed. She was curled up away from him.

'Come, puss,' he said, 'put your head where it belongs.'

She turned over and disposed herself against him, her head on his chest. He placed a hand on her hair. He could quite distinctly feel the dampness on her cheek, but he chose not to pass comment.

'Tell me nice things,' he said.

Mercy said nothing at all. Her flesh was soft and warm as a cat sunbathing. It seemed a crime against nature to find her alone.

'He wasn't worth crying over. Very few people are.'

'It's not that,' said Mercy. 'It's why? Why do they just walk away? What's wrong with me?'

'You are simply too desirable, my darling. They look at you, see how wonderful you are and how well I look after you and realize that they can't compete.'

'I wish that were true,' she said. 'I know I should ditch you to have a chance with anyone, but then I would have no one at all.'

'You say the sweetest things.'

Mercy turned over and put a pillow over her head. Crawford rested his hand on the buttock presented to him.

'You can't quarrel with me,' he said. 'I know you too well.'

She remained obdurate.

'Tell me something nice,' he said. 'Tell me your fantasies.'

'No,' she said.

'You never will. How can I make them come true if you won't tell me?'

'You can't make them come true.'

'I can do most things. It's amazing what money and will-power can achieve. Anything worth having can be bought. Tell me what you want, darling.'

The pillow stayed resolutely over Mercy's head. Crawford saw that neither confession nor copulation was his lot that night, but he felt only the mildest regret. He, and no one else, was in her bed.

★   ★   ★

Mercy cried at nights, briefly, passionately, and then fell into the deepest sleep. She cried over her dead baby, sucked away without ceremony, the babies she could never have, and the man she longed for. She did not try to imagine the baby, for the sight of other women's babies was hard enough to bear, but she often dreamed about the man. She would never have confessed to Crawford that he usually resembled Rewi Mann, whom she had spoken to once or twice as a teenager. Laconic Kiwi bloke to his clipped fingernails, a working man who'd never darken the doors of an opera house. His image had never really left her, the solid kind man, his brown hand holding the miniature hand of his daughter. Sitting on her bed at the lowest moment of her life, frowning with anger at what had happened to Mercy, frowning with concern, offering her a little corner of comfort in her bleak world — a fantasy that it was him, nice, young, sexy Rewi, rather than Crawford Hollander that had been the one.

Crawford would have poured scorn on this fantasy, exposing it for the absurdity it was. In Crawford's world-view, which was the only one conceivable, Mercy was a girl who gobbled up the good things of life — clothes, outings, dinners — a woman who could not live without her annual trips to the châteaux in France, Glyndebourne, the Edinburgh Festival, things unimaginable without Crawford at her elbow to fund them.

Sometimes in the dark of the night, she tried to remember why she had allowed Crawford to infiltrate her life. She remembered how she hated him and how her heart soared when she got on the plane to England because she'd never have to hear his dark brown voice again, and then how her heart had jumped into her mouth when, eighteen months later, the phone rang, and he was inviting her to Paris. And she said yes, because she was lonely and poor and depressed, and besides he *owed* her.

And the years after that, she kept on saying yes to every proposal, because he owed her. And yes, it was such fun to dress up and go to opera, and sit in his swanky car and pretend to be his mistress, and even if in five-star hotels she had to turn the TV up to max and press pillows round her head to drown out whatever he was enjoying in the next room, and even if occasionally she had to politely encounter in the bathroom some woman so unbelievably glamorous that it was amazing to think she was a whore, even if . . . It was Mercy who got the dinners and the dresses, and when she was with him she didn't feel so bad about herself after all.

After a while, Crawford's reality became the only one, and other possible scenarios — ordinary struggling lives, with mortgages, and families, and love and duty and homework — seemed like a rather dull film. In the night she knew his version was the construct, carefully smoothing out inconvenient concepts like corruption, degradation and materialism. Having what one wanted was the natural order. Around Crawford it became so, and for those fortunate enough to be his satellites it was so. *Tell me what you want.*

But at night Mercy knew what she wanted,

and that Crawford and his money prevented her from the possibility of it. In the morning she would resolve to rid herself of him and start again, penniless and friendless. But as the day wore on, she would realize how he had enmeshed her — the mortgage on her house was in his name, for she could not have afforded to live in Harpenden; her head of department was an acquaintance of Crawford's, and she would never have even known about the wonderful job she now had, let alone been considered for it, if they hadn't bumped into him at the Arena di Verona, and his ice-cream made contact with the fabulous red dress Crawford had just bought her in Milan.

And in the evening, when Crawford called, with a new proposal for somewhere to go, something to do, giving her first refusal, with the implication of others waiting eagerly in the wings, she'd think how dull life would be with just a plumber for company, and besides, why should other girls get the goodies on offer, when it was Mercy who had suffered? Crawford owed her, and she had made a pact that he should pay.

But she also paid, crying at night, watching the plain, sexy men who might love her, shy away from Crawford and his works. She longed to break away from him, but feared that he had made her his creature.

He had become so confident of her that he had decided to get married to someone else.

Mercy looked back on that cocktail party with a shudder. It had been just another one of Crawford's little dos, twenty people and quarts of gin. The sun was shining on the Green, the roses were in full chorus. The better-connected of the Gleeful Ladies of Harpenden, Crawford's choir and resident harem, and their spouses, a paste of the people from the tennis and golf clubs, some people from the wine trade — Crawford's habitual gang. Mercy in a red dress doing her usual number — siren crossed with girl-guide leader. From the moment she walked in that day, she knew something really odd was going on. For one thing, Genista, and Genista alone, was already in the kitchen doing things when Mercy arrived to strap on her apron. Mercy did not take this amiss, not regarding Crawford's kitchen as her territory, but she was greatly surprised. She had for some time acted as his presumed partner on social occasions, because it suited them both. No one, she figured, needed to know the details of their relationship.

She knew Genista moderately well, having sung with her in the Gleeful Ladies for several years. Mercy liked her greatly, but would never have claimed her as a friend simply because of the great disparity in their ages. Discovering her in Crawford's kitchen, Mercy was as friendly as it was her nature to be, but did not ask the one obvious question — *What are you doing here?*

Before the party was much older it became clear to Mercy that Crawford had failed to tell her something that anyone else might have regarded as essential. There was a new understanding between Crawford and Genista, which would clearly change her role for ever. She felt no great disappointment, but as the party minutes ticked on she felt anger growing in her at his obtuseness. How could he pretend to her or to himself that this whatever-it-was between himself and Genista did not change things?

But apparently he did so pretend. After an hour, when everyone had arrived, he called for their attention and made a pretty little speech explaining that Genista had done him the honour of agreeing to be his wife, and he hoped that with her coaching he might eventually enlarge into a husband.

Amid the babble of congratulation, Mercy heard Crawford's private tone in her ear.

'Nothing will change between you and me of course,' he said. 'That's part of the agreement I've come to with Genista.'

'What did you tell her about me?' asked Mercy, alarmed.

'That you were my protégée. That there was no sexual relationship between us. The truth, in other words.'

Mercy was so astounded at his version of the truth that she said nothing. But she was slightly relieved that Crawford did not regard transparency as necessary to his marriage.

'I don't see how things can stay the same,' she said.

'Genista understands that boats must not be rocked. She would rather not remain a widow the rest of her days. I'll come over this evening,' he said, and circulated.

Mercy spent the rest of that day in two states of mind. The front part of Mercy was cheerful in the extreme, demonstrating to Genista and the rest of the world that there simply was *no problem. Of course* she wasn't his discarded girlfriend, *of course* she hadn't expected to marry him. This was not a hard part to play, because it was almost entirely true, and besides Mercy loved a party and always enjoyed herself. She finished up mid-afternoon with a group of four middle-aged men laughing at her every remark, while they studiously avoided her cleavage and the glances of their wives.

But all the time she was furiously

wondering what she should do — almost crying inside at the thought of kind and gracious Genista marrying this man — wanting to take her aside and shake her and say: *Don't you know what he's like? You can't marry him, whatever the terms. He's life in death. Just because I seem to like him, don't be taken in!* But what could she say that would not sound like sour grapes? — except to tell Genista the truth, which she could not bear to do. The things between Crawford and herself could not be spoken about. She never spoke of them; Crawford had never done so. Perhaps he had forgotten. Perhaps, like Mercy, he had turned it into a graphic novel of pain — dark, dramatic, but fixed. Something horrible you read once, and then put on the shelf and never needed to get out again. But to tell Genista would make it real again. The drawings would come to life, and the blood would flow.

Should she stay after the party and tidy up, as she always did? Would she be gooseberry, or would she be Mercy carrying on as normal? To leave with all the other guests would imply that things had changed, and that she *had* been Crawford's girlfriend after all.

As she was running these things over in her mind, Genista came to her rescue. She took her by the hand and led her away from the group of admirers.

'Please stay to supper,' she said. 'I know you usually help Crawford after these dos, so if we pull together it will be quicker and then we can whip something up.'

Mercy had a terrible flash of recollection, relating to a hotel room and a woman in high heels and leather, and gulped slightly.

'Yes thanks, I'd love to.'

It was on this footing that they started, and on this footing they continued. Genista and Mercy became the best of friends — older and younger sister, mother and daughter . . . They colluded against Crawford, teased him, and conducted their separate lives with him. They shared many secrets but none whatsoever relating to Crawford. Mercy continued to be in and out of the house, and Crawford continued to take her to the opera, to wine and music festivals, on business trips to France and America, always, naturally, giving Genista first refusal. Genista understood how things were, and almost always declined the invitations she was supposed to decline.

Mercy had grown comfortable with her discomfort. It had always been part and parcel of being around Crawford that she should feel sordid and unreal. That, she felt, was the whole point of it. And so being in this weird asexual *ménage-à-trois* was a continuation of the way she had accepted things would be.

Except at night, in her half-dreams, when a different reality presented itself. A clean, tidy, plain world, in which you took off your shoes and walked on the sand, holding the hand of an ordinary man who loved you because you were funny, and sexy, and homely, and just because you were Mercy Fisher.

★ ★ ★

When Crawford awoke on the Sunday morning after his excarceration, he thought nemesis was upon him. There was a pressing, heavy pain in his chest. Confused by his surroundings he did not at once open his eyes, and let the half-consciousness of his own death sweep over him. *I have done some good*, he thought, surfacing, struggling to remember what it was.

Mercy's golden-eyed cat was sitting on his chest staring at him with the generalized malevolence of cats. From along the corridor came a mêlée of noise, the shower beating on ceramic and Mercy singing in her various registers. Mercy's voice was so low that she sang alto in a falsetto, and she often practised

56

singing pieces in one octave and repeating them an octave higher or lower for the hell of it. Her singing teacher would have been appalled — the voice she said must be pampered and cajoled, not pulled about like a drunken harlot. Mercy liked to play the harlot with her voice, which was possibly why she remained the star of the Gleeful Ladies of Harpenden, and was not belting out numbers in the West End. Crawford was tossed between delight and horror as he listened to her playing the fool, *Summertime* breaking into *And can it be*! followed by a snatch of *Memory* and a bar or two from the Queen of the Night. And all the while, he knew, she was naked, her big generous body all over the place, her breasts lumbering after her as she twisted and turned to get a decent all-over wash.

'Bloody English showers,' she was known to say. 'Even I have to run round to get wet, and if they don't get unclogged every five minutes they piddle like a busload of bowlers.'

Crawford sometimes explained about ionizers to soften water, and French shower technology, but these explanations fell on deaf ears.

'A bath is much better anyway,' she'd say.

He sat up very slowly so as to dislodge the

cat as painlessly as possible, but in common with its kind, the cat was wise to this manoeuvre. It pressed down with all its catty self and extended its claws a microscopic distance, just so Crawford would feel them through the layers of bedding. It purred. And well it might, Crawford thought, having him pinned helpless. Then suddenly it heard Mercy come out of the bathroom and thump downstairs, and it sprang off Crawford's chest with the force of a gin-trap.

Crawford levered himself out of bed and braved the bathroom. It was not that Mercy was messy, or not unduly so; she was a good New Zealand girl, after all, to whom cleaning came as naturally as baking. It was the jungle of ferns and vines and flowering things, in various states of health, the macramé structures hanging from the ceiling flowing over with towels of every hue between olive and cerulean and a bottle of every brand of lotion and gel and foot ointment and massage oil the Body Shop had ever produced. Venturing into Mercy's bathroom Crawford felt he should be armed with a solar topee and a machete, rather than a towel and shaving cream. The surfaces were clean, the towels crisp, but somehow one did not emerge refreshed.

He found a razor in one of the cupboards

and gritted his teeth. His reflection — in one of several mirrors — told him that he had spent a harrowing night. This was all to the good, for Genista must suffer without a word of reproach being uttered.

A little fresher and smoother, he went back to the bedroom and discovered that it was barely eight o'clock. Eight o'clock of a Sunday morning was no-man's time — neither sleeping nor waking, certainly not rising. Mercy, in her lion-coloured dressing-gown, wet and tousled, came up the stairs with two mugs of black instant coffee.

'What on earth possesses you to get up at this hour?' he said, sinking back into the one chair in the room.

'Children's church,' she said. 'The mini-bus comes at quarter to.'

'What a ghastly term. Do you mean Sunday School?'

'I suppose it's the same thing.' She sat down on the floor, on a sheepskin, rather unnecessarily crossing her legs. 'They think it's important to give it validity. Or something.'

'Why do you do this to yourself, Mercy? It damages you emotionally.'

'Yes, I guess it does. Except I am so emotionally damaged that I don't think a few gorgeous six-year-old Christians will make it worse.'

'But why do it at all?'

'Because they mob you — it's so much easier to do it than to explain why you don't want to — I keep trying to drop out — but you know you meet them in the high street and they look so hurt — and you can't possibly admit that you've stopped loving Jesus, or whatever it is.'

'I could help you out.'

'I'll bet you could. But no thanks, I'll handle this mess myself.'

'Genista teaches Sunday School now and then — well not exactly teaches, it's more a sort of lofty child-minding. They have a handful of arrogant overbred children to control. I'm sure she could roster you in once every three months, and then you could tell your earnest friends that you've decided that Church of England children need Jesus too.'

'It's tempting, Crawford, but it isn't me.'

'What *is* you, Mercy?'

'When I've worked that out, Crawford, you'll be the first to know. I shall ring you from wherever I've landed and tell you to fuck off.'

Crawford sighed elaborately, a long and musical sigh.

'Well, come on,' said Mercy. 'Get on with it. What's going on? Only don't tell me you and Genista are going to split, because I can't take that this early in the morning.'

'Don't be absurd, Mercy. As if Genista would even contemplate such a thing. We are far too comfortable for that. No. I walked out of that execrable production of the *Damnation of Faust*. I'm sure I told you about it. She remained behind. I can only conclude that she was enjoying it. I find that incomprehensible. When I returned home, after visiting you, Genista had locked me out. I find that equally incomprehensible. The whole thing is a surreal nightmare.'

Mercy started to rock with silent laughter. She rocked and rocked backwards and forwards, and had to put her coffee down, out of the range of her mirth. Crawford suffered her derision in dignified silence.

'I'm glad my marital difficulties are such a source of amusement. Remind me of this when you come sobbing to me after yet another abortive love affair.'

Mercy stopped laughing abruptly. She started to object passionately, then shrugged her shoulders.

'Sometimes I wish I was married to you, so I could divorce you messily.'

'You'd never divorce me. You have far too well-developed a sense of what's good for you. As indeed does Genista.'

61

'Sense doesn't always come into relation-ships.'

'My relationships are compounded of good sense,' said Crawford.

'Bullshit,' she said. 'Your relationships are about possession, which is not sensible. Anyway if I was able to divorce you, it would mean I had already been married to you, which would mean that you had actually asked me, which would mean you had at least *said* that you love me, which you never have, and that I thought I loved you, which I can only imagine doing in very special circum-stances, so we would have to be very different people to even be in a position to be divorced, which means that we probably wouldn't want to anyway.'

'I don't think logic is your strongest suit,' said Crawford.

★ ★ ★

He decided the best moment to arrive home was just after Genista had left for church. There was a risk that she might forgo God that morning. But he estimated that her love of a chat would win over the desire to confront him. Besides she was bound to be on some duty — teas or hymn books. He sidled the car towards the house, and saw in the distance Genista and the dogs striding across the Green to church, then turned into the garage and let himself in by the front door with a huge exhalation of relief.

He put *Judas Maccabeus* on to play, had a long bath as if he had been somewhere rather grubby, another, decent shave, and thrust his last night's clothes into the depths of the laundry basket. His reflection still reminded him of an Eastern European intellectual thrust into exile on Southampton docks, but at least he was properly shaven. He prepared the drinks for Genista's return, and sat comfortably with a pot of tea and the Sunday newspapers in a square of sunlight by the open window. A warm wind brought the scent of roses and a neighbourly game of tennis into the room, and the distant bark of the dogs as Genista approached.

'Well!' she said, as she flung herself down, limbs all over the chair. 'Aren't we a prize pair?'

'Speak for yourself, Genista,' he said, determined to retain his dignity at practically any cost.

He carried her a g&t across the room; she took it without saying thank you.

'When I got back to the station and saw your car was gone, I walked home and then I found that you weren't there *either*. Initially of course I was worried — I thought perhaps I had mistaken you, and you'd been taken ill at the theatre, rather than dyspeptic. I felt terribly guilty all of a sudden, as one does. But I thought I'd better just check the obvious traps, so I drove round to Mercy's — and there you were, large as life, standing in Mercy's bedroom with a glass of wine in your hand, for the whole world to enjoy the spectacle.'

'I was *standing* in Mercy's bedroom, as you rightly observe. Fully clothed, as you observed. What precisely did I do to deserve punishment? Good heavens, woman, I've taken Mercy to Verona three times and Edinburgh twice. What on earth is so incriminating about her bedroom?'

'I'm sorry if you can't see it.'

'For your information, Genista, when you observed me, Mercy was in fact in bed with a plasterer or electrician rejoicing in the name of Ron.'

'And you were finishing your wine preparatory to joining them?'

'Good God — what a lurid imagination you have! I realized I was not welcome, so I drank my wine and took a hasty departure.'

'Is there any reason why I should believe you?'

'You could ask Mercy.'

'I did rather think of that.' She took a contemplative sip of gin. 'But I didn't want to put Mercy in the position of having to lie to me. She is so endemically honest that any sort of deception is painful to her.'

'Really? Have you experience of this?'

'Yes, actually, Crawford, I do. Just after we were married, when it became clear to me that Mercy was rather more to you than the star contralto in the choir, I asked her about the nature of your relationship.'

'The nature of our relationship? What sort of phrase is that?'

'A fairly precise one, I always thought. You have a relationship with Mercy, which long predates ours, even if it is mildly father — daughter or patron — protégée.'

'I don't care for the insinuation, Genista. I have never been unfaithful to you with Mercy, or indeed with anyone else.'

Genista did not answer, or even look at him. She swirled the tonic round in her glass and watched the ice clunk after it.

'And what did Mercy say when you asked her that highly inappropriate question?'

'It was years ago. I didn't know her very well, though even then I was inclined to like her. She prevaricated, I think that's the best term for it. It was awful to watch.'

'I don't understand any of this. There is

nothing improper in my relationship with Mercy. You know all there is to know.'

One of the dogs got up from the rug and went over to Genista and rested a long red muzzle on her mistress's knee. Genista bunched up the loose skin on the dog's head and massaged its scalp. It looked at her with ecstatic interest and total lack of comprehension.

'Actually, Crawford, that is probably the least veracious statement you have ever made.'

They had never had an argument, nor could this be classed as arguing; Genista spoke with so good-humoured an air that it seemed that at any moment she would deliver one of her jokey lines and the incident would be closed. Crawford was conscious that he was talking like a character in Noël Coward, but this had become natural to him over the last decade or so — since he became rich and settled in England. When he first arrived here, bursting with New World energy and infatuated with antiquity, he soon found the lips ever so slightly curled against him. His immaculate ear helped him to acquire an accent both irreprehensible and untraceable, something like the accent of a South African classical actor. He gained entree into the tennis club, the dinner-party circuit, the club. He became acceptable, though all the while he thought himself absurd.

Slowly the pretence became as comfortable as a raincoat. The accent became his, so that he could no longer recall how he had once spoken, and Rosalia's vowels on the telephone made him cringe. The Sunday afternoon tennis, the carefully informal formal dinner, the little drinks party, the villa in Tuscany, the yacht in Greece ... things which to his old self would have been exotic and delightful, became the stuff of life. The sun shone, far more often than one had been led to believe.

By this time he was well settled in Harpenden, running up to London every day to further his interests, but needing to do very little except watch his ten per cent tick over every year. His French partners lodged the cheque every quarter, and every year Wolf delivered the goods. All the other deals — Portuguese, Cypriot, Alsatian, Andorran or Lebanese — were flourishes, bits on the side, albeit lucrative bits. He took over the Gleeful Ladies six months after his arrival, ostensibly in response to a hand-written notice in the newsagents that Genista had told him to look out for.

Long-established ladies' choir
Enthusiastic amateurs
Seeks new director of music
Kind heart a must, keyboard skills optional.

They had never looked back, the Gleeful Ladies, the love affair *du fin de siècle*, Genista called it.

His bachelor status which had harvested a good crop of invitations to begin with, now became a liability. The Gleeful Ladies, to a woman besotted with his caressing manner and his brown eyes, began to eye him as prey. His social circle became a little uneasy. Both chaps and their wives would have preferred it if he had been more like them — part of a couple, less of a threat.

Happily Genista was not a woman to harbour illusions. She understood from the start that Crawford was not, nor ever would be, in love with her. She understood that his singling her out, when he was surrounded by an adoring horde, was quite flattering enough, without the added need for passion. She enjoyed the first bloom of courtship, the envy and admiration of other women, the delight of his company — expensive dinners in town, surprise weekends to Rome, a good boat at the Henley Regatta, choral evensong at the Abbey. It was all a lot more civilized than life with the Commander had ever been, even if the old dear had loved her to death.

From the outset, Genista had treated her marriage to Crawford as a sensible woman might. She had enjoyed to the utmost the advantages — comfort, status, the giving and receiving of hospitality, large living spaces and room to experiment in the garden — without demurring over the counterbalances. She loved Mercy like a daughter, and never asked an awkward question.

★   ★   ★

And Crawford had, right up until the moment he rose from his seat at the opera, enjoyed the state of marriage thoroughly. His pleasures had not abated nor his habits changed one jot, and in addition he had excellent company when he needed it, and an irreproachable alliance. With Genista had been conveyed all the gratifications of being married, without the emotional tug-of-war that he observed among his circle. He always understood that Genista understood.

Until now.

Bemused, he observed her across the room. She wore the same air of casual authority that had so attracted him from the first, the aura that made her patients across at the private

69

hospital give up the second bottle of wine for several weeks after they had been only gently reprimanded, the air of indefatigable humour that could see you through blitz and shortage without missing a beat. In Genista's company you felt that it was always possible to see the funny side, and to keep your head when all about you etc.

But this same woman had locked him out of his own house and had not yet apologized.

'Did you spend the night at Mercy's?'

'I'm surprised you need to ask.'

Genista's mining of information was legendary; even the perennially fogged Commander, staggering between the golf-course and the clubhouse, had been known to joke about it. It all went back a long way; as a girl Genista had been dragged round the Empire by her father, charismatic headmaster of the old school, shunting his tattered glory from colony to colony in pursuit of a pedagogic world that had never been, never able to find a system to suit his palpable talents. In his wake he pulled his daughters, who had been at school, a term here, a year there, in every shrinking pink bit on the globe. Genista had her father's delightful nature without his debilitating principles. She responded to this uprooting by instantly charming every girl in the form and boarding-house, and then writing to them madly thereafter. It was often said she had never lost a friend, and her Christmas card take was a local phenomenon. She wrote letters constantly, more or less every day, in her handsome blue writing on unlined airmail, letters full of gossip and anecdote, funny, never malicious, sometimes sad, always engaging. By this means, she had connected friends with friends and friends with friends of friends, and wherever she went there was a place to stay and great gales of laughter.

The only person about whom Genista's information was shaky was her husband. She sometimes joked that he'd married her so she wouldn't find out about him.

★   ★   ★

'Last night it all broke over me, the farce that we live in, and I felt I could take no more. I realized that if I trample down the set and turn on the house lights then the whole thing will be over. It makes no difference to you or me or Mercy exactly when the play ends, so perhaps the sooner the better, while we all have other lives to lead.'

'What extraordinary things you say, Genista. There is no pretence in our lives. We all know precisely where we stand.'

'Yes, I am to be eternally grateful to you for being spared the ignominy of widowhood, in return for which I confer respectability on you, and agree to be entirely blind in the matter of Mercy, and whomever else.'

'It sounds a perfectly reasonable arrangement to me, if it were true. But you are not required to be blind because there is nothing to ignore.'

'Don't strain credulity, my dear. Even I know, withered matron that I am, that a man of your temperament has appetites.'

'Mercy is not my mistress.'

'It's a word, Crawford. You probably have a personal definition of its meaning, like the American President. *I did not have sex with that woman*. That poor woman.'

'Genista, do you regard me as a liar?'

'Crawford darling, I did not marry you for your probity. If I had desired truth in the inmost parts, I might have had the Flying Bishop of Sodor and Mann.'

Crawford glided over to the drinks table and started work on two more g&ts. He paused and considered his words carefully. A great deal of comfort hinged on this conversation.

'And what conclusion have you come to? Now you have relieved your anger by locking me out of the house, is that my punishment?

72

Or is there more purgatory to come?'

He presented Genista with her drink, his brown eyes round with unspoken pain at the injustice done him, a faithful lapdog unfairly kicked.

Genista's inclination was to laugh at his performance. As she took the drink from him, he watched the frown struggle to stay on her brow.

'It's insoluble, Crawford. I am not unhappy in any strict sense of the word. I should be less happy if I left you, simply because of the inconvenience. Life would be a tiresome struggle of no benefit to anyone, except perhaps that you would have Mercy more conveniently to hand. But that would not benefit Mercy, whose interests need rather more protecting than your own. So I shall continue to turn a blind eye. It's always been one of my accomplishments, after all.

'Besides,' Genista added, 'it would totally ruin our trip to New Zealand for Dickie Fisher's birthday bash.'

Crawford turned back to the table, plopped another ice cube in his glass. This was motivated not so much by warmth, as by the necessity to hide his enormous rictus of relief.

3

Of the swarm of people who knew and loved Genista Hollander, few, if any, understood her marriages. It was a subject of fascination to her friends, in groups and in pairs, all over the world — *but have you* met *him, darling!* they cried, both of the Commander and then, all over again, of Crawford.

To Genista it all made perfect sense. She understood why she had married the Commander, and having married him, had stuck it out. She also knew the very different reasons why she had married Crawford, and having married him, stuck it out. *Sticking it out* was something she had been schooled to do, and for her it had a virtue all of its own.

But it was not for masochistic reasons that she had married the Commander, nor out of an exaggerated sense of duty. She was motivated by kindness and by love, and the sense that one ought to do good if possible. If, in the latter reaches of the Commander's life, it was hard for others to see him as in any sense lovable, Genista did not forget the feelings and beliefs that had motivated her to save him.

At the end of his career, Genista's father persuaded a group of good men to finance a Christian school, where both muscular Christianity and proper English education might flourish together. He secured the lease of the Catholic Apostolic Convent near Leatherhead, whose broad corridors and narrow bedrooms seemed an ascetic's dream, and in whose impossibly elongated chapel he imagined the angelic voices of girls and boys twisting together celestial harmonies.

The 1960s wasn't a good time to try an experiment in nostalgic conservatism, and Genista, on her father's unheralded and yet quite predictable death, tumbling off the turret where the coping had crumbled, winging his way downwards towards the Surrey green like a veritable Lucifer, was left with a heap of debts which she proposed to ignore for the rest of her life, and a Victorian Gothic megalith, which no one would take off her hands.

She had continued to live in the convent with her mother because it was, currently, their home, and they were used to impermanence. No one appeared to evict them. They reasoned that as soon as the Catholic Apostolics noticed that no payments were forthcoming they would send round a cheery bailiff, at which point the women would pack their things once more and find themselves more convenient lodgings. They didn't realize that that curious band of eccentrics, having failed to provide a process that would allow for later generations of Apostles to be commissioned, had completely died out, leaving oodles of cash and tremendous Victorian piles all over England.

Genista had lived in this pile, not the slightest bit impressed with herself because of it. She knew, none better, precisely how little she had done to earn or deserve the great crags of Gothic splendour under which she attempted to conduct an ordinary life. She contrived to enjoy it, refusing to condemn the dark dankness of the kitchen with its single gas-ring and cracked marble bench, when one might eat the boiled egg and soldiers of toast at a table the size of a foredeck under the gaze of painted angels. There Genista lived, engaging in a perfectly normal life. She trained as a nursing aide, and wore a horrid pink uniform on the wards, but this caused her not to miss a single beat, because she was six foot tall and as striking as a hook-nosed Guardsman, with the chummiest of manners, even at twenty-one, and no one could resist the gusts of her friendship. She was a Brown Owl, a Red Cross volunteer, a Sunday School teacher, a super-enthusiastic ballroom dancer, in spite of her tendency to tower over all the dear old chaps who shuffled out each Tuesday. The old chaps loved her, clutched to her bosom, even at twenty-two as commanding and generous as Mother Russia; the old chaps on the wards loved her, sucking the thermometer practically to death as she bullied them back to health. She took their adoration in her stride, because the real Genista, who lived inside, had only a mechanical connection to the pasteboard Genista, who was jolly and stiffening and who lived in a pile.

When Genista was twenty-five and no closer to being settled, or unsettled, than she had been at fifteen, her mother, worn out by decades of eccentricity, and exhausted by the struggle to get toes and back warm at the same time, declared that magnificence had finally palled, and went off to live with her unmarried sister in Harpenden. Genista was supposed to go into lodgings near the hospital. The convent was to be shut up for the ghosts of the Catholic Apostolics to wander through at will.

It was all arranged, but Genista saw no intrinsic reason why she should waste the two pounds a week lodgings would cost her, and besides she had lived in the convent longer than in any other place. It was as close to a home as she understood, and striding the empty corridors alone, catching through window after window a sight of the Downs, the may trees straining with blossom, the scatter of farm buildings, discreetly turning their backs on the good nuns, she knew she was happy.

Years later, though she was not a woman to repine, she'd declare that she'd never been happier than during her days in the convent, a little joke that confused new friends. In those days, she'd say, it was still possible to dream of love.

She would stand still before the view, and watch as the shadows shrank in the little hollow by the gatehouse, and the shady green grew more intense and exciting as the light increased. The solitude excited her, made her feel each day was an adventure, that Heathcliff might rear up one day on the brow of the Downs and glare down upon her. She thought it would be nonsense to pack up and go into lodgings just for the sake of a bit of company and a dollop of mashed potato. People said she'd be lonely. But Genista knew that loneliness was an inside thing, that one could be lonely though surrounded by friends and constantly busy. People said men might take advantage of her, all on her own there. But there wasn't a man living, in Genista's opinion, who could get the better of her. Of course, she had reckoned without the Commander.

He had probably meant it when he said he had not intended to stay long. A walking tour, a *reconstitutional*, was his word. Breathe the air of the old country, get a perspective, dry out a bit, charge the old batteries, all that stuff. He strode into the village, having done his obligatory five miles from the last pub, and stopped at the village store on his way to the White Swan to enquire about b&b. There they told him about the Nunnery, where Miss Hume took in paying guests. They tried to tell him a great deal more about Miss Hume and her surroundings and circumstances, but the Commander was so transfixed by the thought of sleeping in a convent that he heard none of it. Had he listened he might have concluded that Miss Hume was too good for him, nay too good to live.

By the time the Commander squelched into her life, Genista had begun to take in lodgers, not from loneliness or necessity but from kindness of heart. She had acquired such a collection of eccentrics that she sometimes thought she should record them for the nation. In classic Genista manner, she organized the collection of their laundry, whipped up mashed spud, ham and carrots in

79

the Refectory, and let the peculiarity wash over her.

But she was only twenty-six years old, and beyond the North Downs the world was undergoing a social and sexual revolution. Genista smelt it. On the sly she read the colour supplements in the hospital waiting area, she went to the new British films with her friends; she saw the funny old world of tea and bicycles floating away in front of her, as the skinny people in skinny-rib jumpers and sunglasses proclaimed her, in tones of flat and insidious triumph, to be irredeemably old-fashioned. She had never been anything else, but it had not seemed to matter when one was at school, with all the girls clustering round, wanting to be friends, laughing and screaming at one's jokes. Humour had changed, worse, the contours of friendship had changed. One had one's friends still, but there was an edge to it — we are a couple, you are Genista, wonderful Genista, but still Genista, surreptitiously but irreversibly turning into a peculiarity.

No, she would say to herself, *not* irreversibly. I'm not going the way of all cranks. I'm not going to be the prime exhibit in my own freak show. I refuse. She was twenty-six, and a virgin, and her nipples had not yet been sucked, by man, woman or baby.

And she felt they needed it.

Although she was expecting him every day of her life, the Commander was absolutely unexpected. It was a miserly wet day, ekeing out the rain in little items which hinted at the wealth to come. Genista was comfortably inside the nunnery with her gaggle of lodgers, and they were all sitting round the big table in the Refectory, as they usually did in the evening, playing Mr Pink's version of whist. This wonderful game had evolved over many long winter evenings and had now been enhanced to take account of Miss Cassandra Kearns, whose grasp on the rules of card games, or indeed on anything, was precarious. Miss Kearns was so sweet-natured a person and so much beloved by the parlour boarders that Mr Pink had devised a special sort of hand for her — the Miss Kearns hand, which was rather like a dummy hand, except that it played, in random and with glorious unconcern for the rules of precedence or reneging, any old card that seemed high enough. Miss Kearns was allowed to win tricks at various points, but never allowed to lead. Whenever she was deemed to have taken a trick, whoever had been assigned to her as partner took the next lead. The convolutions of the rules resulted in arguments and enormous hilarity, which Miss Kearns, completely oblivious to the chaos she caused, joined in with all her natural blessedness.

'When you get to heaven,' the Vicar, Fr Moore, would say after his third glass of port, 'everyone will be playing cards like Miss Kearns.'

Mr Pink, who staggered along the unhappy tight-rope of really caring about the game and wishing to please, made endless bitter and funny jokes, and had to wait up for a real game until after Miss Kearns's bedtime, an event Genista engineered so delightfully that Mr Pink, though a lifelong bachelor himself, thank you, sometimes wished she might organize the night-time rituals for him.

The household was engaged in this anarchic card game, and the small rain down did rain, strongly suggesting that no one would come visiting tonight. The convent was sited in a little valley, just visible from the A415, which of course was not its name when the venerable bricks were laid one upon another. It had such a collection of spires that they poked up out of the valley like a very depleted army camping out for the night. Anyone slightly familiar with domestic architecture would have recognized that to site a large building in a little valley would result in dark rooms, shadowy courtyards and a generally penitential atmosphere, but the famous thread baron who paid for and designed the buildings was not familiar with domestic architecture — that is to say, he had, in common with other rich men, no concept of light and shadow following their own dictates rather than his. As a consequence, the convent spent much of its year and part of every day in dank shadow; and on rainy spring evenings, it demanded considerable dedication to go visiting there.

On that wet spring evening the Commander pulled the bell and set up a corresponding clamour in the depths of the convent. All the inhabitants were taken by surprise. Genista ran for the door, surprised at her eagerness. The distance to the door was so great that she was afraid the visitor would give up waiting and depart. He might only be the baker's boy, but there was always the chance, always, of the bedraggled stranger, washed out of his path, the man with a damaged past and a wonderful fund of stories, and a slow and gentle kiss . . . Which, funnily enough, is a good description of the Commander, but at the same time, completely misrepresents things.

Without peering through the grille, she pulled back the bolts, one two three, quickly so as not to be disappointed. On the step was a dirty mac and crumpled bushman's hat pulled down hard over a dark face, and a lantern jaw, and his hand thrust out and over the threshold before you could say Rumplestiltskin. He was taller than Genista, and looked exactly like Heathcliff.

He came into the convent all wet, mumbling apologies and gratitude. He put down his battered leather suitcase and a brown paper bag containing a bottle, and allowed Genista to take his coat and hat and hang them dripping on one of the many conventual hooks. He had been told in the village, and so forth . . . He had obviously come via the pub, but Genista, the nurse, was used to the bad habits of men, and if Heathcliff drank, then it was to salve his tortured soul. Which, again, wasn't a bad description of his reason, but didn't make the habit any easier to live with ten years down the track.

Genista took him into the room of Sister Porteress, extracted a week's board out of him in half-crowns and got him to sign her visitors' book.

'You're from New Zealand! How wonderful!' The Commander did not look as if he agreed.

She took him into the parlour and introduced him, then trekked off to the kitchen to fetch him a cup of coffee and a bun. And also glasses for whisky, however many . . .

By the time she had hurried back to the warmth of the parlour, he was on anecdotal terms with Mr Pink, and had Miss Kearns laughing helplessly at his jokes, though quite why she found humour where she did, one couldn't quite say.

They had such a party. The Commander joined the whist game on Miss Kearns's team and noisily egged her on to play this card or that, to the devastation of the others. Then he got a poker game going, with Mr Pink and Andrew from the library, determined to teach Genista to play. All the while, Genista laughed and sipped whisky which she had never tasted before and did not care for, but which mysteriously never grew less in her glass, and laughed some more.

After the poker, they must have some dancing, so the whole household, protesting and laughing by turn, was dragged off to the big parlour where the nuns had entertained one another of an evening with pieces on the pianoforte. No one had thought to tune the piano since the little girls in plaits and their piano teacher had endured torments on that same stool. But this scarcely mattered in the clatter of the moment, with everybody whirling around and banging into each other.

Genista tried to play a waltz as he demanded, but soon found herself displaced by Miss Kearns and swept into the embrace of the Commander. He propelled her around the parlour with the sort of vigour she had longed for in the old gents in the dancing classes. Miss Kearns's grasp of a waltz was similar to her grasp of whist, but the ensuing chaos seemed to be entirely to the Commander's liking. They tripped over furniture and stood on each other's toes and laughed, and every now and then the Commander grabbed a top-up from his glass, and topped up his glass from the bottle. Andrew, who went to bed on the dot of nine-thirty, so as to be up for Mass at six, was all at once a born-again partyer. The Commander filled everybody's glass, although that everybody had shrunk to the three of them. Andrew didn't play the piano, so they switched from dancing to sentimental songs, with Genista playing requests, all of them the Commander's. He sang very loud without any regard for conventional key, but with a passion that was irresistible. He loved his Victorian parlour numbers, the more emotional and thick-harmonied the better. Genista, who played boarding-school piano, had trouble with the interesting chords of John Bacchus Dykes and Maurice Balfe, but the Commander didn't mind, he roared away on something like the tune, and Andrew picked at the tenor.

Genista played and sang and laughed, and hardly noticed that the Commander's frontage was pressed up against her back. She was quite used to parts of men — the actual part dependent on how tall the man was — pressed up against her bosom, but against her back was a new experience, comforting and unsettling all at once. Then he leaned forward to get a better look at the third verse of *Excelsior Excelsior*, and both arms went round her to steady the music on the piano. Genista was intrigued and excited, and wished she was the sort of young woman who got carried away. Discouraging him was practically impossible, but then he was so benign and bear-like that his fumbles could most easily be taken as accidental.

It was only when she decided that the evening really must be declared over and he shambled after her to the long corridor of bedrooms that it became clear she had not been mistaken, for a kiss is a kiss, and wonderfully exciting, if rather surprising, when it is your first. Genista saw him to his room, made sure the clean towel was there, and the lights and the little electric bar heater worked, and beat a hasty retreat to her own. She sat up with the light on, listening for his footsteps, until she fell into a thrilled and dreamless sleep.

Genista did not want to fall in love. She did not want to fall in love with the broken middle-aged man, staggering out of a brief and catastrophic marriage, the latest in a series of unknown length. She did not want to shackle herself to a drunkard with a past made up of unfinished anecdotes. She wanted a young man with a future and bright shiny eyes. But she fell in love by accident and from the most powerful and humiliating of emotions — from pity. And once it was in her bloodstream, the mosquito poison, she had no choice but to submit, until it had worked its way through her system, and by then it was all too late.

She found him a job at the hospital as a porter, on the early shift, so he had no time for a little drink before work, and most days he made it through. He went down well at the hospital, with his physical strength and his military bearing and accent. Each afternoon she would collect him from the pub and they would bike home together, Genista bowling ahead, the Commander wobbling in the rear.

Some days, however, when she breezed into the George and Dragon by the hospital, she would find him crying silently into his drink. Then he would resist being taken home. He would make her sit down and join him while he told her how his heart was broken and his life ruined for love. How a little girl, a beautiful wild girl, had flung herself into his arms and broken his heart, taken all his money and thrown him, ruined, on the scrap heap of life. 'I loved her with all my heart, as much as a man can love. I'd have done anything for her. We never should have married, it was a mortal sin, and I am justly punished.'

Tears rolled down his cheeks.

'But you have saved my life, Genista. Imagine my finding a wonderful girl like you to take care of me! You can help me forget.'

And he took her hands and kissed them fervently, as if she were a senior and saintly cleric. Genista in her secret heart wanted to be the beautiful wild girl who broke men's hearts, but knew she was destined to be the wonderful one who patched things up afterwards. At least she was connected indirectly with wild passion and broken hearts. She had her Heathcliff, even if she was not his Cathy.

Genista looked on the person of her beloved and did not see that he was middle-aged and drunken and incapable. Or to be more precise, she saw clearly that he was completely unworthy of her, and bound not to make her happy, and she could not help herself. She recognized that it was pity that filled her with helpless emotion, and proximity that eased its course. Her rational person, whom she had always thought was the dominant part of her, looked at him and explained that he was entirely unsuitable, seedy and rather disgusting. Her rational person described his ageing body and his ill-directed lust, but could not succeed in curing the other part of her — the person she had not even known existed — of her addiction.

And he was cunning. He knew that there are magic phrases that work on women in spite of themselves. All my life, he murmured, all my life I've waited for you. I knew you must exist, but I couldn't find you. And now, when it's too late . . . She knew it sounded like a load of old rope, one of his tales, his master line in hyperbole, but she was infiltrated by it anyway. What if it were true? What if she, Genista, who was generally, if not specifically, adored, had found the man who might rightly adore her. That all her special nature which she was aware of, but unable to make use of, as it were a sixth finger, was about to be made use of — that this man, this flawed and unsatisfactory man was the destined discoverer, the pilgrim who had stumbled on for years in search of her holy grail. And if that were the case, should she not submit to his wishes — since they seemed perversely to coincide with her own?

Years of being sensible had left her helpless in the battleground of the emotions. His need gaped at her for healing, at the very moment that his power reared up over her. His stated love for her, expressed at once in poetry and crude passion, crushed any rational opposition. Everyone and everything told her this was absurd, and she went ahead with it anyway.

Years later, when the Commander was restless in his grave and she was married much more suitably, she would look back on the nightmare passion as something to be abhorred and yet visited with secret delight.

There was also the wicked pleasure she took — the only wicked pleasure in Genista's life — in triumphing over the unknown Rosalia, the child bride who had played pat-a-cake with the Commander's heart. Later her dark sense of triumph grew complete when she married Rosalia's brother, so trouncing the enemy on all fronts. Genista's generosity of spirit was appalled by her own feelings, which she hid as meticulously as a bank manager hides his passions for the tellers.

Over the sodden and exasperating years of their marriage, she learnt what little there was to know about the Commander's New Zealand marriage, penultimate in a long series. She also learnt a little of the great deal there was to know about the poisonous brother. Strange then that she should marry him.

4

The Commander stumbled into New Zealand in the dying days of the Malayan Emergency. It was generally felt that he had been in Malaya, though if he were Navy, what was he doing there? His accent was South African in tinge, but he claimed variously to come from British Guiana and Cornwall. He had been all over, and had a fund of jokes and stories, but he wasn't a good man for an anecdote, not really. He was the talking point of a party, but the death of it too. He'd start off on a story, sure enough, settled on a plaited plastic chair on the beach, brown bottle in hand, scent of carbonized sausage in the air, off he'd go into a story about cadets and a night raid, and a brothel keeper in Jo'burg, and something about the Lion of Judah. And just when you felt you were getting to the nub of him, as the brisk wind came in off the sea, and Mum reached her cardy around her naked arms, the stories would peter out and the Commander would be certified pissed as a chook.

None the less, afterwards, when the others had started to crack out the jokes, the whiff of dangerous far-off places hung in the air. That scent had been common enough after the war, when the men came back heavy with sights seen and terrors endured that might not be spoken of, but it had faded by the 1950s, washed out after a thousand good plain meals and days spent fishing and the women determined on ordinariness. Don't tell us and it will soon go away. Mad people go to the funny farm, Sunnyside, Cherry Farm, Porirua. You stay here by me and eat your beetroot, and you'll be jake.

The Commander didn't eat his beetroot, though he drank his beer. He talked about the things they were trying to forget and he insisted that other places not only existed but had equal validity to the West Coast. He did all this without intending to blow his own trumpet or put people down, and he was such a pub character they forgave him, poor old codger, besides he was always shit-faced before tea-time.

What Rosalia saw in him was a mystery. But then she was a batty thing, even though she wasn't old. Young thing, though she acted grand enough to be fifty. Always walking barefoot down the beach with her head in the air and her hair getting all rat-arsed in the wind. Fishing with a bloody great sea-rod she could hardly hold, pretentious bitch. Did she catch anything? Threw them back she claimed, because killing them was horrid — so why fish in the first place, specially when it was so bloody tough and windy out there? Skiting, they said, looks so grand. Gives her something to do while she's waiting for the blokes to come by and chat her up.

Only the Commander obliged, old enough to be her grandfather if he'd started young, dyes his hair, must do, because he went through the war, fairly nobby, if he is to be believed, and there isn't a grey hair to be seen. Unless he's bullshitting of course, all those tales of Gurkhas and the relief of Tobruk.

You'd see him set out, when he'd slept off his lunch, panama hat, creased white jacket, white sandshoes with tarred rope soles, every inch the empire. He'd stroll down the street as if he had just arrived in a foreign seaport and he was taking in the curious sights, sniffing the exotic air. But the air of Westport was unburdened by garlic or decay, and bore only the odd fishy smell and the scent of newly mown lawns. The wind off the sea smelt of nothing except far-off icebergs, which is about as indeterminate a smell as you can find.

He'd end up walking along the beach every day, without fail, and with the same air of happening along. She'd be there playing her man-sized fibreglass rod, if the tide were right, and singing fit to burst, arias, folk-songs, any old thing, who knew and who cared? Or she might be discovered sitting cross-legged on the sand, with a spiral-bound notebook, sucking her pencil or tapping it against her teeth, and gazing creatively out to sea. Or, on special occasions, with a little stool and a paint-dripped easel and a few exploratory daubs, not being sure about her talent in this line.

Not that the Commander was concerned with her talents. He circled about, walking past and doffing his hat, as if she were a casual acquaintance of his generation and class, and sauntering on. Rosalia affected to pay no attention. He would walk to a specific point on the beach, stop, look around vaguely as if he'd forgotten something and swivel back as if he was on tramlines and had to go back the way he'd come, and Rosalia's present position was a terminus through which he must pass. Each time he came alongside her he would raise his hat and engage her in conversation, each circuit a little longer, until finally he was stationary and she was ready to pack up her paints and go with him, one arm resting on his, while he carried her gear in his other. For tea, if she was contrary, a cup of tea that is, or a jug, if his desires were allowed to prevail.

No one was privy to these skirmishing conversations, but enough of the Commander's conversational technique was known to suggest that each time he walked on he would leave a tantalizing reference trailing behind him, which he would fail to pick up on his next round, introducing some new observation on the coloration of the paua shell, the difference in cloud structure in the Southern Hemisphere, the peculiar customs of Trinidadian harbour pilots, or the wonderful dirty remark that Margot Asquith made to Lady Ottoline Morrell, both of whom it was assumed you had heard of. Little Rosalia, with her water-colours and her Mozart arias and her arty-farty aspirations, didn't stand a chance.

Things started to heat up. He was observed one morning heading for the house where she stayed on her visits to the coast. It belonged to some friends of her parents whom the lingering decline of the Coast had forced away. The little house, with its scrubby front lawn and linoleum floors, stood empty most of the year. There was no market for houses, and who, in those days, much cared to holiday in Westport? Rosalia came over by herself on the train, and walked to the house lugging a week's clothes in a duffel bag. She took them home dirty at the end of her stay; no washing was seen to flutter on the rotary line out the back. And what about the sheets? You might well ask, and some did, but no one ever answered.

Just after ten o'clock in the morning, he was seen to approach the front door of the house, an oddity in itself, for in New Zealand no one ever uses the front door; it is there for show and to distinguish clearly between unwelcome visitors — the police, charity collectors, Jehovah's Witnesses — and everyone else, who goes round to the back. The Commander was either unaware of this social nicety, or wished to introduce an element of formality into the encounter. He stood by the front door, looking in vain for a bell, while from the front room came the usual morning sounds of Rosalia's singing practice.

She was pretty darned good, even then, which was one reason why she was treated with amused tolerance in Westport, for a woman who can sing can always silence her critics. She practised every morning, assiduously, squeezing out runlets of notes from the old harmonium which had sat in the front room since its eviction from the Methodist Hall. *Vissi d'arte*, she insisted, *vissi d'amore* that morning as many other mornings, punching the morning air with her passion.

The Commander stood by the front door as she tried and retried a phrase, *perchè, Signor, perchè me ne rimuneri così?* He swayed as he listened, perhaps he'd had one to steady his nerves, or two, even. His head was bowed, as if he were examining his shoes for their suitability to enter the parlour of a young lady, and finding them wanting, but bemused by what he should do.

Eventually, after Tosca had pleaded and pleaded for mercy *Vedi, le man giunte io stendo a te!* in various permutations the Commander gave up the struggle with himself and went away without disturbing her.

That afternoon they were to be observed sitting on the sea wall, her bare legs dangling next to his long linen limbs. He only possessed one suit, and it was a miracle how he kept it so clean, with all his falling against walls on the way home from the pub. His belly settled comfortably on his knees. He was smoking his pipe, or rather sucking it, because he appeared to have no tobacco and no one to cadge off; Rosalia was gesturing out to sea and talking animatedly. She was a good-looking girl, if you could be bothered to look. She had long light-ginger curls which blew everywhere like the most becoming of scarves, and eyes the colour of newly peeled chestnuts. It is possible that the Commander told her this, sitting on the sea wall. It is certainly true that she tore a page from her notebook and wrote down her address in Christchurch, because she was going back home the next day. It must have been that simple act, that indication that she wanted the relationship, such as it was, to continue, that proved her undoing.

It is hard to ascribe much significance to the writing down of an address, but it is quite possible if she had not done so, her story would have taken a much less interesting course. She was the instigator, however innocent, of her own tragi-comedy.

That night the Commander was not to be found in the pub. His absence occasioned a considerable amount of crude speculation; was, for example, Rosalia under age? It was generally thought that she was legal, not to drink, of course, though she had been in the pub with the Commander on several occasions, refilling her lemonade glass ostentatiously from his jug. The local cop, sternly enforcing the licensing laws, six o'clock closing and all, from the vantage point of a bar seat, was of the opinion that she was asking for it anyway, living alone like that, and she knew where to find him if she needed him, but it would never stand up in a court of law. Nor, thought the publican's wife, could the Commander, after so many years of dedicated drinking. She reckoned he'd even have trouble getting it to piss. Crude jokes from women were really not the thing, so the blokes shambled away into the corner to consider their bets for the next day with the pub bookie, leaving the cop at the bar bemoaning today's youth with the priest and the publican's wife.

Rosalia left the next morning, on the one and only train across the mountains, humping her duffel bag and her fishing rod. The publican's wife wondered about the sheets. The Commander was seen walking up and down the beach distractedly, like a dog who has forgotten where he buried his bone. He was back to his drinking ways that night, cheerful because he had received his pension, his pittance, hush or blood money as he variously called it. He was able to shout for the whole pub at last, having been at the mercy of their generosity for weeks, and make a small inroad into his tab. The publican's wife intimated that he might like to pay it all off now, since he might be leaving them soon. He affected to look surprised, and then let the penny drop, and smiled his yellow smile and bought some tobacco with the comment that if he were going away he'd need his money the more sorely for his train fare. After that he disappeared inside a cloud of tobacco.

The next day he went to early Mass, as was his wont. He sat so far back in the church that he could have made out nothing but a vague muttering, but his responses rang out clear and true in public-school Latin. The priest never knew whether to be grateful for this, or irritated because it confused the altar boys. Long after the last black-hatted worthy had stumped off, the Commander sat in his pew staring at the sacred heart of Mary in the alcove near the back. The priest spied him from the sacristy; there was just enough time to slip down a coffee between masses, if you took a liberal view of the ecclesiastical licensing laws, but duty, and perhaps curiosity, called. He had heard the Commander's confession only yesterday, but none the less, or perhaps consequently — we shall never know — the priest felt he must go and sit down next to the Commander.

'Are you OK, my son?' he asked, although the Commander had thirty years on him, but it was tricky counselling someone whose name no one recalls. The Commander didn't answer, nor did he remove his gaze from the Blessed Virgin, who smiled on him with her saccharine smile, knowing nothing of drunkenness, murder, buggery or even, God help her, sex. The priest thought to repeat his question and thought of his coffee.

'I have done some terrible things, Father,' the Commander said, staring hard at the Virgin.

'Everything is forgiven, my son, if honestly confessed and truly repented. Except of course the Sin against the Holy Ghost.'

'You have a definition of that?'

'No,' said the priest sadly, 'if I did, I'd know where I stood. If you know what I mean.'

'It's a bit of a puzzle, this sin business,' said the Commander. 'I sometimes think I must be quite a sinner — but then if you look in the heart — but who sees, who knows . . . '

'God sees, God knows,' said the priest, young Kevin O'Malley, straight from Ireland to the West Coast of New Zealand and loving it, but rather lost for solutions.

The words hung on the air between them, hovering a moment before they disintegrated.

'I'm sure he does,' said the Commander, 'but what about us? How do we know if we're bad or just clumsy?'

'Well — ' began Father O'Malley, 'if you adopt the practice of self-examination . . . I can give you a little book . . . '

'I have heard it all before,' said the Commander, 'out of the mouths of priests from Salisbury to Saigon. Your lot don't know either.'

'The Church teaches . . . ' began brave Father O'Malley.

'It's all a matter of definition, you see. Sin, evil, love, all words . . . '

'But you know sin is real, Commander.'

'I do,' he groaned, 'I do. But this is the puzzle: if I think I'm doing the right thing, how can it be a sin, even if it's wrong.'

Father O'Malley cleared his throat. The Commander carried on.

'Love — sin — they mean what we make them mean. But there must be a way to know. The great warriors of the Old Testament did things that would have had them strung up at Nuremberg. Got a Bible handy, Father?'

'I'm sure to hell to have one somewhere,' said poor Father O'Malley, half rising from his seat, his coffee faintly calling to him, a dying wail.

'It's all right old chap,' said the Commander. 'Pick it up at your leisure, and you'll find them at it, slaughter, rape, pillage, enslavement. Not the baddies, the good guys. Take the sack of Jericho — everyone was sacrificed to the Lord, the original holocaust, don't you think? The only person spared was

Rahab. Do you know who Rahab was?'

'Lot's daughter, was it?'

'A prostitute. Now there's an arbitrary system for you — why spare one prostitute? She'll hardly do for the whole army after all. They spared her on the grounds that she'd done a good deed towards the righteous. Now tell me, Father, is that an arbitrary moral scheme or is that an arbitrary moral scheme?'

'Yes, I'm sure you're right,' sighed Father O'Malley. 'I don't know the Old Testament that well myself, but you won't find any of that stuff in the gospel, that I know.'

'That's not my point — words, deeds — in between them definitions — I love a woman and I hurt her, so how can I love her? But I know I love her, so that makes it all right, because I didn't mean to. But if I didn't love her, which is just a personal definition, it wouldn't be right. Arbitrary, you see what I mean?'

'You've lost me, Commander. But sinful deeds are always sins, even if you think your motives are good. The rules are quite useful sometimes. Adultery, fornication, drunkenness, stealing, lying . . . '

The Commander sighed at the recital, as if avoiding them was as impossible as refraining from breath.

'Go and have your breakfast, son; God and I will wrestle for a while.'

The priest, to do him justice, was seriously concerned with the state of the Commander's soul; he was a cheerful, clubbable fellow, who liked to please, so much so in fact that he had joined the priesthood to please his family and massy array of uncles and aunts and his village. It seemed such a simple way to make them all smile, and here he was in the most cheerful of towns, where every mining disaster became the source of terrific black jokes, and every miscarriage had a scurrilous afterbirth.

He recalled occasionally, when he wasn't laughing and tripping over himself, that his job was to save lost souls, items that seemed in short supply in Westport. But here was one, and it would be both worthy and splendid to do something about him.

'Why don't I come for a chat this afternoon? We'll see if we can sort it out a bit.'

The priest rose hopefully from the pew, scenting the air like a dog being conveyed homewards. *Oh yes, yes, yes!*

'This afternoon may be too late,' said the Commander with lugubrious enjoyment. 'You go on now. Love and lust, now. Love and lust and violence. Where does one stop and the next start? How do you know for sure?'

The sound of these words caused Father O'Malley to scurry in a way that his training told him was unworthy. The stuff of confessions, but who could deal with a conversation on the subject.

'Toodly-pip, Father,' he heard from far away.

The Commander sat on in the church until the sacristan arrived to dress the altar for the next Mass. He was resolutely ignored, as if he had become himself a plaster statue, although not easily identifiable as any common piece of iconography. The sacristan had no time for the understated drama of the Commander's appearance and had never joined his audience at the pub. He would have liked to cover him with one of the purple crêpe veils used in Passiontide to remove distractions from the eyes of the pious.

The Commander slipped out of the church as the next batch were arriving, head lowered, jamming on his hat as soon as he hit the open air. That was the last that was seen of him in Westport, though one or two observed him lurking by the train station trying to ignore his obligations.

He was not such a bad man, it turned out, because a cheque arrived at the Priest's House not so many months afterwards, to settle his debts and make provision for the poor, though who was intended was unclear, the Commander having been quite the poorest man in Westport for many years. Much more interestingly, the cheque was made out by Rosalia's father, not a man greatly noted in the town for his generosity, having repeatedly refused to buy raffle tickets on the grounds that no one, not even a priest, could be *that* lucky *that* often.

5

Niall, for the Commander had a Christian name, as indeed he had godparents and aunts and uncles and a whole smother of relatives, having not sprung fully formed from the pages of *Struwwelpeter*, in spite of appearances to the contrary, Niall, I repeat, could never tell his love. In his darker moments it seemed to him that like whichever Shakespearean heroine it was who stayed stumm about her passion, he too would die of unexpressed passion. On his darkest days he felt his love for Rosalia like a cancer inside him which continued to grow, would never be excised, and would thereby kill him painfully.

There are some ideas that should most certainly stay locked up inside the head. It seemed altogether unlikely that Rosalia's regard for the Commander would have grown stronger had she heard him compare his passion for her to a cancer. If, on the other hand, he had adjusted the metaphor and confessed that he sometimes felt he would die of love, then she would have perhaps forgiven him everything.

There was a great deal to forgive. He was

middle-aged, at once scrawny and paunchy, and unbecomingly pale where he wasn't mahogany. He favoured striped pyjamas, because he had always done so. He preferred anal sex to all other permutations, but rather than allow any discussion of sex to surface from under the bedclothes, lost interest in the act altogether when he detected resistance to his proclivity. He was drunk every night, and generally found it easier to slump down in the sun-room, rather than be needled awake at intervals on account of his snoring.

He liked to wake in the morning in the little curtainless room, with its shaky glass doors straight onto the beach, its walls cheerful with Rosalia's coffee bar murals. He felt himself a bohemian, even though the sun woke him at an unsociable hour. For a few minutes he savoured happiness — the beach washed clean from humanity, the wild southern sea, the prospect of freedom, the little girl whom he adored, ruffled and warm in the next room. Then the sun would assert itself, his bladder would assert itself, the need for a drink, the fear of recrimination, the hopeless wash of his inadequacy — these feelings would snap out of their temporary stupor and take over his mind. His few minutes of happiness were over for another day.

This morning he awoke as usual to partake of his happiness. It was 12 February and he had been married to Rosalia for five months, and tucked up in this little house for four of them. The first month, theoretically their honeymoon, had been spent in the guest bedroom at Hollander House, because they had not a farthing between them to gaze upon. Niall's pension, which had failed to support him for years, was now diverted at source by Rosalia's father until the repayment of all debts was done.

In the few weeks before the wedding, it had become increasingly obvious to Rosalia's father that she was not in fact pregnant, as she had claimed in her determination to marry the Commander. Consequently his mood grew sourer and he absolutely refused to bankroll a honeymoon; instead, he declared, the little rat and the old rat-trap could stay in the house and look after the livestock while *he* went on a decent holiday.

'Don't argue, Mother,' he said to his wife. 'You deserve a trip to Fiji. That man, our son-in-law, has already been there, and everywhere else. He deserves to stay in one place. Preferably in hell.'

From which you will perceive that there was no love lost between the Commander and his father-in-law.

As his final act of paternal duty, he rented them a cottage on the beach at Taylor's Mistake, and found Niall a job on the wharf, and a ride to Lyttelton every morning with a man who would not take a groan for an answer. Then he shook the dust of them off his hands, and concentrated his devotion on his son, Crawford, who was much more promising.

★   ★   ★

This marriage — his third, or was it his fourth — he was often unclear as to the legality of a ceremony conducted in a foreign language — was the Portuguese fellow in a black suit a priest or just a drunk play-acting? — who cared anyway? alas, who cared — the first months of this marriage had no shape. He would not have been able to say up front how long he'd been married — time slithered around the Commander, just as people slid in and out of view. When he was drunk this made perfect sense.

★   ★   ★

On the morning of 12 February 1960 he sat up on the edge of the day-bed and watched the early surfers mounting the water. He sipped his morning happiness. Here was so sweet a place. You could put down your bag on what he called the pavement and the locals called the footpath, and two hours later it would still be there, unmolested. You could leave your doors wide open onto the beach and never fear ransack. You could knock at a stranger's door, ask to make a phone call and be invited in for a meal and a bath. He loved this country, set adrift from the wicked world, a child floating on a raft, smiling at everyone, ignorant of evil.

A child — why had he married a child? He didn't remember making any conscious choices, except the once — standing on her doorstep in Westport and hearing her sing. That moment was sharp and clear in his foggy memory as this very morning. That choice was to turn away from the child who sang with a woman's voice about a woman's agony that she could not possibly understand. It was when he heard her sing that his love for her threatened to burst and destroy him. Not that she was a beautiful singer — accomplished, ambitious, but not affecting. There was a steeliness about Rosalia that was most noticeable in her singing — but to Niall it was the sweet paradox of her competence — all the runs and trills and carefully controlled top notes, the laboured precision of her

Italian — banging up against the little girl, who knew nothing about the heart, about sex, betrayal, violence or the love of God — all the subjects of her song.

Poor little Rosalia, he thought, *how much she has to learn* — all those terrible things that he himself had chosen to forget.

On this spruce morning he had forgotten them all, except that this was a summer's day, this was pay day, and this was his home, and there was his little wife asleep. He kicked around for his slippers. Then he remembered that she'd thrown them in the bin last week crying out that only *old* men wore slippers! He had worn slippers since he was a child, and no delicious young person the world over had ever before objected. He delighted in her spirit, though he regretted the slippers.

Barefoot, thinking how chill the linoleum, indeed the entire outfit would be come winter, he made his way to the toilet, a noisome chemical contraption, whose leavings he was graciously permitted by the council, to bury in the damp sand after dark, Taylor's Mistake having no sewage system, and no subsoil for tanks or long drops. His happiness was trickling away already. He went into the kitchen, cursing the cold floor. Would she give his dressing-gown the same treatment when the weather forced him to dig it out of its trunk? The dressing-gown that had seen him through two wars and four continents — unable to withstand this little waif who couldn't lift a gun, let alone use it with intent. He thought perhaps he would hold his ground over the matter of the dressing-gown. Perhaps if he made it through enough pay days before winter came he could let her choose him an acceptable alternative.

One of the very few items he had brought into the marriage was a small Italian espresso machine. He looked at this sadly wishing he could afford coffee beans to grind. There was a single shop in the town which sold real coffee. He could hardly bear to walk past it and smell the memories; his heart swelled up with a thousand forgotten mornings. But they didn't go into town much, not with the beach and the work and the poverty, and the cheap sherry. Just as well. He had always been poor, except for the brief illusions of army life, and as a teenager had stumbled upon the way to manage — to convince yourself you were too shiftless and exotic to acquire comforts or enjoy them, to be quite sure that if you settled down, even for a moment, you would look just as prosperous as the next fellow. I have drunk away my fortune in the bars of a hundred ports, he would proclaim. This was somehow far more admirable than simply drinking away one's fortune, and several degrees better than not having a fortune to drink away in the first place.

Niall filled and switched on the electric kettle, scraped some instant coffee into a mug and thought briefly about taking one to Rosie. The first problem was waking her — would she welcome it? Or would she scour him with her annoyance at being ripped from sleep? Then how did she take her coffee? To get this wrong was a double crime — not to be attentive to the details of Rosalia, and possibly to confuse her with *someone else*. So much he had learnt in a very few months. Poor darling, how much she had to learn about men and women ... how endlessly destined to disappointment in her men, who would inevitably be inattentive and come trailing fragments of other women's behaviour. If she had had the sense to attach herself to another adolescent, the youth would at least be unencumbered, though probably even more inattentive to the precious details.

Details ... he checked the kitchen clock. It faced him out, the round ugly thing, with its strategic splotches of luminous paint. How could he trust it anyway, since he neglected to wind it? It might be slowing down deliberately to take its revenge on him. The clock asserted it was six-thirty; he had plenty of time. On the other hand, if the clock were lying, at any moment Dickie Fisher might be banging at the door to take him on early shift. He might be shaved and ready and sliding his hand lovingly over the curves on the bed that represented his wife. He might be bristly and disconcerted and have to rush out leaving her ever more disconsolate. How had it come to this — a round-faced clock his sworn enemy?

He decided not to trust it. He abandoned the coffee, dressed himself in his work clothes, shaved laboriously, wondering, as he did every day, whether it was possible to get a good shave with one of those electric things. He cleaned his teeth punctiliously, the one thing in his life he was reliable about. Curious that his teeth remained obstinately beige. He bared his teeth at himself in the bathroom mirror, such as it was. She had married him none the less. Wonders never ceased.

He heard Dickie's Army Indian up the path. His timing was perfect then, except for breakfast and stroking the sleeping Rosalia. He must remember to check the clock and perhaps set the alarm. How was it that one never remembered in the evening what one had resolved in the morning?

As he shot out of the door, Rosalia stirred herself.

'Niall, Niall!' she cried, her voice carrying

all the complex meanings of the opening of an aria — command, longing, distress.

'Yes, darling,' he replied, most of himself just outside the door, hand on the door-frame as if his domineering body was pulling away his reluctant heart.

'Are you going now?'

'Yes, darling.'

'When will you be back?'

'I don't know — I may pick up a little something in the port. Don't make any supper for me — be as free as a bird.'

With that he tore his hand from the door-frame and strapped on the helmet his workmate held out. It was not essential to wear the clumsy thing, but Niall had seen enough men vault out of vehicles on roads such as these. He had no desire to be a cripple nursed into his dotage by an impatient and unfaithful Rosalia.

They bumped up and over the rollercoaster hills, Niall holding on with his thighs, because he would not put his arms around another man. He knew viscerally that there was some message in the way she had farewelled him, a message he had failed to decipher.

If they had been able to afford a telephone he might have rung at smoko to find out what she meant, and the course of this whole tale might have been changed thereby.

He thought of her throughout the day, her slim body naked on the sheets, her face buried in the pillow as she slept. He thought of her running naked into the surf on New Year's Eve to the shocked delight of the beach-partyers. He thought of her curled with her head on his chest in the back of the bus as they trundled over to Taylor's that first time, their worldly possessions in a trunk, two suitcases and a cardboard box. He had thought the world well lost at that moment. He thought of her practising — her diaphragm and chin working, determined. The same phrase again and again, turning herself into her own singing teacher, because there was no longer anyone to pay for lessons.

He rehearsed the same images of her every day, rerunning the home movies of his love for her, until he thought his heart would break. He thus prevented other images from entering his mind — other loves, Rosalia in less desirable moments. Over many years of struggle and inconvenience, years of bungle and snarl-up and shame, the Commander had kept his back erect and his eyes gazing forward by this technique — running through his mind only those episodes he could bear to remember, so that they flooded his heart with admirable emotion. The grey things and the black things lurking in his memory were drowned out until the drink floated them to the surface again, long-dead bodies hideous with gas.

It was good to work on the wharf in those days, after the titanic battle of the waterfront union and the rest of society which had secured for the workers rights beyond the dreams of working man's avarice. The workforce consisted largely of eccentrics and men who had grown eccentric through comfortable pay-packets and extravagant amounts of leisure. The Commander felt perfectly at home — it was perhaps the only place in New Zealand where his oddity would go unremarked. He had spent his entire life in male groups, from the bilge of his genteel-poor boarding-school, into the army, the Malaysian police force, and onto the wharves, with stints in between in places he had forgotten, but always outdoors somewhere, surrounded by men. Sometimes he was the boss-man and sometimes the peon; the vicissitudes of fortune had knocked ambition out of him, though he carried with him always the photograph from Malaya that represented the high point of his career.

On 12 February 1960, just before ten o'clock if the round-faced clock in the kitchen was to be believed, Rosalia smashed the glass of that very photograph, the only framed item in the cottage. She looked at the shards of glass and thought about using them to slash her wrists. It seemed unlikely that they would do the job. The photograph lay face downwards where it had fallen, the slivers of glass sprayed out around it in an aureole. He would not notice this for days — or if he did he would defer commenting on it until absolutely unavoidable. Rosalia was surprised to discover that she knew this about him already. She had so much wanted him to remain a thrilling mystery.

In her cotton nightie, on the morning of her eighteenth birthday, she looked down at the fragments of glass by her bare feet, and saw that love was not remotely as she had imagined it. With the single-mindedness with which she had married the Commander, she determined to dispense with love. She went for the dustpan and brush and swept up the pieces of glass. She did not go back to bed and cry. She did not think about her last birthday, when her mother had brought her breakfast in bed and a pile of presents, and Crawford serenaded her as she came downstairs with a ditty in the style of Noël Coward that he had written specially. Outside the sun was up and doing; the surfies were out, brown bodies taut against the sky. Rosalia decided to make a day of it after all.

The Commander manoeuvred his way down the cliff path in darkness. He might have taken the slower route by the species of road, but at the top, where the bus dropped him off, anxiety had taken hold. He saw no lights in their cottage, and his distress at all the pain stacked up waiting to afflict Rosalia consumed him. He did not speculate; bitter experience had taught him he would always guess wrong.

He patted his breast pocket to see if the remains of the pay-packet were safe, and thanked the fates who had landed him for once in a job where the weekly pay withstood the impact of the pay-day jollities. Rosalia must have dresses; Rosalia must have singing lessons; Rosalia must go to art school — this year — why not?

The front door was unlocked as usual. It gave straight into the kitchen, the room in which they ate and argued and sometimes made love. The inside of the house smelt and sounded wrong. Rosalia always waited up for him, painting her way around the walls again, her *tablier* artistically daubed. There was no sound, no smell of paint. Instead the sound and smell of the beach filled the little space. There was nowhere to look — the cottage had four rooms, each one just large enough to be dignified by a function. Panic-stricken, he switched on the light. The door from the sun-room onto the beach was slightly ajar. Abandoned on the floor of the sun-room was Rosalia's beach towel, in a delta of sand. In the bedroom he found her swimming costume slumped on the floor and the drawers of their lopsided unit pulled open. He surmised that she had rushed in and changed her clothes — to go where?

There was no note on the kitchen table. He sat down with his tooth glass and took the almost full bottle of whisky from his bag. Then he saw in front of him, quite clearly, not illusions conjured by the spirits or his overexercised imagination, two items. He picked them up, put them down, groaned inwardly, downed his whisky, rested his head on his arms and wept. On the table was a birthday card, a puppy holding a bunch of flowers in its mouth, inscribed *To dear Rosalia Happy Birthday from Mum and Dad and Crawford;* next to the card was Rosalia's wedding ring.

The Commander slept where he sat, and woke at dawn, sore and sick at heart. He did not remember why, until he fought his way up to focus, and saw the little ring in the line of his eye, on the surface of the table among the crumbs of Rosalia's breakfast. She'd covered the surface of the table with cheerful plastic, chubby birds and flowers in pots, orange and yellow. The ring against this backdrop seemed over-dramatic, its solidity and carats unnecessarily assertive in the simple optimistic world of the table cover. In this decorative world the men and women were shapes, with smiles and hats and plaits and shoes, but without wedding rings or genitalia. He had given no thought to this little metal object; unable to afford a ring of any kind he had dutifully assented to the family plan to adapt a Hollander great-grandmother's wedding ring to fit Rosalia. Wedding rings came and went on the fingers of women with something to assert. He himself had never worn such a thing.

A woman, he knew, took off her wedding ring for one of three reasons: her fingers had swollen with pregnancy or disease, she wished to run free for a while, or she had rejected her marriage. There were other occasions too, of course; it might become necessary to hock the ring or remove it to deceive authorities — nuns, parents, border guards — but this was storybook stuff, another world from the cottage and the guileless domesticity of his surroundings.

It was dawn, she had left. She had not

come home. There was no note — had she left him or was she lying ravaged in a ditch, her white neck livid from the murderer's hands? Niall sat himself upright and started to shake. There was some whisky in the bottle, and there was nothing for him to do except wait. Fleetingly he imagined himself facing down the local constabulary — a middle-aged drunk alarming because his seventeen-, no, his eighteen-year-old wife had run out on him. Their derision would be barely concealed. Nor could he walk up the road to the phone box and ring her parents to ask after her welfare — if they had not heard from her they would be terror-struck, and would turn their worry into scorn and hatred to pour onto his thoroughly deserving head.

The only person he could turn to was a priest — but in a Protestant country priests are thin on the ground. Where would he find one? Why had he not taken out an insurance policy against this disaster — a disaster he had known was inevitable — by going once or twice to Mass? He had always gone to Mass before — only this past few months, Rosalia's deep resentment of this very unsafe practice had caused him to backslide. Was there a padre on the wharf? Yes, of course, that effete young man with Church of England vowels and excellent Latin, who occasionally sparred with Niall about the doctrine of the Immaculate Conception. On the face of it, such a cleric did not promise to be much use in Niall's pantelone predicament. And he could not go to work today. Turn up drunk on the morning shift and even the tolerant Waterfront Company would get out the black pencil. The Commander was not yet ready to throw away this job.

He staggered to the bathroom and had a go at washing away the ill-effects of his sleep. The mirror was liver-spotted like his hands; his face would not stay in focus. His only thought was a recurrent *Not again*, which was odd, given that this precise combination of events had never happened before in his life. He could not shave with his hands shaking, so he went back to get a drink to steady them and was alarmed how little whisky was left. Where would he find a drink at this hour? *Sacred Heart of Jesus Maria Mother of God misericordia*. He heard the motor-bike of his colleague roar up and stand chuttering while it waited. After a while, Dickie gave up and came straight into the cottage, pulling at the straps of his helmet. He was a generous young man in every sense, scattering vigour and cheerfulness about. He had a spade beard jutting out at roughly the angle of his belly, and spoke with a strong

South African accent.

He contemplated Niall.

'Christ, Commander, that was a good party! Why didn't you invite me?'

'I can't go to work, Dickie.'

Dickie laughed all the way down his chest.

'No, I don't think you can, old chap. No problem, I'll tell them you're crook. Have a cup of tea and lie down quietly. Just stay off the booze for a bit.'

'My wife has gone missing, Dickie.'

'Jesus Christ!' said Dickie. 'Have you been to the cops?'

Niall, slumped at the table, shook his head.

'I expect she went to her parents. But if she did not . . . '

'Didn't she leave a note?'

The younger man went into the bedroom to have a look around. Niall shambled after him on the off-chance that she was curled up in bed after all. But the bed was cold. He sat down on it, unable to restrain his tears at the tragedy of the girl who slept there so often alone. Dickie poked around in the drawers, as if knickers and nylons had a coherent secret to share with him. A tidy man, he closed the drawers. Then he stooped down.

'What's this then? Glass?'

There were many pieces of glass remaining after Rosalia's cursory sweep-up. Dickie

127

started to pick them up. Then under the bed, kicked out of sight, he spotted the photo, its frame out of skew. He pulled it out and sat back on his haunches, cupping the pieces of glass in his hand.

'Well there's a handsome devil.'

The Commander, in the uniform of a superintendent in the Special Malaysian Police, stood in front of a native village. Straw roofs were in evidence behind him. On either hand stood young Malay men in khaki shorts and white shirts, with the bright smiles of those who know they are on to a good thing. The Commander did not smile. He exuded dangerous authority from below the rim of his cap. He held a cane in front of him with two hands, a stern horizontal against the verticals of his tall thin person.

'Piled it on a bit since then,' said Dickie. 'Married life I suppose?'

The Commander sitting on his marital bed made no answer to this.

'She must have knocked it over when she went out.'

'Evidence of a struggle?' asked Dickie. 'Someone cleaned up the glass. Could be fingerprints. We'd better be careful not to smear the evidence.'

'She is perfectly safe. I feel it in my bones.'

'Your bones may not be forensic enough.

128

Has she run off before?'

'Dickie, we have been married for — I don't know — less than a year.'

The younger man continued to tidy up. Niall sat on the bed staring at the proud icon of himself, haloed by broken glass.

'It was her birthday.'

'You blithering idiot, you forgot her birthday? Don't you know anything about girls?'

'Rather more than I did.'

'She broke the picture on purpose, I'd say.'

'I expect you are right,' said the Commander, as if it were a matter of no consequence.

'Well in that case, it serves you right, you big tit. She'll come home. Or she won't. I'll make us a cuppa.'

Dickie went into the kitchen and tinkled the collected pieces of glass into the bin on top of their larger brethren. Niall heard him fill the kettle. 'You'll be late clocking in,' he said, more or less to himself. In his head was a recitation: *gratia plena misericordia gratia plena misericordia gratia plena misericordia gratia plena misericordia.* If he had another drink he might not notice the time passing till she came back. He already stank so much of booze that one little one would make no odds. The smell of burning crumbs suggested

129

that Dickie was doing battle with the grill to make some toast. Niall wondered if there was butter or jam to be found. He thought about marmalade, that exotic substance, Oxford English Marmalade, dark as the inside of his mind, complete with the strange objects emerging from the sludge.

He had a sudden longing for England — the East — Africa even — any place where sin was unsurprising rather than swept under the carpet. A cup of tea would not salvage the Commander. Dickie put his head round the door.

'I've made a pot. There's toast there too. I'll be off now. Ring us at smoko if you need anything. I'll drop in after work and check up on you both.'

The smell of toast sidled into the bedroom. Niall continued to sit. *Bless me Father for I have sinned.* How could she forgive him when his crimes were himself. She had refused to see him for what he was in spite of his passionate but ultimately pathetic efforts to warn her. When he stood on her front doorstep in Westport listening to her girlish attempt to participate in the passion of Tosca — *then* he should have turned tail and fled. In that tiny window of sobriety he knew she would pursue him for what he represented in her childish imagination, quite incapable of imagining what he was. How was he supposed to withstand? Some temptations were beyond resistance, beyond even prayer. And he loved her to distraction, no matter how often she repeated that antiphon of the lovelorn: *if you really loved me you'd* . . . When his love for her was so self-evident — and so useless.

Had he not told her? Surely he had told her on that first dreadful passionate night, in the single armchair, banished from civilized houses for its refusal to conform in any respect to the body. He should have swept her off to bed, but it all came over him too soon — her eagerness, his long drought. Of course it was awful for her, poor little thing, but she was brave, because she had wanted drama, and pain is an undeniable indication of drama. And after that, she sat on his lap and talked about her dreams — such hopes. The dreams of seventeen, he thought, nothing can compare. He felt as old as Methuselah, a dreary old Bluebeard, as she expanded on her plans — singing, painting — she was going to conquer the world, and he would come everywhere with her, protector and friend, to guard her from the evils of the world.

Poor little featherhead, not to see that he was one of them.

Not actively of course; he tried to explain that — he didn't set out to do wrong. He stumbled into it. Not exactly sins of omission, but the closest thing to it — as he tried to explain — but such moral niceties were not in Rosalia's vocabulary.

How could he have done such a thing? How could he not? He didn't want to take her virginity, he didn't want to marry her — to do so was wrong, terribly wrong, but as with everything else, he was carried along in the current of other people's wishes. What Niall wanted — but who knew that? Not even Niall himself.

Actually, he did know. He wanted a drink. There was one teaspoonful left in the bottle on the kitchen table — and then what? Drink it first and get some strength. Like cod-liver oil, it would set one up for the strictures of the day. It was bound to be one of those days.

Once the bottle was drained and the teapot likewise, and she had not come home, he thought he would betake him up to the road and ring young Dickie, assuming he had the requisite pennies. Quite what he would say he did not know, but some action seemed necessary. On the bright road, by the phone box, fumbling for the coins, it occurred to him that he could just as well ring from Dickie's little place, down the road.

His friend's door was unlocked, and Mrs Dickie was out — in fact the Commander had seen her on the beach with the kiddies. He found he couldn't remember the number for the port company, or locate the telephone directory, but he remembered where Dickie kept his Christmas supply of spirits.

★   ★   ★

About half past eleven, though by now the kitchen clock had taken on a blurred, resentful expression, Rosalia banged through the front door, spilling youth and sexual conquest into the cottage. Her hair was wild and her lipstick faded, and there were indications of pressure applied to the lips and neck. He had expected no less.

'I went to a party in Sumner,' she said, 'but I couldn't get a ride home. I would have rung up if we had a phone.'

He nodded, partly because there was nothing to say, partly because the words wouldn't come out right anyway.

'You're drunk.'

'What did you expect? I was beside myself with worry, but there was nothing I could do.'

'You could have tried not to get drunk. It's the middle of the day. What if I had been in trouble? What would my parents have thought?'

'If you were in trouble, my darling, I would not care whether your parents were drowning in hellfire.'

Rosalia pushed past him to put on the kettle.

'I'm starving. Is there any bread left?'

'As hard as a workhouse doorstep, but it will toast.'

'Why is the grill on?'

Niall tried to remember.

'Dickie. Young Dickie was here. He came to take me to work.'

'And you were drunk.'

'I was worried about you. Anything might have happened.'

'I can look after myself you know.'

'You are so young.'

'And you are so old.'

The Commander said nothing. He wondered how to apologize about the birthday, but the words wouldn't come. He should have bought a stupid big box of chocolates at the store, with a ribbon round it. Why did he not think of it at the time?

She made her tea and drank it. She didn't offer him a cup.

'I'm going down for a swim.'

'May I come with you?'

'You can do what you bloody well like. You always do.'

The injustice of this accusation winded him, but he was incapable of rejoinder. When she came out of the bedroom in her swimming costume, still damp and sandy from the day before, he rose to his feet. Both of them pretended not to notice the imprecision of his gait. She sprinted out of the back doors on to the beach; he was as much enchanted by the resilience of youth, which could presumably party and then make love all night, and still run down to the sea, as he was heart-stricken by her cruelty.

He wove his way down to the beach in her wake.

You are a cuckold, Lingerfield. In less than a year. Not for the first time but perhaps the last. The last first time. Unless of course she divorces you and you make the same mistake again no, never again — never never never how could I be so lucky again how could I be so stupid how could I be so drunk?

There was a chunk of Niall's heart which clung to the idea that since fate had wheeled him into the unlikely position in which he now found himself — the penniless, talentless, middle-aged husband of a teenager — pretty, spirited, clever daughter of rich folks — why should he not let fate take him where it would? He had not expected such a stroke of luck (was it luck? was it not tragedy?) so there was no reason why he should put in any effort — she came to him, she married him, she would inevitably reject him. In the meantime, why should he do anything except stumble along in her path, sipping his moments of bliss in the morning, loving her to death?

⋆   ⋆   ⋆

She spurted into the waves. He did not want to sit down on the sand, but was forced to anyway, by the violence of the sunlight and his sudden incapacity to stand upright. There should be a deck-chair or at least a little stool. In England there were deck-chairs on the beach. In France one hired them. Why not take Rosalia to France — show off his war-time French — make her admire him again? Money. Money. What was left of yesterday's? What could he buy her to restore her good favour? It was too hot, too bright, and she too young. It was all impossible. He wept.

⋆   ⋆   ⋆

After her swim, Rosalia flung herself down on the sand, coating herself with grand abandon.

136

'I want to go to art school.'

'And so you shall. In the autumn.'

'Why not now? I want to go now.'

'Because the term — the autumn term — September.'

'Idiot,' she said. 'How long have you lived in this country? Autumn is Easter. Art school starts now — summer — February. They're enrolling next week.'

'Qualifications . . . ' he began. 'Matriculation . . . '

'I met one of the lecturers last night,' she said, her eyes tight shut. 'He said he'd see what he could do.'

The Commander did not even bother to imagine the circumstances. He concentrated rather on how he might shield her from disappointment, should the promise, given no doubt in the heat of alcohol and lust, fail.

'I wonder though,' he said with great care, 'whether you should not concentrate on your singing. I think that is where your greatest talent lies.'

'How would you know? Someone's coming to look at my murals. I described them and he was very very excited.'

'Should I make myself scarce? When he comes, I mean?'

'I don't see why. Unless you're drunk of course.'

'He may not realize you are — ah — married.'

'Oh,' she said, and her fingers fiddled with the non-existent wedding ring.

'I'm sorry about your birthday, darling,' he said, capitalizing on his advantage. 'I swear I shall never forget it again. If I do you can cast me into outer darkness where there is wailing and gnashing of teeth.'

'Honestly, Niall.'

She lay flat on the sand, burning her white flesh to a vicious red under his very eyes. He knew better than to expostulate.

Mad dogs and Englishmen, he thought. Besides if she were sunburnt she would not want to run away from him. The pain would tame her.

'What would you like for your birthday? It's not too late to do something.'

'I would like us to take Crawford to dinner in town. He hates it at school. They persecute him and the food is ghastly.'

'With pleasure, my dearest heart,' said the Commander, lying through his yellowed teeth, for he found no pleasure in Crawford, pretty youth though he was.

6

Crawford. He is the boy in black-and-white striped blazer and cream straw boater, leaning *à la Marlene* against a lamppost on Rolleston Avenue ignoring the jibes of the day boys as they pass. He affects not to hear them, but in fact he has long since processed the insults and worked out his strategy, which is to camp things up magnificently and risk the beatings from the studs, while stealing the girls from under their noses. So far he has scored more heavily in the beatings than the copulation league, but he knows the strategy is working. He is currently sexually engaged with two of his tormentors' girlfriends, and just about to make it with a third. His technical ability improves by leaps and bounds. Naturally, none of the three girls knows of his involvement with the other two, each of them believes him to be sweetly and lasciviously in love with her, and no male person suspects him of any form of heterosexual activity. He is biding his time, and simply fantasizes his way through the punishments he cannot avoid. He has convinced himself that pain is pleasurable, and casually taunts his persecutors with this discovery. The bullies are baffled and losing interest in him because he does not secrete enough fear, and besides you can never find the little bugger.

Crawford is waiting for his sister and her husband with every appearance of calm, although his mind is rehearsing a trunkload of schemes.

They get off the bus. This is not a good start, for Crawford was confidently expecting a taxi. On the plus side, the Commander's stride is impressive in fits and starts. Rosalia walks beside him as if she were accidentally occupying the same footpath. Crawford is bemused by this marriage. Seeing them together one can never quite believe it — that they share a bed, a bathroom mirror, that they make love, which presumably they do, otherwise . . . His experience of sex doesn't extend to imagining his sister and the Commander actually at it, in the elegant phrase used by his contemporaries. They have never helped his imagination by signs of mutual passion — he has never seen them kiss or touch each other — but that is scarcely surprising since their sexual contact is entirely unplanned. She sits on his knee for a moment, and passion overtakes them. Then he holds her and she sleeps like a child.

Crawford doesn't know any of this, and is puzzled by their apartness. Married couples are something arcane and unknowable, but on teenage sex he feels knowledgeable. His sister, even though she is his sister, is still a teenager. But in his sister's interaction with her husband he recognizes nothing of what passes between him and girls. Is it possible, he wonders, that one so old is now past it? What then did she marry him for, and why (if the wind of rumour is to be believed) did she claim to be pregnant in order to be allowed to marry him?

He notices however that his sister looks remarkably well on her married existence. She walks with a swing and her skin is becomingly coloured — not tanned, because she is too fair for that, but none the less the healthy outdoors ad-girl colour. She has acquired sexual confidence along with her married status. Crawford's antennae — already remarkably sensitive to the affairs of women — pick up some activity which is not altogether related to the imposing throwback that stalks beside her. At a mere sixteen he does not feel equipped to deal with the notion that his sister, five months married, is already unfaithful to her husband. He picks up the messages and declines to decode them.

Brother and sister do not kiss; it is not the custom of the country.

'Niall has absolutely no money,' Rosalia announces, as if this is the smartest thing in the world. 'So we are going to the Clarendon, and you can convince them to put it on Daddy's account.'

'Good stuff,' says Crawford, who always rises to a challenge. 'Not much of a treat though.'

'Is the food no good?' asks the Commander.

They stroll past the University, three abreast, taking up the whole footpath.

'It's better than the cabbage sog they give us at College, but I doubt the wine list will be up to much. Sparkling white, served warm.'

'Like your wine, do you, Crawford?'

'I'd like to like it, if I could get enough. Beer isn't a problem at school, smuggling in a half-g is old sport. But decent wine is locked up and counted. It's so hard to come by.'

'Know anything about it?'

'More than you'd imagine.'

'Well, there's something I could show you later.'

'I can hardly wait.'

Rosalia punches her brother, and puts her arm through the Commander's. But that night found them prowling the wharves together by the light of the moon. They had caught the last bus over the hills to the port, without a clue how to get home again. Crawford would undoubtedly be gated, and Rosalia and her husband quite unable to get back to Taylor's, but two bottles of the Clarendon's best, agreed by the man and boy to be a species of horse-piss, followed swiftly by three brandies each, to kill the aftertaste, and not one of them gave a toss about how to get home. They asked for the brandy bottle and filled up the Commander's hip-flask to speed them on their way.

It was a balmy, windless night, just right for adventure of an Enid Blyton kind. The great ships lay creaking in the swell. From on board came the late-night sounds of sailors making the best of things. Rosalia leaped onto a great cable drum and pirouetted, then dived into the arms of her husband and was swirled around till they were dizzy. Crawford teetered on the side of the pier facing the dark waters. He pissed magnificently, in a prize-wining arc into the moonlight, and gracefully accepted a compliment from the Commander on the size of his penis. He took off his boater and skimmed it into the waters of the harbour. They watched it bob away, pelting it with whatever items were to hand — small stones, tin cans, ends of rope — trying to make it sink before it floated out to the ocean.

'Down with school!' cried the Commander.

A night-watchman came out onto the stern of a big ship and shone his torch. The three revellers beat a hasty retreat into the shadows.

'Over here,' said the Commander.

They followed in his unsteady wake, away from the ships, weaving through bollards and parked machinery under tarpaulin, coils of rope and chain, trolley carts shunted together as if having a chinwag. Between the quays at which the ships were moored and the public marina lay a squatter camp of warehouses and sheds, some lettered with a company name, some marked with an identifying code, otherwise anonymous. They were all foreboding in the moon-shadow. Things seemed to scuttle between them — rats or thieving seamen or wekas strayed from the bush.

The Commander, in spite of his unreliable gait, knew exactly where he was going. He stopped outside an unmarked warehouse, well out of view of any nosy night-watchman.

'Does anyone have a torch?' he asked brightly, which considering that they had not a coat, a ten-shilling note or a piece of string between them, seemed a superfluous question.

There was a big fat padlock on the front doors with a very new chain. Niall simply pulled the bracket to which it was affixed and the screws came out of the wood. He pushed the door slightly and went inside sideways on.

Rosalia and Crawford followed him. The darkness smelt strongly of cigarette smoke.

'Favourite venue for the poker school. Pity we haven't a torch.'

'So what is in here that we can't see?' said Crawford, completely ignoring the fact that his sister and her husband seemed to have been suddenly overtaken by lust. He could not see them, only hear a sort of giggling scuffle which it was beneath him to notice.

'Wine,' said the slightly muffled Commander. 'South African.'

Crawford scrabbled around in the dark until he found an open crate. He took a bottle outside into the moonlight to read the label.

'Looks promising,' he said, though there was no one to hear him. 'Nice-looking bottle and very good area.'

He stood by the crack in the door and called out to the Commander. 'All right, Lingerfield, what's it doing here, and why am I interested?'

The Commander answered with some constraint from the other side of the door.

'It's a bond store. The fellow who imported it has gone broke and no one will pick up the bills. Anyone could have it dirt cheap if he could raise the necessary and find a market.'

'Oh I could sell this all right,' said Crawford. 'I could sell this. OK, how much?'

The Commander pushed the door open a little and peered out at Crawford. In the moonlight his craggy face came straight out of Transylvania.

'I overheard a couple of chaps talking in the harbour-master's office. I think a couple of thousand would shift it. HM wants it gone and the receivers are sick to death of it.'

'A couple of thousand. It's one hell of a bargain, but where do you think I am going to get that sort of money from? The old man might stump up a dinner occasionally if put on the spot as tonight, but that sort of money, not likely. I won't get a bean till I'm twenty-one and not much then.'

Nursing the bottle of wine like the baby of his hopes, Crawford led the way back to the road. They flagged down a surprised late-night farmer and bamboozled him into taking them all the way to Taylor's Mistake in the back of his ute. Crawford kept the wine inside his jacket in case he should be browbeaten into parting with it as a recompense. Instead he asked the farmer for his address and promised to send him a small something.

Rosalia scrambled for the key under a rock by the front door. The Commander pushed the door open; the key was a pretence that fooled no one. The french windows onto the beach were wide open.

'I must have a swim,' Rosalia cried and kicked off her shoes.

'Come on, darling,' she said, grabbing the Commander by the hand.

'Hang on a tick,' he said, 'Crawford must have a night-cap.'

She let go his hand and ran out scattily onto the sand. The Commander collected a bottle with two fingers of brandy and two solid glasses of the type designed for holding the toothbrush. He shambled out after his wife, and Crawford, still nursing the wine, trotted behind him.

The Commander stopped short, to watch the white limbs of his wife flashing into the sea. He allowed Crawford to catch him up, and took the fleeting chance.

'Nice arse,' he said, patting it.

Crawford did not move away.

'That warehouse of wine,' he said.

The Commander seemed somehow distracted. Crawford stood his ground. Though old and ineffectual, his brother-in-law was a less offensive animal than a locker-room thug, and potentially a whole order of magnitude more useful.

'You're too young for the wine 'n' spirits

licence. Nice to be young.'

'Yes, but you're not.'

'Who would give me a spirits licence?'

'We can work on that. The old man has vested interests.'

They made slow progress down towards the water's edge. Rosalia was making a great deal of splash to compensate for the bracing qualities of the sea thereabouts.

'Mustn't upset Rosie,' said the Commander and repositioned himself six inches away from Crawford.

The moon flecked the surface of the water. In the middle distance the cliffside reared up secret with caves. In its shadow waves curled up against invisible rocks and hissed back into the dark.

Niall poured two smidgeons of brandy into the tooth glasses and then apparently as an afterthought filled his from his hip-flask.

'You'd need a suit.'

'A suit. I haven't had a new civvy suit since before the war. The European war that is. There was a demob item, a hideous blue. Couldn't be seen in that.'

Rosalia got tired of cavorting in the waves unattended. She came dripping back to her family, her clothes clutched to her bosom, soaking up some of the water but affording no protection. The Commander took off his jacket and draped it round her shoulders. She leaned against him.

'Would you like me to be a wine and spirits merchant, darling?'

'I don't think even Crawford could stop you sampling the stock.'

'Of course I could,' said Crawford. 'I'd count it every day. And check the seals on the spirits. It would be a condition. Anyone drinking on the sly — out.'

'You are scary, Crawford,' said his sister.

'I haven't the capital,' said Crawford.

'Niall . . . ' said Rosalia, but he made no audible response.

They padded across the sand in a silence which Crawford tried to read.

'Hollander & Lingerfield,' said Crawford. 'Sounds good.'

'Sounds *very* good,' said his sister. 'Niall?'

'Letterhead,' said the Commander dreamily. 'Business cards.'

'It's not even a great deal of money,' said Crawford crossly. 'I hate being young. I can't wait to be middle-aged and rich.'

Rosalia dripped away into the bedroom and came back wearing her silk dressing-gown. It was debased oriental in design, electric blue and synthetic orange, the long-tailed birds engaged in a stylized minuet. She put on the kettle and spooned instant coffee into three mugs.

The Commander discoursed on the wine trade. He entertained them with tales of dives in Malacca and pubs in Dublin. He waxed lyrical on wine drunk in the depths of the Spanish countryside, black as the soles of the peasants' feet. He summoned up the smell of the cellars of Beaune — wine-seeped stone centuries old. Crawford sat bolt upright bathing the Commander in the attentive glow of his chestnut brown eyes.

Rosalia sat on her husband's lap and twirled an elegant white foot about, shedding skein after skein of sand. It fell onto the linoleum with a small sigh. At last the Lingerfields went to bed. Crawford made good-night noises and turned out the lights in the sun-room and caused the bed to creak.

Then he got up silently and crept barefoot to the bedroom door. He stood outside and listened. He was aware of the prurience of this behaviour but felt not a shimmer of embarrassment, because what he was after was that elusive piece of information his sister had let slip.

He listened with curiosity and disgust to the palpable evidence of his sister and brother-in-law's love for one another. He was no closer to understanding them and had less desire to do so, now he was slightly better acquainted with the Commander. But he needed that piece of information as he had never needed anything before. So he stood and waited. He would wait as long as it took.

'Niall.'

'Yes, dear heart.'

'You could, you know.'

'Could what, my dearest dear?'

'Do it.'

'Do what?' He started upon several lubricious suggestions, couched in delicate language.

'Don't be silly, and don't be greedy. You know I don't mean that sort of thing.'

'Tell me then.'

'You *know*.'

The Commander fetched a deep groaning sigh from the bottom of his soul.

'I am not a man who keeps promises,' he said. 'I mean to, you know. I try and fail rather often. But one thing I have always managed to do was keep it safe. It's the only thing I've got, you know, and I want to provide for you, my little pomegranate.'

'But this is the best thing you could do! I want you to do it. Please, Niall. For me. I don't care about being provided for.'

The argument went on, the Commander slurry with drink and tiredness, Rosalia merciless. Crawford stood patiently waiting for details until the Commander lurched out of bed to relieve his bladder, and he had to flee. He had no wish to encounter the Commander.

Deprived of the precise details he desired, he still had enough material to work with, and most significantly Rosalia on his side.

★ ★ ★

He lay rigid in the nasty little bed imagining himself in the future. He saw himself the owner of a big house — no, better, two big houses, Hollander House restored to its imperial splendour, with lights blazing and smart people mingling on the lawn, the trimmed lawn, green as a billiard table. The other house must be in England of course, grand but not ostentatious, elegant, under-stated, but visible, so that people could see it and say *There lives a man of substance and a man of taste.* He saw himself at the opera in a velvet jacket, in hand-made shoes, magnifi-cently cleaned, but not by him. He saw his wife on his arm — what was she like? Classy, that's what she was, not the tiresome starlet type who betrayed the tastelessness of so many rich men — he'd seen them in *Life* magazine, he knew. A woman so effortlessly upper-class that money made no impression on her at all, a woman so sure of her place that she could laugh at the pretensions of the rich without a hint of envy. A woman who could go absolutely anywhere and be at home, in a way Crawford longed to be able to do, a woman whose accent did not instantly brand her *colonial* and yet who could sit at her ease on the veranda of the tastefully refurbished Hollander House, look out over the lawn (trim and green as a billiard table) and enjoy the sun going down over the harbour. A person who would walk up through the bush to the pool and place her hand through his arm and enjoy its dangerous mystery as much as he did. A woman you could take to opera and rely on to say the right thing when introduced. A woman who knew about silver even if she didn't own any. It would be better if she didn't have too much in the way of inherited stuff — just the odd bit of engraved silver and a brace of fine eighteenth-century portraits to go with the entry in *Burke's*. Too much possession on her side would unbalance things. He could only bring his money and his charm and cunning and a squatocratic imitation of her great-grandfather.

Of course, he thought, he would have a mistress as well. A much younger woman with enormous breasts, curvaceous, that was the term, not totally dissimilar to Marilyn Monroe, but without the tinny dyed hair. A girl who loved sex, could never get enough of it, but had to be kept at bay, in a little house, not too far away, terribly discreet. A little vulgar perhaps, but always opening the door in her dressing-gown, brushing her hair out of her eyes and smiling at him as she drew him into the bedroom. In English houses, didn't they have the bedrooms upstairs? Upstairs into the bedroom.

He submerged himself into the glory of her breasts, somehow so much more pneumatic than the real breasts of the real girls he had so far conquered. He'd know her when he saw her, as he'd know his wife the minute she opened her mouth.

It seemed to Crawford, sixteen going on sixty, that nothing stood between himself and this opera-going man but the Commander's little secret.

★   ★   ★

The sun came up splendidly on his rich future. He bounced out of bed, compelled, as the Commander was, by the insistence of the light. He felt predictably awful, but his intentions were clear. He would not go to school that day. He would not, in fact, go to school at all, for the time being. It occurred to him with sweet clarity that he was legally able to quit, and could make himself so perfectly beastly that the headmaster would beg the old man to keep him away. Of course there was the small matter of the university entrance exam, but when a fortune is to be made, learning must learn to bow out graciously. And as everyone but a dunderhead knew, even a dunderhead could get into university in this utopia provided he were twenty-one and not certifiable. By twenty-one Crawford reckoned he'd be about ready to let people tell him what to think for a while.

Crawford put on his black school trousers for what he confidently expected to be the last time. He walked bare-chested out onto the beach hoping not to encounter any early surfers, male or female. Boys without money must be big and tanned and good in a tackle. But rich men, he knew, could be pale-skinned and pigeon-breasted, and women still hung on them. Crawford pondered his strategy. He had thought that the fathers of the mob at school would be his natural customers, and he would approach them through casual remarks dropped in the passage between cloakroom and library. But if he were not in school, how could he drop the remarks that would make the orders flow?

How was he to transport and store all this lovely wine when he'd bought it; how was he to invoice people and collect his debts? He'd seen it in operation while working for Uncle Guthrie last summer holidays. He'd followed the mechanisms of his uncle's import/export business with the devotion of a postulant intent on sainthood. Bank accounts, cheque books, ledgers, accountants . . . it seemed all too hard, especially for a boy, his voice not long broken, working as an alcoholic frontman, at one remove, like a diver mending a pipe. University entrance Latin acquired a sheen never in evidence in the dry snarling air of the classroom.

But just for the exercise, as he walked along the beach in his bare feet and school trousers, he tried to work out the profit. He had no idea what the wine would fetch, but it looked expensive. Say he sold it for twelve pounds a case. Three deep, six high, down both sides — say there were three hundred cases in that warehouse — three hundred cases at twelve pounds made a profit of sixteen hundred, minus expenses. But what say he sold it at twenty pounds a case?

He arrived at the rocky end of the beach, and sat down, dangling his feet in the sea and letting the tide encroach on the cuffs of his trousers. He calculated and speculated

— how many could he shift — over how long? How much did storage cost — or if he holed it up in the wool-shed at home, how tricky would it be to get crates to customers in reasonable time? Could the Commander be trusted with a car — assuming they could get hold of one? Could Mother be persuaded . . . On and on went his surmises, growing ever more irritated at his lack of information and lack of years. If he could at a stroke be twenty-one and dispense with the need to propel his brother-in-law before him. So unreliable a puppet . . .

. . . and yet in his favour was this mysterious source of funds, which he must be persuaded to part with. But how?

The Commander came out onto the sand, head first like an Arctic explorer struggling out of his tent. He turned his head this way and that along the beach, as if sniffing his way to the Pole. He spotted Crawford dangling his white ankles in the sea and headed towards him. Crawford was suddenly seized with the desire to run away — he didn't know if it was devilment or dislike.

He steadied himself with thoughts of the future, of a man so confident he never needed to consider what he should do. A man in a Jaguar car, who poured a perfect gin and tonic and presided over his dinner table, making his guests sparkle like the silver.

The Commander came right up beside him before Crawford deigned to notice him.

'I'd lost you,' he said.

'Good night last night,' said Crawford. 'Thanks very much.'

'I think we have to thank your father. Do you want any breakfast, old chap?'

They started back to the house. The Commander was dressed in his work overalls.

'Have to get that suit,' said Crawford. 'Ballantynes, Friday night.'

'Have a snifter first,' said Niall. 'Zetland Tavern, after work.'

'I'm under-age,' said Crawford piously.

'So you are,' said the Commander and placed an unbrotherly arm round Crawford's naked shoulders. 'All ready for school?'

'I'm expelling myself for a term,' said Crawford. 'We need to get the business off to a good start.'

'What business?'

Crawford affected to take this as a joke.

'I thought Rosie could take a little job in our uncle's office. She could learn to type. It's a useful skill for a girl to have.'

'Couldn't agree more, old boy, but Rosie might not.'

'We'll persuade her,' said Crawford and grinned at his partner.

★ ★ ★

It was so much easier than he had expected to get people to do what he wanted. He packed the Commander off to work on the back of Dickie's motor-bike, asking anxiously when they would be home, and whether they would have had a drink.

Dickie promised to deliver the Commander home sober if he could, but it was, he explained, outside his control. He said if Crawford needed to borrow a shirt, he was welcome to go down and see Mrs Dickie, down there with the pink letterbox, and the two men roared away to the wharves.

Crawford stood on the front step and considered whether there was an advantage in getting friendly with Mrs Dickie. He thought perhaps there was, because Dickie was a young man with a motor-bike, and had influence over the Commander.

Whatever Mrs Dickie was like, slag or goddess, he was not going down there without a shirt. Had he been built like the man in the Atlas ad, he would still have hesitated at so blatant a display. If Mrs Dickie was to be his ally, she must first of all find him harmless.

He went back into the cottage and checked that Rosalia was still sleeping. He put on his school shirt, without its absurd detachable collar, tied it at the waist like a navvy, and checked himself in the grudging square of bathroom mirror. He didn't really need a shave, he was sorry to observe, but then neither did he have any pimples today. He wondered about borrowing a toothbrush but thought about the Commander's teeth and rubbed his own with toothpaste on a finger. He wetted and ruffled up his hair a bit, and then wetted it down again.

Then, barefoot, he picked his way out of the cottage, up the path, onto the road and made for the pink letterbox. The little stones were hard on his feet, softened by school shoes, and he found himself walking in a mincing uneven gait. This would not do if he were to encounter Mrs Dickie on the road. He reminded himself of his childhood, now so very far behind him, and how he had run barefoot all day on the gravelled roads and stinging sands. He straightened up and allowed the stones to prick him, and willed himself to walk casually down the rough road as if his feet were faced with leather.

The morning was already hazy with heat. A little brown lizard ran across the road in front of him and took refuge under the fleshy foliage of the ice-plant. Crawford was alerted to the exotic pink flowers, now wide open to the sunlight. He picked one and placed it in the top button-hole of his shirt.

The Fishers' place was a cut above the beach cottages. It had a porch on the back, even if currently nothing more than a construct of building paper and pink-stained timber, which was reached by proper steps, cut into the hillside and framed with timber. There was a rail made of piping, painted the same pink as the letterbox, not very successfully because the paint did not adhere to the piping as well as it did to the pressed tin of the letterbox.

The front door was open. It would have surprised Crawford if it had been shut. From inside the house he heard the radio talking away over the indeterminate noise of small children. Even though he had come all the way down the road barefoot he hesitated at the sound of the children. But Mrs Dickie had seen him.

'Hiya,' she said. Her accent was South African, crossed with American. 'You must be Crawford.'

Crawford was unable to process the curious fact that she knew who he was because he was swept away by her presence.

She was taller than Crawford and naturally wiry, but pregnancy had enlarged her breasts to fantastic proportions, without so far apparently affecting the rest of her body. Crawford, although he knew much, did not know about this phenomenon. He thought her something akin to a goddess, with her white smile and her shirt idly buttoned. Her hair was flame red, but her skin was tanned. His self-composure started out the door behind him. He grabbed it as it fled up the path.

'Hello, I'm afraid I don't know your name. I can hardly call you Mrs Dickie as Niall does.'

'Well, I rather like that! *Missus Dickie.* Niall — is that the Commander's name? Well I'll be blowed! But my name is — well, my given name is Pearl, but — '

Crawford started to laugh the moment the smile spread across her face. Not only did he get the joke, he knew she liked the fact that he got it.

'*O souvenir charmant,*' he sang in a tone so light it was almost speaking.

'Oh yes, you are musical, like Rosalia.' She sighed. 'I miss a piano. Come on in, you poor boy, you're barefoot! You can call me Marg.'

'Thank you, Marg,' he said. 'Dickie sent me down to borrow some sandals.'

'Oh sure. But what exactly . . . '

'I've expelled myself,' said Crawford with a grin of comrades. 'Niall came up with a

162

brilliant scheme last night. It could be the making of him. I thought I'd help him get started.'

'Heavens,' said Marg. 'Come on in.'

Crawford padded after her into the living-room, clearly in the throes of renovation, with stripped plaster and building paper flapping lazily in the heat.

'Dickie's working on the house,' she explained. 'I think this is a state of being, rather than a transition. At least as long as we've been married, Dickie has always been working on the house. Different country, different house, but he's working on them. I guess it uses up his excess energy.'

The radio sat in the middle of the table surrounded by piles of papers, books and materials. In the little space left was a plate and cup, a teapot and milk jug. Glass doors opened out into a little space firmly fenced off from the cliff-hanging garden. Here two small blond creatures were driving lead trucks through hills and dales of sand. From time to time water was applied to the landscape from a plastic bucket. The little kingdom was decked and delimited by shells.

Marg picked up the teapot and shook it a little. 'Needs a refresh.'

Crawford followed her into the kitchen. It was much nicer than the kitchen in Rosalia's cottage and quite unlike the kitchen at Hollander House. It seemed to him to be what a kitchen should be — the light streamed in across the bench, picking up nothing more than the odd crumb. The cupboards were newly painted shiny white and yellow, the curtains white and yellow gingham with blue cords tying them back. White jars labelled *Flour, Sugar, Tea* and *Biscuits* stood in a nice row. There was a magnificent Kenwood mixer, as grand and elaborate as a battleship. On its own little shelf was a plaster statue of the Virgin Mary, in pale blue, with downcast eyes. On the wall a Plunket calendar covered in loopy writing. On the big bowed fridge door a chart of meals for the month. Crawford fell in love not with Mrs Dickie, so much as her kitchen.

She made a new pot of tea. The old tea-leaves went outside at the base of standard rose, doing its best in the dry salty air. The pot was rinsed, warmed, and refilled. Yes, Crawford would like a waffle, though he didn't admit to not knowing what one was. He would have acceded to any suggestion she made.

'Your feet aren't really his size,' she said. 'I guess we can find some plastic ones, but that doesn't seem quite you.'

'No,' said Crawford with a little shudder

164

which he knew he should suppress. 'But they'll be fine for now. I don't mind.'

He wondered if he dare follow her into the bedroom, but she didn't shift from the table where they sat enjoying their breakfast. There was plenty to talk about.

'There's a lovely piano over at my house,' he said. 'No one plays it now — it seems such a waste.'

'Your house in Charteris Bay?'

'Near there. Have you been there?'

Marg threw back her head and laughed. 'Me? How would I get over there? Two and a quarter children and no car?'

Crawford registered the 'quarter' child. To his surprise it didn't diminish her glory. He knew nothing of these matters, except as things girls were deadly keen to avoid. But if the glory of Mrs Dickie was the end result, perhaps the state should be encouraged. Crawford guessed that this was unlikely to be the case, but one never knew. There might be girls who simply became themselves when being someone else.

He tried hard to concentrate on polite conversation, music and school and beach life, when his heart and mind were fixed on two matters, which had nothing in common with each other or with the cheerful subject of their talk. Mrs Dickie took pity on him.

165

'Now this idea of the Commander's — this business — I just don't get it. Since when has the Commander been a businessman?'

Crawford took a large bite of waffle. He risked golden syrup on his chin, but it was essential to buy time.

'I don't know that he has, but it would be nice for him to have the chance, don't you think?'

'Well — ' she began, but was interrupted by wails. Grievous bodily harm was being inflicted by spade in the sandpit. Marg scooped up the wronged child, wet sandy nappy and all, and sat him on her knee, posting portions of waffle into his mouth.

Crawford tried to look on the child with benignity but the effort was beyond him. He took the opportunity to think carefully about his approach.

'My Uncle Guthrie is in a similar line of business,' he improvised, trying to disengage from the child's attempt to unbutton further his mother's shirt. 'He would like to help Niall,' he lied on calmly, 'and I thought I could just oil the wheels a bit.'

'I would have thought your parents would rather you were at school.'

'They'll be so grateful to have Rosie settled they'll soon forgive me.'

Marg looked at him warily.

'You're a bit of a cool customer, aren't you, Crawford?'

At that moment Crawford did not feel remotely cool. He struggled to suppress a blush which was as motivated by anger at not being twenty-one as by bashful lust. He opted for honesty.

'I'd like to be.'

She laughed, a rich mean grown-up laugh. Crawford could not control the blush, and hoped like hell that it made him look boyishly pretty, which was now his only hope.

'Well, let's go for a swim, and you can tell me all about it on the way down. Have you got some trunks?'

Crawford then got to follow her into the bedroom. The bed, true to Dickie's personality, filled up the entire space. It was casually tidied over with a broad-weave throw in ochres and oranges, of a boldness he had not seen before. The walls were covered with patterned cloth — oranges, browns, blocks of white. There were no curtains. The fronds of the kowhai outside brushed hopefully against the glass. Yesterday's discarded clothes lay in a wicker basket in the corner by the door. It was a working bedroom. Crawford tried not to gulp. Dickie was a great big man, so there wasn't much chance of finding anything to fit Crawford.

'I guess you could get away with swimming in the nude,' she said. 'But this is New Zealand, isn't it?'

'If we went round the rocks far enough . . . ' he said, wondering if she would join him.

'It's a bit rough for the kids. Maybe the Commander's trunks would fit you?'

Crawford shuddered.

'We'll go and knock up Rosalia anyway,' said Marg.

They walked down the cliffs. Crawford carried the basket full of drinks and nappies and spades and buckets and sun-hats and lotion. Marg carried a child on each hip. Crawford started to wonder why she had children so close together, then dimly recalled an interchange between his sister and her husband on the subject of Catholicism and conception — he was sure Mrs Dickie's name had come up. Rosalia had maintained that it was all Dickie's fault, while Niall had tried to insist that it was Missus that was the faithful Catholic, and a fine example of the faith to boot.

Crawford inclined to the view that her Catholicism and her pregnant state compounded with his age made it rather unlikely she would commit adultery with him. But there was no harm in watching for any signals, conscious or otherwise.

On the way down the cliff they continued to talk about music — she loved to play and sing, she told him, trashy stuff, songs from the shows mainly, but sometimes easy operetta. Crawford suddenly found he was prepared to accept operetta as real music. But he explained that the piano was his first and only love — but he didn't like accompanying Rosalia much because his ear was so good.

'There's perfect pitch and perfect pitch,' he told her. 'It can be measured.'

'And I guess yours has been.'

He couldn't see her face, for the path was single-file, but he suspected she was teasing him. It was more important to have her as an ally than to impress her with one's brilliance.

'No,' he lied, 'but I don't think it's that good actually. Anyway who cares? Rosie loves music passionately, and that's what matters.

'Though,' he ploughed on, hoping he was now able to reap the advantage from such treachery to his beliefs, 'I think it would be a jolly good idea if Rosalia learned a bit of a trade. If she went to work in Uncle Guthrie's office for a while she could learn to type and that would help Niall no end in his little venture.'

Marg, struggling with two small children and a scrambled path, made no immediate answer. Crawford worried that he had betrayed his principles to no effect.

'I think it's good for a girl to have a skill. I used to work in advertising in Jo' burg. It was so glamorous. Dickie used to wait outside with his motor-bike running. He wouldn't come inside. I was going to be a commercial artist.'

'Oh, so what happened?'

'Dickie happened. It doesn't matter, here I am on a beach every day of my life. And soon we'll have enough saved for the yacht.'

They got to the bottom of the cliff. Marg dropped the children summarily. They started off across the sand towards the sea and had to be roped in, because Marg insisted they all go and fetch Rosalia out.

'Rosalia wants to be an artist. She's going to Art School she told me. She talks of little else. I can't see her in an office. She'd pine away.'

'But she wants to help Niall.'

'I think the wharf is good for him. It's good for Dickie. Lots of time off and terrific money.'

Crawford had to think more quickly than he wished to do in the conditions. 'But the family will never respect him if he stays on the wharf.'

That was pretty good in the circumstances.

'How much does that matter? If they're happy?'

'Of course nothing else matters,' said Crawford, who currently felt not even remotely interested in happiness. 'But I can't help worrying about them.'

The doors of Rosalia's cottage were still flung open. The four of them went inside, yoohooing enough to raise the dead. Rosalia came out of the bathroom in her oriental dressing gown looking much as if she were.

'What happened last night, Crawford?'

'Wonderful things. Come on, sis. We're having a beach party.'

'But it's breakfast time.'

'Brunch,' said Marg. 'Just grab your things.'

Once they were settled, Crawford told his sister a version of what had happened the night before. She had persuaded the Commander to realize his capital. In return she had promised to go to work so they would have access to office facilities. Crawford had promised to take a term off school to help them.

'I don't remember any of that,' she said.

'You do remember the warehouse full of wine?'

'Yes, and the weird ride home in that farmer's truck. But after that — '

'You went swimming nude in the sea.'

171

'Did I?'

'And you and the Commander — well — I'm embarrassed.'

'You are not,' said Marg.

Crawford tried to look manfully out to sea so she might not notice he was rumbled.

'Don't let him down,' said Crawford. 'He was so excited this morning.'

'Did you say wine?' asked Marg.

'South African,' said Crawford. 'Niall says it's very good and a terrific bargain.'

'Don't you think getting the Commander involved in wine is a bit like letting these two loose in the candy store?'

'He promised me,' said Rosalia.

'It's a bit of a test really, isn't it?' said Crawford.

Although burdened with a hangover of mythological scale, with Sisyphean sixteen-year-old lust and sixteen-year-old uncertainties, blinded by the light of a beach in paradise, Crawford understood clearly the meaning of Mrs Dickie's steady regard. It was not in his interests, his business interests at least. He evaluated his choice. He might make her like him or he might persuade her to support him. He accepted, with a deep and terrible sadness, of the uncompromising kind known only to the young, that it was not possible to do both.

7

These days, Marg and Dickie drive a Triumph Mayflower, an interesting car, shaped rather like a hearse, proclaiming them as substantial but not flashy. For indeed they are doing rather well with Fisher's Harbour Cruises and Fisher's Daily Boat Hire. But there's nothing smug about the Fishers, and today there is even an uncertainty in the air, as they draw up alongside the offices of Hollander & Lingerfield, overlooking the river in Oxford Terrace.

'This OK, old man?' asks Dickie, as they slide into a parking spot under the poplar trees.

The Commander is in the back seat, in his best suit, his business suit, oddly displaced by it, like a monster from a child's heads-and-bodies book. The Girephant, half one creature half the other, making no sense at all.

He's had a drink or two, but with the Commander that is quite unremarkable. Sober, what would he be like?

'We'll wait out here.'

Marg and Dickie are dressed up for town,

careful of themselves in their unaccustomed smart clothes.

'No, no,' says the Commander. 'I can find my way back. I'll catch the bus.'

'I don't think that's a good idea at all,' says Marg. 'I think we'll wait, Dickie, and take Niall round to the lawyers. Just to see he gets there.'

'I will be perfectly all right,' says the Commander in faraway tones. 'I do know my way from here to old Harman's.'

'I know you do, Niall, but I expect you'll be a bit upset when you've finished with Crawford.'

Nobody feels it necessary to elaborate on this remark.

The Commander unfolds himself out of rear seat of the Mayflower. He walks, with his head bowed, up the steps of the office building, past the plate that bears his surname, his proud moment of participation in business. It is two weeks since he has been in the office, two weeks since Crawford turned twenty-one and applied for his licence as a wine and spirits merchant, and changed the locks.

The tiny rooms of Hollander & Lingerfield are up two tedious flights, which Niall sprang up in the days of his enthusiasm. Today they cause him to puff and pat the hip-flask in his jacket pocket reassuringly.

There is a new girl at the front desk, pretty, malleable. Her voice suggests the right school and excellent contacts, but rather less acumen. She does not know who the Commander is. He lacks the courage to tell her.

'Just a sec,' she says.

She pops her head into the next room.

'A Commander to see you, Mr Hollander.'

Niall goes into his own office, and sees at his desk another new girl, less pretty, but more alarming. The Commander can see Crawford's paw prints on her body.

'Hello, Niall!' says Crawford, all affability in his twenty-first birthday tailor-made suit. 'How are you?'

The Commander cannot think of a response that packages up into one phrase how he is. He mumbles an answer.

'I've got it all here. Actually Wendy has got it all here. A real whiz, Wendy. Wendy, this is Niall Lingerfield my partner, my brother-in-law. Though I suppose I should say,' Crawford gives a silver laugh, 'my ex-brother-in-law-to-be.'

The Commander wonders why he does not add the ex- to *partner* as well. But presumably the whiz Wendy has drawn up papers and knows full well his status.

'Not officially yet. The labyrinth of the law . . . '

'But it's a foregone conclusion?'

'I think I am if not a trigamist, at least a bigamist. What is the word for four marriages? Polygamist, I suppose. I don't see that the marriage could be legal, if one has had fewer divorces than marriages. Except in the case of death. But they were all so young, it seems unlikely. It seems rather unlikely that one should survive oneself, in the circumstances . . . '

Crawford looks as if he might very well hasten the Commander's end all by himself. The eyes of the whiz Wendy have grown round. The Commander takes some pleasure in this.

'I think technically I have to commit adultery in some sort of public way. This is rather tricky. It would be so much easier if matters were the other way around.'

Crawford purses his lips in a manner not often seen in a twenty-one-year-old. Wendy hands the Commander a sheaf of papers. On the top is a typewritten share transfer form. Niall Lingerfield is selling his shares in Hollander & Lingerfield to Crawford Hollander. Then comes a long white envelope, which contains a ticket on the *Corinthic* sailing in a week's time for Southampton, and a hundred British pounds in ten-pound notes. Then pages and pages of accounts in Crawford's neat black ink, detailing exactly what the Commander has consumed of the company's assets over the past five years. The Commander glances at it — running costs in the Hollander family car, dinners at the Clarendon and Russley, El Segundo, the Mandarin, shirts at Ballantynes, whisky, cash advances, bottles of wine, whisky — Crawford has written it all down, day by day, totting it up at the bottom of each column, until the total far outweighs the putative value of the shares.

There is no way of telling, with Crawford, whether he has kept jottings in his notebooks for five years, or simply concocted the whole sorry catalogue out of his head. He is perfectly capable of either set of actions, knowing full well that the Commander will not be able to challenge a single transaction.

The Commander looks into Crawford's liquid brown eyes and sees his sister, and sees also the great gulf that yawns between the charming and the good. How tragic, he thinks, that the charming will always persuade us to trust them with our hearts and our purses, even though we know that they are not to be trusted. The Commander wonders foggily how often he has been cheated of his heart and his money by a lovely liquid glance. And he pulls together what is left of his shabby pride and resolves that he will never allow himself to be melted out of his senses again.

The young Wendy, charmed out of her better judgement by Crawford, blushes. The Commander enjoys the sight.

'Are you a shareholder or an employee?' he asks politely.

'Sort of both,' she says.

'Make sure you don't sample the stock,' he says. 'Crawford charges full retail, and extracts his due in blood.'

'I think that should tide you over when you get to England. As long as you don't spend it in the bar on the voyage, of course.'

'I was planning on taking my supplies with me.' He fans the pages out. 'I seem to have acquired a bit of stock.'

He chooses not to tell Crawford exactly how many bottles of whisky he has spirited out of the warehouse in the last week. In a mad rush of caution, he has passed several on to Dickie for safe keeping. They have not yet appeared on the inventory of his sins, but now it is too late to add them. He likes the idea of sins that slip past the eternal register — the divine recorder is too distracted by the plenitude to bother with the venial ones.

'Just sign the transfer, Niall, there's a good chap.'

Crawford walks to the window and surveys the river. He can see the stately line of poplars curving around the river with exotic elegance, the heavy-leaved trees in front of the Theosophical Society, the band rotunda and memorial hydrant. The disapproving Ionic columns of the Oxford Terrace Baptist Church are just out of sight.

The Commander loves this view, reminding him of an England that he never knew — sharply coloured, clean, spacious.

'Marg and Dickie didn't come in,' says Crawford. 'Why ever not? I haven't seen Marg in ages.'

Niall enjoys the peevishness in his tone. He hopes that divine justice will work on earth, and Crawford will learn what Marg thinks of him. He hopes, but he does not expect. Crawford opens the window and leans out, calling and waving boyishly.

Marg, strolling by the river, returns his wave with little enthusiasm. The Commander watches for signs that he has taken the rebuke, but is scantly rewarded.

'I love Marg so passionately. She was and remains my first love. Platonic, of course,' he explains to the bristling Wendy. 'Do you think she knows, Niall?'

'I think she knows a great deal about you, Crawford.'

The Commander often wished in later years that he could pretend to have delivered a crushing blow to the young man's ego. But no such pretence is possible. Crawford smiled enchantingly, and as if by remote control, Marg waved with both her arms.

'She's all dressed up. Doesn't she look terrific?'

'We are going on the town,' lies the Commander.

'Don't spend it all at once.'

The Commander, unable to conjure up a suitable retort, signs away his life-savings. As he does so, he thinks how slyly important things creep upon us — here the end of his material hopes, in half an hour at the lawyers the final fissure of his heart. An ordinary day, not a cloud in the sky, seagulls hustling on the river-bank, no thunder crack, no trump. In just such a way lives slip away, honour dissipates, souls are traded. He was always partial to a bit of fire and brimstone, but in reality he knows that melodrama is deeply unrealistic. A rape, a humiliation, the death of hope, the evaporation of love — such ordinary events. Almost dull.

He takes away the leaves of paper, with the intention of getting Marg to read them with her gimlet eye, and Dickie to storm back upon Crawford with the evidence of his mendacity. Then, half-way down the stairs, he stops and tears the papers into pieces, smaller and smaller pieces, scattering the evidence of his misdeeds all down the staircase. He does not care if he has been cheated. On the great day of reckoning it will not be Niall Lingerfield who steps to the left, for all his whoring and drinking. *Oh no, no, no!* he thinks, *watch that boyish face crumple at the trump of doom!*

Dickie relieves Niall of the ticket and all the English money. He gives Niall a New Zealand ten-shilling note by way of surety.

'You might get waylaid, old chap. I'll keep it all safe till you board.'

They drive to the office of the lawyers, up more dingy stairs, this time with a view of the Cathedral. Marg and Dickie come too, steering him as if he were an overgrown child. He does not care about this either, content to relax on the comfortable goodness of these people. Marg does not approve of divorce, and so neither does Dickie. She sits in the outer office, her jaw set, fingering an invisible rosary, her body and her torrent of red hair proclaiming a divergent morality.

In the lawyer's office, pinned in front of the leather desk with brass accoutrements, he is distracted by the word *nisi*. He searches his schoolboy crammers, almost visualizing the correct page in Kennedy's *Latin Primer*, but still can't remember its meaning. A lifetime of drinking has eroded his brain — but then he thinks that even as a schoolboy he couldn't remember those slippery little adverbs or is it a preposition? And then he'd taken nothing stronger than cod-liver oil.

He nods at whatever the lawyer is telling him and decides not to mention polygamy. A legal mind might not see these matters in the same romantic light. He is led away again into a maze of conflicting legalities — would good Catholic Marg disapprove of the dissolution of his marriage less if it were not legal? By the time he is ushered out to his friends, he is none the wiser but one step closer to the end of another marriage, whatever its status.

He knows that Marg and Dickie do not want to spend their special day in town hauling a great mountain of failure behind them, but equally he knows their good nature will not allow them to discard him. They are afraid he will drink himself into a coma, go missing for a week and fail to board his ship. And not without some reason, for that is exactly what the Commander envisages for himself — not that he wishes to behave so, but that he accepts as inevitable that he will.

'Without other people's goodness,' he would tell Genista, 'I would have died in gutters a dozen times over. What a waste of goodness. What a waste of you.'

It's lunchtime. He likes to be seen on the town with Marg, so handsome a woman, even if too fleshy for his personal taste. Dickie steers them into the smart restaurant where is laid out that most modern of feasts, the smorgasbord. The Commander, emboldened by his hip-flask, makes a joke relating to Swedes and orgasms. Marg frowns at him. The Commander, blissfully rebuked, tried to think of another such joke, but they have slid the way of the prepositions. *Unless*, of course *unless*, he remembers.

'There are two classes of people in the world,' he tells them. 'The successful, and their victims. Some of us are born victims, so others can succeed. It's taken me all my life to find that out.'

'I'm planning to be successful without having any victims,' said Marg. 'I want to prove that we can do well without doing a Crawford.'

'Will anyone notice?' asks Dickie.

'God will,' says Marg.

'And,' continues the Commander, 'there are two kinds of sinners, the accidental and

183

the deliberate. I'm an accidental sinner. Crawford is deliberate. I have done terrible things, but I expected to be forgiven. But Crawford . . . '

'Crawford is only a lad,' says Dickie. 'I expect he'll see the error of his ways.'

'I don't see why he should,' says Marg, 'because no one is ever going to point it out to him.'

'Someone should try,' says Dickie.

They see him to the bus stop in the Square, where he waits obediently. As soon as they are out of sight, he toddles over to a different bus stop.

It is a long trip to Hollander House. On the bus to Lyttelton, across on the ferry to Diamond Harbour, and then on foot round the bays to Hollanders, except for the stretch when a local contractor gave him a lift, along with the bales of wire.

Hollander House has one of the loveliest settings on the Peninsula. One of the many bays, a small, shallow bay, sweeps round in front, leaving a toenail of sand. Across the road and back towards the hills, the grounds of the house bank upwards, English green in front, dark native forest behind, and above and beyond, far above, the bare excoriated faces of the hills, still jagged with the memory of a mighty eruption.

The first Hollanders, ruthlessly practical, chopped down a paddock full of mighty native trees, sold off the timber at a good price, and filled the ugly gaps with an avenue of English trees which they could never hope to see. It curves around, splendid now, following the shoreline, from the road to the site of a grand house — which they were in no hurry to build. Practical people, they favoured convenience and thrift, and stayed in their wooden homestead among the sheep yards, shaded by a few surviving totara.

The grand house is there now, and very fine it looks with the sun glinting on its many windows, teasingly visible amid the trees. It is not a house that daunts those used to European mansions, but in the New Zealand landscape, empty for the most part, stands out like a duchess on a dosing strip.

The Commander was not daunted by its splendour, but greatly enjoyed the view of harbour and hill from its many large windows, a view, he reckoned, as fine as any in the world. His father-in-law had warmed to him for a moment, until Niall began a discourse on Naples versus Valetta.

He stands under the trees at the entrance to the avenue. He has not been here often, but the place is charged with memory. He does not even know if Rosalia is at home.

Home. Her home was once a little place on the beach, as insubstantial as the marriage proved to be. His home — is everywhere and nowhere. He thinks of this and sheds a tear, fuelled perhaps by the emptying hip-flask.

He sees her through the trees. She's wearing black and is barefoot. She's trailing across the grounds towards the sea. He is stricken with terror and embarrassment. How old and absurd he is, in his city suit and his dusty shoes, his fusty old English ideas and his middle-aged fumblings. If it were possible to flee, he would flee.

But would she see him in the distance, if he turned back? If he hid — He would not hide. He would wait for her, since he had already been so thoroughly abased that he could fall no lower. There was always the chance of something better. Always the chance.

It's a lovely setting to say goodbye to the last love. After Rosalia, it was sensible middle-aged love, being warmed by a hot water bottle, instead of sunlight. He did not say as much to Genista, for the hot water bottle is a wonderful comfort and one does not wish it away.

He never forgets the last image of Rosalia, slender as a lily, springy as willow, golden-red hair impossible in the breeze. His heart turns over and over with tenderness, and regret,

regret that she will never again be quite as young and lovely as she is today, regret at the disappointment that will grow inside her, eating away at her spirits. He knows that everything disappoints, even love, and everything fades, even beauty, and that one day she will know this too.

'What do you want?' she says, but she's not angry with him — not yet. He has rehearsed so many different speeches on the way over, that he is unprepared.

'What do you want?'

'To say goodbye. I sail for the old country next week.'

'Crawford did that for you after all?'

'Crawford has bought me a ticket. I suppose I am grateful. I shall like to see Blighty again before I die.'

'Don't be silly.'

'It has changed more than I have changed. I am a throwback, as you often told me.'

'I'm sorry, Niall. I didn't mean it.'

'No it's true.'

Neither of them can think what to say.

The late afternoon is so beautiful, he thinks everything that needs to be said about the world is contained in the tip of the bare mountain caught in sun, and behind it, cloud casually streaked across the bleached sky.

'I wanted you to know how much I love you,' he says.

Rosalia looks down at her bare feet.

'I know you do, Niall,' she says, and then turns and runs away.

He cries. He casts a last fond look at the avenue, the house smug against its grand backdrop of trees, the hills behind, on which no trees are suffered to grow. He does not love the house, or the household, the grasping, morally superior Hollanders, replete with pioneer virtue. But the house contains, for the moment, the dying strain of his real life — everything afterwards will be a coda, but, as it turns out, a surprisingly long and beautiful coda.

Part II

Part II

8

Up the back of Hollander House, where civilization lapped at the shadow of the hills, Rewi Mann was pouring concrete. It was time to break for lunch, but the pesky serpentine path that Rosalia had insisted upon was proving harder than he'd expected. Rewi generally did his concrete nice and straight, so perfectly square and flat you could calibrate off it. Curves were a nonsense thing, but Rosalia had insisted, and Rewi had thought it smarter not to argue. He had been working for Rosalia barely a month, and it was not his policy to argue with the boss until he had proved himself indispensable.

He straightened up to clear the sweat out of his eyes. We had better have a good look at him, for he is what passes for a hero in our story.

In spite of his name, Rewi had no Maori blood, or none that anyone owned up to, but he could have passed for a Maori. The sun had burnt him chestnut brown, and he had the broad face, clearly defined features, Roman nose and buttress build of a Polynesian, and a rich dark voice of whose power he was unaware. He was named not out of sentimental attachment to the *tangata whenua*, but in honour of the great Socialist visionary Rewi Alley. Rewi himself didn't greatly care either way, a name was nothing more to him than a flag of convenience. He hadn't put up much of a fight when Janis wanted to call the children things like Flame and Sky and Aroha. He let her work all the names out of her system, and was relieved when she settled on Tom and Zoë, which had seemed fairly ordinary names when they lived in town. They seemed rather less ordinary now they had moved out here, to the Peninsula. He felt rather angry about their names, as he had never done before. It seemed to him that if Janis was going to inflict oddball names on them, the least she could have done was hang around to see the project through.

Most of the time he concentrated on whatever he was doing and gave no thought to anything else. This strategy provided protection from anger and doubt, and was a great advantage in getting the job done well. He'd always taken a pride in doing things well, as with this path of Rosalia's, and he always managed to make a tidy job, no matter what. He had no mechanism for dealing with failure, and so was making no inroads at all on the great black swamp in the middle of his life. It was not being drained, nor likely to be. He tried to act as if it were not really there. In his simple universe of give and take, right and wrong, if a woman left her husband it meant he was a bastard or had managed marriage poorly. But Rewi held that this could not be true of him, who took such pains to do things well. Practical things, that is, for in his mind there was no other kind of thing.

The swamp was still too treacherous for him to venture into. He had talked to nobody about his feelings and he did not intend to start. He thought people blathering on and on about their feelings, exploring the inner man, bringing out the child, launching into the primal scream — all that was nothing but wankers' tosh. It was the sort of thing espoused by Janis's feminist friends in their sacklike dresses and dyke jeans. He could see no possible benefit in dwelling on what had been done to him. However aggrieved he was, and he knew he was aggrieved, for everyone told him so, it would do no good to think about it. It would keep the things in the swamp alive, when left alone they would shrivel up and die.

So here he was pouring concrete, and that's all he was doing, and as he was pretty good at emptying his mind of everything but the task in hand, he was thinking only about the best way to box curves, and not about the iniquity of Janis.

He was pleased he'd come to live out here on the Peninsula, in the very comfortable bungalow built by old man Hollander against his retirement. But old man Hollander hadn't made it that far, keeling over in the Addington stockyards one Nor' Wester day, as the auctioneer passed sentence on his prize mob.

Taking the job here was the only radical thing Rewi had done in his life, and made him feel that he was even with Janis. His mate Brian, whom he knew through the Vintage Car Club swap and meet, had told him about it.

'Suit you down to the ground,' Brian said.

Brian and Julie lived more or less next door to Hollander House, half a mile round the road towards Diamond Harbour. Julie, who'd done domestic science, cooked for Mrs Lingerfield when she had guests staying. Rewi knew Julie from socials, knew her rather better than Brian realized, but that was no reason not to be a mate. So you can see that Rewi is not entirely conventional in his approach to life.

At the time Rewi was trying to keep down his job in operations at the computer centre in town, juggling shifts and children. It was a private nightmare that he didn't let on about, leaving his kids at night and screaming back to them as fast as he dare before they woke. Hunching over the macabre lights of the terminals, hoping against hope that no one would have a nightmare or wet the bed.

But they did.

Mr Hollander thought there should be a man about the place, since many of Mrs Lingerfield's paying guests were gentlemen, who were not quite gentlemen. Mr Hollander thought that the caretaker could live in the bungalow and eat at the house in return for his constant presence and assorted odd jobs. Rewi was interviewed by Mrs Lingerfield and a nameless man in a suit, but not by Mr Hollander. It turned out this was just as well, because Rewi, though wanting the job more than he would let on to anyone, including himself, insisted on being paid a salary over and above the keep. He had a strong suspicion, entirely well founded given our knowledge of Crawford, that Crawford would have taken one look at him, and used the demand for money as an excuse to reject him. But Rosalia took one look at his handsome forearms and decided otherwise, and so he was able to strike a good deal. He negotiated his accommodation, all found, and enough besides to feed and clothe the kids, to take them on the occasional modest outing, and to shout himself to the pub now and then.

★ ★ ★

Rewi had reason to be pleased, and didn't at all mind doing the chores around the house and making himself available. It was a bit like being a husband without any of the crap. He had determined to care for his children better than any woman. Punctual at the bus stop, a dragon on the homework, the house clean as a show home, the cut lunch as nutritious as a Plunket pamphlet — you weren't going to fault Rewi on his parenting. And he swore he wouldn't inflict a stepmother on his kids until he found a woman he could trust, and he wasn't at all sure she existed.

The concrete mixer ground out its bass. It is quite possible that Rewi loved his concrete mixer more than anything else on earth. He shovelled the last of the mix out into the boxing and thought that maybe a concrete mixer was the right sort of thing to give love to. You look after it and it never lets you down. You get exactly what you expect, and what you pay for.

The same, in Rewi's view, ought to apply to women, whom he sometimes opined would find life a great more straightforward if they behaved like the average concrete mixer. All this: *I can't, it's just — it's just —* and the tiresome refrain *You don't love me, do you?* Rewi pronounced himself fed up with the fluctuation of women. In and out, like the tides, only not so predictable. All over him one minute, miles away the next, and him, perfectly consistent throughout, never promising what he couldn't deliver, never promising more than he intended, no vows, no romance, no crap.

He noted that once again he had judged it perfectly — there was almost nothing left in the concrete mixer, and his path, as far as he'd boxed it, was complete. There was plenty more path to make, but he'd decided to do it in sections, in case Rosalia (as he called her internally, though not to her face, yet) or one of her arty friends decided his design was all insensitive. When it was all done, he planned to lay thin slices of shale onto the concrete to make it look like flagstones, and build the soil right up to the edges. He would like to have done the job properly, but he could see that the tight fist ruled at Hollander House. He tipped the remnant of the concrete onto the ground roughly where the path would continue, and trundled the still grinding mixer back to the shed, reeling in the power cord as he went.

It was a relief to be in the shade, sloshing water to clean up the bowl of the mixer. It had to be pristine by the time he finished, water shortage or not. Not a speck of cement could be suffered to be left on it — exterior and interior had to be surgically clean. It was important to look after things, to take trouble and take your time. Small things mattered. The concrete mixer must be spotless, but the water should not be wasted. He positioned himself so that the surplus water ran down the slope of the yard into one of his concrete gutters and onto the flower-beds in front of the old house. He remembered his mother getting upset about alkaline in the water killing the flowers, but flowers, like children, he reckoned, had to learn to survive in less than ideal environments. Water was water, and they should be glad to have it.

The path was designed to lead from the old farmhouse, the original homestead of the Hollander family, up to the big house that replaced it. Rosalia wanted it finished by the coming Saturday, before what she called her *soirée*. Rewi saw nothing wrong with the existing path of beaten earth and old pine needles, and considered the construction merely a hurdle set in his way to prove his mettle.

But none the less he would do it without complaint and as well as he possibly could, just to show her what he was made of, should she be in any doubt.

He washed his hands under the hose, one hand, then the other, carefully, in sequence, as if he had a work instruction for it. Small things mattered.

★   ★   ★

He thought he would go up to the house and have his lunch there, since food was one of his perks. He also thought — but this is unworthy — that Mrs Lingerfield might enjoy his company. It was by no means clear what she wanted of him.

Hollander House had been built by Crawford's grandfather as a homage to the American South. He had raised himself a gracious mansion with windows from architrave to parquet floor, broad verandas, a great curved staircase, in incidental imitation of Sir John Soane, and massive problems for his progeny. The mod-cons of 1905, although doubtless the best of their breed, did not endure for ever. The renewal of systems — heating, wiring, filtration for the Hollywood pool, obscure hydraulic communications and even, God help them, a lift — and the constant niggling of flaked plaster, mournful wallpaper and blistered varnish required an income that subsequent Hollanders could not achieve without selling off assets. This they absolutely refused to do. Consequently in the time of Crawford's father the house had sunk slowly into a gracious decay. It was Crawford who had come up with the bright idea of installing his sister as hostess and taking in paying guests. He had set her up a little company, wheeled her and her elegant silks into a bank manager's office, raised her the capital, called in the decorators, and away she went. From time to time, she told Rewi pitifully, he sent out a man in a suit to tell her off. He also restricted her *mistress classes* to once a month, and although she was, of course, not one to complain, Rosalia took this very hard, and somehow all the parents of her pupils and prospective pupils *knew*.

★ ★ ★

Because of the generosity of Crawford's acquaintance at the bank, the approach to Hollander House was very grand. Not only was the old avenue of trees properly trimmed and paved and freed of impertinent grass, but when the visitor swung round the corner in front of the house she emerged on to a scene fit for a movie. The lawn, surrounded by shrubs and trees, was so perfect as to look artificial. The white wall of the house shone like an advertisement for British Paints (*sure can!*) — and the acres of glass glittered like in a fairy-tale. No one could tell how many hours Rewi had already spent cleaning those windows, even with his cunningly adapted hose-dooffery.

Rewi had been impressed by the house for all of five minutes, but by now had entirely forgotten that he ever was. It now represented to him a damned inconvenient dwelling and, as he liked to describe it, a bugger of a lot of unnecessary work. People who built those houses, he said, should have to clean out the gutters. That would give them pause for thought.

Rosalia was not in the kitchen, which was hardly surprising. Rewi made himself a fine sandwich of cold chicken and salad. The pickings in the fridge were always good. He had begun to suspect that Julie over-catered specially for him. What could that girl be after? he asked himself smugly.

He wandered into the front of the house, looking out for jobs to be done, and listening for evidence of activity. He did not quite know what Rosalia did with her days.

Sometimes he heard the piano, sometimes the sounds of singing. Sometimes he saw her sitting elegantly in front of her easel, or plodding down to the beach with her fishing gear. All the cleaning, cooking, laundry and arranging were done by other people. Rosalia's sole task seemed to be greeting the guests graciously on arrival, presiding over the dinner table and staying sober long enough to bid them good-night.

She failed on the last.

Then he heard it quite distinctly, and his only thought was to flee. He was only the handyman, and he was only just getting his own life straight. But she was upstairs, and she was crying. It was none of his business, and he recoiled at the merest suggestion of a woman's tears, as if from menstruation. But then the phone rang in the hall. Rewi knew that there was no instrument upstairs, since he had been tasked with organizing this, and he was bickering with Telecom about it.

He hesitated before answering it, thinking it was not his job, but decided that what was good for the household was probably good for him. It might be a new client. You should always be ready.

'No, I'm afraid she's unavailable,' he said in his poshest manner.

He was curious about the voice at the other

end, a girl's voice, but so low and sexy as to seem not quite real.

'Tell her it's Mercy,' she said. 'Mercy Fisher. Dad and me are running a bit late but we *are* coming.'

Rewi put down the phone and refused to speculate on what kind of girl Mercy Fisher was.

Rosalia appeared at the top of the stairs. She was wearing a lilac silk robe and had her head wrapped in a white towel.

'Who is it?' she called.

Rewi went half-way up the stairs, trying not to observe Rosalia too closely.

'It's a girl called Mercy Fisher. She's late but she is coming.'

'Oh good,' said Rosalia faintly, 'at least someone is.'

'Can I get you something? A cup of tea?'

'Oh,' said Rosalia. 'A nice tonic water would be nice.'

'OK.'

'With the tiniest splash of gin.'

'OK.'

He took her literally, even though he was clearly intended not to. But he mixed it carefully, with ice and lemon.

When he took the drink back upstairs, she was lying on her bed once more, with her head buried dramatically in the pillow. She threw out her hand for the drink without looking at him.

'Are you OK?' he said.

She fetched a great sigh which transmuted into a sob.

'No. Evidently not.'

'I'm sorry. Can I do something?'

She sat up and sipped.

'Well, you might have put *some* gin in this.'

'I did,' he said, and grinned. 'You said the tiniest splash, and I always do as I am told.'

She laughed and patted the side of the bed. Rewi, without much reluctance, sat down upon it.

'Do you?' she said. 'What an exciting idea.'

Rewi was at a loss what to say.

'Everything is going wrong,' she said. 'My brother Crawford won't commit himself to coming out on Saturday. I was relying on him. He adds such cachet.'

As Rewi didn't know what *cachet* was, he said nothing.

'I so wanted him to accompany the girls in their pieces. They enjoy it so much when he does, but he really must come and practise with them. I insist.

'Of course,' she went on, 'Hillary is probably a better accompanist, but she is such a frump. I have a very glittering company coming, I did tell you.'

'You did,' said Rewi, watching her bare foot snaking towards him as if disembodied. He obediently put his hand out where it might be met by her foot. He had not known this was in the contract, but had no particular objection.

'My life is so dreary usually,' she said. 'I look forward to these little *soirées* with all my heart.'

'I don't see why your life should be dreary. It's very nice here, and you get plenty of company.'

'Not the right sort,' she said, and wriggled her toes happily in his hand. 'I'm never going to get married again,' she declared, 'and I suppose men can tell somehow.'

'Nor am I,' Rewi said. 'Once is enough.'

'Certainly if that once was the Commander. Poor darling, he loved me to death and then went off and married a nun.'

Rewi laughed.

'Well he got the worst of it. But there's nothing wrong with being on your own. I like being my own person. It doesn't mean you can't have a bit of fun.'

'No,' said Rosalia, 'it doesn't, does it?'

★　★　★

An hour and a half later Rewi heard the school bus whining round the corner. He

205

leapt out of bed, cursing, threw on his clothes, cursed about forgoing a shower, and jogged down the drive to collect his children, the very picture of parental rectitude.

He was crossing the road, clutching Zoë's hand, Tom tagging close, when an aged Land Rover, with the logo *Fisher's Boat Hire* painted on the side, came up behind him.

It slowed, turning into the drive, and then stopped to wait for him.

A girl poked her head out of the passenger's window, a white-skinned, dusty redhead, a smile too big for her face.

'Hi,' she said. 'I'm Mercy Fisher.'

'Hello,' said Zoë. 'I'm Zoë Mann. With a zed.'

'That's cool. To start with a zed.'

'I'm the only one who does.'

'I bet.'

'Are you a guest?' asked Zoë.

'Not really. I think we're in the cottage.'

'Oh goodie. I'll come and visit.'

Mercy Fisher laughed. 'Please do.'

The big bearded man driving called out that he would go and park round the back as usual.

The Land Rover followed the drive to the left, disappeared behind the great stand of macrocarpa pines, and then stopped briefly in front of the house. Mercy got out and lifted her bag from the back seat. The Land Rover, familiar with the layout of the place, drove on round to the parking area.

Rewi and Zoë trudged up to the house. Tom sensibly went home with the school bags, but it seemed that Zoë wanted to consolidate her relationship with the bigger girl.

Mercy Fisher, at sixteen, was big, uncertain. She wore jeans, which, she was later to discover, suited her rather less than baggy pants and flowing skirts. She hoisted her bag and gawped up at the house.

Rewi looked at her as he walked up the drive. She had a narrow waist and big hips. He came up beside her, trying not to notice her breasts. She walked up the steps, her eyes round with awe.

'Hi. Rewi. I'm the caretaker.'

'I know. Rosalia's talked about you.'

'About me?'

'You're her touchstone, she says. When we're singing, she says, if you can touch my Rewi's heart, you have made the emotion true. Stuff like that.' She grinned.

Rewi was taken aback to discover that he was already part of Rosalia's personal mythology. This was mysterious, as he thought she had shown no interest in him till that afternoon. Women were to him entirely inexplicable. Girls, however, were pretty obvious in their hunger for experience. He knew he must give them a wide berth, especially now he had his hand on the tiller.

'You're welcome to try,' he said. 'Not my favourite entertainment, opera.'

'That's the point. We have to sweep it out of the opera house and into the hills.'

'That sounds like Rosalia.'

'Shall I give you a sample?' she said and laughed. 'To see if it works.'

This seemed dangerously like flirting, and he was already far more chatty with her than he judged sensible. She reminded him of a prize dairy cow — big and beautiful and slightly scary, but at the same time uncertain of who you were and prone to startle. Her confidence felt fragile.

'Can I take your bag?'

He watched her hesitate, new-fangled feminist principles struggling with the tiresome fact of her bag's weight.

'Yes,' she said with a terrific smile, 'thanks.'

He hoiked it over his shoulder with one hand, not really trying to demonstrate how strong he was, well, not trying very hard. Zoë took Mercy's hand.

'Wow,' said Mercy, still staring at the house. 'I never realized.'

'You not been here before?'

'No, I'm a new pupil. I've been learning off the nuns. Rosalia's an old friend of Mum and Dad's. I've had a few lessons in her studio in town. She says I'm a natural.'

'Well she would. But,' he added hastily, 'I'm sure you are.'

A great big man with a jutting beard and jovial girth came round the corner from the parking lot, scattering energy and goodwill about him.

'Hello there!' he said, his South African accent as pronounced as when he had left the ever-to-be-lamented fatherland. 'I'm Dickie. Dickie Fisher. Old friend of Rosie's. And the Commander's. You must be the new man she's talked about so much. Rewi, is it? And, no, let me think — Zoë!'

Rewi shrugged off the remark, not being a man to whom inference was dear. They went in through the front door, with its laboriously polished brass knob, and into the hall of gleaming parquet hung with framed water-colours of the surrounding landscape.

'Wow!' said Mercy, standing in the hallway and surveying the square miles of floor. 'I didn't know. Gosh they must be rich.'

'You're supposed to think that, but actually we take in guests. The bank owns it. No, I tell a lie, the shareholders own it.'

'I remember when young Crawford didn't

have a brass razoo to his name,' said Dickie. 'Had to sweet-talk every penny out of other people. Even touched me for a loan — he called it offering me start-up shares.'

'Did you buy them?'

'Well yes I did, though Marg was dead against it. Of course I sold to Crawford at a small loss, just before the whole outfit became profitable. Looking back, knowing what I now know about young Crawford, I'm not a bit surprised. But I learnt a valuable lesson. Holy hell, he's not lurking in the parlour, is he?'

'No, Mrs Lingerfield's all upset because he won't come out for her party.' Rewi grinned as if everyone present would see the absurdity. 'She's lying down, a bit overcome just now.' He grinned again, but this time at a private joke.

'Well, I'm greatly relieved he's not going to be here, sniffing around my little girl,' said Dickie, but contrived to make it sound like a joke. 'I never liked the way he looked at Marg, even when she was pregnant.'

'Dad!'

'I thought he was camp as a row of pink tents,' said Rewi.

Zoë looked from one adult to another, and a certain uncomfortable silence fell.

Rewi had not yet met Crawford Hollander,

but based his evaluation mostly on the black-and-white portrait photos artistically placed about the house, which showed the beautiful young Crawford, by turns seated at the piano, gazing into the distance and shaking the hand of some man in a suit while grasping a silver cup. He was Rosalia's constant theme — Crawford's supernatural charm when dealing with bank managers, foreign orchestral conductors and other frighteners, his talent, his kindness, his clever business deals that had restored the fortunes of the house of Hollander. Rewi knew his approximate age, but Rosalia, in all her torrent of anecdote, had never mentioned a girlfriend or fiancée. He therefore concluded that Crawford was discreetly gay and had not divulged this information to his doting sister.

'Nothing would surprise me about that man,' said Dickie. 'Well, we can look forward to the party now, can't we, sweetheart?'

'I was anyway,' said Mercy.

Rewi got them both drinks, a lemonade for Zoë, and took a drink up to Rosalia. This time he put a decent slurp of gin with the tonic, because he thought she deserved it.

Dickie Fisher chatted amicably about the bush, sailing, concrete and other matters dear to Rewi's heart. They got on so well that Rewi

THOMPSON-NICOLA REGIONAL DISTRICT LIBRARY SYSTEM

declared the sexy daughter even more firmly out of bounds.

'Better go,' said Dickie at last. 'Got to meet a client at six, in Lyttelton. Wants to hire a yacht for the whole summer. Definitely not a man to disappoint. A pity though. I wanted to see old Rosie. We worry about her. Look after her, old chap. Toodly-pip, as the old Commander used to say.'

Rewi shooed Zoë off home, protesting, and then took Mercy and her bag over to the old farmhouse where she and the other two girl pupils were to stay. He took Mercy in through the back door. The ingenious pioneers who built the house had squeezed in more rooms than you would believe possible. There could have been no possibility of privacy in that wooden tent, but it was solid and comfortable. All three rooms downstairs now contained beds, as well as no fewer than five upstairs.

'Take your pick.'

Mercy instantly took off up the stairs with an energy that belied her bulkiness. Rewi lit a cigarette and heard her banging around in the upstairs rooms.

'I like it down here,' she said, and plumped her bag on the double bed.

Thoughts of cheerful copulation entered Rewi's head and were shown the door severely.

THOMPSON-NICOLA REGIONAL DISTRICT LIBRARY SYSTEM

'Will you be OK here on your own?'

She grinned at him. He couldn't decide whether she was brazening out fear or teasing him.

'Why, are there dangerous men about?'

'Well round these parts there's only me and Crawford, and like I said, he's — '

'As camp as a row of pink tents. You said. So I should be OK, then, shouldn't I?'

★ ★ ★

That evening, after he had put his cleaned and replete children to bed, Rewi went up to the big house, summoned by Rosalia to check out suspicious noises.

The lights were on in the old farmhouse. Through the uncurtained window he saw Mercy Fisher sitting at the old table with her school books.

Disembodied strains of U2 — *And I still haven't found what I'm looking for* — reached him through the night.

Rosalia had no guests that night. She had kept the night free for her pupils and her brother, failing to accept that her pupils were mere children and her brother slippery. She was alone, and hating it.

Rewi sat down with her in the big bay window at the end of the pool room and watched the rich black sky. Conversation was stilted; physical intimacy would not make it any easier for them to chat. He sipped a beer, contemplated his future, and thought he could put up with it.

'I am so disappointed in Crawford,' she was saying. 'He knows how much it means to me. He really does not care about anyone else.'

Rewi found this all very tiresome, but he thought he would pass on the little bit of information he had, just in case it was helpful.

'Apparently he used to care quite a bit about Mercy's mother, Dickie said. You'd think he'd like to come for old times' sake.'

'Don't be ridiculous, Rewi! Such a thing wouldn't affect Crawford. Marg is at least ten years older than Crawford! He isn't like that anyway. You don't know him.'

If Rewi felt that he was glad not to know Crawford Hollander, it was impolitic for him to say so.

Rewi reckoned he had an instinct for a nasty piece of work. He acknowledged this himself, but took no pride in it, since it was a characteristic he shared with any sensible dog. He trusted his intuition absolutely, but sometimes found it a burden to be unfailingly civil to some of the shits entertained by

Rosalia, who was not endowed with his discriminatory radar.

The evening of the day after Mercy Fisher's arrival, Rewi watched Crawford Hollander get out of a sleek, ancient Jaguar, watched him reach into the back seat and bring out a polished leather music bag. He noticed the slacks, the bottle-green cord jacket, the white shirt casually open at the neck. All the inconvenient hairs on the back of Rewi's neck rose with dislike. He could not have explained why, although we who are better acquainted with Crawford are not at all surprised.

He watched Crawford proceed up the steps of the house with a little mincing run. Then just as he was about to go into the house, Mercy appeared around from the back, her head down, not seeing him. She was wearing jeans and sandals and a red and black check shirt, which was partially unbuttoned. Crawford stopped half-way up his little run, turned in his tracks like a principal dancer acknowledging his fans, and went back down towards her. Rewi confirmed at once that Crawford Hollander might be loathsome, but he was certainly not gay.

At about the same time he felt a desire to protect Mercy from Hollander that took him by surprise by its fierceness.

But he carried on his oblique course towards the swimming pool which was in need of a clean.

★ ★ ★

Two days later, three girls were cosied up in the little cottage and Crawford was still in residence and the preparations for the party were almost complete. Mid-morning, Rewi was sent over to the cottage to fetch the girls for an extra rehearsal.

As he approached the cottage he heard Crawford's voice, his strained English vowels, his fluting and cooing. This was most peculiar in itself, since Rewi had overheard him after breakfast saying he was driving over to French Farm where, according to Crawford, the good people were fantasizing about opening a winery. Rewi failed to see that there was any call for him to be entertaining the girls in the cottage, but somehow was not surprised.

He hesitated by the open front door, and admired the lovely job he had made of sanding and polishing the kauri floorboards. He heard the sound of water beating on the tin of the shower. Over it, Crawford's voice carried perfectly. 'Oh, I seem to have your towel. How careless of you to leave it out

216

here. You'll have to come out and get it.'

Mercy's answer was drowned by the water.

'Oh I don't think so. Carelessness like that should be punished. Fancy leaving your towel lying around where anyone could pick it up. All you have to do is come and get it.'

Mercy turned off the water.

'Please give it to me, please.'

'I've got an even better idea. You come here and I'll dry you myself. Now that's a nice idea, isn't it? Your servant Crawford. Come on.'

'No, please, please don't do this. Please.'

'Mercy, are you losing your sense of fun?'

'Please, Crawford. Please give me my towel.'

Her voice, husky and unreliable as a superannuated chorister's, started to break.

Crawford had not heard him arrive. Rewi considered turning around and coming back at some later point when his anger and disgust had subsided. But being the man he was, he ploughed on in, making a fair bit of noise.

'Oh, Crawford,' he said, although he was supposed to call him Mr Hollander. 'What are you doing here?'

Crawford backed out of the bathroom and came calmly into the living-room without Mercy's towel.

'Much the same as you are I suspect. In fact, I found someone's towel on the grass. I suppose the girls had been sun-bathing out there. Where are the other two?'

He opened the window at the front which looked down over the lawn towards the bay. The figures of the other two girls were just visible picking their way across the rough grass towards the beach.

'Oh, there they are!' he said. 'Sun-bathing already. So silly, they simply burn a patchy unattractive red. Mercy is much more sensible, preserving her delicate white skin.'

Mercy came into the room, wrapped in her towel, and padded into the room with the double bed without a word, looking at the floor. She didn't acknowledge either of them, and shut the door with a firmness that its frame could not accommodate. Crawford looked out the window.

Between the cottage and the sea stretched an empty green paddock. Crawford had got rid of the sheep, as being uneconomic. Beyond the paddock a million-dollar view of glittering sea and golden hills.

'I don't know why I don't develop this into a golf-course. I think that every time I look at it. All it requires is a business partner. Japanese. Korean might be better.'

'Place swarming with foreign golfers,' said

Rewi. 'Mrs Lingerfield wouldn't like it.'

'Mrs Lingerfield does not know what is in her best interests. She never has. Every decision she makes for herself turns out to be disastrous. I have tried to explain to her that we will stay poor till the day we die if we don't sacrifice something we hold dear. True success requires you to make a pact with the devil. I just can't pin him down to an appointment yet.'

An answer was called for, something simple and stirring, to counterbalance the evil forces of materialism. But Rewi, though shocked and righteously sickened, thought of nothing to say, except 'Tell the girls that Rosalia wants them up at the house by ten-thirty.'

He went out by the back door, pausing to open the bathroom window so the steam would not damage the window frame. As he passed, he admired the curves of his new path, and congratulated himself on a job well done. He wished that life were so easily managed.

He squatted down in the darkness under the macrocarpas and lit himself a guilty cigarette. He watched as Mercy and Crawford came out of the cottage together and walked towards the beach. She walked apart from him, but somehow his hand contrived to reach and rest on her buttocks. Rewi did not understand how it was possible for her to tolerate him. It might be fair to say he did not particularly want to understand either.

It did occur to him that someone should be alerted to Crawford's behaviour. While not illegal, it seemed to Rewi wrong, but not quite wrong enough to require his intervention. Should he mention it to Rosalia, presuming on their new relationship? Should he drop a hint to Dickie Fisher, who'd be over in a flash, shotgun blasting?

He thought defensively that he had enough on his plate with two small children to parent all by himself. He was aware that Mercy produced in him the same painful wash of protectiveness that came over him when he saw Zoë playing the fool at the school bus stop. Larking about, so young and silly and confident, so easily damaged, racing up like a young clematis climbing a fence. One spot of wind or a clumsy foot, and all that vigour gone . . . Rewi was determined to protect Zoë with every drop of himself, and he didn't see how he could be expected to have anything left over for Mercy.

He watched the two figures disappear under the avenue of trees and told himself it was not his problem. Surely she was old enough to know? He allowed himself to believe that it was too late to save her from herself.

★ ★ ★

Mercy wore a scarlet dress for the recital, and Crawford his brown velvet jacket. Mercy had made the dress herself, and it fitted her like a very impertinent glove. It was cut so low that it was a wonder anyone listened to her singing at all. Crawford was grateful that he was seated slightly behind her as he played. Her intonation was suspect, but mendable, and her phrasing showed the amateurish hand of his sister. As for her breathing — *well*! But the voice had the unteachable thing — you wanted to keep listening to her, and Crawford was aware of this, since he was not distracted by the dress.

He played well, the unobtrusive accompanist, a role he had discovered gave one great credibility in the world of egos. Real power, he was discovering, like real wealth, did not display. A man who shows himself off has something to prove. Crawford wished to prove that he had nothing to prove.

He was glad he had changed his mind. He had not really intended to withhold himself, but Rosalia must be taught not to take his presence for granted. The promise of the

221

youngest Fisher tipped the balance in her favour, though glancing around the rather lacklustre company, he was confirmed in his opinion that it was only marginally worth his while to be there.

After the recital he mingled his way through Rosalia's guests, charming all in his path, but, as he had expected, found few that were of advantage to him at present. He needed venture capital and he needed contacts in France, particularly someone who would offer to accommodate him during the Prix d'Or. The company was rich in minor patrons of the arts, lowly arts administrators and operatic season ticket holders, but short on the owners of châteaux. There was however a useful chap who loved his opera and wrote a wine column. A silly fat lecherous old bastard, but the column was syndicated. Crawford obligingly introduced him to the girl in lilac silk, but somehow failed to hear the request to meet the one in red.

Wolf was haunting the edges of the gathering, exciting speculation. Crawford had invited him specifically for this effect. He wished to create a legend around Wolf, if only in the local folk-lore.

Wolf was a heavy young man, with a cliché of a black beard and long curling locks, as if he had strayed out of an artistic salon of the nineteenth century. He looked far less like a wine-maker than an overgrown student radical, from whose pocket you expect a scribbled-over typescript by Ulrike Meinhof to protrude. He was solid and stubby all over, his fingers obstinate, and his blue eyes belligerent. He looked too untidy to be the perfectionist he was, but every bit as obdurate.

Crawford sometimes felt as if he was in love with Wolf, although being strictly heterosexual this could not be the case. But he had no other way of describing the fascination Wolf exercised over him, and his concomitant desire to master the young German. He wanted Wolf to be murmured about in this company of blazers and Italian shoes; he wanted Wolf to feel uncomfortable and angry. He must not become cosy anywhere; if he did, like the great artist he was, he would lose his edge. Crawford wanted to propel him into circles and wait to catch him when he spun out of them again, spitting his anachronistic radical notions in Crawford's face. It was all so beautifully appropriate; a wine-maker was an artist, and should look and behave like an artist. Wolf gave no thought to his appearance, he did not care one jot what another person thought of him, except whichever unregarding blond young man he was currently pursuing.

He was standing at one of the windows in the big billiard room, his shoulders hunched and his fingers curled around a beer glass, watching the game of pool in progress between Rewi and the young blond boy called Michael whom Rosalia kept as a house pet. Crawford observed him with a proprietor's eye and saw he was falling in love with the blond boy. It was about the right timing, for his heart was beginning to mend after the last disaster. Although Crawford had known Wolf for less than a year, he had been working on him closely for several months, in his diligent appraisal of the Platts' vineyard. It was important to know all that could be known about the principal asset, his moods, work patterns, tastes. Crawford had not personally observed the arc of Wolf's love affairs, but from the long drunken confessions half in German that he had absorbed so far, he knew that Wolf had a propensity to fall in love, was single-minded and monogamous when in love, and had never been the terminator. His heart had been broken by Kurts, Stefans, Pieters and even the odd Bruce.

And now there he was transfixed by Michael's grace — little Michael whom

Rosalia claimed to have saved. Crawford filed the matter for further consideration. In the meantime he would neither encourage nor discourage it, which meant that Wolf must be prevented by simple mischance from plying his suit until Crawford had made up his mind about it.

He happened into the billiard room to disinter his best brandy from below the bar, and wandered over to Wolf's side to watch the game. He handed Wolf a brandy as if a balloon had just chanced into his hand. Wolf sniffed it with concentration like a police dog at the trials, before bolting into the substance.

'Rewi may be winning,' said Crawford into his ear, 'but Michael has so much more style.'

'Michael,' said Wolf, savouring it.

'He's a darling,' said Crawford. 'Rosalia adores him, and he adores her. He's like a member of our family. But a word to the wise, old chap.'

'Also?' said Wolf.

'He's here with a bit of a big-wig, friend of Rosie's. Very important to her next project. I know Michael's unhappy with him,' Crawford improvised, 'but I wouldn't like there to be a scene, if you follow me.'

'Absolutely,' said Wolf. 'Will you give me his telephone number?'

'I will. Later. I will also introduce you now,

225

if you promise to bide your time.'

As Crawford's luck would have it, Rewi had just completed his slaughter of the innocent and was looking around for female appreciation. Crawford duly introduced Wolf to Michael as his vintner, and Michael as *practically his adopted nephew*. These two men looked longingly at each other, but Crawford kept up a stream of engaging talk and steered them into the next room, introduced them separately to other guests, and kept them slightly apart until he had engineered Wolf a lift back to town. Officially, Wolf lived at the Platt family winery, up near the Hurunui river flats, but that mild and bucolic place took its toll on urban Wolfgang, and he spent most weekends sleeping in someone else's bed. He scarcely seemed to mind whose, so long as he escaped the countryside.

Crawford watched the precious rump into the back seat of someone's car and turned back towards pleasure.

Fortune was on his side tonight. Mercy was standing by herself at the top of the steps, in the red dress, framed in the doorway. She was clearly thinking about leaving the party which was winding down behind her. The other girls were nowhere to be seen. Crawford had observed them sneaking off earlier about some business of their own. He was glad because she was left alone. He ran up the steps and took her hand between his own and kissed the back of it.

'You know,' he said, 'when I was your age I was terribly in love with your mother, but I think you are far sexier than she was.'

This opening line was a terrible risk, but if he pulled it off he knew he'd win. She looked confused by his compliment for a moment.

'You sang beautifully,' he continued. 'I think you could go far.'

'Do you? Do you *really* think so? Or are you just saying that?'

'Mercy, do I strike you as the sort of man who just *says* a thing? I am an entrepreneur. A fixer.'

'I don't think I've met one of those before. Dad's friends are all drinkers and sinkers, as he calls them.'

'I liked your dad too,' said Crawford. 'Enormously.'

'He's great,' said Mercy without enthusiasm. 'They both are.'

'But it's you I'm interested in,' said Crawford. 'You sing with such confidence. How can a girl so young sing so like a woman?'

He steered her over towards the bar, keeping up the talk. He guessed that taking a paternal line was his best bet. If he pretended to be young and trendy she'd see through him anyway and despise him as only the young can despise. If his age was no barrier to her favours, then he might as well play it for all it was worth.

'I'm going to mix you my favourite drink,' he said. 'It's called a Maiden's Prayer. If you ask for it in any bar in Europe or the States, they'll murmur respectfully.'

He kept up this line of talk while he filled her up with alcohol. It was a new adventure, intoxicating a girl so young. Inside Crawford a guilty twitch told him that the message of her body was not to be trusted, because he must also look into the face of the child. But as if to confuse him further, she smiled and flirted like the woman he knew she was not.

He drank orange juice liberally spiked with tonic and slices of lemon. He began to hate himself and delight in his cleverness. He topped up the vodka in her drink.

She struggled manfully, you had to admire her. She knew she was starting to disconnect, but she kept on cutting back in.

'I can't imagine why they call it that,' she said, referring to the concoction. 'Maidens generally want to know what's happening to them.'

'Ah, but that's the peculiar beauty of

vodka,' he said, 'you can be stupendously drunk and still clear-sighted. Hence the magnificence of the Russians against all odds — perpetually drunk, but nonetheless our superiors in all matters of the intellect and all matters of the soul.'

She was lapping this up.

'I thought you would have preferred the French.'

'Oh the French — well, yes of course. But you see, one can acknowledge a person as an intellectual and spiritual superior without wanting to emulate him. I am sure the Archbishop of Canterbury runs rings around me in both those regards, but I wouldn't want to *be* him.'

He delivered this witticism into her very bosom, and she laughed gorgeously. 'Especially at this very moment.'

It was deliciously easy, his seduction of Mercy. Before an hour was up, he had persuaded her that if she was game for his dare, he'd buy her a ticket to London. He was not specifically drunk, but euphoria had crept all through his body, and he felt he could climb the tallest tree on the estate, dive naked off the rocks or run round to Diamond Harbour for the first edition of the *Press*. Everyone else had gone home, and Rosalia and Rewi were circling like the Chinese grandmothers who clear up your crumbs in McDonald's, Kowloon.

Crawford whispered in her ear.

'I'll meet you outside the cottage in ten minutes. Change into something less sexy and bring a towel.'

She glided away, bidding Rosalia a sweet good-night. Rewi scowled at Crawford, no doubt envying him his success with a nubile, when he himself was stuck with poor old Rosalia, leaning on the door of forty, shut fast behind her and hating every minute of it.

'Good-night darling,' Crawford said and went up the stairs.

He changed into his old cords and his nice walking shoes, a check shirt and cashmere jersey. Yes, the clothes proclaimed middle age; Crawford did not feel that forty-two was remotely old, but he knew his image and he saw no virtue in distorting it. At sixteen he had been an amusingly olde-worlde and smart swinging girls had wet themselves over him. The curious magic seemed still to work. There was no accounting for women.

He made his way silently to the back stairs, noting that his sister was taking to bed that inarticulate lump of testosterone. This was no bad thing for the short term, for it effectively distracted and contented Rosalia. But Crawford wondered whether this man should be encouraged. Sooner or later he would surely don pretensions and wish to marry into the Hollanders.

Right that moment he did not care a jot. He ran between the house and the old cottage breathless with fear that she might have changed her mind or been impossibly joined by her friends.

But when he got to the cottage, it was in darkness, and there was no indication of anyone inside. The other girls were still out wherever they had gone. And by the door stood Mercy in jeans. The white skin of her face and forearms was all that was visible.

He ran towards her and began to kiss her all at once. It was as well that this was what she was expecting, because he would not have endured it if she had drawn back in surprise or modesty. She kissed him as if she was born to do so. He felt he had always known she was set apart for him, that she was the child in Marg's womb generated by his lust alone. His calculating mind had already told him that this was impossible, but he liked to believe it.

'This way,' he said, and led her along the path so conveniently laid between the cottage and the forest.

'I thought you said the pool.'

'I did say the pool.'

'But the pool is that way.'

'Not that pool, darling, the secret pool. My secret pool.'

'Where is it?'

'I'll take you there.'

And so he did.

★   ★   ★

It was a devil of a long way. He'd forgotten how steep the path was and how far. She was completely unfazed by it, being young and fit and full of high spirits. He was aware how much he had neglected himself latterly. And made several promises to the domestic gods of the body that if he got up to the pool without embarrassing himself he would do them due and rigorous homage.

The darkness of the forest was rich with possibility. Crawford felt tremors of fear himself, not at any human threat, but at the reverse, the absence of anything to suggest that his family had owned this place for well over a hundred years. It breathed malevolence at him, the darkness, older than the squatters, older than the Maoris, a chain of vegetation swinging back to creation, in a place in which God had not chosen to deposit humankind.

He called a breather — officially a pit-stop

— and went a short way into the trees. Almost at once he was swallowed up in the forest. He dared go no further than the second tree from the path, convinced he would be lost. He imagined Mercy standing on the path, growing cold and restless, calling out for him and wondering what to do. He felt a huge regret at dying so young and missing out on Mercy. He shook his cock dry and told himself to grow up.

He called out to her, and heard her answer. He followed her voice back to the path, thinking what a lovely sound she made in all circumstances, and how very much he would like to hear her say she loved him in that voice, even though he did not remotely want her to fall in love with him. The very thought made him shudder.

They reached the pool with very little conversation. Crawford was not going to waste his breath on unnecessary chat, and Mercy had nothing to say. She did not seem apprehensive, which surprised him. Perhaps after all she was not an innocent?

The pool, his secret only because it lay on his family's land and precious few people could summon the puff to climb up to it, was formed at the bottom of a waterfall, a brief respite in the course of the stream before it coursed on down the hillside. The water fell so noisily into the pool from its prominence that conversation could only be conducted in shouts or gestures. Although Crawford relied on his honey tongue to get him through most things, he was quite grateful to be spared the tricky minutiae of the next conversation. He took her by the hand and led her to the edge of the pool where the water plashing down formed a back eddy. He knew that the water there was calmer and slightly less perishing.

He started to undo the buttons of her shirt. She shouted at him that she would change.

'No,' he said above the roar. 'Naked. That's the deal.'

She pulled away from him and started to expostulate. He failed to hear what she said, and shook his head, smiling at her.

He decided to take the upper hand, and sat down on a rock near the water's edge and unlaced his shoes. He put his socks carefully inside them, because he had neglected to bring a torch, and he did not fancy walking back down that track sockless. Then he started on his trousers.

She saw that the outcome was inevitable and ripped herself out of her clothes, as if suddenly eager for the event. In the moonlight she was as white as a goddess, but he affected not to look until she had run yelling into the water, and plunged in to breast height.

'Fuck!' was all he heard which hardly surprised him even though Mercy was not given to swearing. He knew from experience there was no other response. None the less she was game and he admired her for it, swimming around a bit to warm up, agitating her white limbs through the dark water. He watched the breasts and thighs swarming through the blackness with unadulterated pleasure. He took off his underpants and made towards the pool, hoping that his shirt concealed the enormity of his erection, for now at least.

He put a naked foot into the water and exclaimed at its coldness. He explained by dumbshow that he wasn't getting in after all and fetched the towel from where she had dropped it.

'You'd better come out,' he called. 'It's far too cold.'

There was no way of hearing what she said in response, but she swam about a bit quite vigorously, which did not add to Crawford's comfiture. He tried to encourage her to get out, but she seemed impervious to his pleadings, so he walked along the edge of the pool to admire the waterfall as if he were a Romantic poet on a night outing. He took the towel with him.

He knew the trees about the edge of the pool like his brothers. He had spent a lot of time here as a boy, when he thought he was destined to be a composer writing his New World Piano Sonatas and other works. The trees were woven into the luscious late-romantic chords he had scribbled down by the pool. But that was a past life, before he discovered the much sweeter delights of making people make him money.

While he was strolling among the fringes of the pool, she clambered out of the water and joggled about looking for the towel. He went towards her with it, but would not actually part with it. He started to dry her off as swiftly as he could because she was shivering and crying with cold. But one thing led to another, as was inevitable. He was surprised at how strong he was.

'No,' she cried. 'No, no, please don't. You're hurting me.' But it was easy not to hear.

He knew he had hurt her, and felt ashamed, but not as ashamed as elated. It was only afterwards, when he was washing himself off with water from the pool, and felt the blood on his fingers, that he realized the full implications of what he had done. But there was no going back now. She was crying and shivering as she got herself dry and dressed, but she wouldn't accept any comfort from him. She ran off down the path while he was still tying his shoe-laces.

He did not hurry because there was no point. He would not catch up with her unless she chose to wait for him. He started off down the hill at a good clip, but careful not to stress his system. Much further down, where the path turned into the forest and away from the stream-bed, he found her sitting on a log which some enthusiastic early Hollander had formed into a bench. She was still shivering and crying.

He sat down next to her, but didn't try to put his arm around her. It seemed an unworthy gesture.

'I will keep my promise,' he said. 'I will take you to London.'

'I'm still at school.'

'When you've left school. You can trust me, you know.'

'Can I?' she said, without the satisfactory level of conviction.

'Let's get you back before you catch your death.'

'I'll race you,' she said and took off again. He fancied she was crying.

He strolled down the hill, singing *La chi'darem la mano* at the top of his voice to ward off the demons.

9

Six weeks later, Rosalia and Michael were gathered in a worried huddle by the front door of Hollander House.

Tonight was the night. Tonight they expected Wolf for dinner. Tonight they expected to hear about the Prix d'Or. Crawford was in France, hovering about the judges. Tonight was morning in France, and therefore last night was the judging. He had said he would ring them, with bad news or good. A commendation would be nice. The Pinot Noir was lovely, everyone agreed. A little mention, a nod from one of the judges, would be enough. They did not know when Crawford would ring. If the news had been very good he'd have rung straight away, last night, French time, this morning. But he'd ring, he was sure to.

They were worried, not on account of Crawford's call, which was somehow inevitable, but because Wolf was expected for dinner. He was late. Michael's soufflé was not made of waiting substance.

'I did say *not* a soufflé,' said Rosalia. 'But you never listen to *me*.'

238

'I do nothing but listen to you. *You* said we should ask him. *You* said he was perfect for me. *You* said tonight was a perfect occasion because he'd either be elated or sad.'

'I did not!'

'Stop fighting you two,' said Rewi, coming from the dining-room. 'He's here. I can hear the bus. I'll go and get him. You get everything perfect in the dining-room.'

He plunged into the darkness, hoping like hell that Wolf was on the bus. If not, it was better to be out of it anyway. He liked being outside in the dark, you could pretend for a minute or two to be anyone, with any number of chances. He liked to be alone. Often he dreamt of being by himself in the bush, him and the trees, or on a yacht in the middle of a blue harbour. Sometimes there was a woman there too, but he couldn't imagine who she might be, so he airbrushed her out.

He decided that he must rig lights along the avenue. The darkness was wonderful, but would scare some. Who knew what was lurking in the trees up there? *Crawford Hollander?* he joked to himself.

Wolf was standing by the bus stop, still. He was visible only because there was light reflected off the sea behind him. He hadn't moved, maybe because the avenue up to the house looked too daunting. Rewi set off towards him, dribbling his torchlight in front, so Wolf would see it.

'Hiya, mate. We should put in some street-lamps.'

'No, it is wonderful this darkness. Never let them take it away.'

'Each to his own. You OK?'

'No, I am desperate with nervousness.'

They walked along under the trees together. Rewi had got to know many gay people over the years, what with working in the computer centre, and through the groups he collectively titled Janis's bunch of dreamers. He still felt uncomfortable round them, but would never let it show. The strategy he had evolved to deal with them was to treat even effeminate Michael like an ordinary bloke. To his surprise and suspicion, this made him very popular.

'The big competition, eh?' he said to Wolf.

'No, not at all. I am not caring about prizes. I know how good my wine is. It is very good, whatever the silly old Frenchmen say. No, I am in love.'

'Ah,' said Rewi. This was a concept on which he was unclear and one he did not normally associate with men. Living at Hollanders was proving educative.

'It is six weeks since I saw him. I have thought of nothing else but his beauty and grace. His vulnerability, his sweetness. Crawford gave me his phone number, as he promised, but I was afraid.'

'He's OK, is Michael,' said Rewi, wishing that Wolf would not go on so.

'Did he invite me tonight? Tell me the truth.'

'Well,' said Rewi. 'It's a bit complicated in our household. Things get suggested. Ideas sort of slide into the mix.'

'It was not Michael's idea to invite me.'

'Look, mate, if Michael didn't like you, there's *no way* he'd cook you dinner.'

'Then I must be content with that.'

The two men walked up to the main door where Rosalia was busying herself with the dried flowers. Wolf kissed her on both cheeks, and gave her the bottle of wine concealed behind his back. His smile suggested that it was a great prize, but Rosalia had been brought up on bulk sherry and fizzy white at Christmas. She looked at the label and saw it was French.

'Oh thank you, Wolfgang. Shall we keep this do you think?'

'I do not mind when you drink it, as long as you do not share it with Crawford.' He laughed very loudly, and Rosalia joined him without at all seeing the joke, if there was one.

Rewi took the wine away to the kitchen. Michael was quivering over a saucepan. Rewi showed him the wine bottle.

'What do you reckon?'

'Oh I don't know. It's bound to be good, isn't it? He's a champion wine-maker. I'm only a little cook.'

'He told me he was in love with you,' said Rewi, 'so shut up. Shall I open this or not?'

Michael tissied.

'Oh of course, you idiot. But don't serve it straightaway. Give him some of that McLaren Vale that's open.'

'The one from the back of the cupboard? I'd better check.'

Rewi took the opened bottle out into the main room, where Rosalia was being charming to Wolf about Germany.

'Michael and I fished this out of the cupboard, but don't know whether it's any good. It could be in the back because it's rot-gut.'

'Was it lying down or standing up? If it is good, he would not keep it standing up.'

Wolf sniffed the wine and studied the label. 'I don't know about other men's wine,' he said and laughed very loud. 'But I know Crawford. Let's drink it for him.'

'Oh Rewi, do you think — ' said Rosalia.

'We already opened it,' said Rewi. 'He

wouldn't want us to keep it for his return, would he?'

Wolf poured himself a glassful and drank most of it off as if it were blackcurrant juice.

'Thank you, Crawford,' he said and laughed loudly. 'Is there another one in the back of that cupboard?'

Michael was a wonderful cook, there was no question about that. His employability was more moot; Rosalia believed in it passionately, but she was at odds with the proprietors of the better restaurants. Rewi, shuttling back and forth between the kitchen and the dining-table, could quite see the point of view of the restaurateurs. He pined for the straightforwardness of Julie, who normally cooked for the guests, even though she presumed on their undercover relationship to boss him unmercifully. He did not care in the slightest about being bossed, because the job got done brilliantly, and that was what mattered.

To Michael, however, cooking was not the job of feeding his guests or further impressing his new admirer; cooking was an art in itself, and there was nothing base or even craftsmanlike about him in the kitchen.

After Rewi had been reprimanded because the shallots were chopped into slivers and not tiny squares (you might wonder, as Rewi did, how you cut a shallot into squares), because the plates were too hot, and the sauce dish too cold, he was fantasizing about retreating to his house and sharing a spag bol with Julie. But he knew the aim of the evening; it was to wait for Crawford's phone call and to aid Wolf's match with Michael. Rosalia wanted this so very much it was painful; Rewi was quite prepared to work at whatever Rosalia wanted, as long as it didn't conflict with his own interests, or those of his children.

The first course, the soufflé, made it to table. Rewi was so hungry by now that he fell on his insubstantial portion, almost fighting with Wolf for a decent helping. Rosalia and Michael picked at their splodges of air and egg as if eating food somehow desecrated it.

The first bottle of wine was gone already. Wolf was telling dreadful jokes end on end, many of them about faeces, at which Michael laughed hysterically. Rosalia tried not to look disgusted. Rewi just grinned to himself, and listened out for the telephone, keeping his ears tuned to the children being vociferously herded out of the indoor pool. Julie was supervising with an ill grace, and had let them all stay far beyond their bedtimes, no doubt to spite him. He analysed the noises, and thought how odd it was that the noises people make are no indication of how they are really feeling. He thought of this chiefly in relation to sex.

Once the jokes were temporarily exhausted, finding something to talk about might have been a bit of a problem. Michael went off to the kitchen, watched every inch of the way by Wolf, and Rosalia launched into chat. She had never been to Europe, she told Wolf, but her heart was there. Her husband, the Commander, had been very fond of Germany and had also spent time in Italy after the war — and so on. Wolf laughed away as if everything she said was the funniest thing.

When the phone rang it was something of a relief. Rewi ran for it in the hall and found he was quite drunk. He hoped it wouldn't show. Maybe Crawford would have a stinking hangover.

It wasn't Crawford on the phone at all. It took him a while to register whose voice he was listening to, it being too deep for a girl.

'Is Crawford Hollander there?' she asked.

'No, no. He's in France.' He recognized the voice of Mercy Fisher. 'He doesn't live here, you know.'

'No,' she said as if dreadfully disappointed. 'I know he doesn't, but I don't know . . . '

'This is Rewi anyway. Do you want his number in town?' He pulled open the desk drawer, hoping like crazy that Crawford's number was in the teledex, because he sure as hell didn't want to ask Rosalia for it.

'Yes, yes I do. He's not in the book or anything.'

'No, he likes to keep things dark.' He found the number and read it out to her. 'Is that Mercy?'

'Yes. How did you know? How long is he away for?'

'Dunno. I think he's going to Germany after France. I know I've got to take his Jag for a warrant and it isn't due till next month.'

'Next month,' she said.

'Yeah, might be six weeks.'

'Six weeks,' she said.

'Can I give him a message? We're expecting him to ring.'

'Oh I don't know — I don't know — I need to talk to him, urgently.'

Rewi heard the misery in the girl's voice, and knew immediately the nature of the problem. He felt anger so intense in the pit of his stomach that he wished to put his fist through the french windows, and for follow-up to reduce Crawford's pretty features to a pulp that even his sister would find repellent.

'Is there anything I can do?' he said. 'Or Rosalia?'

He knew that this was inept, because what

could either of them do? But then perhaps Rosalia could speak to her parents, protect her, tell them it wasn't the girl's fault that a predatory middle-aged man ... would Rosalia do that?

'Please don't say anything to Rosalia. I was so afraid she'd answer the phone, but I had to call, you see. I'm glad it's you. Please don't say anything.'

'I won't. I promise. Do you need some money?'

'What for?' she said.

'Sorry, I just didn't know whether it might help.'

'I don't know what you're talking about.'

'No, sorry. Stupid bugger. Give me your number and I'll get him to ring you. We're expecting his call because of the big wine competition yesterday. He's hoping for a commendation for Wolfgang's wine — you know he's buying the Platts out.'

'No I didn't,' she said. 'He didn't tell me things.'

'No I guess not. Well, I'll speak to him.'

When Crawford's call did come, it was something of an anti-climax. Rewi was in the kitchen being busy about the dishwasher. Zoë came padding in, half dressed, leaving a charming pattern of wet feet on the slate.

'I hate Tom! He whipped me with his

towel. And he splashed me in the pool. Right in the face.'

Rewi sent her packing without sympathy. These petty hurts and crimes were somewhere else, in a world of innocence where an injury was a faceful of chlorinated water. Rewi wanted to shout at her for allowing some trivial hurts to raise so much as an ouch, but he was above their hurts as he was above Mercy's. He could not afford to be otherwise. It seemed to him only logical that if you let yourself grow angry with kids over absurd breaches of civility, what were you to do about Crawford Hollander, the child-seducer? Rewi had no techniques in his head or heart to deal with the anger, or with Mercy's plight. He didn't know if he should do anything at all. He didn't know if there was anything he could do, or if his anger was in any way justified. He had no one to ask and no moral signposts to refer to. He was in the middle of the high country with a dodgy vehicle and a track that bumped into oblivion.

He heard the phone ring, and knew this time it was Crawford. He hurried into the elegant parts of the house, tea-towel draped over his forearm, and tried to hover beside Rosalia as if he was eager to hear Crawford's news. He *was* eager to hear Crawford's news, but not half as eager as he was burning to bore a few words into Crawford's ear.

'It's a great year for Pinot Noir,' Rosalia reported breathlessly. 'Everything is going really well. People have been very encouraging.'

'And?'

Wolf shambled in from the dining-room and stood breathing behind Rewi. Perhaps after all Wolf did care to some minor degree about the opinions of the French wine lords, whom he was constantly heard to ridicule.

'And the competition? The judging? Oh. Is it? We all thought — I'm sure you said — It's not until tomorrow.'

Wolf exclaimed and turned sharply away. Rewi stood by the phone trying to cut through Rosalia's stream of encouragement and brittle excitement.

'Yes,' she said, 'yes I understand. Russell, at Harmans, at once. I'll tell Rewi so I don't forget. Rewi, you are to call Russell, you know, the lawyer, in the morning — oh immediately — no, first thing in the morning — and tell him to proceed. With all haste. Yes of course, dear. Rewi wants a word, Crawford darling — can Rewi just — '

But he had hung up.

'Where was he calling from? I need to speak to him urgently.'

'Oh I'm sure it can wait,' said Rosalia. 'Russell will know how to contact him. What a disappointment. It's not till tomorrow, and here we are waiting to hear. How silly. Never mind we are having a lovely dinner, aren't we, Michael?'

But Michael was unable to speak because the delay had practically ruined his zabaglione which had flambéed gloriously almost as the first peals of the phone sounded. They all declared it delicious, but Michael said it wasn't right and finally did burst into tears. The others continued to eat in silence after his retreat into the kitchen. Rosalia kicked Rewi under the table once or twice before he realized that she wasn't displaying her amorous intentions in a novel way, but suggesting some action. He was so obsessed with the matter of Mercy that even when he had taken the hint, he did not see why two gay blokes couldn't sort out their own affairs, when all they had to worry them by way of risk was some obscure disease or a dose of clap.

Wolf was exploring the possible explanations for their confusion over the date of the contest.

'It is perhaps because we have been judged badly, that he is deceiving us.' He smoothed out on the table a printed brochure in French.

'The dates are quite here,' he said. 'We have not mistaken. He is deceiving us but why?'

Rosalia delivered another kick under the table. Angry, Rewi said: 'Why don't you go into the kitchen and help him with the coffee. Or we'll never get through.'

Wolf stopped mid-sentence, waved the brochure in a vague gesture of incomprehension, and went into the kitchen. Rewi shut the dining-room door. He poured Rosalia a bucket of Cointreau and himself one of Crawford's best brandies.

'I wonder what Crawford's up to,' he said.

'It was me he spoke to, and I am his sister, and I would know if he was being clever. If he says the main judging is tomorrow, then it is tomorrow.'

Rewi knew better than to argue. He wondered how long it was before they could call it a night. If he went on drinking at this rate he'd be no use to Rosalia, or to Julie, who would be in no hurry to depart when he finally made it home.

He thought of the girl sitting alone in her room, hoping for the phone to ring against all odds, midnight, one o'clock, before she fell into some sort of sleep, and woke sick and frightened. His impotence made him reach out for another of Crawford's brandies, the only revenge that came immediately to mind.

He made his way home on auto-pilot, having made Rosalia the expected offer and been contemptuously rejected as a drunken lecher. He failed to take this personally, knowing that she was no more responsible for the cruel things she said to him, than a drunkard was for his tears.

Rewi felt sorry for her, as he felt sorry for all kinds of people. He felt sorry for his children abandoned by their mother, and so he felt he should not burden them with a stepmother. He felt sorry for his ex-wife, cutting herself off from the effortless love of children, shielding herself in righteous anger against his pity. He felt sorry for Julie, a wild spirit writhing in an ordinary suburban body. And now he felt desperately sorry for Mercy Fisher.

Feeling sorry for other people was not something he admired in himself, though we may legitimately admire him for it. To Rewi, it was an unmanly thing, a form of weakness, something to be hushed up. But none the less, he persisted in it, in secret, though, as he sometimes reflected to himself, it didn't do anyone the blindest bit of good.

He stumbled into the house, longing for his unencumbered bed, but Julie was waiting to unburden and unbutton herself to him, and he must, of course, sit down with her and pay some attention to her woes, however hard he reckoned she'd worked to dream them up.

And indeed Julie curled herself up on his sofa and person and told him at some length what a shit of an evening she had had while he played Lord of the Manor. She also told him what had been on TV and how pathetic it all was, and how foul they had all been in the pool, and also how grotty it was eating the sort of food the children would tolerate and what did Michael cook for dinner?

Rewi had only one thing on his mind and it was neither food nor sex, contrary to Julie's stated opinion of him. He didn't mean to mention it, but Julie's constant prodding questions drove him to it.

'What *is* the matter with you tonight?'

'Nothing.'

'Nothing, my arse. Usually you can hardly wait to get my knickers down.'

This was in fact quite untrue, for Rewi, gentleman to the core, always waited to be invited.

'I'm OK.'

'Well I'm not. Have you met someone?'

At last he gave in.

'It's that bastard Crawford. He's got her up the spout.'

'Got who?' said Julie. 'Don't tell me, that

silly cow. She was asking for it. Didn't you see her fooling around, flashing her boobs at him?'

'She's only a kid. Jeeze, don't you remember being sixteen?'

Julie remembered very well being sixteen. She referred to her youth often, as a balladeer remembers the highlands before the raids. She remembered squeezing herself into the tightest jeans and hanging out at motor-cycle swap meets on the chance of being swept off on the rump of a Harley. That was how she met Brian — and how life turned instantly to not even anything as interesting as shit.

'There's nothing to it now, you just go to the doctor and they write a referral to the clinic, and it takes fifteen minutes, and you don't feel anything.'

'Yeah, but aren't those Fishers Catholics?'

'You don't actually believe they do things any different, do you? They say things, but they do it just the same. That's just a few old priests and wrinkled-up nuns getting publicity.'

Rewi was by no means sure, but had no evidence to disprove her. He could not understand that the careful mother of three, the woman to whom he was prepared to entrust his own children, could talk so calmly of the disposal of life. But then he was a simple man, and women understood these things. Her reassurance did not reassure him. He worried about Mercy to the extent that he was unmanned and Julie finally went home in a temper. Such a thing had never happened before.

In the morning he packed his children onto the school bus with ruthless efficiency and went up to the house far earlier than necessary. On the dot of nine he rang Crawford's lawyer, who was not, needless to say, yet in the office. He rang at fifteen-minute intervals until he achieved a result, but it was not a satisfactory one. The lawyer was most interested in Crawford's instructions. He understood that he was to conclude the purchase of the Platt vineyard immediately, without even an hour's delay, even if that meant conceding a little on price. Crawford was most insistent. The lawyer was, by contrast, totally uninterested in calling France or passing on messages. He did have a contact number for Crawford, but he saw no reasons why —

Rewi, armed only with a telephone number on scrap paper, no knowledge of international dialling and no word of French, picked up the phone. He dialled, received beeps and heard disembodied instructions. Tried different combinations, consulted the battered phone book in the desk drawer, tried a fourth and a fifth time. Then he dialled the international operator and talked unavailingly to a bored young woman in Singapore. Tried the local directory service and chatted to an equally bored young woman in Palmerston North who was no more use though much more fun. In the end he tried Telecom Faults and quite by chance was given the right information. He got through to France successfully, but no amount of repeating Crawford's name could elicit anything except a stream of French. At the end of this process he was as angry and humiliated as the boy in the back of the fourth form who cannot understand the substitution rule.

He stomped out of the house slamming the door with terrible disregard for the safety of the glass, and got on with his chores.

★ ★ ★

About the middle of the afternoon, distracted by something he could not put a name to, like a bluebottle that buzzes round the house, goes quiet on you when you reach for the fly-swat, and starts again the minute you put the thing down, he suddenly straightened up from his saw-horse, left the saw half-way through a piece of four-by-two destined for the laundry window-sill and went back to the big house, where Rosalia was entertaining two jowly men in over-priced suits who looked heavily like the golf-course developers they in fact were. Her brittle tones overlaid their relentless bass; they were men used to doing the talking. Rewi stood by the back door taking off his boots, and tried to remember why his errand was so urgent it could not wait till the evening. He was plagued by a fragment of memory, the girl's smile, too wide for her face, the child peering out from inside the woman's body, like a novice deep-sea diver. He recalled Crawford's proprietorial hand resting lightly on the girl's buttock while she walked as far apart from him as the hand allowed. He felt angry, and went boldly into the house to use the phone. 'Yes, Rewi, what is it?' asked Rosalia sharply.

'I have to use the phone,' he said, and ignored her further twitterings by closing the door between the hall and dining-room with a manliness he thought she would not dare to challenge.

He called the Platts' winery, and got Christine Platt in the kitchen of the house. There was no phone line down to the winery on the river flats.

'Gidday, Rewi!' said Christine. 'How's it

going, mate? Yeah, hang on while I get him on the walkie-talkie.'

Wolf was a long time responding. Rewi stood twisting up the phone cord, and listening to the louder of Rosalia's two guests discoursing on the World's Most Difficult Holes. Golf, he supposed, though his mind ran briefly to more ribald interpretations.

'*Ja?*' said Wolf at last.

Rewi explained to Christine Platt who relayed to Wolfgang that tomorrow would be a good day for him to come over and pour that concrete slab out the back that Crawford had told him was required.

'Tomorrow is not good,' said Wolf.

'He says tomorrow is no good,' said Christine.

'Well tell him today then.'

'He says no day is good.'

'Jeeze, Chrissy, he can't be that busy.'

There was a crackled discussion in the background.

'He says,' announced Christine, almost consumed with mirth, 'that he isn't busy, he's in love.'

'Oh tell him to get a grip. Well, OK, very funny. You know. Pull himself together. Look, that's enough of that, Christine, you grubby-minded woman!' he continued as Christine chuckled richly. 'Tell him I'll be up tomorrow anyway, sparrow fart.'

'You know the way? Just take the Port Robinson road as far as the Cathedrals and look for PLATT on the oildrum,' Christine said.

Rewi was tempted to feel smug, but Mercy's predicament pressed on the inside of his eyes. Wolf's state seemed to him like pure self-indulgence, of the kind only a queer and a foreigner would wallow in. He got out the teledex and found Mercy's phone number.

'No, she's at school, of course. Who is this?' said a highly suspicious Marg.

Rewi tried to explain, very unconvincingly, left his name, and said he'd ring back at four. He felt a fool, not remembering she was a schoolgirl. He also felt more than a fool because her mother would now think he was her boyfriend, and assume he was the father of the baby, when it all came out, as it would.

Towards four o'clock he was delayed at the school bus stop by someone who wanted him to stand for the PTA, and once he'd got free, he had to sweet-talk Julie into delivering and collecting his children the next day, so he could get a good day's run at the concreting over at the winery. Julie wanted revenge for his failure to reward her for baby-sitting, and went on for some time about why didn't he get a wife instead of making use of her all the time, every time he needed something.

Rewi took his punishment like a man, secretly smug that he was not any more a married one. Julie agreed to his request, and suggested she also cook his tea tomorrow, since he would have such a long day.

'Might be a bit too knackered to appreciate it,' he said.

By the time he got the children sorted, it was well past four, and he didn't have the Fishers' phone number, which meant a trek from his house to the big house to get it. He contemplated calling Rosalia to ask for it, and dismissed the notion. He consulted the phone book. There were dozens of Fishers; he tried two with hopeful initials, but neither knew a Mercy. The third R. Fisher did not answer, and the number had a sort of familiarity which made him assume it was correct. He thought he would call later, but in the insistent clatter of homework and tea he ceased to hear the terror in Mercy's voice. Next morning he was up at an hour no self-respecting man rose unless he were going fishing. He tidied the house with the ferociousness of a nun, so that he couldn't be accused of needing a woman, in *that* sense anyway, and crept guiltily away from his sleeping children.

It was a long drive over the hills onto the

plain and up the road north to Port Robinson, where the Platts had their market garden, and their fledgling winery. Rewi loved every moment of it. The broad welcoming roads were empty, the countryside bare as if swept clean, the morning sky at once innocent and uncompromising. He leaned in the generous curves of the bays, raced up the mountainsides and expanded into the emptiness. He felt equal to anything.

Once over the hills and onto the plain, the driving was less fun, but still the roads were broad as a football pitch, and empty, even the main road north, and its two whole miles of motorway. There wasn't a traffic cop to be seen. Great stuff, but surpassed by the terrific switchback dirt road that led to and fro, round and down, skirting the limestone striations called the Cathedrals, to the Platt gardens.

On the side of the road he recognized the oildrum on legs, which served as a post box. PLATT was painted on the crinkled side, with the word WINERY added more recently.

The Platts' place, Rewi noticed, showed signs of the hard times they were experiencing. He bounced down the track, thinking how Zoë would have screamed with delight. But the place made Rewi sad. The fences sagged and its gates were ingeniously rigged;

weeds flourished along the borders of the potato fields. Panes were cracked in the glasshouses; others were missing, replaced by flapping plastic. Miscellaneous sacks and boxes and pyramids of rejected spuds suggested a farmer forgetful or careless of his work. Rewi knew this not to be so, but that Pete Platt was hard-working and effective, and from his ragged plots emerged sack after sack of lovely white potatoes, with a dusting of black soil to prove their country origins. Or had emerged; for cyst nematode — a phrase as terrible as *Black Death* to potato farmers — had struck him down, and the apparent disorder was overlaid by a real threat of despair.

There was no sense of tragedy in the kitchen of the farmhouse when Rewi yoohooed his way in through the back door. There was a great deal of miscellaneous stuff about, a plastic trike, perilous stacks of crates, huge balls of twine, their intestines spilling out, an ancient tractor parked bum-on to an even more ancient predecessor, which for some reason had a greater share of the shelter. Rewi did not care for untidy places, but he recognized a genuine Kiwi working space where amazing invention flourished. As indeed it had, for back down on the river flats, where nothing much was to be found except gorse, sheep droppings and the occasional disoriented fisherman, Pete Platt had planted vines, much to the derision of his mates. And in the dark sheds out the back of the farmhouse he had installed Wolf and his vats and a miscellany of odd machinery, home-made for the most part.

Rewi found Christine Platt, broad, handsome, part-Maori, getting on for six feet tall, and eight months pregnant, with her elbows in the sink and a toddler at her ankles. She was pleased to see him, put on the kettle, full of news. They had all known each other for many years, ever since the days when Pete had a passion for the reconstructing of the Hillman Minx.

'You never guess what!' she said shaking the suds off her rubber gloves with a terrible firmness. 'We had the *Press* on the phone just before, and they're sending out a photographer. And just now, Radio New Zealand rang.'

'Radio New Zealand!'

'Yes, it's just brilliant. Apparently Wolf's wine got a gold medal or something, over all the French and everyone. I think it was the Pinot Noir.'

'No! Crawford didn't say. Gee when's the party — I bet Pete's over the moon.'

'Well, no. He's a bit miffed. We just signed.

We only got back from the lawyers when the Radio rang. I can't believe that Crawford's timing — it's great for Wolf though, isn't it? We always knew he was a real beaut — '

Christine chatted on, trying to make the best of it, telling Rewi as much as she knew about the wine competition. The news had come through the wire to the *Press*, but nothing official had been heard by the Platts. Apparently it all had happened the other night, but news takes a while to travel all this way, doesn't it? Wolfgang was absolutely made now, apparently the French were green, because such a thing had never happened before. He could get a job anywhere in the world now, and never need worry about his qualifications.

It took Rewi some time and half his cup of coffee to twig. Crawford had already bought the winery off the Platts, after the medal was won, but before the news had made it to New Zealand. He had known all along, hence his indecent haste to sign the papers. He had appeared to concede on the price, buying it all, including Wolf, over whose qualifications doubt had been cast, for a snip. All the Platts had for their gold medal was honour and glory.

Rewi continued to grunt his half of the conversation, while rolling over in his head if it were possible even for *Crawford* to be so perfidious.

Out the back, beyond a straggle of potato sheds and structures which seemed unsure of their use, he found Wolf pacing round and round his kingdom like a mad king in his observatory.

The room in which Wolf operated was a nest of equipment, and racks and benches, ziggurats of bottles and monuments of barrels. Between the bottling machine spewing tubes and insulating tape, and the labeller with its vicious glue stick poised to stab the unwary passer-by, Wolf had worn a track. He could just walk round the whole of his work area, clutter notwithstanding, and he was walking around his track, in a species of figure-eights with autistic intensity.

His denim shirt was half untucked from his jeans; his hair was unwashed and stuck up in a crazy quiff. Rewi hoped the press photographer would line up Platt family rather than wine-maker.

'Shit hot!' Rewi said. 'You showed the buggers, Wolf! You're a made man now.'

'I am unmade, unmanned,' said Wolf, groaning in a histrionic European way.

'Yes, I know Crawford's a bastard, but you don't have to stay with him.'

'I do not care about Crawford, except that

I hate Crawford with every bone that I have in my body.'

'So what's eating you, mate?'

Wolf flung his elbows onto his workbench and thrust his face into his hands.

'It is Michael,' he said through his hands. 'He does not call me.'

Rewi shook his head at the nuttiness of the man. He wins an award no one but he himself could have expected, and it has virtually no impact because he is so consumed by love. Rewi himself had never been in love, and had no time for its nonsense; he found men in love absurd and embarrassing, and a man in love with a man, unnatural into the bargain. Love was a women thing — tears and pleadings and stuff. There was something incomplete about a man who allowed his behaviour to be modified by irrational feelings.

'Well ring him up then.'

'I have, I have. I leave messages — but I cannot leave any more or he will run away from me. If he not calls back, he cannot care for me.'

'Doesn't follow with that Michael. He's a delicate flower, our Michael. He's probably sitting in a darkened room biting his nails and waiting for your next phone message and saying 'If he really loved me, he'd ring one more time.''

'How comes you know this?'

'Feminine intuition. Michael stays with Rosalia whenever his life falls apart. You two make a right pair.'

'I do not think that you have ever been in love, Rewi.'

'Nope, and very happy about it. Now, where do you want this concrete poured, mate?'

Wolf straightened himself up and led the way outside to a patch of cleared ground abutting the back door.

'I need to tear this wall down, doors which open right out onto concrete here, and a roof over.'

Rewi knocked the jamb of the back door, leaned his weight on the wall, scuffed the ground with the side of his boot.

'Tall order, mate. I can start it today, but we've got to level this and get the boxing in first. Don't know about the wall. I don't think Crawford wants to spend money on this place. He'll want to move you in a new shiny place where he can bring visitors.'

'I will die in a new shiny place.'

Rewi worked without cease until smoko, further clearing the area outside the back door, and levelling the ground. He guessed that Crawford would barely thank him for his efforts, but this did not stop Rewi from doing the best job possible. Wolf pottered around in the sheds behind him, appearing to do nothing, but Wolf's chaos and apparent ineffectiveness were misleading. A man more steelily determined on his course would be hard to find.

Rewi plodded back to the house and left his boots at the door in deference to Christine's newly washed lino. He gladly took the coffee she pressed on him, reconstructed the toy train that had got all twisted and mixed up, and asked to use the phone in the hall.

He shut the kitchen door and then realized he didn't know Michael's number. He called Hollander House and after many rings raised a bothered and tetchy Rosalia.

'I didn't *know* you weren't here!' she said, 'I hunted everywhere, until Julie told me.'

'I left early,' said Rewi who didn't apologize. 'Can I have Michael's number?' and in a rush of courage, 'And Mercy Fisher's as well, while you're at it.'

'What do you want their numbers for?'

Rewi wasn't good at this stuff.

'Just something Wolf — '

'A surprise? Something for Crawford?'

'Yeah.' That would do a treat.

He wrote both numbers down carefully in the Platts' *Yellow Pages*, on the *What To Do* in *Case of Earthquake* page, and tore the portion of the sheet away. He reckoned Christine Platt would always know what to do in an emergency without needing the *Yellow Pages*. He wondered if he should talk to her about Mercy.

Michael, naturally, did not answer the phone. When the answerphone cut in Rewi started in at him.

'I know you're there, Michael, pick up the fucking phone. It's Rewi. Pick up the phone. Now.'

Michael picked up the phone.

'You are horrible, Rewi. I hate you.'

'Good-oh. Hate away. I thought you'd like to know that Wolf's wine won a gold medal at that competition in France. The top prize.'

Michael started to squeal.

'Oh, how fabulous, how wonderful, isn't that wonderful! I always knew he was the best . . . '

He continued in this vein for some time until Rewi grew impatient.

'He wants to talk to you. If I get him now, will you talk to him? Nicely?'

'Oh I have to congratulate him!'

'He wants a bit more than that.'

'Oh, Rewi, I don't think I can cope. I mean he's so German, so intense and scary.'

'He's a good bloke.'

'How can you possibly know that?'

'I'm like a dog. I can smell a bastard a mile off. Wolfgang is all right.'

'Do you swear? How do you know he won't hurt me?'

'You watch too many war movies. He wouldn't hurt a fly. Just do us all a favour. Put him out of his misery, will you?'

'I'll blame you if it all goes wrong.'

'Blame away, mate.'

Rewi got Christine Platt to press the buzzer used to summon Wolf to the house. He was at the door before she had finished buzzing, panting, his black hair over his eyes.

'Michael, for you,' said Rewi, and went away sharpish.

When Wolf finally returned to the winery Rewi was thinking about lunch. Wolf was no more useful than he had been before the phone call, but instead of walking obsessively round his workspace, he stood in one place, roughly where Rewi was trying to work, and stared into some distant landscape, presumably more beautiful than the corrugated iron fence immediately in his vision.

'I need you to do me a favour, Wolfgang,' said Rewi.

Wolf didn't hear him at first, and had difficulty concentrating.

'I need you to ring Crawford for me, and

give him a message.'

'I will not speak to Crawford.'

'I wouldn't ask if it didn't matter.'

'He is gone to my brother in Hamburg. I do not want to talk with my brother. He shouts at me.'

Rewi straightened up from setting the boxing. He took himself right in front of Wolf, and fixed him firmly in the eye.

'I need you to ring Crawford and give him a message. It matters like shit.'

'What does *matters like shit* mean? Much or not anything?'

'Life and death, mate.'

Wolf frowned at Rewi, as if unable to believe that anything in his world could be so important.

'It is night in Europe.'

'Not now, later.'

'OK. What is the message?'

'He must ring Mercy Fisher urgently. Do you understand me? Mercy Fisher. I've got the number here.'

'Why?'

'I don't know, nothing to do with me. I'm just the messenger, but I can make a guess.'

'She loves him,' said Wolf.

'Something like that. And you know how that feels, mate, don't you?'

'Yes,' said Wolf, sighing like an opera

singer, 'every minute you are away from the one that you love is an hour of agony and ecstasy.'

'Hmm,' said Rewi. 'Will you ring Crawford?'

'Yes, yes, I am a man who keeps his word.'

'Tonight?'

'Today evening night I am with Michael. He is cooking a special celebration dinner for us two alone. Will I remember?'

'I'd like it if you did.'

The next day Rewi went back mid-morning to finish off the job. He found the Platt household full of people — friends of the family, assorted large relatives, a lecturer from the Agricultural College who had always known that Canterbury could produce red wine equal to the world's best, and a nice blonde girl from one of the papers — but no sign of Wolf. Christine Platt's mum was running a shuttle service between kettle and Tupperware, and there was a great deal of noisy conversation. For a while Rewi held up his end in the congratulatory buzz, said he was *definitely* coming to the party, as long as they had it before Crawford got back, which got a good laugh.

Wolf had not come in from his evening with Michael. The assembly in the kitchen would have had a jolly good laugh about this if he'd been out with a girl, but as it was, they didn't like to discuss it.

Rewi went and got on with his work, but couldn't take his mind off poor Mercy Fisher, for whom the days must be endless. Unless of course she'd panicked too soon, and everything was now OK. Rewi remembered several such scares in the blistered years of his marriage. And that would leave Rewi bothering quite unnecessarily. He began to get annoyed, before he realized that the girl could hardly be expected to ring him up and set his mind at rest, when she hadn't burdened him with her problem in the first place. He determined to ring her up that afternoon, when he got home, come hell or high water.

Though he thought the news must all be good, Rewi fretted because he doubted that Wolf would have remembered to call Crawford.

When he finally got the children settled and himself near a phone, he found he no longer had Mercy's number. Once again he started the search — scanning the phone book until he found a number that seemed familiar. He swore that when he got the right number he'd circle it in red, even if Julie did notice and think something of it.

After several mildly uncomfortable calls, he

found the right Fishers, and reached at once for a red crayon of Zoë's. One of Mercy's brothers answered, much to Rewi's relief. He had a collection of things ready to say to Marg, if necessary, messages for Dickie about bush-walking — that kind of thing. He made it clear to Mercy's brother that it was not Crawford calling.

Mercy was a long time coming to the phone. Rewi didn't waste time on chatting.

'I'm trying to get through to him,' he said. 'We think he's gone to Germany. Wolf, Wolfgang, his wine-maker, is trying to get him in Germany.'

She didn't say, *Oh it doesn't matter.* She sounded like a dead person.

'Thank you for trying,' she said. 'I'll never forget it.'

'You heard about the gold medal?'

'No. What gold medal?' though it was hard to imagine anyone sounding less interested.

'Wolfgang's wine won a medal in France. That was why Crawford went over there. Crawford's bought the winery, and Wolfgang along with it of course.'

'That's good, isn't it? Will he come home any sooner?'

'I don't honestly know. He's gone to stay with Wolf's brother. But I suppose he might go back to France now.'

'Oh Jesus, do you think so?'

'Or hurry back to get on with hogging the limelight.'

'You don't like him.'

'Not specially.'

'Nor do I,' she said.

Don't cry, Rewi thought, don't cry. This is nothing to do with me.

'I'll keep on his case,' said Rewi, 'I'll ring before tea-time the day I get any news. If anyone rings before tea-time, you'll know it's me, OK? If I get your mum, I'll have to make up some story. Something about cutting a track up to the bush. Your Dad and I were discussing it the other day.'

Mercy passed no comment.

'Thank you,' she said. 'You're a great guy.'

★ ★ ★

Rewi felt no such thing three evenings later when he finally pinned Wolf down.

Wolf said, 'I left a message with my brother, and the telephone number, but he was reading me a lecture on homosexuality, so I do not know what he did afterwards.'

They were crushed up together in the Platts' front room, with plastic glasses of red wine in their hands. Wolf had his other hand tucked in the far side of Michael's belt, as if letting go of him might allow him to dematerialize.

Michael was not looking his prettiest; days of Wolf's attention had caused him to neglect his hair, and the black roots formed a reverse halo around his face. Nor had he been getting enough sleep; his eyes were tired, placing him much more firmly in the correct age group, and he had a spot or two. Rewi was of the opinion that, pre-Wolf, Michael would never have gone to a party with a spot; he'd have stayed home under a face-pack.

So many bodies were packed into the room, many of them of the dimensions of the Platt family, that Rewi and Wolf had to shout to be understood, and Rewi was disinclined to shout about the private affairs of Mercy Fisher, so he had to leave things as they were.

He struggled out of the crush to refill his glass, and when he glanced back, Wolf had filled the space in front of him with Michael, holding him face on, by both sides of the belt. Michael stared back into his eyes, seeing no one else. Rewi had seen Michael in other social situations, and had marked him down as one whose eyes did a circuit of the room every thirty seconds, on the off-chance that James Dean had dropped by. He marvelled at the transformation. There was no accounting for these gays.

He found the contemplation of their mutual infatuation nauseating, as did many of the Platt family, but all were far too courteous to let it show.

Rewi filled his glass and went out the back door into the yard. There was no view to admire, though a stupendous vista of sea and mountains was, in fact, just beyond the macrocarpas, nothing but jobs that needed doing, and there was no fun in that. But he felt unable to go back into the mass of bodies, unable to chat and flirt and get drunk and hope to score.

He could see Pete Platt, back there in the kitchen, red-faced and early balding, a good kind funny man, though he looked like a troglodyte on steroids. He was sniffing the wine in his glass with a delicacy that filled his big person with grace. A short man with an expensive haircut, whom Rewi recognized as Crawford's lawyer, was talking in his ear. Pete's face, half distracted by the scent of the wine, was puzzled and sad.

Rewi was alarmed at a feeling he did not recognize. It seemed to him that there was rottenness at the heart of everything, and where people were not rotten they were going to be made sad. He wondered what he could do about Mercy Fisher, he who could fix anything broken.

Christine Platt came out into the yard, feeling the heat, and settled her broad bottom on a side-on plastic crate.

'That doesn't look too safe,' said Rewi. 'Got to look after that baby.'

'Are you kidding? This baby's tougher than I am. And kick! I tell Pete, if he doesn't make an All Black I'm sending him back.'

'You and Pete for parents he'll be a Forest Meads.'

There was an unusual silence in which Christine Platt watched the future All Black gyrate in her stomach. She sipped her wine. She had been heard to assert that she didn't mind if drinking alcohol in pregnancy led to smaller babies.

'You OK, Rewi? You should be in there having fun.'

'Not in the mood really.'

'You got problems? Women, money?'

'Not me. Own nothing, owe nothing. Got a home for my kids and a job to do.'

'You're down though.'

'Yeah, I'm not quite in the party mood, that's all.'

He looked up from the contemplation of the concrete of the yard. She was smiling at him, her broad-beamed, light brown face written with quizzical concern. She wouldn't pry, but she took an interest.

Confiding wasn't Rewi's thing. When his wife left he had the greatest difficulty telling anyone about it, except in the simplest, most practical terms as in *I'll have to bring the kids when I come over to fix your lawnmower because Janis has left me.* Followed by, *I don't know. She had to find herself or some such crap.* Followed by, *Yeah, I'm OK. Just buggered and pissed off.*

Deep inside him was the notion that because he had ridden the rage and hurt the way a cowboy is supposed to ride a bronco, and had not yet fallen off, he was sentenced to ride his pain for ever, because it had not stopped kicking and thrashing.

He hoped that confiding in Christine would be a different process from his unsatisfactory attempt to engage Julie in the small matter that troubled him. He thought he would give it a try, just to see what it felt like.

'There's this girl,' he started.

'Right,' said Christine.

'No, it's not that. Nothing to do with me. It's that bastard, Crawford.'

'Geeze I hate that man,' said Christine. 'I don't think there's anybody in the world so mean. He's ripped us off mega.'

'Someone in there said Penfolds had been on the phone trying to buy you.'

'Too bloody late for that, eh,' she said. 'Still we were the silly buggers who didn't know what we had. But tell me about this girl.'

'I don't know anything, and honest to God I'm not involved, but there's this girl, and she's pretty young. And a few days ago she rang me up in a right old state trying to get hold of Crawford. And I think he's duffed her up. And I've been trying to pass on the message to Crawford in Europe.'

'Oh shit, how old is she?'

'Still at school.'

'God, what a bastard. Someone should take him out.'

Rewi grunted, thinking of the immense satisfaction it would give him to give Crawford something to think about in the kidney and bollock department. And grunted a second time at the genuine impossibility of such a thing.

'I think the family are Catholics.'

'Oh shit,' said Christine. She spread her hands over her unborn baby to protect him from the cruelty of the world. 'You know right now that little girl is thinking only one thing: how to get rid of it. She's dreaming of that every night, and throwing herself into things — exercise and hot baths and drinks and anything — all she wants is to see blood on her pants. And you know, from the minute that baby gets born and for the rest of her life she'll be horrified to think that's what she wanted.'

'And what if she gets a termination?'

'Well I dunno, Catholics have rules don't they? It's murder. And even without that — well you never forget a baby, even one you lost after five minutes. I kid you not.'

Rewi shrugged, unable to believe so extreme a statement, had it not come from her.

'I got Wolf to ring him in Germany, but there's no way to know if the message got through.'

'You can't do anything, Rewi. A girlfriend could, but you can't. You did your best.'

'Yeah, but it doesn't feel like enough. I could have stopped that bastard. I saw what he was up to.'

'You couldn't have, Rewi. You aren't her dad or her brother or a boyfriend. Just accept it. Bad things happen. You aren't responsible. Crawford is. He's a bad man.'

Rewi was not entirely convinced. He was quite prepared to accept that Crawford was a bad man, but he did not see that that excused Rewi. He shrugged.

The three of them sat in contemplative silence.

'You're down too, Christine.'

She sighed. 'We all make our choices and live with the shit.'

'Aw come on, Christine, you don't have any shit to live with.'

'Yes I bloody do. I pushed Pete into selling to Crawford. I have to live with that shit. He didn't want to sell, reckoned he could hang on, but I was worried sick about the mortgage. I thought we'd lose the lot. I knew there was something wrong, especially when he caved in on the price like that. I never trusted him, but I just wanted us to have the money safe. So I went on and on, as you do . . . '

'As you girls do,' said Rewi grinning, though his wife had been too busy spinning about to nag him.

'So now we've sold it, and Crawford's going to make a killing, and not us. And it's all my fault.'

'Pete nice about it?'

'Of course Pete's nice about it. But I just wish I'd kept my bloody mouth shut. And I always will. It happened so quick, you don't realize that you've made a choice at all, until it's too late, and you're looking at a mistake — like your little girlfriend.'

'She's not.' Rewi was determined not to reopen the subject. 'You guys should take Wolf and start up again. You know how to do it now. There's much better places up country.'

'You kidding? Crawford Hollander let Wolf go? Hell will freeze over first.'

As if he had heard mention of his name, Wolf came out into the yard, trailing Michael behind him by the hand.

'Is this true?' Rewi demanded. 'You signed your life away?'

Wolf stared at him, momentarily uncomprehending. He forced himself back into the world of Rewi and Christine and the muddy concrete of the yard.

'My life? No one has that, only of course Michael.'

Michael blushed, and both Christine and Rewi, unkind though they knew it was, laughed.

'But,' continued Wolf, as if nothing had happened, 'I have only signed a short contract. If I had not signed, they would not have sold.'

'But you didn't want them to sell, did you? Not to Crawford?' said Michael.

'No. But the Platts are my friends. I owe them my living — they gave me my job which made me a wine-maker. In life we must always pay our debts of honour or we are not men.'

Michael looked down at his foot, scraping mud off the concrete with the side of a soft leather trainer.

'But it is not for long. Soon I am away.'

Michael jerked his head up to stare at him. 'Wolfgang! You promised!'

'No, no, I shall never leave New Zealand. I cannot bear to live anywhere else, even before I found you.'

Michael blushed and smiled like a child on prize-day. It was Rewi's turn to study the constitution of the yard. Christine laughed.

'You are a hard case, Wolf,' she said. 'So you're out of it?'

'My contract with Crawford is for a year. Of course I shall honour that contract. After that, Michael and I will go away and start a winery and restaurant all our own. I am knowing the perfect place. Michael will cook and I shall vint, and we will be the best in the world, and our own masters.'

'What a lovely idea,' said Christine and sighed. 'It sounds too good to be true.'

'What can stop us?' said Wolf. 'What in all the world?'

10

Crawford rarely succumbed to excitement. He felt the thrilling rush when a deal was about to succeed. When in pursuit of a woman, he relished each pace of the chase and the conquest. He had felt a huge surge of sexual pleasure as he strolled into Archibald's, on the river, to collect his new car — but excitement, no, it was an adolescent's emotion.

None the less, he could find no other word to describe what possessed him now. It was so improbable that he should feel such emotion, and had it not been so curious, he would have dismissed the possibility at once.

Crawford loved to explore the intricate interior of the person. It was the key to his power. And sometimes, he extended that examination to himself, to keep his hand in.

Therefore he did not simply dismiss his excitement. He looked at it clinically. He concluded that the thrill associated with entrapping Wolfgang was related to the oddity of his undertaking, the unspoken elements of what he was about, and the strong possibility of failure.

He had been back in New Zealand for six weeks, by far the most turbulent weeks of his life. He was now a made man — his wealth was completely assured, for Mayaud, Père et Fils, French wine magnates, had already approached him with an offer, which, after suitable flirtation, it would be impossible for him to refuse. Crawford wished to be a big player in the world of wine, but he recognized that there is big, and there is massive. However large he grew, he would be a pigmy beside Mayaud. But he did his calculations and decided his pride had its price. If he allowed them to buy him, he would be rich enough to make himself much richer.

There were two black holes in this master plan. Mercy Fisher and Wolfgang Mark, so-called Herr Doktor.

All through these exhilarating weeks, Crawford had been hauled down to the gutter by physical events he could barely contemplate without nausea — gestation, blood, foetal development. He had put all that behind him now. It was over and did not need to trouble him again.

That hole had been as black as hell, but it was closed over now. But the little local difficulty surrounding Wolfgang was not resolved.

Without Wolf's goodwill he had nothing.

Nobody in the world knew this secret. The deal with Mayaud Père et Fils was predicated on the contract he had with Wolf. Through their interpreter and very politely they said, *No vintner, no deal.* There is no problem, Crawford replied, smooth as Shiraz and lying like hell, no problem at all.

He had lain awake at nights, more troubled, it must be confessed, by Wolf's intransigence than by Mercy's torments. He knew how unworthy this was. He accepted that he could no longer regard himself as a feeling man. He wondered, about four a.m. every morning, whether he had ever been worthy. He wondered if it could possibly be worth the price.

Perhaps if he had expended as much energy on procuring a more professional abortionist for his son, as he did on securing Wolfgang, this story would never have needed to be told.

He arranged for Wolf to visit the best wine merchant in town, spend five hundred dollars of his money, and bring the booty, and Michael, out to Hollander House for the weekend. The abortionist cost him rather less, and the telephone call was shorter.

They duly arrived, in Wolf's ancient black Lancia. Crawford stayed quiet while Michael and Rosalia hugged one another. Later he took them all to a very fine restaurant on the head of the peninsula, with a view out to sea that a romantic painter would have cut off his ear for. That night, he sat up late with Wolf, drank port and talked about women, power, Goethe, port, socialism, architecture, hydraulics, Le Corbusier, Richard Strauss . . . and you get the picture.

They spent Saturday apart — Michael and Wolf went for a walk up into the hills behind the house. Crawford and Rosalia engaged in a little music, for as long as Crawford's patience could be made to last. Then there were some men about the golf-course — two practical men measuring and surveying, and two others who sat down with Crawford to go through draft brochures and discuss the refreshment side of things. Rosalia was needed for this discussion, but she had removed herself upstairs and would not come down. In the end Crawford was forced to phone for Rewi to come over and thrash out the arrangements for staffing the bar. He arrived in shorts, t-shirt and sandals, spilling heat. It was Saturday, he explained.

Crawford observed how civilized New Zealand was becoming when men did not confine business to five days a week, and how quickly, now, she would grow prosperous. Rewi suggested that the price of the prosperity might be too high, if a man might not spend Saturday afternoon with his children. The businessmen continued to talk about staffing the bar.

In the late afternoon, when all the golf-course men were gone, leaving behind them nothing but flags and warratahs at intervals all over the green sward, Wolf and Michael returned, and the hour Crawford had been waiting for arrived.

Michael disappeared into the kitchen, Rosalia donned a frilly apron to help, and Crawford and Wolf took the basket of wines down to the beach.

Crawford had asked Wolf to bring the best and most interesting wines he could find. He was to drink them with, and explain them to, Crawford. Crawford felt that the dual pleasure of drinking the wine and patronizing his master would flatter Wolf and soften his mood. This is how he expressed it to himself, although other phrases may seem to us more appropriate.

It was a perfect evening. The two men strolled down from the house carrying the provisions between them. The earth was still warm from the day's sunlight and there was no sign of the mean evening breeze so common in those parts. Wolf had his supermarket basket full of bottles. He explained to Crawford that living alone in one room, he had never needed more than one basket full of groceries, so found it easier to have a basket for his own use, in which he selected goods and carried them home.

'But with Michael, now, we need the trolley. The basket is become neglected.'

'Is it better, now you need a trolley?'

Wolf shrugged.

'It is more expensive.' Then he laughed. 'Sometimes when he screams at me for being untidy, I think, well, nobody's perfect, and I remember the ending of the Marilyn movie — you know?'

Crawford did not. So Wolf told him the entire plot of *Some Like It Hot* with great hilarity and as many gestures as the basket of wine allowed. Crawford found himself helpless with laughter, and wondered how he had missed so simple a delight as a Marilyn Monroe comedy.

They walked through the avenue.

'We must go to the beach!' Wolfgang asserted. 'I have had enough trees today, even for a German.'

Forests, he explained as they strolled along, were European, even these forests of great New Zealand trees, they were dark places of the soul, cathedrals of the dark forces. But the beach, he said, was pure, like the hills out there on the plain, scraped clean of vegetation and guilt, neutral, with nothing for him to connect with — neither church nor ruined castle, nor prison wall, nor the ash paths of death.

★ ★ ★

Crawford said very little, entranced by the effortless way Wolf carried his culture — philosophers, poets, musicians, statesmen, ancient cities, sieges and imprisonments, sackings and enthronements, gilded courts and barbaric prisons, café societies and radical cells — Crawford found him the quintessence of Europeanness, and envied him. They had walked down to the beach, Wolf explaining all the way under the avenue of Hollander trees why property was theft, and that the landscape of Europe was a thieves' kitchen — every parcel of it stolen and sold and resold and stolen and restolen from the *Volk*.

'But this beach,' he cried, as they stepped onto the sand, 'this beach is free! This beach is both ours and nobody's.'

Crawford was taken aback. Without realizing it he had always regarded that particular stretch of beach as *his* beach. When he was a little boy, before he became an aesthete and retreated to the shade and his piano, he lived on this beach. He protected it from any stray neighbourhood boys and populated it with place-names and characters, each rock, each driftwood tree. He sailed and swam and castled, by himself for the most part, though Rosalia was sometimes allowed to join in.

Crawford's stretch of beach was bounded by outcrops of rock at either end. It was about a quarter of a mile long and followed the amenable curve of the harbour. It was a shallow beach, sloping gently from the road to the waterline, not a particularly attractive picnic spot, and there was better swimming to be had beyond the rocks. Its lack of features had enabled Crawford to keep it for himself all through the summers of his childhood.

'I used to think of this as my beach,' he said lightly, 'but that was no doubt, because I was a lonely little boy, with no one to play with.'

'But you are not a lonely little boy no more?' said Wolf, looking at him quizzically.

Making no sense of this question, Crawford selected the best spot, up against the rocks, where the sand was firm and warm, but not damp.

He spread out the blanket he had brought, the glasses, corkscrew, water and pieces of cheese. Wolf started to open a bottle of wine as casually as a man opens the door of his home. He told Crawford with great amusement about Pete Platt and the Canterbury Television interviewer. This smart young woman had come out with a film crew to talk to the heroes of the hour, and Pete had started to explain about the trials of potato-farming, the terrors of cyst nematode and horrors of rot, and insisted on leading her out into the water-logged field to see for herself the rottenness of the rotten potato. Half-way across, her white high-heeled shoes became mired, and so Pete simply picked her up bodily, to the enormous delight of the television crew and Wolfgang, standing safely on terra firma.

Crawford laughed, and Wolf sniffed the cork and peered at it. Then he showed it to Crawford and explained what to look for.

They drank the first glass. Crawford had sat on a blanket and Wolf on the sand. Wolf took off his shoes and buried his long white feet in the sand. Crawford wanted to take off his shoes too, but felt it might be interpreted as a sexual move.

He tried to remember when he had last sat on a beach. He tried to remember when he had ever enjoyed himself like this.

'Well you have it all now, Wolfgang. I hope we will be happy together.'

'Happy?' said Wolf. 'Happy?

'*Erhabner Geist, du gabst mir, gabst mir alles, Worum ich bat.*''

He laughed uproariously at his private joke.

'I'm sorry, my German isn't quite up to that,' said Crawford.

He had understood the words, but not the meaning.

'Goethe,' said Wolf vaguely, 'I have this habit — this, how you say, tic? How does it go: *exalted ghost, you gave me, gave me all for which I ask*. It is never good to get what you want.'

'On the contrary, I always find it even better than I had imagined.'

'Ah but you see, my friend, what you want and what I want are in different universes. You want to be rich. You can measure rich, so you can be rich. You can enjoy it, because you do not need to look at any other things. But I live for my art and for love, and I want also to be a man of integrity. In all these things it is not possible to be sure you have achieved, because one cannot measure it. It is all choices. If I live for my art and my love, I must live here in New Zealand with my Canterbury reds and with this sweet Michael, you know, but if I am a man of honour, I must go back to Germany to care for my mother. It is not *right* that my brother does that alone. But the choice — how can I be happy, like you?'

'But surely you are not going back to Germany?' said Crawford, his happiness suddenly under threat.

Wolf shook his head, sadly, and then laughed noisily.

'What sort of fool do you think me? The old mother or the young lover? Besides,' he added, laughing hugely, 'you heard what my brother has said to me. He does not even wish to wipe his arse with me.'

'Yes,' said Crawford, very very carefully. 'I did hear him say that. And a great many other things.'

Wolf said nothing at all. The sun started its slow decline. Wolf put the cork firmly in the half-drunk bottle, swilled his glass with water, drank a mouthful or two himself, and opened another wine.

As he sniffed the cork, without looking at Crawford, he said, 'I did not know your German was so good.'

'It is good enough. Your brother was very angry. He made matters clear to me.'

'And you are making them clear to me, yes.'

'I have a new contract waiting for you, Wolf. But that will not change our friendship?'

'Do not call me by that name, I am Wolfgang to you, or perhaps even Herr Doktor Mark.'

'I think not, Herr Doktor. I have never seen any proof of qualifications of that sort.'

'*Wandle den Wurm wieder in seine Hundsgestalt.*'

Crawford chose not to understand that a higher power was being exhorted to turn him from a reptile back into a dog. He reflected that the Germans had a much greater capacity for insult, as they had a greater capacity for suffering. His eyes met those of Wolf, blue and uncompromising as a high country lake. Crawford felt an ecstatic rush of pleasure, that he had Wolf in his power, even as he recognized his greater strength of character. There was no pleasure in mastering the weak.

Then Wolf snapped away his eyes and looked out to sea and started to talk with considerable erudition and hypnotic eloquence about Goethe.

Crawford, enraptured, marked this down as the best moment of his life.

★ ★ ★

Two days later, Rewi was clearing a drain by the old house, of its sludge of soap, hair and balled-up tissues, and thought about the girls whose beautification had caused this drain to block. It could have been any of them, they came and went. It could, he reflected, even be remnants of Mercy among that grey conglomerate of matter. One of Mercy's hairs — perhaps — ginger no, it was that nice word, auburn . . .

He had tried to ignore the worm in the back of his mind. *It'll be over by now*, he told himself comfortably — all safe and sorted, and paid for.

He saw the dust of Crawford's new car coming from the house. The new car had the curved outline of true affluence; Rewi had seen such cars on the other side of the glass in showrooms; he had occasionally wondered what sort of people would, in his terms, tie such an absurd quantity of dosh up inside a piece of swanky tin. Now he knew. People who wanted you to know that they had made it. People whom you seriously wanted to take out and do over, except you got more satisfaction from telling yourself that their kids probably hated them.

★ ★ ★

Crawford's car stopped on the drive. Rewi felt a ball of nausea, as he did every time he thought Crawford was going to speak to him. But instead Crawford merely lowered the window and called out to the contractor who was carefully building defects into the smooth green between the big house and the sea. The golf-course marched on apace even though Rewi pretended otherwise, and made access to facilities as inconvenient as was consistent with obeying his orders.

Rewi turned his back on Crawford and his car and thought it was time he rang Mercy. He wondered what he could say to her, and what point there would be in his saying it. But he felt so strongly that he wanted to hear her a little bit cheerful again that he did not like to examine the feeling for fear it might bite him.

At four o'clock he took the telephone into a corner of his kitchen and dialled Mercy's number. Her mother answered, and he made stilted conversation about a plan he and Dickie had hatched to walk the Heaphy, and would Marg come, and what about Mercy? If Mercy didn't want to tramp, would she be interested in some well-paid baby-sitting. Oh yes, he had children. Mercy had got on with them very well when she was here . . . Is she OK? Marg was enthusiastic about the plan, which meant that Rewi was trapped into it, until he thought of an excuse, but she was entirely non-committal about Mercy, and Rewi's crude attempts at pumping her for information were entirely ineffectual.

Well, Rewi said to himself, *I tried. You can't say I didn't try. I tried quite hard and was quite smart.* But it was unclear quite to whom his protestation was addressed.

Shortly afterwards his phone rang and his heart leapt a little with the notion that Mercy was calling him back. But it was Pete Platt in great jubilation over the birth of his new All Black — ten pounds six ounces and with feet on him the size of a saucer. He described the birth, the first he had attended, in all the loving and ecstatic detail of fathers in this circumstance. Rewi, who remembered vividly, half listened, enjoying, vicariously, the best two hours of his own life. 'Yeah, great, I'll go and see her, where is she, Women's?' He wasn't going to let on to Pete or anyone else that he loved the smell of a newborn baby, and the sensation of the thistledown hair against his skin. He wasn't even going to let on to himself how much he loved it, but he persuaded Zoë that she would really like to see Christine's baby, even though Zoë didn't think she cared much for babies.

'Zoë wants to see the baby,' he told Julie, and repeated the same mantra to Rosalia to explain his absence. Rosalia pursed her mouth up in a most unbecoming way and murmured scraps of complaint about guests that evening and the veranda needing a sweep. Rewi said acidly that sweeping the veranda was not his job, and was it occasionally possible to have his days off, off?

He left Rosalia in a huff and drove all the way into town to the Women's Hospital. Zoë chatted about the Barbie horse and stable set that her best friend Francine had got, and how she, Zoë, didn't want one. Then she chatted about how her other friend Tania was going to Disneyland for Christmas, and how she, Zoë did not want to go to Disneyland yet because she thought she would enjoy it more later. She then described to her father in minute detail every ride and every outsize cartoon character one was likely to encounter in Disneyland. This recital filled up most of the drive and did not require Rewi to respond beyond a grunt. He wanted very much to take his children to Disneyland, in the same way he wanted to buy a yacht and sail around the islands.

The Women's Hospital, vast and unadorned, proclaimed an era when childbirth was centre-stage and nobody's business. Do not enter here, the great white walls declared, unless you are an initiate. Vast women in matron's uniforms seemed to guard the doors.

Rewi's wife had gone for alternative places with water baths and mood music; the Women's was associated in his mind with the purgatory you ended up in if the water birth went wrong. Low mutterings among the midwives.

They had to park way down the street, for all visiting was confined to a narrow space in the afternoons, so as not to interfere with the necessary regimentation of babies and their unruly mothers.

All around Rewi and Zoë people were streaming up to the hospital clutching flowers and teddies and parcels wrapped in paper depicting flowers and teddy bears.

'We need something for the baby!' cried Zoë.

There was no nice flower shop at the entrance to the hospital. They walked into the big avenue and found a dairy, with bunches of dusty flowers out the front. Zoë selected some carnations and went inside and poked around the miscellaneous areas of the shop for something that seemed more present-like to her. Rewi stood and let the front covers of the magazines parade past him. Spice up the Barbeque — new recipes for summer; Christmas novelty knits; the G spot and how to help him find it; Cellulite the silent enemy

— it sometimes seemed to him that women did communicate in a secret language. It wasn't, he thought, that he didn't know the words — it was more that he couldn't see the connection. Why would you call cellulite the silent enemy? Cancer, air pollution, coastal erosion — but cellulite?

Zoë found a fluffy white bear attached to some chocolates, which she deemed suitable, the bear if not the chocolates. They carried their spoils away back towards the hospital.

'This bear is grubby,' said Zoë after an intimate examination. 'We need to clean him.'

So Rewi obediently trekked back to the dairy and bought a white eraser. Zoë plied this vigorously over the bear's fur all the way back to the hospital, giving it a surprised, mottled appearance. Rewi carried the flowers down and to one side, like a package he wished to leave on a bus.

The corridors of the hospital had been polished by an obsessive compulsive. Zoë skated around while Rewi frowned over the notice-board and finally accepted he must ask the guardian behind the grille.

They stood in the gloom of the main hall looking at the lifts — Rewi reluctant to trust such aged machinery for a mere two floors. Bustlers full of the confidence of a new grandchild, pushed past them. Rewi thought of the stairs.

'No I want to go in the *lift*,' Zoë cried, as if this clanking mechanism was the newest ride in the kingdom.

They found Christine without difficulty. She was sitting up in bed in a pink bed-jacket some kind relative had knitted, pinned down by the neatly tucked covers. Ranged around her like a showpiece in a florist's shop were flowers of every pastel shade, interspersed by balloons proclaiming IT'S A BOY and BUNDLES OF JOY, and various teddy bears wearing blue ribbons.

Flanking Christine were a selection of her relatives and friends, large people, who seemed to block out the light. They had the air of those who have moved in for the interim, and regarded the transients with only glancing interest. Rewi chatted to those he knew, and had a hold of the baby, an improbably small and self-contained creature like a shelled walnut. He held the baby's head against his cheek and felt the tenderness that it was inappropriate to show. He remembered his own precious newborn children, and the newborn fear of his inability to protect them adequately, a fear he had never lost.

Zoë held the baby perfunctorily and handed him back, smiling so cheerfully that

Christine's mum made a joke of it.

'No,' said Rewi, 'I don't think there'll be any babies in our house.'

They left their offerings on the end of the bed and trooped away. Just out of earshot, Zoë said, 'I don't want you to have any babies, Dad.'

'You need a mum for that, Zo.'

'I know that, Dad. We do Civics at school.'

Rewi knew better than to ask for an explanation of a subject that had not existed when he was a boy.

'I'm not going to get married again,' he said. 'So no babies.'

'You don't have to be married to have babies.'

They came to a big curved staircase with lovingly polished banisters. As Zoë wanted to slide down these, and Rewi felt that stairs were generally to be preferred to lifts, they went down to the next floor where the corridors seemed to stretch endlessly away into light. Sun streamed in from windows at the ends of the corridors, but the floor was dark and quiet. The dark-stained doors were mostly half shut and there was no mewling of babies or raised laughter of visiting grandparents. The scent of flowers hung over the disinfectant, as on the upper floor, but could have suggested a funeral parlour. A sign pointed them imperiously towards the WAY OUT.

Zoë skipped along the corridor reading out the names off the white cards in little brass holders, to see if anyone else had a name starting with zed, as was her habit, now she could read well.

'Laura Knight. Mrs Feinstein. J. Barford. Why are some of them Mrs and some of them just J.?'

'Perhaps some of them are older ladies who like to be called Mrs.'

She got well ahead of him with her skipping and chanting, so he thought he had misheard her when she read out 'Mrs Dickinson. Angela Brown. Mercy Fisher.'

Various thoughts flashed through his mind — he was hearing things, obsessed by the thought of her, so hearing her name everywhere — that she had had the baby — no of course absurd — another Mercy Fisher — a miscarriage —

He got up to the door, and read the name. Mercy Fisher. He stopped. Zoë came back to haul him onwards, but she also stopped.

'Is that our Mercy?' she asked, although Rewi was only vaguely aware that Zoë had so much as met Mercy. 'Has she had a baby too?'

'I don't expect so,' said Rewi, angry

sickness rising in his stomach.

The door was not closed. Zoë could not be prevented from pushing it open and poking her head round.

'It is!' she said, with far more excitement than the baby had induced. 'It is you, Mercy.'

She would have launched herself on Mercy, with a hug, had not her father caught her by the arm.

Mercy was lying in bed, all alone in the room. There was one vase of garden flowers with the water jug and school books on her locker, and a huge florist's bouquet, lopsided and still in its cellophane, stuck in a vase on the floor. At the end of her bed sat a lumpy collection of teddy bears guarding a big wicker sewing basket from which scraps of bright patterned cloth bled onto the counterpane.

Mercy's face was as white as the sheet drawn up over her breasts. Her eyes had been closed until Zoë burst in. She opened them and produced the ghost of her smile. Even when dimmed Rewi thought it was as lovely a thing as a white beach at sunset.

'Hello Mercy, are you sick?' asked Zoë. 'We came to see Christine's baby.'

'Hi there, how nice to see you,' she said, sitting up. 'No I'm not sick. I'm better now. It's nice to see you.'

Then she burst into tears.

Rewi sat down on the bed. He didn't know why he did this, because this wasn't his scene, nor his doing.

Zoë looked away from Mercy's tears and started to play with and chat about the teddy bears. Rewi wanted to take Mercy's hand, because she was crying and it seemed to him so dreadfully sad.

'I did try and ring him, you know. He went off to Germany. I got Wolfgang to ring.'

'It doesn't matter,' she said, wiping her eyes with her hand and sniffing as if she wanted to put him off. 'Even if he had rung back it wouldn't have made any difference. I'm OK now.'

Rewi was inclined to disagree, but didn't think he could say so.

'I could arrange for someone to beat him up,' he said.

'Don't be silly,' she said. 'What good would that do? That wouldn't . . . '

She started to cry again. Zoë made one of the bears walk up the bed and cuddle up to Mercy. She took the little stuffed body in her arm.

'I guess you can't really — ' Rewi started.

'He's been very kind. He keeps wanting to buy me stuff, like a car was the latest thing, but I can't even drive.'

'You could have lessons. I'd take it if I were you. He's rolling in it.'

'But Mum doesn't know who. And I won't tell her.'

'Why not? You have to tell her something.'

'I just feel so disgusting. I mean he's so *old*.'

'So what did you say?'

'Nothing. And Mum told Dad and the nuns I had an ovarian cyst. She's beaut my mum.'

'My mum went to Australia,' said Zoë.

'You poor kid,' said Mercy.

'She sends us lots of neat presents though. And we're going over there for Christmas aren't we, Dad?'

'Not as far as I know,' said Rewi. 'How long are you in for, Mercy?'

'I don't know — the doctors talk to Mum and whisper away as if I was some kind of moron. I suppose I must be — an idiot anyway.'

'That's crap and you know it.'

'I'm not going back to school, I told them that. The other girls are so bitchy. Those two who came to the party — they're at my school, and they saw Crawford pick me up from school one day, and the story was round the school next day, about like, over fifty and really gross and married and had tried it on

308

them as well but they turned him down. Which just isn't *true*. He didn't even *look* at them.'

Rewi, who had seen Crawford looking appreciatively at many young girls, including the two in question, said nothing.

'You'd better not stay. If Mum found you here, she'd think — She already thinks — '

'Me?' said Rewi.

'You rang up, though.'

'Well if anyone wants to have a go at me, I'll send them straight round to see Crawford.'

'No please don't do that. Please don't. I don't want them to know. It's just so disgusting.'

Rewi was incensed at the thought that he was silently being blamed for harming this poor kid — as if — as if he'd — but what would he have done, he wondered, if one thing had led to another? Well he'd have offered to marry her and braved out the baby, however much he didn't want a baby or a sixteen-year-old. But even if Crawford had done the decent thing, she'd have turned him down. Not that you could imagine Crawford lumbering himself with a baby. No doubt he'd moved heaven and earth to procure an abortion, legal or otherwise. Looked as if he'd made a pig's ear of it, though, for all his money, or she would not be in hospital right now. There was no decent thing for Crawford to do. The only thing he should have done was keep his cock in his trousers to start with. And perhaps have remembered afterwards what he had done.

Rewi felt his loathing for Crawford maturing inside him into a hard round entity, like one of those big cheeses the Dutchmen out at Loburn made. He felt he could cut slices off it to share around and still have plenty to keep him going.

Two more of Mercy's bears made the progress up the bed, one of them wearing a new skirt of red and white flowers. Mercy took them into her arms. Rewi pondered on what he might do to assuage his anger. Then, although not a man for schemes, he came up with a cracker of a good idea.

'Well I'll tell you what, Mercy,' he said. 'I'll make a deal with you. You can let them all think I'm the guilty party if you like — your girlfriends, nuns, priests, what have you — as long as no one comes knocking on my door. But you've got to do something for me.'

'What? I mean, what am I any good for?'

He wondered how to answer this, and was defeated.

'That's crap, Mercy, and you know it.'

'You're good at sewing,' said Zoë riffling

through the workbasket.

Mercy closed her eyes and crushed the bears to her breasts. Rewi had to stomp hard on the thought *lucky teddies.*

'What I want you to do is this, take that bastard for all you can get. Car, clothes, university fees, the lot. I don't care if you think it's too much. Milk him. Get him where it hurts, in the pocket.'

Mercy kept her eyes squeezed shut, but she nodded.

'Will you do that?'

'OK.'

'And keep on doing it, so he never forgets what he's done to you.'

'OK.'

★　★　★

Zoë held his hand as they walked away down the corridor. In the distance, he caught sight of a tall red-haired woman who could only be Marg. He'd met her once or twice, but he wasn't brave enough to face an encounter today. He ducked away hastily down the stairs.

'I didn't understand,' said Zoë.

'You don't need to, Zo, not yet.'

Part III

11

In the middle of the gleaming glass and steel headquarters of the Hollander Estate was the cave of the sorcerer.

Wolf crouched there, much as he had done in the back shed on the Platt farm, neither aged nor improved with the passage of years, the establishment of reputation or a decade of married bliss.

From the windows of his office it was possible to view the perfect ranks of vines, which through tricks of perspective seemed to stretch all the way to the mountains. But Wolf had closed the state-of-the-art blinds against the view, so that his room was perpetually in the half-light of his computer. This helped him concentrate on the screen, he said, where much of his work was done these days. Nobody believed him on either account. It was generally felt in the winery that Wolf blocked out the vines because he could not bear to be reminded of the wealth of the Estate, to which his contribution was incalculable and for which his reward had been imperceptible. As for the computer, although Wolf was mostly to be discovered surfing the Internet, no one had ever seen an article on his screen relating to wine-making. One of the clever young things employed by the French had examined the log of his surfing, and ploughed through a bewildering catalogue of sites, from anarchy to cartoons to learned depositions from German universities, by way of the Jesuits, Neo-Nazis, pornography, art galleries, feng shui, classic car dealers, Beethoven, Frank Zappa, transactional analysis, limericks, French slang and the growing of truffles. It seemed that Wolf was interested in everything except wine-making.

When asked what exactly he did these days Wolf replied that his contract simply required him to be, not to do. He would explain patiently, as if to novitiates, that he employed the best young wine-makers out of college, and while they stayed with him, he would sample their wine once a year and then renew their contracts. He did not make wine, because, he said, only free men could make wine, and he, Wolfgang Mark, was a slave.

His auditors would nod seriously and agree privately that there was no dealing with the German sense of humour.

On a glaring hot day in September 1997 Rewi sought out his friend in the darkness of his office. He picked his way into the room, around the cardboard boxes labelled *Stuff 1991, Mütti, Recipes, Tax 1990*, discarded garments draped over teetering towers of magazines, photographic equipment, miscellaneous old wine-making gear, its red Italian enamel persistently cheerful. Wolf did not look up to see who had entered. He peered at the computer unconcerned that his screen was filled with the interlaced limbs of naked boys.

'Disgusting,' said Rewi. 'I'll tell your wife on you.'

'He likes it too,' said Wolf without turning round. 'It turns him on.'

'Put me off my lunch.'

'Sometimes,' said Wolf, closing down the site, 'I look at the heterosexual sites out of curiosity, and you know, Rewi, I feel the same way.'

He laughed uproariously at his joke, and Rewi found he was joining in, as he always did.

The two men trooped out of Wolf's office into the brilliance of the corridor, where ever more glass proclaimed the searing beauty of the Canterbury landscape. Wolf put his arm over his friend's shoulders. Over the years Rewi had learnt to tolerate the oddities of continental behaviour. There was a part of Rewi that enjoyed confusing people.

One of Wolf's privileges as Chief Vintner was free run of the extremely swanky restaurant which fronted the winery. In theory this was for him to entertain his overseas contacts and important visitors. In practice Wolf took no one to lunch except his rag-taggle of local friends, the scruffier the better. Wolf himself dressed like a man who had once visited a charity shop and been amazed at the bargains. He was always, in Rewi's terms, in need of a shear, and Michael's attempts at smartening him up hung expensive and pristine in the perfect wardrobe in one of the perfect spare bedrooms of their perfect house.

Wolf liked to be very loud on the occasions he took his friends to lunch and to drink beer.

He settled himself at the best table by the picture window, and sprawled back to survey the room.

The French maître d' and the tightly laced serving staff acted as if he were the window cleaner who had mistaken the time.

'They never stoop to complain,' said Wolf. 'They will serve us with the greatest politeness. I complain of course to the management. They should not allow one to lower the tone.'

He called across the room, '*Bitte* two Steinlager.

318

'They are mostly French, of course, though one is Australian and another French-Australian which is the marriage of two evils. What can you expect from a French-Australian? Arrogance and no sense of humour.'

The beer arrived without a word in two tall chilled glasses.

'I will have my usual,' said Wolf to the waitress.

While Rewi ordered, Wolf kept on a stream of talk over the top.

'They have sent faxes to Crawford complaining about me. Why not email I ask? But of course Crawford is not evolved beyond the fax. His replies are very amusing and very beautiful. He writes by hand in an italic, about how I am a living treasure, and he does not wish them to upset me in any way. I love this very much, how he perjures himself.'

'How do you get to read the faxes?'

'In the morning I am here at dawn — I must be here for eight hours, but which eight it does not say. Then after lunch it is time to go home. I read the faxes, the emails.'

'You'd think they would notice that.'

'They become very angry and write to Crawford almost daily. They change their passwords, lock offices — it is no good. I have hours and hours to torment them, and good friends to help me.'

'Wolf, it's bloody stupid, this game. It's not doing you any good. Just get out and do what you always talked of doing, start your own place.'

Wolf laughed uproariously.

'How often have I told you, my friend? It is impossible.'

They had had this conversation before, and Rewi had never understood why Wolf could not or would not break his contract with Crawford. He knew little about law, but he was convinced that all contracts had escape clauses.

'You've told me before, but I still don't get it.'

'I have told you nothing, only that it is impossible.'

Rewi tore into one of the bread rolls. Caraway seeds, why did they have to do that? What was wrong with bread?

'Would you like wine, Herr Mark?'

'No, I would not like wine. I do not drink the wine you serve here. It is not good enough. I will have some of my reserve, but you will not serve it me.'

The waiter sighed like a parent of an autistic child who is destined to play out the same ritual every day of his life.

Wolf leant forward and said in a loud

whisper, clearly audible to many of the diners around him, 'There are several crates of the '94 reserve which they have lost. It is very embarrassing for them. Of course the crates in my garage wait for Dickie Fisher's party.'

Rewi allowed the delivery of his steak — *you can call something by a fancy French name, but it's still steak* — to buy a pause. But then he decided to go for it. With a mouthful of steak, a man feels strangely brave.

'You do know that Crawford is coming to Dickie Fisher's do, don't you?'

Wolf did not know, and Rewi knew that Wolf did not know. He himself had only discovered the day before, when Rosalia dropped one of her elegant little bombshells. *You do know*, she said, *that Crawford is coming out specially for Dickie Fisher's party?* Her words, artful in their casualness, arrested the conversation as effectively as bone china hitting marble. He did not know and did not know what to say. For what had Crawford to do with Dickie Fisher?

Wolf was far too controlled a person to let his surprise and anger show. He might act the boor in the restaurant but his louche behaviour was studied to cause the maximum embarrassment to his enemies.

Rewi watched him concentrate his attention on the food placed before him, bowing his nose low to sniff the salmon, on the off-chance it might have been kept too long, or perhaps frozen.

Then he swept his arm across the table. The tall glass flew onto the tiled floor, spraying beer and shards in a satisfyingly wide arc. All the diners in the restaurant looked up and across at the two of them, but Wolf paid no attention to what he had done.

'I hate him,' he said to the salmon. 'I will not see him.'

Rewi was, as frequently in his dealings with Wolf, confused.

'But he's your boss. How can you avoid seeing him?'

The maître d' came over to their table and stood guard while lowlier forms of life brought out the dustpan and brush and the bucket and cloths. He said nothing to Wolf, but disdain was written on his face in block capitals.

'When Crawford is in this country, I am on my holiday. Or sick. It is easy to be sick when Crawford is nearby.'

'You should deal with this situation,' said Rewi, wondering to himself if he had ever dealt with a situation, or indeed ever had one to deal with.

'A bucket should do it,' said Wolf laughing uproariously. 'What is it, you kick the bucket? Let Crawford kick the bucket.'

Rewi wondered vaguely who would inherit the Hollander estates, what would happen to Rosalia and his job should Crawford kick the bucket.

'You want him to die?'

'No, I want to kill him.'

The maître d', who could not help overhearing this conversation, fetched a deep patient sigh. Rewi felt much the same way.

After lunch Wolf took him for a tour of the great processing engine behind the glass and wooden showplace. The attendant in a white coat told him he couldn't take a visitor in for health and safety reasons. Wolf was genial and offensive all at once and carried on. There was nothing to see. There had been nothing to see in Wolf's winery since he was shifted out of the back shed of the farm. The stainless steel vats reared from floor to roof. There were rooms with glass fronts and bottling machinery beyond. In the bond store were rank upon rank of new bottles, cardboard boxes of wine labels, and great plastic bags of oak chips.

'Chips!' said Wolf. 'Oak chips. They use them instead of barrels to give the taste.' He spat. 'They take not plastic corks which everyone knows are better, and use oak chips.'

He took a penknife out of his pocket, opened the longest blade and split a bag of oak chips across its belly. A stream of dark chips of wood issued out onto the perfect concrete floor with a soft clatter. Wolf walked on.

'They have left me a few casks,' he said, 'because they hope to keep me quiet. And they hope to show the important people.'

They passed into a dark adjoining room, a cathedral of great oak barrels. Wolf stroked them as if they were cart-horses.

'Why is he coming to the party?' Wolf asked. 'He is no friend of Dickie Fisher's.'

'Rosalia was a bit vague. Something to do with Mercy.'

'Mercy?' asked Wolf, theologically confused.

'Dickie's youngest. I think he is paying her fare.'

'She is his mistress.'

This explanation of events had not occurred to Rewi. He tried to equate the pale girl clutching her teddy bears to the word *mistress*. And failed.

'I don't know.'

'He will have a mistress, you may be sure of that.'

Rewi shrugged his shoulders. These European ideas left him cold. New Zealand men had bits on the side, embarrassments or transitions to the next marriage; they did not have mistresses.

'I do not see,' said Wolf, caressing the flank of a barrel, 'why Rosalia did not say no, it was not convenient for him to come. Such a simple thing to say. She is so weak.'

'You've got to understand poor old Rosie's situation. It's Crawford's house, and he lets her use it for her paying guests. He doesn't take any money out, but the business is all technically his. In return she has to do what he wants. Like last month we had to cancel all the bookings for December because Crawford had arranged a visit for his Korean partners — the ones who developed the golf-course with him. He wanted to block-book the house, and that was that. Rosalia can be as stubborn as a goat, but she can't say no to Crawford. I've never understood why.'

'Crawford has a nose for weakness. Rosalia is weak, which is why she plays at being so impossible. But Crawford is not deceived.'

Wolf led the way through the dark aisle to a door marked FIRE EXIT ONLY. He pushed the bar to open it.

'Isn't that alarmed?'

'It may have been, but it is not alarmed any

longer,' Wolf said. 'I have all the passwords to all the systems. I like to go out of the building this way, so they cannot discover me.'

The fire exit gave onto a big concrete yard around the back. Here two men in brown coats were messing about with a forklift truck. The floor of the yard was perfectly flat, the storage sheds had large metal doors which closed flush. There was no miscellaneous stuff lying about, only tidy piles of boxes on their way in or out. It was hard to tell that grapes were the raw material and pleasure the end result of this operation.

The two men wandered into the yard. Wolf greeted the storemen with a wave, which was cordially returned.

'You get on OK with them?'

'I am the friend of all workers here. My enemies are the managers and their lackeys.'

Wolf led the way to the big steel gates. Beyond lay plains, apparently empty except for the regimented rows of Mayaud vines, stretching away into the brightness of the mountains. The light was too bright to bear. Wolf put on a pair of sunglasses which made him look even more like a terrorist. Rewi scrunched up his eyes against the light.

'You can just see it,' said Wolf. 'My windmill.'

'I don't reckon you can, Wolfgang.'

'In my mind's eye you can see it. Every day when it becomes intolerable, I come outside the door and look at my windmill, and I know that one day, when Crawford is dead, I will be over there by my windmill, picking my own grapes and making my own wine.'

After a while Rewi could see it too, lazily flexing its blades in the beginnings of a wind. Every year for the last five he had helped Wolf harvest the grapes from his plot in the saddle of the foothills. Every year for the past five he had driven Wolf's entire crop of grapes to market, because Wolf would not make so much as a drop of wine on his own account.

'Why don't you tell him to get stuffed, Wolf?'

'If you knew that, Rewi, you would know what Crawford knows, which no one else must know.'

Rewi chewed on this admission for a while. In all the time he had known Wolf, no mention had ever been made of a secret. He thought better than to follow up on the information just yet.

'What shall we do then?' asked Wolf.

'About what, mate?'

They wandered out of the double doors towards the car park. Rewi's old truck stood awkwardly head and shoulders above the sleek late-model Japanese and French cars, like an amiable uncle who has wandered into a teenagers' party.

'Crawford, about Crawford. I will not breathe the same air as him, but Michael must go to the party, or he will not be forgiven, and I must go with Michael, or I will not be forgiven.'

'It's only for one night.'

'You don't understand the nature of hatred.'

'Actually,' said Rewi, 'I hate the bugger too.'

'Why?'

'I can't tell you that.'

'Also,' said Wolf.

Rewi climbed into the cab of his truck. He had to shout as he started her up. 'Thanks for lunch, mate. You coming out in the weekend? To plan Dickie's party?'

Wolf frowned in the general direction of his windmill. He might have been a romantic hero looking out at the plain on which the fate of nations was bloodily determined. After a long pause he said, 'Yes, Rewi, I will come. I think we should make this party an evening for Crawford Hollander unforgettable. Let us form a welcoming committee.'

★ ★ ★

The sole pleasure of flying is not to fly economy class.

Crawford argued with Mercy over her determination not to join him in first, but once he had graciously admitted defeat, he was able to indulge in this simple pleasure to a double degree. The discomforts of other people's flight were embodied in Mercy herself.

London to Hong Kong he tried to content himself with dozing and reading. He worked his way through *The Wine Trader, Vintage Wine, Bloomberg Money*. Genista was no use at all. She had a worthy novel on her lap, but clamped on headphones and laughed her way through hour after hour of film.

Crawford amused himself by watching the cabin staff compete for his favour. He speculated on which one would be the most entertainingly delicious, but soon tired of this, as memories of the intense tedium of such encounters threatened to engulf him.

Time in Hong Kong was very agreeable. His two women were in high spirits and suffered him to spend a great deal of money on them, Genista exhibiting her perfect good taste and discrimination, and Mercy her naïve and bottomless glee in expensive things.

Crawford had cause to congratulate himself that Genista and Mercy got on so exceptionally well. He attributed this to his careful planning and shrewd judgement of character.

There was one episode, however, which clouded his happiness. On the last day in Hong Kong he and Genista were breakfasting in their room, pausing between bites of toast to look out on the morning buzz of the city. The exigencies of booking travel obliged him to share a suite with Genista, but he looked on this as a sort of holiday experience.

'I am so excited,' Genista said. 'I have always wanted to go to New Zealand — practically all my life. The Commander was so in love with it, he talked about it constantly — especially the West Coast.'

'I'm surprised he could remember anything about it at all.'

'Crawford, there is no need to conduct a lifelong campaign against the Commander. He's been dead long enough, poor dear, and there was not a jot of harm in him. He loved your sister to distraction.'

'Then he had an eccentric way of exhibiting his feelings.'

Genista ignored this remark.

'And although he didn't love me in the same way, for which I am rather grateful, he was devoted to me, charming to be with, and endlessly grateful.'

'And so he should have been — since you contributed everything, youth, possessions, energy, good humour — and Niall, as far as one can tell, contributed nothing, except a wonderful opportunity for you to be kind.'

'Which only goes to show how little you understand about relationships!'

'On the contrary, I understand a very great deal, by honest and unsentimental observation. I do not let my vision become blurred by such vaporous things as expressions of love and outbursts of good intention.'

'You are altogether a superior being,' said Genista, with a perfectly straight face.

* * *

On the flight from Hong Kong to Christchurch, boredom threatened to kill Crawford.

He took himself down from the blessed realms to find Mercy. She was seated next to a lean, youngish man, in expensive, casual clothes, with no wedding ring. He and Mercy were watching the same tacky action movie on their personal screens, with a headphone on one ear, so that they could exchange remarks and hear each other laughing.

Alarm bells rang in Crawford's head. He had seen this before — so many times. He did not want to deal with yet another entanglement of Mercy's. He had enough to deal with already on arrival in New Zealand: the possible hotel development of his house, and

Rosalia's reaction to it; the hysterical complaints of his New Zealand managers against the insubordination of Wolfgang . . . The extra burden imposed by Mercy chasing some man the length of New Zealand was not to be endured.

She removed the headphone.

'What do you want, Crawford?' she said.

'To underline to you the folly of refusing my offer.'

'I'm having a good time.'

'But first class affords so much more comfort for casual copulation. The lavatories are so much more spacious. It depends on one's proclivities, of course.'

He cast a surreptitious glance at Mercy's neighbour to see how he was taking it. Satisfactorily, he looked properly uncomfortable.

'Piss off, Crawford. We're enjoying the movie.'

'I can see that. Though I don't suppose the film has a great deal to do with it.' And just in case the man had the idea that Crawford was a kind relative, he leant down, placed one hand firmly on Mercy's left breast, and kissed her roundly on the mouth. Then departed for the upper realms, swiftly, before she could counter-attack.

His tactic must have worked, because when

he strolled past two hours later, she was reading *Captain Corelli's Mandolin* and crying, and her neighbour was asleep.

★ ★ ★

Rewi, for the most part, lived in the Hollander bungalow in great comfort with his children — now so large and determined that he failed to recognize them, except when he recognized Janis in them, and wished he had not.

The bungalow was very well appointed. It had not been designed for any mere farm worker, but built and decked out for the older Hollanders themselves. Old man Hollander, Crawford's father, had intended to remove himself there, as soon as Crawford married. It had not occurred to him that Crawford might not marry, or, when married, might not wish to take over the family halls. In the event, although the bungalow was fitted with the latest everything, and caught the sun in every nook and cranny, and had a wonderful view of the harbour, it was all a waste, since the old man died before Crawford evicted him. His widow packed up and moved to a tiny warm flat in Wellington, with her sister and her sister's cats, and purred out her days with bridge and concerts. Crawford installed his sister in his New Zealand mansion, and she, in turn, installed Rewi in the bungalow.

Rewi was still amused by this, years and years later. It amused him every time he cleaned up his whiz-bang kitchen, or sat on the patio in the sun enjoying a fag and a beer and watching the sea change colour. It amused him in the winter when he wrapped the little house around him and stayed warm; it amused him when he sat on the loo with his legs stretched right out, while Zoë was camped out in the other bathroom getting ready.

The house, with all its understated comforts, was one reason he was still here. The house, the sea and the bush up behind. The house gave him comfort and stability, the sea and the bush so close reminded him of what was out there waiting, as soon as he was free. He should have been happy, and he told himself most days that he was. Of course he was happy.

He was whistling in the shower, enjoying the easy-to-keep gleam of it all, the venetian stripes of early evening sun on the tiles, when the bathroom door opened and Julie walked in. He felt no embarrassment, though considerable irritation. But instantly checked himself, recognizing Julie's need to assert their relationship, and then deny its importance. He did not know why she did this to him, except to pass on some kind of hurt, and because he felt sorry for her, he let it pass.

'I've come to take you to the pub,' she announced.

'No can do. Sorry. I'm up to the big house for dinner.'

He turned off the water, even though it provided a great excuse for mishearing.

'I know you are. She's having one of her private dos, isn't she? I saw the poofs arrive in their sports car. So of course she doesn't want me around.'

'You wouldn't enjoy it much,' Rewi said. 'Fancy food and smart talk. I don't.'

'So why go then?'

'Because Rosalia likes to have me there.'

He came out of the shower cubicle and started to dry himself vigorously (clean towel — good housekeeper, Rewi). She watched him derisively, as if he had let a once-fine body go recklessly to seed. Since he was rather vain about his body, for all its middle-aged outlines, he took this amiss. She was a fine one to sneer!

'Well I need you to take me to the pub.'

'I can't. Get Brian to take you. Isn't that what husbands are for?'

'I can't go with him. Besides he wouldn't.

335

He won't stir out of his shed after tea. And Dwayne will be there.'

'Oh gee yes, Dwayne. I forgot.'

So that was it. He was to take Julie to the pub, walk in, buy her a drink, sit in the corner and exchange a few laughs and yarns, while she positioned her charms near enough to the pool table for Dwayne to notice. Then he was to bugger off and leave her.

He wrapped the towel around his waist and went into his bedroom. She followed him in and watched critically while he finished drying and stepped into his underpants.

'Dressing up?' she said as he took a newly ironed shirt, his favourite emerald-green Italian number, from the wardrobe.

'You know Rosalia,' he said.

'I don't see why you have to do things for her. You don't owe her anything. You don't have to get dressed up like a toyboy and dance attendance on her.'

'I like the nosh,' said Rewi.

He wanted to explain that he owed nobody anything, nobody in the whole world — not the memory of his wife, not his kids, not Julie, not Rosalia, not the bank, the Hollanders, neither God nor the devil. No one owed him or owned him. He thought this fleetingly, and then wondered why he did not feel a free man.

Julie gave him her considered opinion of the food Michael extruded. Half-listening, Rewi grinned at her thinly disguised envy. Poor bitch, he thought, poor bitch, makes everything hard.

'Michael's a sad case,' he said, to cheer her up. 'He's so temperamental he can't hold down a job anywhere. If he didn't cook for Rosalia occasionally, he'd go mad. I just wish that silly bugger Wolfgang would open up his restaurant. At least if there was a crisis in the kitchen, the management would be sympathetic.'

'Well why won't he?' asked Julie, her envy temporarily fed.

'Don't know,' said Rewi, stepping neatly into his best jeans. 'He won't leave Hollanders Wines, but he won't explain why.'

'Of course he's foreign.'

Rewi thought of nothing to say, so busied himself in front of the mirror.

'Are you wearing that jewellery?' she asked.

He made no answer, since he was clearly putting on the silver and malachite bracelet that Rosalia had given him one Christmas.

'Don't you think it's a bit poofy?'

'Do you think I'm a closet gay, Jules?' he said grinning at her in the mirror. He flapped his wrist in imitation of Michael, and stuck out his arse. She scowled.

'What will they say in the pub?'

'I wasn't going to the pub.'

In the end, he took her anyway.

'Tell you what,' he said, his foot on the running board of the truck. 'I'll do you a deal. I'll take you down, buy you a drink, then I'll disappear. You can tell that Dwayne that the bastard Rewi has buggered off because he's jealous, and he'll take you home. Or to his place. Or whatever.'

'Don't be disgusting,' she said, but she must have accepted his terms because she climbed in.

★ ★ ★

So he was late. He parked the truck behind the sheds and walked through the shadows towards the house. He was looking forward to the evening. Michael was giving them one of his dinners, and Dickie was coming over to work on the details for his party. Wolf had called it a meeting of the Welcoming Committee.

Rewi enjoyed the notion — it gave a focus to their anger and affront that Crawford had invited himself where he was entirely unwanted. It allowed them to speculate about endless practical jokes and minor acts of revenge, without admitting to their hatred or its causes. Indeed Dickie was surprised at Wolf and Rewi's enthusiasm for the project, for neither of them had told Dickie, or each other, what particular cause he had to hate Crawford Hollander. Dickie was quite open about his own dislike and its origins, and by their silence was forced to assume that Rewi and Wolf disliked Crawford merely because he was as easy to dislike as to envy.

Various projects had been mooted — getting the whole Fisher clan to appear at the airport with banners and babies was one favourite, but it was felt that this would seem no more than a genuine welcome for Mercy, which Crawford would calmly ignore. The Fisher clan had no animus against Crawford — and Rewi was not going to be the one to tell them that he had raped their sister. Sabotaged vehicles, joke cushions, fraudulent dinner invitations, repackaged wine — these were some of the many jests that the Welcoming Committee had come up with, rocking with vulgar and, it must be admitted, drunken laughter. But they were coming to the conclusion that the party itself had to be structured around the humiliation of Crawford, and that whatever was done to him must hurt, and hurt seriously. Rewi found that he himself, now he was forced to consider Crawford Hollander regularly, was visited by fantasies of hurting Crawford so seriously and repeatedly that his smug face was miraculously transformed into a demonic mask.

He did not know he had such imaginings in him. He remembered the odd occasion from school — rumbles, punch-ups, encounters with the bullies — but he had never consciously plotted violence. He did not think he was consciously plotting violence now, but none the less the images rose and stayed in his mind, and contaminated the conversation.

He walked through the darkness behind the sheds trying to slough off these thoughts, and restore himself to the good humour that was the normal mode, at least of the surface man. He did not know about the man below the surface, because he was not given to introspection.

A big sleek car came along the drive towards the house. Rewi was a little surprised because he hadn't known anyone else was invited to dinner. It was typical of Dickie though — the world was his friend, and he often forgot that for every person fed at the table, someone had to cook the extra portion. Rewi hoped fervently that Michael had been warned, or they would never scrape him off the ceiling.

He was heartened by the thought of new arrivals. He was always hopeful when new people arrived at the house — as they did most weeks for some reason or other. He was always hopeful when he went to a party, as he walked in the door, looked around the room, that she'd be there — the funny, sexy, kind-hearted woman of the right age for him, free from neuroses and nonsense — earthy, bold, flexible, calm and passionate all at once. He didn't think he expected too much, but he was none the less constantly disappointed. In the places he went there were women aplenty — lots of them of the right age too, since he was flexible in this regard. He wasn't obsessed by looks or body shape either; he had early on in his sexual career discovered that there was almost an inverse relationship between conventional beauty and what he would term sexiness. He did not know why things never worked out for him. Sometimes he thought it was his ambivalent relationship with Rosalia that smothered relationships at birth; sometimes he blamed his own fear of abandonment. Other days he thought it was because he had an image in his head that no one quite matched. Deep down, he suspected, he was a perfectionist, and if he couldn't have *her*, he'd just get by. But who was *she*?

Mostly he didn't think about it, hoped momentarily and then threw the hope away.

But tonight as he made his way towards the house, hearing the big car stop on the gravel, and doors slam, and voices he did not recognize, he realized that he had become depressed, deep down gloomy. He was well turned forty, and he was more or less alone, except for his obligations, and it was a sad place to be.

He heard Dickie's voice rumbling through the darkness, a cheering sound, no matter the circumstances. He could hear Rosalia's voice soaring and diving like a seagull with pretensions, but not Wolf's laugh. Why not? Wolf should be installed on the veranda by now, beer in one hand, gesticulation in the other, in full joke or rant. Dickie matching him joke for joke, but deflecting the rants with anecdote. No Marg, of course. Marg spent her weekends in the bush, leading groups of women into the wild, strong legs in shorts, thick woolly socks and tramping boots. Rewi offered to go along and carry the bags. *All those women!* he'd say. *Precisely why you're forbidden,* Marg would reply. *They'll pay to be allowed to carry their own bags.* Rewi confessed to not understanding women at all.

The lights upstairs in the big house went

on — flash, flash, flash, all of them, one after another, and illumination poured into the grounds. Such a waste! Rosalia abhorred waste, even the paying guests found lights turned off behind them.

But these lights stayed on. The voices were dimmed — the visitors must have gone inside.

Rewi stepped into the house, entering by the front door. The entrance hall was piled with expensive luggage. He looked at it in surprise. No guests were expected this weekend. He examined the labels, as was his right to do, and swore viciously under his breath. So much for the Welcoming Committee. Crawford and his entourage had already arrived.

★   ★   ★

Rewi stood in the hall counting the bags, amazed that anyone needed so many. He didn't know about the cost of luggage, but he knew that the Louis Vuitton shop in town was one he wouldn't venture into. And it was mostly new, except for one wonderfully battered leather suitcase with manly straps and the labels of priority clubs for four different airlines.

He heard voices upstairs, and voices from

the kitchen. Dickie and Wolf had retreated to help or calm Michael, Rosalia was allocating bedrooms and pointing out the facilities. She was inordinately proud of the fact that between them, she and Rewi had installed *en-suite* bathrooms in the six largest rooms. While Rewi was standing eyeing the luggage, knowing full well it had been left there for him to carry up, Mercy came downstairs.

It was more than ten years since he had last seen her, a pale girl with her teddy bears, and now she was a woman, as solid as a Stalinist statue of Mother Russia, and as splendid. She was frowning a bit as she came down, perhaps because the cases were heavy and she felt she should take hers up all the same. She was wearing jeans, which might have been a mistake, had she cared to conceal the generous proportions of her body, and a check shirt whose buttons seemed to have a mind of their own. Her hair was lank from travelling, but was the same golden red he remembered, perhaps less abundant and glossy than it had been, but then the poor girl had been living in England for years.

She saw Rewi standing in the hall, and her face broke into the smile that he had not forgotten, at once innocent and inviting. It was so broad and encompassing that it seemed to take over her whole person, and you could hardly believe that such a mouth fitted, even in her big and handsome face. Rewi received the smile, looked in her eyes and knew he was a lost cause.

'It's you!' she said. 'The one I used to pretend was — '

'Rewi.'

'I wouldn't forget your name! Not after all that . . . So you're still here — still with Rosalia.'

'And you're still with Crawford.'

'Ah, no, you see, I'm not *with* Crawford.'

'And I'm not *with* Rosalia.'

'Oh good!' she said, then covered her mouth as they both laughed.

She came down the stairs, avoiding his eyes now, because they both knew perfectly well where they were headed. She stood among the suitcases and tried the handles of hers.

'I'll take them up,' he said.

'No it's OK. Serves me right for bringing so many presents for the family.'

'I'm going to take all the others up,' he said, 'so I might as well do yours. I'm probably stronger than you.'

'Yes, but it's a matter of principle.'

'Well I can't thread a needle, so if you fix the button on my work trousers, we'd be square.'

'But I could easily teach you to sew.'

'And you could easily do a bit of manual work round here and get stronger. But we've still got to fix what we've got now.'

'Fair enough,' she said. 'I'll take the lighter one.'

Rewi picked up her larger case, which indeed was surprisingly heavy, and another one to counterbalance it, not, he swore, to demonstrate his strength. They struggled up the stairs. Rewi dumped one case and followed Mercy along the corridor.

'Are you staying here?'

'Well I am supposed to be going home, but there's some sort of classic Dad confusion — he's redecorating my room, and it's not finished.' She laughed merrily. Rewi smiled, recalling Dickie's reputation as a perpetually overextended DIYer.

'He hasn't changed a bit!' she said, as if it were the best thing in the world.

'We weren't expecting you tonight.'

'No, that's a typical piece of Crawford behaviour. He doesn't want to be met at the airport in case people are not sufficiently pleased to see him. Poor Rosalia, poor Dad, having their dinner ruined.'

'Poor Michael,' said Rewi, feeling that *poor Rewi* might be more appropriate. 'So you're in here?'

She was in the third best room, done out in

blue and scarlet tartan, with polished kauri floorboards and a bed the size of the *Ark Royal*. Rewi eyed the bed, though he'd taken cases into that room a thousand times before. Then wished he hadn't because she saw the direction of his glance, and laughed gorgeously.

'And Crawford will be *right next door*, listening out for every creak.'

'Let me get you a drink.'

'I'd kill for one, but let me help you with the cases first. I couldn't enjoy it while you were working.'

'You could admire me.'

'I could.'

They laughed and went out of the room together, to meet Genista in the passageway. Mercy introduced her to Rewi.

'I've heard about you! You are Rosalia's rock!' said Genista. 'It is so kind of you to bring up our bags. One does feel so pathetic.'

Mercy and Rewi were making short order of the suitcases when Dickie emerged from the kitchen, glass of wine in hand. Behind, before the door swung shut, came the tempest of Michael and Wolf's joint and separate unhappiness.

Dickie, these days, was shaped like an elongated barrel, but his beard had kept pace, and jutted out in sympathy with his stomach.

He twinkled, not with any sort of sanitized Father Christmas jollity, but with the dangerous cheer of a Visigoth cowed by a little Irish monk.

'My little girl!' cried Dickie. 'You're not making her work, Rewi, old man!'

'She insists. Modern women.'

Dickie insisted also, and between the three of them the cases were taken up and distributed. Crawford was in the bathroom when his cases were taken into his room, so it wasn't necessary for anyone to speak to him.

Rewi took the two female guests into the billiard room and poured them a drink. Dickie propped up the bar as was his habit when at Hollander House and admired his daughter out loud at length.

Rewi and Genista chatted, or more precisely Genista told Rewi amusing stories about going shopping in Hong Kong with Crawford and Mercy. Then Crawford and Rosalia came downstairs talking nineteen to the dozen, and Rewi slipped off to the kitchen to calm Michael down, and see if it were remotely possible to feed three more. It was all right, Wolf said, he and Michael would not join that man at table. If Rewi were in solidarity with them there would be three less. The speech went on for some time, but as it was mostly in German Rewi only followed the gist.

'But I'm hungry,' Rewi protested, drooling slightly over Michael's hors-d'oeuvres.

He was told to take the horrid things away, so before Michael changed his mind he took out the great platter, so pretty it seemed a shame to eat them.

Dickie, slumping on the bar, ignored by Crawford, was silent. Rewi murmured to him that Wolf was dangerously drunk and should stay in the kitchen.

'I'll go and keep him there.'

He wandered off, followed not long afterwards by his daughter. From the kitchen came raised voices and laughter. Rewi sighed and checked the settings on the table. Would they like to eat now? he suggested, conscious of the six gins inside Rosalia.

'Oh no, we are not hungry,' said Crawford, addressing Rewi for the first time, but without any recognition. 'No matter how often one flies, one is never *quite* inured to airline food.'

'Well I am ravenous,' said Genista. 'The smells from the kitchen are simply divine. I didn't realize you had such a resident cook, Rosalia, as well as such a wonderful steward.'

Rewi didn't know he was the steward, but he quite liked it.

Genista got up and went to the table. Rewi

blessed her for it and sat her down. The others trailed in her wake as if eating was a tiresome formality like queuing for stamps.

'I say,' said Genista confidentially to Rewi, 'it does sound like a good party in the kitchen.'

Rewi replied in an undertone that the other two might notice if they slipped out.

Crawford explained at length over dinner to the admiring audience of his sister, his various acquisitions and sly pieces of business over the past year or two.

'Goodness,' said his wife, 'I had no idea you were so successful, Crawford. The settlement's going to be even better than I thought.'

Rewi, who was hoeing into the claret on the grounds that it was the one Crawford had specifically requested, laughed more loudly than was altogether polite. Crawford gave him a look which said quite clearly that an employee was only tolerated at table because he pleasured the mistress, and she might one day embarrass them all by marrying him.

Rewi liked being talked to by Genista, though he couldn't fathom why she was married to that man. Some of his attention, however, was concentrated on the kitchen, and wondering if he could somehow persuade Mercy to go for a stroll on the beach, or up into the bush. He was a bit ashamed of himself for this adolescent urge, and cross with himself for only half-attending to this exceptionally pleasant Englishwoman, but his urge to dally would not go away simply because of his discomfort.

He found plenty of excuses to go into the kitchen to fetch parts of the dinner. Mercy was playing camp mother magnificently, and was being allowed to help, which was unheard of in Michael's kitchen. She was wearing an apron around her waist which pulled her shirt down in such a way that one could hardly fail to notice what it failed to contain. Dickie, now officially pie-eyed, was slumped over one of the kitchen islands, watching her every move with adoration.

There was so much commotion in the kitchen, with Michael's banging of lids and Wolf's preaching, that Rewi was able to make his suggestion without being overheard.

'Yes,' she said. 'But first I'll have to put Dad to bed here, he's not going home like that. I can't believe Mum's gone tramping. I mean at her age.'

Rewi didn't mention the many occasions on which Dickie, widowed for a weekend, had wobbled his way back to town miraculously preserved. He maintained that the bike knew the way home by the back streets, where no cop was ever known to venture.

'I'll meet you back of the old house at eleven,' he said, feeling every inch a seventeen-year-old going on forty-five.

12

It had been lovely to come home. Crawford felt such extraordinary satisfaction at seeing how well his plans had worked out. The golf-course, even in the darkness, smooth and pampered, the drive to the house clear of the broken branches and stray structures that blighted the approaches to many a grand old New Zealand house. And the house itself so well kept and imaginatively decorated, something only a commercial motivation could have achieved. Nothing would have inspired Rosalia to have performed such wonders with the old place had she rattled around in it with a few singing pupils and the odd resident penniless painter, as would doubtless have been her fate had not Crawford had a care for her future, and for the preservation of his house.

Immediately on his arrival he went into each room of the house in turn to see what had been done. The front bedrooms had been redecorated on his last visit, but he noted the continuous improvements — a new Italian shower, handsome kauri towel-horses. Rosalia must keep a sharp eye on the place for deterioration, because there was scarcely a frayed edge or a faded surface to be seen. This seemed so out of character for her that Crawford, opening and shutting the glass door of a bathroom cupboard to try the hinge, was forced to consider that it might be her factotum's doing.

After he had inspected the front bedrooms he turned into the western quarter of the house, intending to look through the rooms one by one, but on a whim went to the back of the house. There had once been a long narrow room, with big windows looking out of the back of the house towards the hills and trees, but with a glimpse of sea and hill out of the very furthest on the eastern end. The family had claimed it as a picture gallery, although they had little more than an etiolated collection of water-colours and portraits of a couple of starchy Hollanders in wing collars. It had dark-varnished boards and striped wallpaper. Crawford had annexed it as his music room. In it had stood his grand piano, the harpsichord he assembled from a kit sent from England, his cello and the big desk at which he wrote his music. To this room as a boy he invited select company to play chamber music, and here sometimes Rosalia was allowed to bring her performance *Lieder* and arias to try out. Even after he put away childish things and concentrated all his efforts on making his business fly, he kept the piano polished and the ink fresh in his pen, and sheets of perfect manuscript paper in the drawer should inspiration catch him unawares. He played from time to time, well-oiled favourites, gazing out of the windows at the variously lovely views the different windows presented. Rosalia had sent him plans and sketches and photographs, so he was well aware that his long gallery had been transformed into two smart rooms with a bathroom between them, all, as the brochure said, *with interconnecting doors, to make one charming if idiosyncratic suite, with views of forest and sea!*

But the shock was greater than he cared to admit, as he opened the door of the end room, and saw in place of the long vista of his artistic dream, a little bright square room, with thick white carpet, white and yellow curtains, a quilted bedcover, frilled bedside mats in white and yellow, and a nice armchair in white and yellow which positively insisted that one sit down in it to enjoy the view.

Into his memory flooded a piece of music, *Death and the Maiden*, not as played by himself and his friends at fourteen, but by the Juilliard. But the memory of playing it intertwined with the music itself, and he could see his own forearm and fingers, and the extraordinary moment when they got something right, and nothing else in the whole world mattered.

He felt an absurd desire to go downstairs at once and assuage his melancholy at the piano. But they would laugh at him, successful middle-aged man regretting his youth. He did not regret his youth; he had taken control of it and dispensed with it.

He shut the door of the truncated room firmly, and looked into each of the others firmly. The job had been done extremely well; the revenues from the house were generally satisfactory, which was just as well since the drawings sent through by his partners in the golf-course for a hotel were positively mouth-watering. It would be a pity to gut the place for a gloriously elegant frontispiece, when it had so recently had quite a bit spent on it — poor return on investment — though actually when one thought about it, the work had been done for remarkably little. Crawford trawled through the account books in his head and nodded appreciatively at how cost-effective the latest round had been. Which meant of course, that it was less of an issue to throw it all away, given that the returns on the hotel would be in rather a different league. But the Japanese and Korean golf-tourism markets had not really quite recovered, and although one wanted to be slightly ahead of the recovery, having the facility ready more or less when the punters were ready for it, the venture capitalists did not see it in quite the same way. Crawford privately thought that a cautious venture capitalist was a contradiction in terms, and found it hard to believe that anyone would doubt his business nose. But facts must be faced, and in the meantime everyone was very happy with Hollander House as it was, and Crawford was determined they should all enjoy their holiday there.

But he sensed trouble ahead. He walked down his staircase, wafting expensive soap, and saw that Mercy was under siege already, and her gates were wide open.

He appeared to pay no attention of course, since to do so would merely alert her, and entice her to annoy him. But he was acutely aware of the way the man's eyes followed Mercy, and how eager he was to follow her into the kitchen. When she came out steaming with laughter and kitchen heat, he could tell at once that she had made an assignation with him, because they never so much as glanced at each other. He pondered what his course should be? Sarcasm or intervention?

Both had their role in keeping Mercy safe. Sarcasm usually helped her see an admirer in a different light, and intervention tested the man's metal, which inevitably proved to be inferior.

Crawford assessed his rival without appearing to pay him any attention whatsoever. He knew a great deal about him already. He had been with Rosalia for over a decade, her unacknowledged lover, very tawdry, the gamekeeper without the sex appeal; he was forty something — young compared with Crawford himself, but far too old for Mercy. He was dull, unsophisticated and penniless. All Crawford really needed to do was point out to Mercy his age and charmlessness, and his long, rather sordid association with Rosalia, and she'd turn tail.

Mercy liked the things his money could buy. She liked travel and dressing up in a new frock and going to the opera; she liked dining at the smart new restaurant and being taken by him to little cocktail parties. She liked riding in his car, and taking his arm for a stroll around the picnic grounds at Glyndebourne. What could this Rewi possibly offer her instead?

Under Rosalia's prattle of long-discarded friends he pondered his strategy. How long should he let things go? Tomorrow surely she should be packed off to her parents' house, and it could be contrived that she didn't get near him again. Until the party . . . now there was a risk. Mercy was notorious at parties. And in this place there were so many cracks to disappear into . . . He was probably only likely to make a pantalone of himself if he attempted to prevent her rutting with that man.

And besides it did her good to experience a certain amount of raw sex from time to time, to remind her just how dull the conversation became afterwards. She had a considerable appetite for sex, which needed to be fed occasionally (a fact that gave Crawford great vicarious satisfaction), in a manner that did not end with the poor creature going off the rails. A short vigorous holiday fling would probably do her no harm; at forty-odd this man's performance would be starting to go off, and flab was creeping about him. He was not an Adonis to whom she might become addicted. She would be whisked away home soon enough, and one could imagine the sort of letters that man would write, if he wrote at all, which was unlikely.

On balance, Crawford decided that he could turn a blind eye to the pair of them, though he saw no reason to smooth their path.

He savoured his wine and picked at his plate — admittedly garnished with very good food indeed. Wolfgang's rudeness was upsetting him. The loud German voice could be clearly heard, his great vulgar laugh forming a duet with Dickie's.

Crawford calculated when he had last spoken to Wolf directly. Although he could work it out almost to the day, he flinched from doing so. Wolf's ingratitude hurt him — it was the only thing in the world that hurt Crawford. It was the injustice that embittered him — for had not Crawford made Wolfgang into a vintner with an international reputation, given him everything that money could buy, and turned the blindest of eyes to his disgraceful, childish behaviour? For year after year.

And now not even to come out to greet him. Indeed Crawford knew that Wolf had fled into the kitchen on hearing his master's voice.

It occurred to him, winding strands of seaweed around his fork, while Rosalia explained at length the comings and goings and escapades of her regular guests, that he might simply walk into the kitchen and confront Wolf. Kiss him on both cheeks, clasp him to his chest, as he used to do, to show that he too was a European. He was sure Wolf used to like him; he had been convinced once that Wolf was in love with him . . . that would, Crawford believed, explain why he was once so happy to comply with all Crawford's plans, and was now so surly. Rejected love — perhaps even a broken heart.

The neatness of this explanation had always appealed to the part of Crawford which kept his string quartets in numerical order within composer, and had never mislaid a sheet.

Crawford, in spite of being an aficionado of opera, was mostly in the dark when it came to the workings of the human heart. It suited his sense of order to attribute Wolf's behaviour to a broken heart — since there must be a rationally irrational explanation — but he understood the concept of a broken heart in the same way as he knew what a hare looked like from Dürer's water-colour. Operatic heroines and the singers of *Lieder* suffered from this malady; love was apparently a species of virus, a sort of *herpes simplicissimus*, which when contracted was without remedy and excused all aberrant behaviour.

> *Amor e palpito*
> *Dell' universo —*

He had heard those words sung how many times? — allowing for repeats — how many productions of *Traviata* — how many unanswerable declarations that love is the heartbeat of the universe — in music so powerful that even Crawford bent before its message.

He did not quite dare deny it, but he no more took it into account in his calculations than the contradiction between Newtonian and Einsteinian physics. Things might well be asserted to be true, without actually *mattering* at all.

Mercy, wearing an apron, brought out a tray of *crème brûlée*. Crawford used the dessert as an excuse to ignore his sister, who was beginning to irritate him already. He pondered that it was not logical to ascribe Wolf's foul behaviour to a broken heart while at the same time disregarding the notion. He thought to himself that he really had two choices — to find another reason for Wolf's behaviour or to admit that there was some truth in the romantic catechism *amore misterioso, misterioso, croce, croce e delizia al cor. Mein Herz! Mein Herz!* Repetition, he thought sternly, does not, in itself, make things important.

Crawford sometimes wished that he might have these conversations with another. Ironically, Genista was almost perfect as a conversational partner — shrewd, acerbic and warm-hearted all at once. But the matters closest to Crawford — Wolf, Mercy, the existence of love, the power of music — these things he found insurmountably difficult to discuss. He did not recall he had ever talked about them — except of course to those named but interchangeable women whose services he called upon. *My therapists*, he called them, in the privacy of his head. He talked to them, often garrulously — but once he had spilled too much, he requested a different girl. He knew that the second time she would remember the names, the odd fact, and ask the unaskable: *But what about Mercy? What about the baby?*

So many unspoken matters. Genista and Rewi talking animatedly, with never a hint of the pasteboard life she was forced to lead, so alien from him and his peasant ways that it was surely miraculous they found common cause. Mercy, never uttering a word about the pain that bounced around inside her; she'd fuck herself stupid with that man and never tell him what she wanted, what she could never have. Himself and Rosalia chattering away like the children they had been, never mentioning the Commander or the house — the two matters that hung between them like carcasses on the chain.

So much chat, so little said.

Why was he taking part in all this — why allowing himself to be dragged down into the whirlpool of words away from — from what? What did Crawford want that light conversation could not give him? He had money, success, friends, projects — what more did he want than cheer and pleasant times?

He wanted Wolf to speak to him.

Suddenly without warning even himself he rose from the table, his spoon still half full of *crème brûlée*. He pulled the napkin from his throat and threw it onto the table. Genista half-rose.

'Are you ill, Crawford?'

'No.'

Rosalia, Mercy and Rewi watched him in silence. He stalked across the dining-room floor towards the kitchen, from which now issued the sound of singing. Wolf was teaching Dickie a German drinking song.

The kitchen doors had double hinges which allowed the staff to push them most satisfactorily in either direction. Crawford placed one hand, arm straight, fingers splayed, on the door and walked in.

The singing stopped. Wolf turned away so he did not have to meet Crawford's eyes. The other men were silent. Crawford went up to the German and put his hand on his shoulder.

'Why won't you *speak* to me, Wolfgang?'

'Ha! He asks me why I will not speak to him? As if he didn't know.'

'I don't know, Wolfgang, that is why I'm asking you. I've given you everything — you know how much you mean to me. Nobody is more important.'

'He says nobody is more important. But first you must ask the question, is *anybody* important to Crawford Hollander?'

'That's very cruel, Wolf.'

Dickie left his perch at the kitchen bench and sloped across towards the two of them. He placed his arms around both men's shoulders.

'Now, children,' he said, 'there's no need for this. Let's behave like grown-ups.'

'Oh yes there is,' said Michael. 'It's time Wolf said something. He's been brooding for ever.'

'I could remind him,' said Wolf, 'of what he knows very well, but he thinks I will never talk of it before folk. But he is wrong, Dickie. I will tell the world our secret.'

'There is no need to be melodramatic, Wolfgang.'

Wolf laughed. 'Bring them all in here, Dickie, everyone — '

'Wolf,' Michael pleaded, 'there's no need for a scene — '

'No, I have a better idea,' said Wolf, pulling away from Dickie and stalking off across the kitchen to the outside door. He opened it onto the night and made as to go out.

'Invite all his acquaintances, Dickie, invite all Rosalia's friends. Invite all Canterbury to your party, and I will tell in front of them all, what Crawford Hollander has done to me.'

★　★　★

Crawford stood where Wolf had left him, and watched his grand exit into the night. He felt a tear spring up into his eye, and wondered if he were a little drunk. He felt Wolf's departure into the night as a physical wound, but he did not understand why. He told himself he no more understood Wolf's outburst than he understood why Genista had locked him out of the house after their abortive evening at the opera.

★　★　★

Silence fell on the kitchen, a dense silence full of little sound, Dickie pouring himself a drink, Michael clanking a pot. From the next room came a madrigal of three women's talk and laughter, weaving in and out, high and low. It seemed to come from very far away. Crawford stood still for what to him seemed like an unnaturally long time.

'I think I am tired. I shall go up to bed.'

He turned on his heel. As soon as the door swung shut behind him, Dickie and Michael burst into excited conversation. As he returned to the dining-table the counterpoint of women's voices stopped. All three of them looked at him while Rewi glared at the table settings.

'I am going up to bed,' he announced. 'There is no need for you to follow. I don't imagine the sounds of revelry carry through the walls do they, Rosie?'

'I don't think we are making much noise,' said Genista.

'No, my dear, you are not. But I am sure that once I have gone up Dickie and Wolf will rejoin the party and the singing will start up in earnest.'

'Oh dear, we can't have that!' said Rosalia. 'Not on your first night!'

'I'll send him to bed,' said Mercy. 'The silly old duffer.' She went into the kitchen.

Crawford kissed his sister good-night, and then his wife. As he did so, he registered Rewi's surprise. Of course — the peasant did not understand a world where it was

367

unnecessary for husbands and wives to sleep together.

As soon as he started to go up, the party disbanded. He stood in the dark at the top of the stairs and noted that Mercy had gone to deal with her father, Genista was clearing the table, and obviously about to retire, Rewi and Rosalia were having a conversation *sotto voce*.

In his room he did not turn on the light. He stood in the middle of the room and listened until the footsteps had climbed the stairs and the good-nights were all said and the doors had banged. He counted heads, and knew who was in, who was out. He knew that Michael was still in the kitchen, waiting up for Wolf who had not returned.

Then he changed his shoes and put on his navy blue cashmere sweater, although the night was mild.

He went down the back stairs, avoiding the stair that once used to creak, even though he was fairly convinced someone would have mended it by now.

Once outside the house, he stood in the shadows behind the house, in deeper darkness because a full moon stood over the bay. He wondered where Wolf's passion would have taken him.

There were so many places to wander into

— the grounds were large enough before you took in the forest up behind and the foreshore and beach. He recalled that in the days when they had been friends, Wolf had preferred to walk along the beach rather than climb through the forest.

He scarcely thought of the beach these days. One might walk along the strand at Nafplio or Nice, but that did not remind you of Charteris Bay. He supposed, as he issued from under the trees and stood beside the road, that he had not felt sand under his bare feet for some forty years. What would it feel like to walk barefoot now?

The bay was particularly lovely tonight, as if nature had laid on a full moon, clear sky and tiny warm breeze for his benefit. How lovely to share it with someone, how agreeable to hear what Wolf would say about the ramifications of moonlight on water — something about Schubert perhaps, or a quotation from Goethe.

He remembered when he had last spent time with Wolf — how civilized and content he had felt, sitting on the sunset beach with the basket of wines, looking ahead at their shared future, a marriage made in heaven.

Crawford somehow expected Wolf to be sitting on the beach waiting for him, but he was nowhere to be seen. The stretch of sand was entirely inviting. Crawford crossed the road and went down as far as the wet sand. There were footprints here and he followed them.

It was not long before he saw them, sitting on the rocks on the Diamond Harbour end of his beach. The smack of the waves against the rocks prevented their hearing his footsteps on the sand, and prevented his hearing their voices. But the brilliance of the moonlight allowed him to see them clearly.

They were sitting on the rocks at the edge of the water. They had taken off their shoes, which were on the rocks higher up, and presumably from their posture they were dangling their feet in the sea. They were neither embracing nor even touching each other, but far enough apart so that Rewi's profile, turned towards Mercy, was perfectly clear. Silhouetted, he was someone else — not the lumpen working man whom Crawford despised, but a participant in one of those moonlit romantic paintings that Wolf loved so much — all mountain, lake and moor.

Mercy, set against such a background, was a figure worthy of Wagner. Crawford regarded her with a mixture of admiration and furious lust. She was looking straight out towards the hills on the other side of the harbour, and

Rewi was looking at Mercy. They were talking to each other with such intensity that Crawford was aware of the tenor, without hearing a word.

He watched the conversation between these two statuesque people — creatures of the romantic imagination — and he thought of Tristan and Isolde, and then with rising gall of Aida and Radames. He heard romantic arias in his head, and he hated them.

The stuff of opera was merely stuff. It was not the substance of human relationships. A man and a woman, face to face in the moonlight, did not break into torrents of Wagnerian excess. They talked of simple, silly things, they touched, and then they would kiss, and then they would make love, in the standard manner. The earth would not move, nor the mountains clap their hands. The lovers would wake next morning to furry teeth and recrimination. But Crawford, as he watched Rewi and Mercy, these people whose habits he knew, could hear only the insistent refrain *amor e palpito dell' universo*.

He did not know how long he stood and watched them, as if standing there would assuage his desire to know what they were talking about. How could they know each other so well as to talk like this? Crawford, inveterate observer of the behavioural minutiae, recognized that two people who have just met, and are circling around each other, do not sit still, apart, and talk intensely. They flutter and dive in their conversation, catch each other's eyes and look away, flick the hair off the face, fiddle with anything to hand. Only people deeply engaged with each other sit still, and talk and talk.

In the inner part of Crawford there was a worm which suggested to him that he had missed something. A hint that the price he had paid to be Crawford, and successful, had shut him out of a market. He had never sat with anyone and talked with that intensity — except perhaps on this very beach, with Wolf, talking about Caspar David Friedrich and Schopenhauer and the meaning of will and the essence of being, as the sun went down and the wine grew warm . . .

Crawford wondered how much longer he could bear not being able to read or comprehend the situation. He wondered why he was inflicting such punishment on himself, for watching them not kiss was far worse than watching them kiss. He had seen Mercy embracing other men more times than either of them would care to enumerate. He liked to watch Mercy kiss other men; it gave him thoroughly unworthy pleasure, both allowing him to imagine himself in the place where she forbade him entry, to feel ownership, and to experience the unadulterated lubricity of the voyeur.

Crawford was about to turn away and seek Wolf elsewhere. Rewi lifted his hand and placed the palm on her cheek. She turned her head and looked at him directly, but neither of them moved again.

A great burst of emotion surged into Crawford, from the groin, up through his stomach, into his throat and head. It felt something like nausea, something like lust, something like grief. He feared that he was watching the very moment of two people falling in love, and he could not endure it.

★ ★ ★

He turned away from the sea-shore and walked back under the trees. There was a slight movement in the darkness of the avenue. Wolf was watching him. They started to walk back to the house together.

'Do you love her very much?'

'I don't love her at all,' said Crawford. 'I have a care for her.'

'I thought so. Do you think you have ever been in love, Crawford?'

'I have no idea. How does one tell?'

Wolf may have shrugged. It was too dark to tell.

'I believe I love my wife,' Crawford continued.

Wolf made no reply. Crawford felt that something was missing but he could not decide where the lack was centred. He did not know whether it was related to Genista, Mercy or Wolfgang himself. He rolled the idea of loving his wife around in his head, trying to decide what he meant by it.

'She was the girl that you seduced, all those years ago,' Wolf said. 'When it was necessary for me to telephone my brother. I think if I had not spoken to him then, perhaps my brother and I would not have quarrelled. And if we had not quarrelled, perhaps he would not have shared our family secrets with you so easy.'

'I don't recall,' said Crawford, though he recalled perfectly.

The fat white face of Wolfgang's brother, Pieter, rose before him. The face which so genially conducted him around the late-night sights of Hamburg, creasing with falsely innocent delight at the services offered and the things to be bought, explaining the terms in his cunningly broken English, while Crawford, whose German was better than he admitted, took amazed note. The broad burgherly face, creased with anger, as he shouted at his brother on the telephone: *Why have you called me? Why have you reminded me of your existence? Why don't you come home, come home and help with Mother. It is your duty. What is love against duty? If it was a proper decent love, it would not be enough, but yours! And you, whose shame brought this affliction on our mother! You who are most to blame* . . .

Much of the tirade was lost on Crawford, but he understood enough, and he understood clearly what Pieter told him afterwards. Wolf was so seriously in love that he would not come home, even though his mother was, as Crawford had seen for himself, a lost soul creeping towards death.

Pieter, dutiful son, bachelor, lip-smacking grazer on the delights of the red-light district, carried away trays of untouched food and hid scissors. Of course he shouted at his brother.

'If it were a woman!' he shouted, 'a woman, I might understand you! But this is unnatural, disgusting.' He tailed off into words that Crawford recognized only in implication.

Afterwards Pieter remembered that there had been a message, a message from a girl. But Wolfgang had not given the correct number, or Pieter, in his wrath, had written it down wrong.

He had misrelayed Mercy's number, but he had given Crawford all the information he needed to make his fortune serious.

It was all so very long ago it was hard to see how it could matter now. All that mattered now was averting the crisis that loomed — that Wolf might choose to unearth the past and make them all suffer.

'Will you do as you threatened?' Crawford asked.

'Yes.'

'You understand the consequences?'

'Yes. But the time has come, Crawford. I must be free, though I lose everything. I have been your slave too long.'

Crawford stopped. Between them was a patch of moonlight as bright and unlikely as a Halogen headlamp, but they stood in the shadows of the trees.

'There is no need to be melodramatic, Wolf.'

'*You* can call me by my proper name,' said Wolf. 'It is Wolfgang or Herr Doktor Mark, to you. I am not melodramatic, only truthful. Let us see what the rest of the world says, at Dickie's party.'

'Don't do it, Wolfgang, don't ruin the party. More importantly, don't ruin your life.'

'You mean, do not ruin Crawford Hollander's chances of making even more money. Do not take away my reputation that is based upon the excellence of Wolfgang Mark's name.'

'No, Wolf, it is simpler than that. If you tell the world, then the world will know, and sooner or later, someone will come knocking on your door.'

'I no longer care, Crawford. Our contract is ended. I shall descend into misery, but you will burn in hell.'

★ ★ ★

Wolf walked away very swiftly, so that Crawford would have needed to run to catch up. Crawford leant his back against a sycamore tree, and breathed deeply. He tried to make sense of the random emotions that bombarded him, great blobs of feeling like colour in a lava lamp — up, flourish, disintegrate, without a shape or a name. The only thing he could grasp was his overwhelming desire not to lose Wolf — his whole world had been built on Wolf, Wolf's contract was the dearest thing he owned, his reputation, his fortune, all rested on that signature. His ability to bind Wolf to him year after year had raised his standing in the eyes of his French

377

masters to something mythic — *Mark is impossible, but he is a wine-maker of genius and absolutely loyal to Hollander. Hollander made him, and Mark has never forgotten the debt. These Germans are men of honour.*

Crawford had fed the myth so much that he believed it himself. Crawford had made Wolfgang, had nurtured and protected him, and still continued to do so. Now Wolfgang was spitting in his face. Should he take revenge or simply turn away?

Why was there nobody to turn to? To whom could he spill out his secrets? He thought at once of Mercy. He had always turned to Mercy, though sometimes she wasn't listening when he arrived at the nub of the problem. It didn't matter, because merely talking in front of her was usually enough to clarify his thoughts. But he could not use Mercy in this way, not tonight, when she was all sheep-eyed with the handyman.

Perhaps Genista? One's wife was supposed to be the repository of secrets. He started back towards the house, looking up at her bedroom window for signs of activity. Her room was dark, for sensible woman that she was, she had doubtless ignored the dramas in the household and gone to bed. Crawford felt he might as well do the same thing.

As he walked along the avenue towards the

house, the lights of a car approached. He secreted himself behind a tree. Wolf and Michael drove past, quite slowly, in their little black convertible with the roof down. Crawford could hear and see them talking and laughing as they passed him.

When all danger of being spotted was over he set off again. He was amazed to find the front doors of the house unlocked. Entering, he saw light under the kitchen door and heard voices, and was surprised at how peeved he felt. In the kitchen, Genista and Dickie Fisher were sitting very comfortably at the bench on stools, drinking from large mugs. They greeted him hospitably, as if it were their kitchen.

'And what have you done with my little girl?' demanded Dickie, cheerfully enough.

'She is on the beach with Rewi,' said Crawford, trying for a neutral tone.

'With Rewi!' cried Dickie. 'Now there's a marriage made in heaven! I can't bear to think of it — it's too nice.'

'He does seem a lovely chap,' said Genista, 'and awfully attractive too. But I always thought he and Rosalia — '

'That's a convenience,' said Dickie, and laughed as if he had made a terrific joke. 'Like a loo. Something for an emergency.'

'Marriages of convenience have their

place,' said Genista.

'Mine is very convenient,' said Dickie, still chortling to himself. 'Marg goes tramping every weekend and I go for a little drink.'

'Your daughter is hardly likely to marry Rewi or anyone else, Dickie. Genista and I live through a new affair of Mercy's every month, don't we, my dear? It's our charity work.'

'She certainly has a rapid turnover,' said Genista, then, realizing that this was not what a father likes to hear, added, 'but that's because she is simply waiting for the right man, and doesn't want to get too involved with the wrong one. Wouldn't it be wonderful if Rewi were the right one? Sad for Rosalia of course.'

'I can hardly wait for the day,' said Dickie. 'Mercy needs babies. She's just like her mother, born to have babies.'

'Well, unfortunately,' said Crawford, 'that's the one thing Mercy will never have.'

Dickie's face, normally a picture of good cheer, suddenly resembled Mr Micawber's on the wrong side of the arithmetic. For a moment Crawford wished he had not said anything, but swiftly reminded himself that it would save Mercy embarrassment in the long run, if Dickie inclined to drop heavy-handed hints about grandchildren.

'*Crawford!*' said Genista.

'I don't see how you can know that,' said Dickie, 'since her own father doesn't.'

'In a sense we are *in loco parentis*,' said Crawford, 'Mercy living away from home as she has chosen to do.'

Tears appeared in Dickie's eyes.

'I can't bear what you are telling me. How do you know — how does she know? She is still young — no babies? Why should I believe you?'

'I really am amazingly tired,' said Crawford, and turned on his heel.

★　★　★

He lay in the darkness for hours listening to the movements of the household. Genista did not come upstairs, nor did Dickie. He imagined Dickie crying on Genista's shoulder, growing drunker and drunker, and testing even her legendary patience. But what could Genista tell him, except the bare reported fact that Mercy could not have children? She did not know the reason why, and even if she had known the surgical cause, she did not know what part Crawford had played in it all. His secret was safe.

He fell asleep, finally, but was half-woken towards dawn by disturbances downstairs. He

381

was not sufficiently alert to register what was happening, but he heard voices raised in emotion. He heard Dickie's roar, women's voices laden with tears, confused shouting — but he must have been dreaming. He banished from his semi-conscious mind the notion that Mercy would tell her father the truth.

The shouting and crying subsided, footsteps on the stairs indicated that all three of them were finally going to bed. He heard intense whispering, then closing of doors. He let slip into nightmare the idea that he was about to be attacked.

He submerged himself in nothingness, so that he did not have to hear, even in his dreams, the sound of desolate sobbing from the next room.

13

Sunday was Zoë's day off, and so the household rocked.

On weekdays, if she was at home, she got up even before her father, biked around to Diamond Harbour to catch the first ferry, then biked to the QEII pool to get in a bit of serious training before school. That she dozed through school, reeking of chlorine, was politely overlooked, for she was a sporting hero. Her room at home was festooned with medals and ribbons and cups, but she was in it so rarely that Rewi called it the Zoë Mann Memorial Parlour. Most nights she slept over at her friend Francine's place, near the pool, to maximize training time. In return Rewi did odd jobs for Francine's mum, who was a solo, so they were all squared away.

On Sundays, if she hadn't stayed over at someone's place after a party, she slept in, till about eight, and then compensated by rousing her father and Tom by a bewildering combination of rock, television and clatter.

The morning after Crawford's return to his estate, she was up and about, jiving to an exercise programme on TV, while singing along with Britney, turned up loud on the stereo, so as to be heard over the aerobic instructor's pieties, and eating a bowl of muesli. But above all this noise she could still detect sounds.

She danced along to Tom's room and bashed on the door. She knew he would not answer, so she barged in. Tom's windows were curtained fast against the light, and his head was under two pillows. Only his computer monitor winked in the dark, and the luminous aliens on the indigo ceiling. 'Pooh, what died in here,' she said.

Tom groaned poisonously. He was a creature of the night, mostly found crouched over a computer or a TV screen, watching horror movies or setting the world to rights, or embroiled in tortuous adventures of the imagination with his friends. Rewi had given up reprimanding him about his hours, or indeed about anything else, because he reckoned that the web site, newsletter and subscriber database Tom produced, at his father's mild suggestion, for the Native Forests' Protection Council outweighed any number of unsavoury personal habits.

'Socks,' Zoë pronounced. 'Dead socks, rotting. You're disgusting. Come and listen to this. You won't believe it.'

'Bug off,' said Tom.

'No you've gotta.'

Zoë took a lot of refusing. Tom said she had an imagination bypass, which was why she never stopped and never gave in. Zoë didn't get it, though she knew it was an insult.

'Wake up you lazy sod, just listen.'

She pulled the pillows off his head. Since she was wide awake, and very strong, this was no contest. Tom clutched his head with his hands to shut out her presence.

'You mustn't miss it. You'll thank me. You will.'

She flung the bedroom door wide open.

The sounds of television, voices and pop music flooded in. Also the sound of a copious shower running, as their father punished the plumbing in his enthusiasm for cleanliness.

'So,' said Tom. 'Noise pollution.'

'You can't hear it can you?' She shook her brother vigorously.

'Hear what? Crap music, junk TV?'

'No, it's Dad.'

'Yes he's in the shower. Unless of course it's Norman Bates come to do us all a favour.'

'Dad is singing in the shower.'

'OK, Dad is singing in the shower. Can I go back to sleep now?'

She shook him some more, for fun.

'You don't get it, do you?'

Zoë was fiercely protective of her father's heart. As a little girl she had fought several successful battles against women who might have been just about to turn serious. She had warded off Julie and Francine's mum, and several other opportunistic women, all of whom were allowed a portion of her father, but not his heart. She turned a blind eye to his relations with Rosalia, for whom she felt deeply sorry, poor old bat with her big house and pretensions.

'He never sings. Not even at weddings or on New Year's Eve.'

'Well he must be happy. Or it's an alien who's inhabiting his body.'

'But why has he suddenly got happy? What makes people go like that?'

'Is this a pop quiz? Because I'm not a contestant.'

'I think he's met someone. Do you know what time he got in last night?'

Tom regained possession of his pillows.

'It was about five,' Zoë continued. 'I thought it was you, but I'd heard you at four. He was up all night.'

'So?' said Tom, to whom this was normal behaviour, and his sister's diurnal habits aberrant.

'He never stays up all night. He's always in bed at midnight.'

'Well go and tease him about it, and leave me alone.'

'But, Tom, what if he has?'

'What? Turned into Norman Bates?'

'Fallen in love.'

'Oh for Christ's sake.'

'What if we loathe her?'

'Might be a him. That might explain why he never remarried. Our dad was a closet gay.'

'Oh, stuff you!' said Zoë and slammed his door.

She met her father dressed in a towel, coming out of the bathroom.

'Put that away, Dad.'

Rewi merely grinned and made no attempt to cover his naked chest, of which, as Zoë perfectly well knew, he was rather proud.

'What's her name then,' demanded Zoë.

'Mercy.'

'What?'

'Mercy. Mercy Fisher.' Spoken by any other man, you might have thought it contained a sigh.

Zoë frowned.

'What sort of name is that?'

'A woman's.'

He grinned all over his person.

'Honestly, Dad!'

'Come and meet her,' said Rewi. 'Soon as I'm dressed I'm going over. You'll like her.

You met her when you were little, and you liked her then.'

'I did?'

'Well, you liked all her teddy bears.'

'Dad, it takes more than teddy bears now.'

'I know. I'm serious. It won't take long to say hi.'

'No way. No time. I probably will like her. If you swear it's the real thing, I promise to try if you promise not to sing in the shower any more, but I've got to get to Denny's for some tennis.'

'It is the real thing and it's only next door.'

'What d'you mean, next door?'

'Up at the house. Mercy's staying there.'

'With *Rosalia*? That's awful.'

'Why?'

'Well how do you think Rosalia will feel? I mean she does have feelings, you know. You men. Shit, she'd better be worth it.'

Rewi didn't want to think about these matters, so he kept up the grin as he went into his room and started to agonize over what to wear. In the living-room and kitchen music and voices competed for space with Zoë, now noisily on the telephone.

He thought about what Zoë had said about Rosalia, but it was too hard to concentrate. He sang as he buffed himself up and dusted himself down; he admired his manly outline, but only as a tribute to Mercy. He went into the kitchen, fighting his way past Zoë's exploding phone call, and found he had no appetite for breakfast. This was unprecedented.

He took a coffee out onto the patio and tried to drink it standing in the sunshine with a view of the sea. Every moment he hoped he'd catch sight of Mercy walking along the beach, thinking about him . . .

He found he couldn't finish his coffee. This had never happened before.

It was barely nine o'clock, and it was Sunday, but he found he just *had* to go up to the house. There was bound to be a job that needed doing, Sunday or not.

'You don't work on Sundays,' yelled Zoë at his departing form, but he was strangely deaf.

★　★　★

At any moment he thought he'd see her. Somehow he thought she'd be running towards him under the trees, like a movie, even though running didn't seem quite Mercy's thing.

But as he felt like running himself, anything was possible.

Rewi didn't dare to examine his feelings;

officially he didn't have feelings. He did things.

No vision of eternal womanliness appeared before him as he made his familiar plod across to the big house. He'd walked that route, with a few variations, thousands of times, but never had it seemed to take so long. He was anxious that at any moment a car, by some misunderstanding bearing her away, would zoom past him. She would not go away without saying something, but knowing this did not stop him fearing it.

'What a fuckwit,' he told himself repeatedly, though the repetition of abuse did not increase its impact.

He entered the house by the kitchen because he didn't want to be taken by surprise. He had expected a war-zone, knowing of old Michael's cooking and Dickie's drinking. There was evidence of the latter, but efficient people had tidied up the former. In the fridge was a regimented supply of leftovers, wrapped in cling film, amazingly appetizing, if not immediately recognizable, like plaster meals in dolls' houses. Lunch was assured, for those, unlike Rewi, who had an appetite.

The house was quiet, except for a tinkle of classical music from a radio. The inhabitants,

Rewi supposed, were sleeping off booze or jet lag.

He made himself a cup of coffee, to buy a bit of time, but was too impatient to drink it. He knew Rosalia was probably about, and he wanted to avoid her, but as he prowled about the kitchen looking for things to put away or fix, he knew that he should not, and so could not, duck away from the conversation he must have with her. And the sooner the better.

She was in the front hall rearranging the silk flowers, something she did when she was at a loose end but wanted to feel artistic. Beyond her in the morning room, the table was laid for breakfast.

'You've been busy,' said Rewi, indicating the table.

'Oh, Genista did that,' she said crossly. 'She spent years running a boarding-house. That's how she met Niall. He was a lodger.'

Rewi couldn't work out if this was cited as evidence of Genista's poor calibre as a person, or simply as explanation.

'No one's come down yet,' he said.

'Evidently.'

He stood and sipped his coffee and watched her fiddling with the flowers. He knew he must say something to mark the end of their years-long relationship. A coward would let it just fizzle out. He didn't want to think he was a coward.

'Don't you have anything to do?' she said.

'No, not really. I'm waiting for Mercy.'

Rosalia acted as if she hadn't heard him.

Rewi heard himself speak, but could not believe the words came out of his mouth.

'I've always been waiting for Mercy. I just didn't realize it. I'm afraid she's the one, Rosie.'

'I am sure you are very well suited,' she said. 'Quite how Crawford will take it I don't know.'

'It's nothing to do with Crawford,' he said.

Rosalia gave a little laugh. 'She obviously didn't want to upset you too much. She has always been Crawford's mistress, and probably always will be. A girl like Mercy doesn't have any trouble double-dipping.'

Rewi's temper was rarely ignited, but exceedingly fierce. He stood stock-still and gripped his coffee mug, and told himself that Rosie only said those things because she was jealously disappointed. He told himself that he must at all costs be kind to her, since he was so unceremoniously dumping her. He told himself that unpleasantness was her way of coping with misery. He would not let her get to him, poor dear.

He held onto his coffee mug for dear life,

and somehow managed to get the better of his anger.

'There's lots of Mercy to go round,' he said mildly. 'We'll get by, you know. I won't let you down.'

It didn't make much sense as a series of statements, but she seemed to understand his attempt to be conciliatory. And he wouldn't let Rosalia down, even if she was determined to be poisonous. If Mercy expected him to, she was not the woman he had dreamt of.

Rosalia sniffed.

'I think I'll go and find her,' he said, not sure that his temper would hold. He put down the coffee mug on the dining-table, right on the French polish, even though he knew it would upset her, and started upstairs. Then he saw that she was crying and stopped in his tracks, having no idea what to do. Life had not equipped Rewi to deal with emotion. The night before, for the first time in his life, he had admitted to himself, and to another, that he felt love — that in fact he was overwhelmed by, transformed by, helpless in the grip of love. Such an admission, and such feelings, were new and frightening. He was bewildered, like an Amazonian Indian at an amusement park — it was brilliant, it was thrilling, but was it safe and was it real?

And now this.

All these years, he thought, all these years, not a loving word, not a single tender moment. He would have responded if she had allowed him, not effusively, but he knew in his heart, insofar as he knew his heart, he knew that he would have responded. A sweet word from Rosalia, and he would have smiled and joked kindly in return, patted her lovingly — made between them a little warmth.

But Rosalia had kept their love-making contractual. *Be here, do this, and I will never ask for more nor talk of love.* It was understood. Rewi did not know if she was afraid of rejection, or simply afraid of emotion. He did not ask. He told himself he wanted it this way, and certainly he could never have loved Rosalia in any romantic sense, had she allowed him to. But he felt for her, though he had no emotional vocabulary to explain how this feeling was different from that for Mercy which now overpowered him.

'Don't look at me,' she sobbed. 'I know I am so ugly, so old, and now I look so much uglier. Do look at me — '

'I'm sorry — ' he began.

'Don't be sorry! I don't want people feeling sorry for me. I want to be adored and admired, I don't want to be pitied. But that's what everyone does! You only make love to me out of pity. And duty. Do you think I don't know? Do you think I don't know how you go running for relief to that Julie and all those other fat wenches? And now Mercy. It was the only thing I had. The only thing I could cling to — my house here, my establishment, having you here. It made me happy. I've been a failure at everything else, I wanted to be a singer, I wanted to be an artist, I wanted to be a famous singing-teacher or at least a famous hostess. I failed at all of them, but at least we were here, you and me, and our friends, and our lovely place, even with the golf-course and paying guests. It is lovely. But now I'm going to lose that too — Crawford's going to build a hotel — '

'I didn't know that!'

'I was tidying his room . . . ' said Rosalia.

Rewi allowed the gross unlikelihood of this to pass by. It seemed reasonable in his moral scheme that she should snoop among her brother's papers, when her way of life was at stake.

'So I shall have nothing at all — not even my house. And you will go away — '

'No I won't.'

'Mercy won't stay here. Even if I was here, but I won't be here either, because of what Crawford's done to me, but Mercy wouldn't stay here.'

'She's not like that, she's not the jealous

395

type,' said Rewi, presuming, correctly, but on very little evidence.

'No, not that, she hasn't reason to be, and if she's marrying you she'd better not be had she?' Rewi hung his head, but she went on without enjoying her hit. 'She wouldn't want to, not after what happened to her. It would remind her all the time.'

'How did you know about that?' Rewi shouted.

'You all think I'm stupid, all of you, even you, who aren't exactly superman in the brains department. Of course I knew what was going on. But what good was it my talking about it, or trying to get involved. It was my fault, don't you think that was bad enough, knowing that? Do you think I can look Dickie in the eye, even now, without shame? And as for Marg — '

'You *knew*!'

'I wanted to help,' said Rosalia, crying more heavily, 'but what was there *I* could do? Crawford always had the money. If I said anything Marg and Dickie might guess it was Crawford, and . . . I have to support him. He's the only person I have to love . . . '

Rewi went down the stairs and put his arms around her. He held her firmly against his chest, with his arms wrapped tightly around her insubstantial body, as he knew she liked him to do.

'You have Michael and Wolf, and a lot of friends, and you will find someone else, if you just keep looking for him. And I won't let you down, Rosie. I'm not like that.'

'Promise?'

'Promise,' he said, though he was at a loss to know how he would keep his promise. But it must be kept somehow, or he was not Rewi Mann.

'I'll tell you what. We'll go upstairs and I'll run you a nice deep bubble bath of that smelly stuff Mercy brought you from London, that you like so much, and then I'll bring you a nice deep gin, *just this once*, and then you go back to bed, and when you wake up, you call me and I'll bring you brunch in bed.'

After he'd successfully decanted her into the bath, with the gin, he felt he had earned his reward, and so took himself off to the room which contained his heart's desire.

★ ★ ★

The rooms were so familiar, in every state — derelict, stripped, restored, beautified and maintained. He knew them better than he knew any woman's body, but hoped, very much expected, that all *that* was about to change.

Mercy was asleep in the tartan bedroom, in the bed so big it seemed a crime against nature to sleep in it alone. She did not want to wake up, not even for Rewi.

Rewi didn't mind this, because sitting on the side of the bed and watching her asleep seemed to him the best thing in the world.

After a while, being fairly tired himself, he wondered if it would be OK to get into bed with her. He thought about the night before, and the things they had said to each other. Did they constitute a warrant?

He leaned over and applied his mouth to the ear that was just visible.

'Can I get in?'

She made a sort of noise which might be construed as affirmative. Rewi decided to take the risk.

He took off his clothes deliberately, so if she woke up he couldn't be accused of being in a disgusting lecherous hurry. He even folded them over the kauri towel rail he had lovingly turned, but never, of course, used. Folding his clothes up did strike him as a bit excessive, but he now wanted to get into bed with her so badly, he had to slow down. He started to talk generally round the subject, not that small talk had ever been his strong point.

'Are you sure about this?' he said. 'Because I can't be quite sure of myself.'

It was too late now, he thought he'd die if he had to retreat, so he pulled back the bedspread and slid in beside her.

She felt as warm and wonderful as he had imagined — as he had always imagined women would, and they never quite did. She immediately redisposed herself so that his body could fit around hers, or would have, except for the inconvenient and urgent member in the midst of it all.

'Oh geeze, how wonderful,' she said, and arched her back and wriggled her buttocks to accommodate him, 'I didn't dream you after all.'

14

'Goodness,' said Crawford, as the cars swept up the drive, 'I didn't know you knew all these people.'

'I don't,' said Dickie, 'but you do.'

Crawford was graciousness itself, welcoming to his house person after person with whom he was acquainted. Naturally there were among the guests a great many of the odd and rough who were Dickie's friends, but so many arrivals greeted Crawford as if he had invited them that he began to think that Rosalia had laid on a surprise party for him.

Unsettled by the event, he was none the less delighted to look around and see that everything around him spoke of money tastefully spent — Mercy had even deigned to wear the new silk dress which he had insisted upon buying her in Hong Kong. A gnome of a tailor had made it especially, from dragon-brocaded silk, so that it exactly fitted the unfashionable but spectacular contours of Mercy's body. Crawford looked at it in contentment. How agreeable it was to spend money on Mercy.

He had hardly spoken to Mercy recently. In

theory she was now staying at her parents' house, but whenever Crawford touched down at Hollander House in the gaps between his business outings, she was either down at Rewi's house, or just about to arrive, or had just left. On the rare times when she was in none of these states, Rewi was off the premises also, as if the two of them could not bear to be separated for so much as a day. Crawford felt such irritation with her that, in the last two weeks, the very sight of her made him turn away with bile in his mouth. But he had forgotten all that now, seeing her here, standing with her mother, who provided a fine contrast, in a tank top and blue jeans, as lean and husky as a longshoreman. Wonderful though they looked, there were no men in attendance, as if they were awaiting Crawford's pleasure. Yes, things were, in essence, as they should be, Mercy, without a man, repentant and anxious to please, in *his* house, wearing the dress *he* had bought her.

He looked around with pleasure at his contingent, Genista horsily handsome, in a cream silk suit, Rosalia, not yet arrived at the *unfortunate* stage, in layers of pink floating stuff. But then he frowned. Dickie was in evening dress, and very fine he looked too, his great barrel of stomach tidily contained. But Crawford, who felt he had never got the measure of Dickie, didn't understand the evening dress. He himself had opted for a plum-coloured jacket with a sumptuous white cotton shirt and cravat of Italian silk, black, gold and a hint of the precise plum of the jacket. But Dickie outclassed him. He had a surreptitious feeling he was being mocked.

The impression was intensified when Rewi turned up in evening dress, obviously hired, but nonetheless a good fit. He looked, Crawford was forced to admit, terrific. Rewi took his place next to Dickie and Crawford in the hallway, greeting guests. Crawford felt that Rewi's role was surely to be parking cars and opening doors, rather than standing at his front door aping the toffs, but it was impossible for him to say anything.

Then Wolf emerged from the kitchens, his hair and beard washed and brushed. He came and joined the others. He also was wearing evening dress.

'What are you three playing at?' said Crawford.

'We are the Welcoming Committee,' said Wolf, and guffawed.

As the stream of arrivals continued, it became clear to Crawford that Dickie and his friends were intent on playing a joke on him, the precise nature of which escaped him. The guests were the oddest mixture — people whom Crawford had known well, and people he knew only by reputation — business luminaries, society figures whom you would expect to be busy elsewhere. Crawford had long ago discovered that mildly famous and even famous people still had gaps in their diaries, but they would try to make you feel as if they had shifted a couple of glittering events to fit you in.

Some of those invited he would have classed as his enemies, but perhaps Rosalia was not to know these things. He greeted them graciously, perhaps more graciously than was strictly necessary.

The three men beside him shook hands with everyone too, as if they were the lords of the earth, and not a rag-bag collection of hangers-on. Crawford determined not to let himself be irritated.

Effort had been made for this party, far more effort than seemed altogether appropriate. There were festoons, rather expensive ones, fantastic professionally arranged flowers, six feet high with peacock feathers and driftwood trees and all manner of avant-garde inclusions. There were hired people in rather smart outfits handing around tiny pieces of food. Crawford had only been vaguely aware of the activity, having spent much of his time since arriving in New Zealand inspecting the various arms of his own business and being conducted round the more sinuous and wider-reaching arms of his great French partners. He had been through Marlborough, up to Martinborough, and then down south as far as Geraldine, poking soil with his foot, smelling grapes, watching tick over electronic readouts on the walls of giant vats. He had pored over marketing briefs and admired mock-ups; he had breakfasted with venture capitalists and charmed little wine-makers with lavish lunches.

In all, he'd had a most delicious and useful holiday, with so many possibilities raised as to quite take his mind off Mercy's waywardness. The visit to New Zealand had confirmed him to himself as a man of achievement and ideas, and now to round it off, there was a rather good party.

Rather too good a party, he was beginning to think. He looked around him and was slightly appalled at all the expense. A string quartet of handsome young people in evening dress struck up in the corner of the billiard room. Crawford immediately started at the quality of their playing — where the hell had Dickie found such brilliance? That too came at a price. Crawford had seen the seven-piece swing band unpacking their instruments in the pool room by the well-stocked bar.

He absent-mindedly accepted a thumbnail-sized piece of sushi, smiling at the girl in a becoming uniform who served him.

'I say, old boy,' he said to Dickie, 'this must have cost you a few bob.'

'Not at all, Crawford,' said Dickie. 'Hardly a brass razoo.'

'But this food — the wine — ' Crawford paused for a perilous moment as he suddenly totted up how much Hollander wine was in circulation. 'The decorations — '

'No no, old matey. You're paying for all this.'

At that moment there was a bit of a cheer, as Mercy and Zoë pulled the cords that released two big painted banners. One read HAPPY BIRTHDAY DICKIE, the other WELCOME HOME CRAWFORD.

'I don't understand,' said Crawford. 'I never under any circumstances agreed to a homecoming party.'

'No,' said Dickie, 'but we felt you deserved one.'

'Who are we in this context?'

'Us,' said Dickie, 'Wolf, Rewi and me. The Welcoming Committee.'

Crawford looked at the three men, but they would not look at him.

'Is this some kind of elaborate joke?'

'Yes,' said Dickie still refusing to look at his

interlocutor, 'in a way I suppose it is.'

Dickie was not smiling now, neither were his partners in absurdity. Crawford looked from one man to the next, all three of them, unnaturally smart, like so many funeral directors.

Crawford felt the creeping onset of uncertainty.

He was pinned to the entrance for some time longer by the arrival of guests, far, far too many of them, and all drinking his best wine.

When he could get free he sidled up to Mercy and positioned himself at her elbow. He was distracted momentarily by her breasts, both concealed and displayed by the slit neckline of the silk dress.

'What's going on here, Mercy?'

'I think the blokes are having a bit of a joke, Crawford. Don't react or they will just love it.'

She sounded more disturbed than Crawford felt the occasion warranted. Perhaps she had already fallen out with her stud. Mercy's affairs were generally of this profile — intense, all-consuming and then suddenly over. Crawford had hoped that the suddenly-over phase had already arrived. He had particularly disliked this relationship with *Mellors*, as he was inclined to call Rewi in private. He did not know why he felt such particular dislike, and he certainly was not going to expend energy finding out.

But now he felt confidence rising in his breast.

'What have I done to upset *them?*'

'Honestly, Crawford.'

'Yes, honestly, Mercy. I do not understand. Please explain.'

'I have a feeling you will find out soon enough.'

As she refused to be more forthcoming, Crawford oiled his way around the room, having, he had to admit, a splendid time. The committee had assembled a wonderful party — the right mix of characters and class, of wit, style and worth. There was none of that awkward clumping that characterized a poor party. Although the swing band attracted one clientele and the string quartet another, there was a continuous thread of people from one area through the house to the other; there were people sitting on the stairs and others talking through the banisters. There were constant forays on to the veranda and turns about the lawn.

Crawford succeeded in cornering Marg Fisher on the end of the veranda, where she was leaning against one of the slim wooden pillars, looking out to sea. He thought she looked perfectly splendid, though now too old to trouble him. He had gained the impression that she was avoiding him, and was determined that she should not succeed.

'How long has it been, Marg?'

She wouldn't look at him, but continued to scan the horizon, as if a sea-eagle were due to dip by and take her away from all this.

'Oh, years and years.'

'You look every bit as wonderful.'

Marg made a scornful noise in her throat.

'I am absolutely in earnest.'

'I suspect you wouldn't recognize the Truth if she stood in your way. Unless she were well-endowed, of course.'

'You are harsh, Marg. I always loved you for your moral certainty as much as for your beauty.'

'You loved me for neither. I doubt if you have ever loved anyone. Except perhaps that lovely man Crawford Hollander.'

Crawford decided that she was probably menopausal and embittered. Perhaps even had turned lesbian as her charms faded. Certainly her marriage was a sham, for he knew she spent most of her time tramping in the bush with women. What a waste, he thought, remembering his boyhood dreams of her — dreams of a very specific nature, which still occasionally visited him. He would not let the sharp-tongued old woman, who thought jeans appropriate wear, and lecturing her host appropriate behaviour, for a smart party, interfere with the Marg Fisher of his memory.

He left her to her contemplations and strictures. Thank heaven, he thought, that Mercy took after her mother only in appearance. Mercy, so mercifully devoid of moral certainty, so amenable and loose. Perhaps loose to a fault, but even so, the contemplation of her promiscuity had its appetizing moments.

As the sun went down, in the satisfyingly *fin-de-siècle* colour-scheme, concealed lights came on around the lawn, spilling gold across the lawn and silver onto the handsome exterior of the house. Crawford, who had been outside admiring the contours of his bay in the sunset, in the company of Mrs Harry Williams (the Williamses of Hawkes Bay, of course), saw his house anew, and liked what he saw.

But he muttered 'Damned Rewi' under his breath, feeling that the excellence of the new lighting was somehow designed to insult him.

At ten o'clock supper was laid out in the dining-room, a supper so lavish that even Michael was surprised at himself. Wolf called for silence. Crawford felt a wash of fear. Wolf was about to tell the world, ruin himself, shame them all. He had not expected Wolf to carry out his threat. He had imagined that the silly idea Wolf had entertained, of confessing his past in public, had been subsumed into this embarrassing outlay of Crawford's money and the wanton consumption of Crawford's wine.

'Thank you all for coming,' said Wolf.

There were two hundred or so guests milling about the tables, clutching their plates and waiting to lay hands on the imperial spread before them. Wolf's voice was so loud and his manner so commanding that silence fell, as respectful and deep as if he were about to say grace in Maori.

'Dear friends and honoured guests, my name is Wolfgang Mark, and I am vintner at Hollander Wines. You may have heard of some of our wines. We hope you are enjoying the very best of them which we have given you tonight. I would like to tell you something about myself.'

Crawford's stomach contracted into a balloon and rose up into his throat.

'Before I was with Hollander Wines, I was wine-maker at the Platt winery, of which you may never have heard. You may have heard the story of the origin of Hollander Wines, the first vineyard in North Canterbury, and its legendary gold-medal Pinot Noir. But it was Pete and Christine Platt who started it all. Both of them are here tonight, as our honoured guests. It was they, not Crawford Hollander, who planted the first grapes on the river flats and were laughed at by the local folk. It was they, not Crawford Hollander, who employed me, a penniless, undesirable, long-haired, bad-mannered homosexual with a shady past. It was they who took the risk of their lives and properties to set up a winery. And it was with the Platts that I made my gold-medal wine, the Pinot Noir that won the Prix d'Or at the judgement of the Société Internationale de Vins des Côtes-du-Rhône. It is this wine that Crawford Hollander would like you to share with us tonight. The young men have all the remaining stock of the Ste Marguerite 1985 Pinot Noir already opened for your delight. When it is finished, my friends, it is finished. There is no more! Please enjoy with our compliments.'

★   ★   ★

The waiters began to take the wine around; there was something of an undignified rush towards them.

Crawford's relief mingled with his fury; each emotion rose in turn and choked down the other. He watched the hordes reaching out their hands for a measure of his precious fluid — not perhaps the best wine they had produced, but the legend, the special event, a bottle of which was brought out perhaps once a year to impress exceptional clients with the tale of Hollanders. Crawford knew how many bottles were left — precious few — and as he saw them circulate, he knew that Wolf was not fooling, and the last drops of the '85 were indeed disappearing before his eyes. He wanted to cry with rage and affront — how dare the man? How did he get his greasy German hands on the wine? It was locked up in the electronic treasury, safe in the heart of his kingdom, guarded by cynical and technologically sophisticated Frenchmen. He caught Wolf's eye. Wolf grinned at him, his mongrel's grin, conveying at once to Crawford that no part of the empire was safe from the Goth. Few things had been more precious to Crawford than this cache of wine. No doubt it was the very preciousness that drove Wolf to steal the bottles.

'I kept back one,' said Wolf in his ear. 'It is opened in the kitchen.'

'Well, do enjoy it, dear fellow,' he said. 'You made it after all. It is a pity you never made another wine as good.'

He walked smartly away, denying Wolf the

counter-argument that many of his later wines had been as good, if not better. Crawford knew that his partners did not bother to enter the best wines, the Hollander Estate boutique wines, in competitions, since their sales were assured to the *cognoscenti*, who were above such vulgar lotteries. Mayaud père et fils concentrated on bolstering their middle-range bulk vin-de-table with stickers from the world's wine festivals. A gong in this market, any gong, no matter how obscure, doubled sales.

Crawford determined to enjoy as much of the party as he could. It seemed unlikely that he could repudiate all the expenses contracted in his name. A reputation as a poor payer, and worse a poor sport, would haunt him in this monohyppic place for ever. Not of course that he *cared* about his reputation in Canterbury, not he. But none the less his family home was here, his business was founded here, his name was known . . . He did not like to think that anywhere groups of people were uniting in thinking ill of him.

He surveyed the room and picked out the likeliest young woman. About twenty-six, no obvious hanger-on, low-cut black dress, voluptuous but shapely. He didn't like thin, hungry-looking women; he had found them to be fortune-hunters, neurotics, drunks, husband-hunters. Women with flesh on them were, by and large, in Crawford's experience, fond of the flesh. He started his slow congé across the floor towards her. He was conscious of Genista watching him, not with alarm or disapproval, but as a bird-watcher watches the heron at his work.

He was doing rather well, he thought, keeping a general amused conversation going, while not slackening his noose around the young woman in black. He sighed with pleasure when he discovered she was studying singing at the conservatoire — of course his luck held. He began to think that his holiday was nudging towards a delicious conclusion.

About eleven-thirty, when he had let the group around him loosen so he could concentrate on his catch, he was aware of Rewi approaching Mercy. He watched the pair out of the corner of his eye, and the hope he had entertained, of their cooling off, faded away. They stood a little apart but their bodies inclined towards each other, as if the owners were unaware of it. Crawford understood this secret language, using it was his infallible guide when approaching women. He read the communication between them, and established that the affair was, sadly, far from over. It was so intense that they seemed connected through their vital organs while simply in conversation. After a few minutes of urgent discussion, Mercy left the room.

Crawford speculated on the reason — perhaps a presentation to her father, a stripper in a cake or a pantomime horse? Perhaps nothing more vulgar than flowers for Rosalia.

Mercy did not return. Rewi, Dickie and Wolf were all over the place, rounding people up, Rewi was bringing people from the outside — lawns, shrubbery, avenue — Dickie, the upstairs landings, Wolf, the swimming pool and its surrounding bolt-holes. A presentation was to be made, but by whom and to whom?

Surely not to Crawford himself?

★　★　★

Mercy was nowhere to be seen. It was now some time since she had disappeared. Dickie climbed upon a stool behind the bar and tried to quieten the assembly. They crushed into the billiard room, clacking and laughing, glasses of Hollander's best — Ste Marguerite, of course — in their hands. Crawford stood obscurely in the corner, shoulders in his line of vision. The young woman in the black dress, on whom he had expended so much energy, was distressingly swept away in the flood of guests.

Dickie finally succeeded in hushing the throng. Crawford studied his shoes, sure that Dickie was going to cover himself with egg in his drunken attempts at humour.

'Thank you for coming tonight,' said Dickie. 'I'm Dickie Fisher, if you don't know me. It's my birthday and I'm having a rip-roaring time!'

Someone launched into *Happy Birthday*, taken up by a trombone on the outskirts of the crowd.

When the clamour died down, Dickie carried on. He sounded entirely sober, and as confident as if he had scripted his words and learnt them for an audition.

'Thank you, thank you. Now if you don't know me, you are probably wondering why you were invited here tonight? It's wonderful to see everybody — I always think nobody can resist a good party.

'Well, you see, me and my mates, Rewi and Wolfgang, decided that it was all very well to celebrate a birthday, but sometimes you need to do more than that. Sometimes you need to mark a life.

'Now, my friends, you probably think like I do, that when someone dies and you hear all the tributes and read the obituaries, you think, don't you, that it would have been better if the dead person had heard those things? Maybe when he was alive — if he knew people loved him — if he knew people hated him — wouldn't it be better to know? If it was you, my friend, wouldn't you like to know before you died, what the obits were going to say?

'Well that's the thinking we came to, my mates and I. We heard that our old friend Crawford Hollander — there he is in the corner, modest as ever — was coming home specially to celebrate my birthday. And we thought, well that's a pretty special thing to do. Let's celebrate Crawford's life too.'

There was an odd sort of buzz in the crowd — a laugh crossed with an appreciative or apprehensive murmur.

'So here you all are — my friends and Crawford's friends, and I would like to tell you a bit about me and a bit about him, because we go back a long way.

'I think it was at the start of the 60s. I was a young scamp from South Africa, and working on the wharves. It was a good life — lots of dosh to be made on the wharves. And we had a bach on Taylor's Mistake — right on the beach. Marg will tell you what a great life it was. She was surfing every hour God made, when we weren't making babies. Out on the beach with the babies, in the sea, and I was down on the wharves having a

417

good time. And sometimes we did some work, eh boys?'

There was a surge of laughter from Dickie's fellow watersiders, a group of men so disparate in appearance that only their proximity to each other while sharing this joke could identify them. Crawford remembered the smell of the wharves, the smell of his excitement as he carried away his cache of wine, case by precious case. He remembered the endless good humour and caustic wit of the watersiders, smoking, gambling, drinking and joking their lives away.

'I had this mate while I was working down there, an older guy nicknamed the Commander. He was our neighbour too, a wonderful, spaced-out Englishman, been everywhere, done everything — the handsomest man you ever saw, wasn't he?' He addressed this remark directly to Rosalia, who was perched on a little chair quite close to him, listening eagerly with her head on one side, braced to concentrate on his every word. She turned a delicate pink, much the colour of her scarf, and smiled with joy, as if her marriage had been long and blissful.

Crawford, who had banished to the loft every photograph that contained the Commander, was surprised to hear him described in such glowing terms. He recalled chiefly the smell of the man, booze mingled with unwashed fear.

'Well the good old Commander's crowning achievement was to marry the lovely Rosalia, whom I'm sure you all know by reputation, even if you haven't had the pleasure of her famous hospitality before. She and the Commander set up a love-nest in Taylor's. What a way to go when you're supposed to be past it! How many of you remember the Commander?'

There was a bit of a cheer from the group of watersiders.

'He was a great guy, not an ounce of harm in him, as long as you took the guns and the natives away. No, seriously, folk, he was a good old boy, even if he liked a drop rather more than he should. I still don't know about that disappearing bottle of whisky, Rosalia. We lived next door to them, and Marg and I used to laugh at the pair of them, canoodling on the sand, and frolicking in the surf, and we used to think we were the young lovers!'

Crawford tried to adjust his version of the Commander, but failed to do so. He glanced at Genista, far across the room from him. She caught his eye and smiled, apparently pleased too with this shameless romanticization of the past.

'Well, my friends,' Dickie continued, 'that

419

was when I met Crawford for the first time. How old were you, Crawford? Sixteen I think. He was still at school, ladies and gents, but it just goes to show what an amazing person our friend Crawford Hollander is!

'Crawford took one look at the poor old Commander, who was his brother-in-law, and saw that here was a chap of a superior caste, working down the wharves, making a packet, living on the beach with his teenage wife, blissfully happy. But Crawford was smarter than that. He saw that the old Commander was a bit too top-drawer for the wharves, and what he needed was a business career — selling wine was perfect, because after all the old boy really enjoyed a drop. Nothing like a wine merchant who loves his work! So good old Crawford sets him up in business. Amazing, really, when you think about it, at sixteen to have that sort of acumen.'

There was a species of noise, centred round, but not confined to, the watersiders, something between a groan and an ironic cheer. Crawford did not like the tone of it at all.

'Hollander & Lingerfield. The wine merchants — remember them? Lingerfield didn't linger though, sadly. He put young Crawford in the way of their first consignment of stock, a warehouse full of orphaned South African wine. It was perfectly safe on the wharf, because none of us chaps ever touched a drop. Of wine that is. Beer, whisky, rum — too right! But wine was for poofters. Nowadays we're all drinking wine — don't know what that tells us . . . '

There was a jolly laugh from the whole room.

'Anyway, Holland & Lingerfield. The old Commander had a bit of a nest-egg tucked away, but Crawford persuaded him to invest it and he fronted the business, because of course a sixteen-year-old can't get a wine and spirits licence, not even in these trendy lefty days, though a drunkard can. Crawford really pushed the old boy from behind. It shows you what sort of chap he is, Crawford, that even at sixteen he could motivate the Commander. I remember the old boy coming to see me. 'Dickie,' he said, 'Dickie, is this the chance of a lifetime?' Marg said — lovely Marg — told him it was. 'Make you or break you, Niall,' she said. 'My money's on break you,' she said, and she was right of course. 'So is mine,' he said, poor bugger, 'but I'll do it for Rosalia.'

'Well, I said to Marg afterwards, 'There's a novel way of laying down your life for your love.'

'But you have to hand it to Crawford, he

really tried. And even when things became untenable, he made sure the Commander was OK. He paid his fare to England, isn't that true, Rosalia? He booked the Commander's passage back to the old country, so the old boy could see the green fields of home once again. Poor old boy didn't have a sou left.

'I remember the day he left for England. We went down to see him off, didn't we, Marg? He took us round the ship, as proud as punch as if he owned her. And he gave us a drink in his cabin, very grateful he was. Good old Crawford — good young Crawford as he was then — paid for a decent cabin to ship his business partner, the old drunk, out of the country. Damned nice of you!'

There was a murmur from the company. Crawford, trapped in the corner, wished the parquet would fissure and drag him anywhere — to hell would do just fine.

'You see, he's a good bloke underneath that suave exterior. Do anything for you!

'I had an interesting life after that, because Hollander & Lingerfield gave Marg the idea of starting a business. She used to say, if a drunk and a teenager can do it, so can we. And so we set up our harbour ventures — our little cruises and boat hire, and we owe it all to Crawford. Marg saw what I couldn't see — that a little bit of money and a lot of effrontery can make a business go. Crawford knew it from the cradle — we learnt it from him. So thank you, Crawford! We didn't need to go to the same lengths to get started, unless you've got some old drunks hidden away, Marg, who I don't know about?'

There was fairly general laughter; Marg, sitting on the stairs, took all of this in good part. She threw back her head so that her wild, red hair brushed the riser behind her. 'But there's more, folks. Good old Crawford didn't stop there. My friend Wolfgang can tell a story or two, but he's a bit of a shrinking violet.' Sustained laughter.

'But I'll give you the short version. Young Wolfgang came out to New Zealand from Germany quite some years ago — fifteen, is it Wolf? He had a bit of a past, didn't you, old chap? Convictions, not to mince our words. Two convictions, to be precise. Two convictions in Germany. One for smoking cannabis. One for under-age sex. With a boy. Well when I heard that about Wolf, I *was* surprised.' A portion of the crowd laughed obligingly.

'Is that your understanding, Crawford?'

Crawford shuffled in a mime of vanishing.

'Let me explain something to you, my friends. When you apply to be a citizen of our fair country you mustn't have any stain on your character, not *one* blot. It's the only way to keep out the riff-raff — all those bloody South African freeloaders! But this is strange, isn't it, friends, because Wolfgang is such an asset to us, isn't he — he wins gold medals with his wine, he put us on the map for wine, little old Canterbury, a wine-growing centre! And all because of Wolf — a piece of riff-raff apparently. But Crawford came to the party, didn't he, Wolf?

'Let me tell you how. You all know the story of the wine-maker no one heard of, who beat the French at their own game. I think everyone in Canterbury knows and loves that story. What not everyone knows is that right at the time the gold medal was won Crawford was buying the winery and the big asset, Wolfgang. And he's a lucky bugger, our Crawford, because the deal was signed and sealed just before the judging took place — what a commercial nose, what a lucky and clever man, eh? Some malicious people say that it's only because news travels slowly to the back-blocks of Canterbury, and Crawford was on the spot. But that's just envy, isn't it, mate? Envy of your acumen.

'But he isn't just canny, our Crawford, he's big-hearted. When he found out that Wolf had convictions, he didn't dib him in to Immigration. Crawford did the decent thing — he said to Wolf, 'Wolfgang, my dear friend, and dearer asset, you work for me, and I'll protect you. I won't tell a soul about your past, so you can stay here with Michael in the country you love so dear. As long as you work for me, making me those wonderful wines, I'll look after you. I'll keep our little secret.' And he did, all these years! Keeping Wolf in employment and keeping quiet. Now there's a generous man! All these years, no one said a word to Immigration.

'And you guys with friends in the Ministry, you won't either, will you? We need our Wolf here, and the civil liberties people tell me they'll fight his deportation every inch of the way, with the gay rights people as cheerleaders. So we should have some fun. Wolf wants me to tell you his secret because he reckons his time's come, because he's going out on his own. He's leaving Hollanders, saying farewell to Crawford and his protection, and he and Michael are opening a restaurant and a little winery up country, with his golden handshake from Hollanders. Isn't that so, Crawford?'

There was a round of polite applause. Crawford allowed his gaze to lose focus, so that he could see nothing except a bright blur.

'But you know my friends, Crawford's kindness doesn't stop there! It reaches out to all sorts of people. It reached to my own family. This is a bit of a personal tale, so for those of you who don't know me and Marg, a bit of background.

'Marg is the light of my life, friends, the wonderful woman like a pillar of fire by night and a pillar of cloud by day, you can always follow her lead. I'd be a shell without her; I'd be down on the wharves drinking away my life. But Marg dreamed of a business, she thought good people should get into business too, and we have, and we did, Fisher's Cruises, Fisher's Cat Hire, Fisher's Wind-Surf, Fisher's Bushwhackers — we're small beer I know besides you kings of industry, but we did it all on integrity — Marg's integrity. My wonderful Marg is a pillar of rectitude too, and fierce on moral issues. It's a bit hard to talk about these family things, but my family is the heart and soul of my life. I'm very proud of my children, all of them, Patrick and Gregory and Bridget and Dominic and Philly and last but certainly not least, Mercy. They've all had adventures and got in and out of scrapes and while they were growing up into the beautiful people you can see around you today, Marg and I had to learn the hard way to be more understanding and less strict.

'I want to share this with you, because it's

one of the hardest things a parent can learn — that his children have their own lives, and start leading them much earlier than we like, but they have a right to their own lives. We try and impose our own ideas of right and wrong on others, and we shouldn't do that — I learnt the hard way. Values can't be imposed — you have to hand them on, like an inheritance, and leave the young to use them their own way. When our youngest girl, our little Mercy, got herself into a spot of trouble when she was a teenager, we were still too rigid to understand this.

'But our gallant friend Crawford wasn't like that. Even though he's not a parent, he knows a lot about young people and takes a great interest in their welfare. He came to the rescue of our young Mercy, and looked after her, even though she was only sixteen.

'You may wonder why a man like Crawford, well-to-do, man-about-town, would concern himself with the troubles of a little girl. Crawford takes a big interest in the arts, as you all know, and he particularly likes to nurture the careers of young singers, help them on their way. Our little Mercy when she was sixteen was a promising young singer, still is a lovely singer. And our dear old family friend — I know you weren't old then, Crawford, and you're not now — not from my perspective anyway — you're a spring chicken! But Crawford, acting a bit like a dad in some ways, though I can't say I ever acted quite like Crawford, took her under his wing, and he helped her out in her spot of bother back then in '86.

'And you know, he's such a decent fellow, because he's been helping her out ever since. He can't do enough for our Mercy, which shows you what he's made of. Of course he hasn't stopped helping other young singers on their way, he's made something of a career of it, I think it would be fair to say. It's nice to see a man of means being so generous with his time and money to help young women get a start.'

Crawford scarcely dared look at Genista, to whom the insult of this insulting inference seemed greatest.

'So because Crawford is such a man, hiding his deeds under a bushel, we — that's Wolfgang, and my dear friend, Rewi Mann, whom I'm happy to tell you all is going to help me celebrate my birthday by becoming my son-in-law' — cheers, applause, and a blast from the trombonist — 'the three of us decided to throw a bit of a bash for Crawford too.

'In conclusion, friends and guests, I'd like to say this. And I want you to listen very carefully, because this is the distillation of my many years. Marg often laughs at me. 'What's the smallest book in the world?' she asks. And the answer is 'The Wit and Wisdom of Dickie Fisher'.

'But what I think is this. We're all moral cowards, me included. But we should not be afraid to stand up and say — this person is good, that person is bad. There are good people in the world, not saints, but people like you and me. It's healthy to be able to praise them. There are bad people in the world, not monsters, not criminals, but people who look like you and me, but spread misery and pain. It would be healthy if we could expose them. But the bad people get away with it because you and I are moral cowards . . . '

There was quite a bit more in this vein, but Crawford could not listen. He stood with a glazed expression of benevolence, appalled beyond reason at what was being done to him in his own house. The mendacity of these slurs, the enormity of the ill-manners . . . the crude bully-boy sneers . . .

★ ★ ★

Crawford didn't know how he got out of the house. He was terribly afraid that everyone in

429

the room had seen the blind panic of his departure. It was impossible that they should not have seen it, for he had to fight his way out of the corner. He knew that to face down Dickie he had to stay and smile as if each word had carried its surface meaning and not been a barb aimed at his heart. But his self-control had deserted him. He felt cold and yet was sweating; he felt his head spinning and his vision unreliable. He felt that if a single person spoke to him he would surely vomit, from anxiety at their meaning.

He made it out of the house. The air was warm. He tried not to run, choosing instead the fervent walk of a doctor in an emergency hospital.

★　★　★

He got away from the lights around the house, across the yard, which was absurdly filigreed with tiny coloured lights, and made it into the shadow behind the cottage. There he sank down on the back doorstep, his back against the door, and breathed deeply.

Mercy was standing in the shadow of the cottage. He had guessed that she might be. She had changed into jeans and a shirt and trainers. She sat down on the step next to him.

They sat in silence. Crawford wanted to know if she knew what they had done to him. He was afraid to ask, in case she should be party to this outrage. He was shaking. He put his hands on his knees to steady himself. She put her hand over one of his.

'Was it bad in there?'

'Did you *know*?'

'Not in detail. I was afraid to find out. Dad was all set to castrate you at one point.'

Crawford continued to shake.

'We talked him out of it,' she went on. 'Rewi and Genista and me.'

Crawford groaned. 'Not Genista too! Why?'

'Because I'm tired of pretence. I want to start a new life with Rewi, with the past in the past.'

'Romantic twaddle,' he said. 'The past is always in the past. It is merely things that have happened. The only people who dwell on the past are romantics and religious fanatics.'

She didn't say any more. He wanted her to argue, so he could tell her how stupidly she was behaving.

'I'm not going back to England, Crawford,' she said. 'I'm staying with Rewi. I'm going to spend the rest of my life with him.'

Crawford shook his head. How to prick this bubble of hers? This girl who loved city life and dining out — how long before she got tired of scrubbing the decks and being polite to rich Americans? Six months?

'Mercy, Mercy. How long did that riding-instructor — the one with yellow plaits — how long did he last?'

'Jack?' said Mercy. 'I don't remember — about a year, I think. I never saw him after we got back from Barcelona that time. Do I *have* to remember him now?'

'Not at all. Forget him by all means. About a year. Would you say he was the longest-lived of all your lovers?'

'I don't keep an account book, unlike you.'

'You were certainly very keen on him. But then you really wanted that fortnight in Spain with me, didn't you? And he didn't like that.'

'We had a row about it.'

'And you came on holiday with me, and never saw him again.'

'Yes, it hurt. It hurts. But you aren't going to upset me that easily. I was waiting for the right man and now I've found him.'

Crawford shook his head sadly.

'I always said you read too many novels, puss. Look at the facts. Your relationship with me has lasted twelve years. No other man has lasted longer than twelve months. What can we make of that?'

'That you are a possessive and manipulative bastard who knows my weaknesses, and I am a sad bitch.'

It pained him to hear her talk like this, but he knew he had struck home.

'I don't care,' she said furiously, 'I want you to ship my stuff, sell my house, pay yourself back the loan with interest and send me what's left. Rewi and I are going to buy a yacht and sail people around the islands, Fisher's Island Cruises.'

'Ah, your house,' said Crawford.

There was the little matter of the house — was this the right moment to tell her that the monthly payments she made him, with such grimace, were merely some part of the interest payments, and the house was, in principle, rather less hers than it had been at the outset? On the whole, he did not think that now was the moment to initiate her into this particular truth.

He had run out of talk. Dickie had struck him dumb. All his kindness exposed to the world as self-seeking. All his little ways of helping others portrayed as manipulation.

'You can't leave me now,' he said. 'Now you have betrayed me to my wife.'

'I haven't betrayed you. I didn't tell her the half. I told her and Dad that it was you who got me pregnant, and you who insisted on the abortion and found that bungling murderer to do it. I didn't tell Genista about your whores. I haven't told *anyone* you raped me. Not even Rewi.'

'Never use that word! How can you?'

'What, *Rewi*?'

'That word too,' he said shuddering. 'How can you, Mercy, after all I've done for you.'

She shook her head.

'And now especially,' he added piteously, 'after all that they have done to me.'

'Let's go for a walk,' she said.

Crawford didn't trust himself to talk. He had been transported into a surreal universe, where everything familiar was twisted into a new but just recognizable shape, like an object in a Dali landscape.

Mercy stood up and offered him her hand to rise. He absolutely did not want to go for a walk, but he could not think what else to do. He could not go back to the house for fear of meeting his guests. For fear of meeting Genista. He wanted to hide, in a bed, a wardrobe, an attic, away from all those people who would stare at him and say things.

But Mercy had not yet deserted him, and she at least understood his motives. He wanted to ask her 'I'm not a bad man, am I?' but he did not dare, in case she gave him the wrong answer, out of perversity.

He followed her lead, feeling like an old man being taken for a walk by a kind nurse. She took him up the back of the farm, up into the bush. It was pitch black up there, but she had a big Maglite torch. They found the path and started up the hill.

He knew where they were going. She was taking him up to the pool by the waterfall where he had first made love to her. Perhaps she would allow him to make love to her again, for old times' sake. He wished for that more than anything else in the world.

None the less, he dreaded the climb. His physical condition often embarrassed him these days. He knew he would have to ask her for many halts before they reached the top, which would give her the advantage. They didn't talk during the climb. She had nothing to say, and he was too short of breath.

When they reached the top he was panting so hard he thought he would die. There was nothing else in his mind except the urgent necessity to catch the next breath, to calm the gasping, to wait for the pain in his chest to dissolve. He sank down on the fallen tree-trunk and reached for breath. Mercy wandered away, leaving him alone. The pounding of the waterfall matched the pounding of his heart. Strangely illuminated, as if their energy generated white light, the flecks of water leaped up as they hit the rocks.

Gradually his breathing returned to normal, though his chest hurt perilously. He tried not to think about dying, which had always struck him as a remote and tiresome possibility, like a stock market crash.

Mercy came and sat down beside him.

'Do you remember?' she said. They had to shout to make themselves heard.

'Yes. Of course I remember. As if it were yesterday. I loved you then and I love you now.'

Mercy said nothing at all for quite some time. He thought she had not heard him.

'You're despicable,' she shouted. 'You are only saying that in a last bid to win me back. You don't know the meaning of the word *love*.'

Crawford wanted to explain that of course he did, that everyone understood something by the word *love*, but the tragedy was that one person's understanding differed so radically from another's. Of course he loved Mercy. He had always loved Mercy. Had he not cared for her, lavished presents upon her, guarded her from folly and harm?

He wanted to tell her all this, but feared she would not hear him out of stubbornness.

'Let's go back, so we can talk,' he called to her.

'No. I don't want to talk. I don't want to hear your serpent words. I want you to sit here by yourself and think. I want you to try and remember what you did to me, what you did to the others. I want you think about the baby we killed, the only baby I will ever have. I want you to try and figure out why so many good people hate you so much.'

But what was he to think? How was he to remember? He remembered the night by the pool, her white limbs, her gorgeous youthful resisting flesh, her vigour and innocence, the unbelievable surge of power, and the rightness of everything — the waterfall, the girl whom he had as his for ever, because no one else would have her as he had. His to protect, his to possess, surely he had thought, too, that she was his to love?

. . . But here by himself, with no one to set a framework, he did not know what to think any more. Everything he thought about himself had been held up to ridicule before a horde of people. What he thought of as entirely admirable had had its garments flipped to show dirty netherparts.

Mercy stood up and set off down the path. She walked briskly, and by trotting, painfully, he kept up with her stride. But he could not find enough breath to talk to her.

He refused to give in. He *would* persist

until she heard him.

Further down the path was a big totara trunk, sawn into a bench. It was here they had sat the night he first made love to her.

She sat down and let him catch up. They sat in silence for some minutes while Crawford recovered himself.

'You can always reconsider,' he said. 'At any time.'

Mercy said nothing.

'I understand how it is with him. You find him sexually attractive. He's straightforward, capable, masculine. All the virtues of the New Zealand male. I see the attraction. But it doesn't last, Mercy. The fever passes. You fall in love, like everyone else — '

'Except you.'

'I may have done,' said Crawford, trying not to think of occasions. 'Mercy, you fall in love. It possesses you. It's a very powerful emotion, but the fever passes. What do you have then?'

'A man who loves me.'

'Yes,' said Crawford, 'and what else? Is he amusing? Mildly. Is he rich? No. And what sort of things do you do on your weekends, on holidays? You tramp in the bush. You sail. You work in the garden. You fix the lorry. You paint the boat.'

'Yes. I can hardly wait.'

438

'Let me remind you. Next month, I am going to Palermo for six days as a guest of the Sicilian Wine-producers Guild. Genista will not come. Indeed I imagine Genista will be busy with her lawyers taking me for whatever she can get. But you would enjoy Sicily. Wild and homely all at once, devilish and domestic. Wine and sun and blood on the pavement . . . Dangerous beauty. And on my way back from Sicily, I have business in Milan. And of course some complimentaries for La Scala.'

'I don't care, Crawford. You know how much I enjoyed it all. You don't need to taunt me. If you cared about me, you would shut up about all this.'

'It's because I care about you that I have to remind you. The offer will always stand, Mercy. Any time, any place, ring me up, and you can be on a plane to England within the hour. I will say nothing — no snide jokes, no recriminations. You can come back to your proper place, and it will be as if none of this happened.'

'No,' she said. 'No. No. No. No.'

'You do not need to be so vehement. It suggests vacillation. Because of course, you know I am right. You *will* grow bored . . . '

Mercy leapt up and ran away down the path.

She ran as she had run once before down that path. Then, she remembered, it had hurt her to run, but she did not care if it tore her apart, so long as she got away from him. She did not care then if she swelled up and died, or ran headlong into the sea and drowned, as long as she got away, and did not need to think about him.

She remembered those feelings now, as she pounded down the path in the darkness, she felt them again, as hideously as if her hymen was still torn and bleeding, and her inside desecrated. *You never get over these things*, she said, to whoever was listening. Once torn, never mended.

She remembered also the sense of power she had derived from facing him and taking things from him. Every gift taken without a thank-you was an act of defiance. *You raped me and humiliated me, and made me sterile, but you did not destroy me.*

She said these words in her head as she ran away from him again. She was appalled that she was running, but she could not stop herself.

No, she said, *no, no. I will not listen to you any more.*

She could not believe that she needed to say it. Surely the strength of love was entirely sufficient? She did not want to believe that she could even *hear* his blandishments, let alone be swayed by them. She slowed her running, to show herself she was not afraid.

In the distance she could hear the dying sounds of the party. Voices calling out, car doors slamming, a saxophonist on the veranda filling the night with the anguish of his soul. She remembered how, when she had run away from Crawford those years ago, she had come down to the same cheerful sounds of departure. She had thought she would run up to the first person and scream out that Crawford Hollander had raped her, but as she came down the hill towards people and lights, she realized that they were in another world. Between raped Mercy and the rest of them was a membrane, like cling film, that would bend and stretch but prove impenetrable for ever, unlike the inadequate protection nature had given her virginity.

She had told no one, that night, nor ever afterwards, but she had repeated to herself time and again, as Crawford beguiled her with gifts and his own particular brand of endearment. *You raped me*, she said to him in her head, *but you have not destroyed me.*

Now, walking, half-running, towards the safety of the lights, she wondered if perhaps he had won. Otherwise, she would not be running away.

She skirted through the trees, to avoid meeting anyone who might recognize her. If they spoke about Crawford, or did not speak about Crawford, it would be equally unendurable. She must find Rewi, and nobody else.

As she came up to the house by the back door she heard Wolf and her father laughing in the kitchen. She did not feel there was anything to laugh about, so she hesitated on the doorstep. Then she heard Rewi's voice, and took courage.

'There you are, I was worrying about you,' he said, coming to her across the kitchen at once.

He looked so handsome in his smart gear, so solid and strong, and his expression was so kind, that she burst into tears.

He put his arms right around her. They were about the same height, but she still managed to cry into his shoulder. Her father and Michael suddenly decided to check the bar out for unfinished drinks. Rewi and Mercy were left alone, their arms around each other's bodies.

'Can you keep Crawford away from me?' she said.

'All I can do, Mercy, is put my arms around you and give you a hug. I can't keep you away from him. You have to do that.'

'I don't know whether I'm strong enough.'

'You've got to be. If you aren't, no one is.'

He let go of her, and smeared the tears on her left cheek away with the back of his hand. 'I'll make you a coffee,' he said.

He busied himself with the kettle and mugs. He had his back to her, perhaps to make it easier to talk.

'I reckon you can stop now, making him pay. I think you've done enough. Any more will just end up hurting you. And us guys had our fun out of him, and any more will make us no better than he is. Be happy some of us are different. So let's just forget him, and get on with our own lives.'

He brought her coffee. She took it, leaned forward, and kissed him.

'Yes,' said Mercy.

★ ★ ★

Mercy leapt up and ran away down the path.

Crawford saw the little circle of light bobbing along the path, away from him. Mercy was leaving him, and he could not bear it.

He stood up, though his body bade him sharply to sit down, and called after her. She did not hear.

'Mercy, Mercy!'

The circle of light bounced down the hill, further and further into the darkness, leaving him behind.

He went after her, completely unable to see the path, trusting to vague memory and Crawford luck. She drew further and further ahead, she must be trotting, if not running.

He called out to her.

'Mercy! Please help me. I need to talk to you — I need someone to talk to. You can't leave me like this, I need you!'

He started to run, stumbling and weaving in the dark. Behind him the noise of the water quietened. He called again, surely she could hear him? He could no longer see her torch. He tried to run faster, but his body surged with overwhelming pain, and he fell headlong into the earth at the base of a tree. He lay there with his cheek on moss, his shoulder hunched against the bark. His body lay awkwardly along the path, the feet slightly higher than the head. His left side, which was uppermost, seemed not to wish to move at all, such was the pain sweeping through him. There was no reality any more, he was a disembodied creature, whose twisted body lay at the base of a tree in the darkness.

He could not move.

The only thought he could frame was that he was about to die, and at first he felt strangely calm about this. It seemed the best way out of an impossible situation. Then they would be sorry! Dickie and Wolf and Rewi, sorry that they had killed him. Their cruel joke had killed him. He would not have to look Genista in the eye, and face her reassessment of him. He would not have to smile at reports of Mercy's wedding. They would all be mortified that they had killed him, when he was not so bad a man after all.

After a while, the waves of unreality ceased to break through his mind and body, and he thought perhaps he was not about to die. But he could not move, and cold and pain coursed through him like a ghastly insult. He began now to be afraid in a more conscious way that he *would* die.

He did not care about God or any sort of after-life. He had no such convictions and through lack of practice could not find any now. He thought only of the terribleness of slipping away — of being nothing — of being a fat, empty thing, in muddy clothes, the hideous effigy of what was Crawford Hollander — the guy to be carried along in an old pram, pointed at and jostled, as he had been pointed at and jostled at school. And worse. So much worse. Old fears of humiliation and pain, from far far away, and deep down, burst to the surface, and he was a third-former crying in the locker room, with no one to tell.

There is no one, he thought, *no one to tell. I am alone as I have always been alone, and now I shall die alone, and the women who weep for me will brush their tears away and get on with life, relieved to be rid of me at last.*

He thought with envy of Dickie Fisher and Rewi Mann; he thought of their funerals, of the pale widows and whey-faced children, the grandchildren clinging onto hands and asking pitifully after granddad. He thought of eulogies delivered by friends without a trace of irony, and rip-roaring wakes where they were loved and remembered. Dickie Fisher and Rewi Mann, two nobodies, whom he, Crawford Hollander, envied.

If only he could move his body a little, there might be hope for him. He would die of exposure out here, unless Mercy told them soon where he was to be found.

But why would she, when she had left him alone to think?

Think, I must think.

But he could form no sensible thoughts. All that came into his mind, riding just above the pain and panic, were memories, little pieces of scene. The Commander kissing Rosalia passionately on the waterfront, while in young

Crawford's bosom swelled a passion for success induced by the sleek forms of unwanted wine. Oh how delicious had been the formation of that plan — that moment in the dark when he saw it all fall into place, how everyone had a part to play, how simply and painlessly he, Crawford would become someone, someone who could not be touched and could not be mocked. He remembered the feeling of power, that the silly old Commander was his, that Rosalia was his, that he could pull their strings and distract them from their kissing.

He remembered too the moment, many years later, in Hamburg, standing frozen in the hallway of the apartment, while Wolf's brother ranted over the telephone. Understanding what was said — *du Knastbruder!* — *you jailbird!* — and thinking — *got him!* The maverick, brilliant, uncontrollable Wolf — *got him. He is mine!*

But none of them was his, neither the Commander nor Rosalia, nor Mercy, nor Wolf. They had all slipped out of his grasp, leaving his hands around the empty form of their hatred.

The hours ached away on him. Surely someone would come for him?

Pieces of his life that he had successfully forgotten floated past on the dark stream of pain and desperation.

Oh the desperation, the desperation of it all. The child that had to be disposed of, even though it was well past the legal term for such things; the abortionist that was recommended, but was a cack-handed bungler. The sweating and screams and the blood. And the woman hustling past with a black plastic bag, containing the body of his child — his only child.

In Dante's version of Hell, the first people you met were the shades of children dead without baptism — neither sinners nor saints, simply nothing, literally in Limbo. But where did the children go, who died without even being acknowledged as human? No burial rite but a hospital incinerator, no shroud but a black plastic bag. Did his and Mercy's child have enough substance even to haunt them?

But it haunted them none the less, bloody rag of matter.

He had never wanted children, never contemplated mortality or what would be left of him. When he died, the world would end. He would leave behind measurable achievements. He was a man who had made good, had done well for himself. Not even his enemies, not even the Welcoming Committee, could deny that.

It occurred to him in his stupor, induced

by pain and cold, that in the kitchen of the big house was an opened, but otherwise untouched, bottle of his precious '85 — the very last. He thought he would crawl back to the house, wait till all was quiet, and drink it all. Then this period of his life would be over for ever, and he could put behind him the Commander and Mercy and Wolf and Genista.

He tried to start the crawl — but couldn't move at all. The cold began to alarm him more than the pain — how long could one survive without warmth or fluid? How long before they came to look for him — and who would care enough if he were missing in the morning?

Genista? He could not even be sure of her. How was it possible? He had married so sensibly — a woman without beauty, youth or possessions, a woman who understood how matters were, who could be relied upon to be perpetually grateful. But he could not be sure that even Genista was loyal enough to come to his rescue.

On what could one rely?

This seemed to Crawford such a terrible question: if one could not buy loyalty, nor engender it, how was one to live?

He had no one to ask, for in Crawford's head there was no longer an interlocutor, no longer a conscience. He was alone, even in the space of his head.

After a long blank time, he started to imagine the child. It had been a boy. At least he believed it had been a boy, though how he knew, he couldn't tell. He would have been about twelve now — ready for a new school. Where would he have gone to school, this precious, beautiful, vigorous, musical boy? Christ's, Crawford's old school, to prove a point? Or some ancient expensive school in England?

A son who was nurtured and protected and showered with good things — perhaps he could be relied upon? Perhaps he would go so far as to love his father? Perhaps it was not too late after all — a new young wife — a new lease of life, people for whom one had done so much that they were duty-bound to be loyal.

But then he thought he would be an old man before the child grew, and in the meantime nothing but demands and tantrums, not to mention the acerbic amusement of Genista — for how could he rid himself of her, or of Mercy — these people who were so implicated in his past, woven into his very being? And Wolf — what of Wolf? Wolf who had broken his heart and spurned his protection — would he conveniently disappear?

Realistically, and he prided himself on being a realist, he would never be rid of them. They would prey on his imagination, eating away at his self-image. If he did not have them in his power, they would have him.

He saw no way out, and thought that perhaps, after all, the best thing would be to die. *And then they would be sorry!* He wanted to laugh at himself for this thought, but he had forgotten how to laugh, desperately humiliated by his impotence.

'I will *not* give in!' he cried to himself. 'I will *not* give them the satisfaction of my death, or of walking away from them. I will humble them as they have humbled me! I will make them watch me rise above them, and be even more successful — whatever it takes . . . '

He'd show them all. He'd face them down, let Mercy get married to that man if she must, let Genista divorce him if she must, he'd find a new wife and a new mistress, a proper one this time. There was no shortage of candidates. And as for Wolf — he'd find another vintner and make even more money. In a year's time he'd throw a big party in his house and invite everyone who came tonight, invite his enemies along, and gloat, discreetly, invite even Mercy and her hanger-on, even the vitriolic Fishers, even that ingrate

451

Wolfgang and his catamite.

Though he'd have no '85 Ste Marguerite to serve the guests.

He determined on one superhuman effort to pull himself to safety.

He clawed at the tree roots next to him, and succeeded in levering himself up with the arm that was not riven with pain. He rose a few inches and dropped back to the ground, exhausted. He gritted his teeth and pulled again, gained some momentum, and twisted himself over, so he was belly down on the path, his chin on the red earth, his eyes glaring down into the valley. A strand of aria ran through his head, urging him on. *Chi l'anima mi lacera? Chi m'agita le viscere?*

Mozart. Yes, defiance. He reared up his head, and thought in the distance he could see the dawn. If he could move, he could live, he could struggle —

He tried to pull his working arm from under his body. The pain and awkwardness, the sheer recalcitrance of his body, infuriated him. How could he be defeated by such inconsequence — Crawford Hollander, who had overcome bullies and doubters and snobs — to be brought down by a mere accident?

'I will *not*!' he thought. 'I'll show them all.'

He heaved himself up into a lopsided parody of a press-up. He pushed hard with his working arm, and toppled over onto his back, fell a few feet down the path, and landed against a rock, half-suspended over the valley.

If I fell, he thought, down and down for ever into oblivion. Nothing left but to fall. And here, so suitable a place — my valley, my trees, the place where my child was conceived and I sealed my pact with humanity. But I do not want to go down — not yet — not yet.

He wriggled and rolled, twitched and bucked, like a man on the gallows, and succeeded in righting himself for a moment, then fell heavily, down the path, over and over, a bundle of flesh and bones without volition.

He was flooded with horrifying panic into which seeped gradually the unreal sense that this could not be happening, and yet it was. He was no longer real, he was nothing but fear, without name, without shape, without hope, without resolution — he was nothing, nothing except fear.

He did not know how long it was he lay still, unable to move, screaming with terror but paralysed, suspended between life and death.

At last he opened his eyes and saw them.

The three men came towards him, in dark suits, their white shirt-fronts vivid. Absurdly he could distinguish their bow-ties better than their faces. The Welcoming Committee had come to get him.

'Is this the end?' he asked them.

'Oh, it never ends,' they said, smiling terribly.

THE END

We do hope that you have enjoyed reading this large print book.

Did you know that all of our titles are available for purchase?

We publish a wide range of high quality large print books including:
Romances, Mysteries, Classics
General Fiction
Non Fiction and Westerns

Special interest titles available in large print are:
The Little Oxford Dictionary
Music Book
Song Book
Hymn Book
Service Book

Also available from us courtesy of Oxford University Press:
Young Readers' Dictionary
(large print edition)
Young Readers' Thesaurus
(large print edition)

For further information or a free brochure, please contact us at:
Ulverscroft Large Print Books Ltd.,
The Green, Bradgate Road, Anstey,
Leicester, LE7 7FU, England.
Tel: (00 44) 0116 236 4325
Fax: (00 44) 0116 234 0205

STRANGER IN THE PLACE

Anne Doughty

Elizabeth Stewart, a Belfast student and only daughter of hardline Protestant parents, sets out on a study visit to the remote west coast of Ireland. Delighted as she is by the beauty of her new surroundings and the small community which welcomes her, she soon discovers she has more to learn than the details of the old country way of life. She comes to reappraise so much that is slighted and dismissed by her family — not least in regard to herself. But it is her relationship with a much older, Catholic man, Patrick Delargy, which compels her to decide what kind of life she really wants.